MW00583370

Two
Halves
of
New Haven

TWO

HALVES

OF

NEW HAVEN

by

Martin Schecter

CROWN PUBLISHERS, INC. NEW YORK

This is a work of fiction. All characters, events, and dialogue are imagined and not intended to represent real people, living or dead.

Some of the quotes appearing in this narrative are taken from the following sources: Keith Moore's *Clinically Oriented Anatomy*, The Williams & Wilkins Company, 1980. Eric Kandel and James Schwartz's *Principles of Neural Science*, Elsevier Science Publishing Co., Inc., 1981.

Published by Crown Publishers, Inc., 201 East 50th Street, New York, New York 10022. Member of the Crown Publishing Group.

CROWN is a trademark of Crown Publishers, Inc.

Manufactured in the United States of America

Library of Congress Cataloging-in-Publication Data

Schecter, Martin.
Two halves of New Haven / by Martin Schecter. —1st ed.
I. Title.
PS3569.C4783T88   1992
813′.54—dc20
91-33493
CIP

ISBN 0-517-58418-2
10 9 8 7 6 5 4 3 2 1
First Edition

Book design by Lenny Henderson

For Ted

Acknowledgments

The author wishes to thank the following people for all their help and encouragement: Richard Russo, Elizabeth Evans, C. E. Poverman, Linda Chester, Laurie Fox, and David Groff. Thanks also to readers David Sarich, Bill Marsh, and Joe McGreevy.

Also thanks to my friends and family, to the Yale Medical School class of 1988, and of course to Ted, my joy.

Contents

Part I: Structure

1. Nerves   3
2. Cells   26
3. Heart   68
4. Eyes   91
5. Teeth   132

Part II: Mechanism

6. Circulation   149
7. Biochemistry   187
8. Metabolism   221
9. Psychology   247

We live out our grammars with our bodies...
—Charles Bernstein

PART I

Structure

1

N*erves*

A week after I came to Yale, they arrested one of the medical students for being an impostor. This is true; you can look it up. The police came right into the anatomy lab: handcuffs, search warrants, everything. The idea of someone posing as a medical student, in itself, didn't altogether surprise me. As far as I was concerned, the question wasn't *why* you would want to go to medical school, but *why wouldn't* you. This particular impostor's motives, however, weren't the ordinary ones; it later became known that he'd made a whole career out of posing as everything from a pediatrician to a third baseman for the Detroit Tigers. His name was Lyle Montgomery Cash, but I'd known him as Daniel C. Anderson, or more simply, Daniel. He was my lab partner. In a week, he'd learned as much anatomy as the rest of us.

They arrested him on the day we were looking for the liver. I was cutting back skin with my scalpel while Daniel hunted with his forceps, the anatomy atlas in his lap. The liver has three lobes, the texts assured us, but at the moment, we'd only found two: a large one and a smaller one. We thought the large one might be two smaller ones merged together; we searched for telltale lacunae, any sign of aberrancy. According to our textbooks, the liver should have been just about the easiest organ to identify. It should have practically leapt out of the abdomen with all its bile-filled hepatocytes and purple integument and announced, "Hey, folks— over here!" But the world is always much more complicated than the systems we use to describe it—the first thing medical students tend to forget. Dr. Grant had told us a joke to illustrate the point: An old lady stops a medical student while he's shopping in the

3

grocery store. "Young man," she says, "do you know where the liver is?" "Right about here," he tells her, holding his hand at the base of his ribs.

We were all slightly giddy when it came to anatomy, anyway. As the instructors in the psychiatry department would soon inform us, this was known as a *defense mechanism* (appropriately mixing the metaphors of war and machinery in their long march across the human psyche). Daniel had a habit of shaking the cadaver's hand whenever we'd begin a day's dissection. "How you doing today, Mr. Zorba," he'd say, overpronouncing the name, as if he didn't know why we'd named him that and felt slightly embarrassed for him. The arm was stiff and moved only a few degrees up and down as Daniel shook it. Who would shake a hand with gray skin and black fingernails? But the rest of us had our hands in Zorba's abdomen, pushing aside intestines. Personally, I thought the abdomen wasn't so bad, once you got used to it, once you were already soaking in it. What worried me was the brain, which we'd do last. Rumor had it that badly preserved brains contained kuru, an exotic African virus that could worm its way inside you and, twenty years later, turn your mind to mush.

The arrest began with two guards stepping into the entrance of the anatomy lab, shoulder-to-shoulder, forming a barricade. People across the room stopped what they were doing and looked up. Two uniforms can only mean one thing. It only meant one thing to Daniel, at least, who slowly pulled his hands out of Zorba's body. He watched the guards as they glanced about the room, apparently trying to match a description from a photograph. Daniel's eyes met mine, and all at once I understood the implications of his nervousness. He didn't look away, but held my gaze, trying to tell me something. We shared, in that moment, a silent and complete communication; yet he still held something back, some mystery. It wasn't at all the look of someone trapped, discovered— his eyes were joyous, almost gleeful, as if he'd been waiting for this moment all his life. As if to say: A-ha! Before anyone could move, a pair of forceps clattered to the ground and Daniel ran out the nearest door, pages of someone's anatomy text fluttering in his wake.

The cops bolted after him. We heard them in the halls, their footsteps echoing, the cops shouting, "Hey, there he is, stop him!" Some of us watched out the doors, but the rest gathered around the windows to look down on the courtyard below, at the dingy street with its phalanx of NO PARKING signs and the hot-dog vendor on the corner. That's where he'd have to eventually appear. The windows were slightly opaque, having absorbed the oil of formaldehyde, textbooks, sweat—Yale windows, holding years of tradition in a texture of metal and glass. We'd never looked through them before.

None of us knew what was happening, what Daniel had done, but it crossed my mind that perhaps they wanted him for failing an exam, for not knowing his biochemistry. This didn't seem so unreasonable—one of my classmates, for instance, had earned three advanced degrees by the age of twenty-one, and such paragons had intimidated us common folk, at least until we discovered their tendency to dribble Thousand Island dressing on their shirts whenever they ate a Reuben sandwich, or other foibles for other paragons. But such revelations were, during those first few days, still weeks away.

"What's going on?" Julie asked. She was another of my partners. She looked out the window and shook her head. "Now, this is something. This is really something. Daniel of all people." Julie believed that everyone at school was smarter than she, and that, therefore, misfortune could only befall herself. She was, of course, smarter than she gave herself credit for (as we all were, most likely . . . although some maintained their modesty better than others). Below on the street there was nothing going on, just an anonymous doctor in a lab coat calmly buying a hot dog.

We waited. Daniel never appeared outside. They must have caught him inside and done whatever they'd wanted to do out of sight of the rest of us. We went back to Zorba, disappointed and still curious. Our team was now one person short, and Julie, John, and I just looked at each other and shrugged. We were too startled to speculate. We'd find out soon enough—maybe Daniel would come back and tell us himself. At any rate, we had work to do.

"He left his tools and stuff," Julie said, sifting through his books. She picked his forceps off the floor and put them back in their case.

"Yeah."

"Well?" She looked at John and me for an answer.

"Look at the book," John said. "Read what it says to do next."

□   □   □

As it turned out, this story about Daniel's arrest became, for a while, something of a regular recitation for me, associated almost more with *me* than *him*. I was there standing next to him when it happened, of course, so that was part of it. But eventually it came to be known that anyone who wanted information on Daniel should come to me. Perhaps they simply liked the way I told it— throwing in sound effects, secondary voices, hand gestures. But the person to whom I especially wanted to relate these events was my father. I'd have my chance soon enough. A few weeks later, I would fly home for a family emergency, and as Dad met me at the airport, he'd ask me to tell him something, a story about medical school. And, of course, the story I related about Daniel more than satisfied his expectations. When I mentioned Daniel's elaborate impersonation, my dad told me that such disguises weren't so unusual—just last year, for instance, they'd found out that one of the lawyers in his building had forged his degree. My dad, though—I knew he had sedulously earned every diploma on his wall.

Periodontistry was one of my father's most reliable loves. He attended conventions. He subscribed to journals. He went to periodontal dinners. I remember how, as a kid, on Saturday mornings when he was away working, I'd sneak into his study and look at the somber graphics of his periodontics periodicals, wondering how much the colorful gingival and skeletal structures in the photographs and diagrams had to do with *him*, his office and his machines, and the women he hired to help run them. Dad was always telling me stories of his old dental school days—all the pranks and practical jokes he and his buddies had played—and I knew he'd been waiting, all this time, to hear something even better from me.

Dad's other love (aside from Mom, of course) was our living room. Whenever he wasn't busy being a periodontist, he'd be sitting in front of the tube. He'd talk to it the way you'd talk to an old friend. He'd tell it to do things—shoot the guy on the roof, tag the batter out at third, get on with the weather report. Our family was always the most contented when we'd watch the _____ Night Movie together—take your pick. Whether it was the television or his work that had given him his insatiable passion for detail, be it his own, his son's, or anybody else's, I didn't know. But tell Dad a story, and you had his attention.

"Okay, Paul, don't hold out on me. I know there's something more to it. I know there's something you're leaving out."

So I told him as much about Daniel as I could, while we walked to the Indianapolis Airport parking lot, while we loaded my luggage into his car, a brand-new Cutlass. The interior was black, authentic Naugahyde. The car chimed when we opened the doors, lights flashing on the dashboard, the car saying, *"Seat belts... seat belts... seat belts..."* in a soft, female voice, until we put them on. You could tell this car must have cost. Maybe it was my youth, but I didn't think it was the sort of car I would ever spend my money on, a Cutlass. A car that talked—my dad was doing well.

"That's so?" he said throughout my spiel. Or "No..." And when I was finished, he concluded with, "Paul, you don't know how happy you make me." He said it without even taking his eyes off the road. "You're becoming a real *mensch.*"

* * *

What I told my father was that after we finished our anatomy that day, we went immediately back to the dorm—Pete DuPree and I and some of the other guys from the eighth floor—to discuss Daniel's feat. I had wanted Julie and John to join us; who else but his lab partners would know Daniel's most revealing habits? But they'd declined to partake in our rampant speculation—we'd get the official debriefing soon enough. There was a biochem review to study for.

The more insatiably curious among us sat in a semicircle on Pete's floor, comparing information. Among five of us, we were able to gather that (1) Daniel's name was really Lyle Montgomery Cash; (2) he was a criminal, responsible for the theft of six hundred and seventy dollars from various medical students (including fifty dollars he'd borrowed from me); and (3) he was wanted for jumping bail in Arkansas, having already once been imprisoned for just such shenanigans. Apparently this was the information being circulated so far, in bits and pieces, by the administration, although no one could verify the original source. It didn't seem so outrageous that someone should get arrested at Yale, which, after all, had a long and illustrious tradition of notoriety, but no one could figure out why Mr. Cash would want to impersonate a medical student. What did medical students do, except study medicine?

And what could be the attraction in that? I personally thought that any one of his previous incarnations—including the full-fledged doctor—sounded a lot more interesting.

What had tipped Daniel's hand, apparently, was that he'd mentioned to Pete something about having had three admission interviews. "I never did think everything was right about the guy," Pete said. "But three interviews? I knew there was something fishy about that." Two interviews was the standard operating procedure at Yale; but how could an impostor have been expected to have known that? I'd noticed irregularities about Mr. Daniel Anderson myself, but nothing I could have so definitively put my finger on. It was Pete who had given his name to the Office of Student Affairs. The school was already on the lookout for an extra person—a hundred and three names had been appearing on rosters that were supposed to have only a hundred and two. After that, it was only a matter of time, of checking everyone's credentials.

His destiny was as sealed as that of the passengers in a disaster film.

"Sure," Pete told us. "He must have done research. Look at all he knew about this place—tuition, the grading system, everything."

"Everything except how many interviews," someone said.

"Yeah, so he made one mistake. Not bad."

"It's those insignificant details that kill you."

"Ain't that the truth."

"So, Paul, tell us something else about him."

I told them all I knew, all I felt comfortable with, but there was at least one thing I consciously held back, to them as well as to my father, later: the look Daniel had given me, moments before he fled. There were no right words for what had happened between us, the complicity we'd shared. And even more significant, it seemed that with his penetrating gaze, Daniel—or rather, Lyle—had bound me to silence. As if it had been my secret, rather than his, that was at stake. Daniel had known nothing about me personally, but if the truth be told, I wasn't all that happy to be on Yale's doctor-track. And who knew—perhaps he'd sensed my discontent, had thought of it as something to use to his advantage.

For the first time, thinking about Lyle Cash, I started to feel the unremitting danger of this place, its desire to lead me off down a path, alit with anatomical nomenclature and psychoanalytic indices and cellular mechanisms, concepts designed to redefine the vague former sensations that I used to think of as "myself." And it wasn't just my feelings about medical school that I was worried about—normally, I could put out of my mind these problems and doubts. I could bury them in my subconscious and lead an ordinary waking life. But there were times when they came rushing back, when they became overwhelming, reality. Which was the true reality—the waking dream I lived ninety-nine percent of the time, or those few, exceptional punctures of clarity, when the rest of my life seemed like a blatant fog? Either way, I had to play it cool. In the supercompetitive world of medicine, if you showed any sign of ambivalence, you were dust.

After everyone had seemingly tired of the topic of impostors, and enjoyed some additional discussion of their skills at human dissection, it took hardly any effort for Pete to shoo the others from his room. They did as he commanded—he'd been a fraternity president. The boys said good-bye and dispersed to the far corners of the dorm, back to their desk lamps and anatomic atlases. With the vanished crowd, Daniel seemingly vanished, too, his whole mystique and his whole mystery, as suddenly as the police had appeared. That left only me and Pete; we were practically roommates, since we lived across the hall from each other.

"So do you think he had a room in the dorm?" I asked. "Or a locker in the labs? Maybe he left some stuff around."

"Maybe."

"Want to check it out?"

"What for? I'm sure they've confiscated everything. Or else it's locked. Or empty."

Those didn't strike me as the only options. But apparently Pete wasn't the type to go breaking into an escaped convict's anatomy locker; at least, not with me. I still couldn't believe that someone like Daniel was dangerous. He'd seemed so innocent, so wide-eyed.

Without warning, Pete pulled off his anatomy shirt, then pants, turning a pant-leg inside out over first one foot, then the other. I looked away, not wanting to be discovered ogling, by either Pete or myself, but still having caught enough of a glimpse of his torso to sense my interest growing, despite my best efforts to deny it. Why did there have to be so many Petes in the world, and so many situations where I couldn't get them off my mind? Why Pete, for instance, and not Julie? Why couldn't my desires orient themselves in the direction I wanted them to? Perhaps it wasn't so much the nakedness as the act, his innocently baring his body in front of me, that unexpectedly fueled my heart and distorted my intentions. Hell, he'd played tennis, squash, football, Frisbee, and Hacky-Sack, all in our first weekend on campus; it would have been a body well worth staring at.

"What's the matter, Paul? Looking for something? Shit, do these clothes stink. I hear we're going to smell like formaldehyde all year."

"Your girlfriend will sure appreciate that." I turned the pages of his anatomy text: rectus sheath, rectus abdominis, epigastric artery. It was all so sexless and dry, the way the various imaginary planes articulated the body into right angles, the way the photographer had washed out everything in stark black-and-white contrast. Why the need to make the human animal seem abstractly mathematical, clean as a postulate? I wondered how much time Pete actually spent on this stuff, how much it all meant to him, what he made of it.

"Girlfriend?"

"Well, Pete, it's been a week. Don't you have one yet?"

I thought the comment might not have sounded quite right. Pete simply chuckled and drew a towel from his closet. "Give me at least till Saturday."

"Pete, after you shower, do you... have plans?"

"Plans?"

I looked at him full on. He stood there holding up his towel with one hand, plastic container of soap in the other. A thick bath mat of hair covered his chest. I swallowed. "I thought you might want to do something."

"Yeah, like study."

"Like go out for a beer. Or a game of squash."

"What, on a Tuesday night?"

There was nothing more terrifying than an enervating Tuesday night alone with Stryer's *Principles of Biochemistry*—a Tuesday night alone in any case, with its small suggestions of mortality. I wasn't about to let any destructive, studious routines begin. Besides, who could concentrate with images of Daniel and armed guards dashing through your head? I wanted company, and Pete was the most tempting I could think of.

"That's the beauty of the Yale System," I told him. "It's forgiving."

"Yeah, well, it sounds nice on paper."

"It sounds nice in a beer stein."

He shrugged and walked out of the room. I lay back on his bed and stared at the ceiling, wondering what it must be like to come home to this side of the dorm instead of mine, everything opening to the left instead of the right, everything so organized and sure-footed—it was like an entirely different part of the country, a place where you might be content with everything you had to do. And after a moment, Pete stuck his head back through the door.

"Yeah, okay. Let's grab a yard. What the hell."

We walked toward the Green until we spotted a good bar— old, run-down, homey, beer-sodden. Pete said he'd heard the name before—a hundred-year-old English bar with steadfast Yale tradition—so that clinched it. We pushed our way inside.

It was the beginning of the semester and the place was packed—undergraduates, graduates, locals. Most everyone seemed to know most everyone else. One of the bartenders talked to some women at the bar, while the other handed out pitchers over the customers' heads. There were pictures of ancient scullers, rugby heroes, football players, all up and down the walls. The special was Harp by the half-yard—these long-neck pilsner glasses, with a bulb at the bottom, like an Erlenmeyer flask. It was just how I'd always pictured the Ivy League would be. Not like the medical school at all. We signaled the bartender with our money.

"So Yale's going to be a blast, huh?" Pete said while we waited.

"Just like they promised."

"Where's your family from again? Montana?"

"Indianapolis."

The bartender handed us a pitcher, and we found a booth and sat down with our brew. Pete had already met my folks, but we hadn't had more than a day together, or an opportunity to just talk. Recently, it seemed as if he'd been ignoring me, and I'd practically given up any hope that we'd get to know each other better, that we might become truly thick.

"So."

"So . . ."

I took another sip, groping for a subject of conversation. Interviews. "Interviews, Pete. How about them, huh?" It was perhaps the only common history we shared. So we got a real discussion going. Pete told me that he'd been to one school where they'd interviewed seven students at once. I told him my own horror stories: being yelled at, intimidated, asked to recite the chemical subtleties of photosynthesis.

Once the subject was exhausted, we reached another impasse. We were almost done with our beer, so I suggested we order another round.

"Oops, sorry. I think it rolled over there." He winked at me as the waitress bent over to pick up the loose coins. She stood up and made change from her portable box, "all in quarters," as Pete had requested, and replaced the empty pitcher with a full one.

"Hey, dudes, I thought I might find you here."

Trust Fergie to be out—like us—during the middle of the week. He parked himself at our table and asked the two women with him to pull up extra chairs. Nurses, they were, or so they claimed. Fergie was dressed complete with porkpie hat, thin tie, and wraparound sunglasses, which made him look like an android. Reggae Fergie, of the nurse brigade. Halloween's in two months, *dude.* He sat down and took over the conversation like a one-man brat pack.

"They've got to be new quarters. New quarters are always better." Fergie examined one of Pete's quarters, then wordlessly, with serious concentration, started it bouncing. "Not bad. Should do the job."

"So, Pete. Tell me about growing up in California."

No one answered me. They'd entered a new plane. The quarter ritualistically made its rounds. The nurses giggled in stereo whenever the coin rolled to the floor. Apparently Fergie was getting enough intellectual stimulation during the day. Between him and Pete, it wasn't going to matter which guy left with which doll. It was as if Fergie had walked in with a six-pack or a bag of doughnut holes.

"Whoa, girl! Your turn to chug." Pete held one of the nurse's bulbs while she drank. "No wasting any. What's your name, honey?"

"Rhonda," she said breathlessly, and wiped her chin.

"Help me, Rhonda . . . help, help me, Rhonda."

"I think that calls for a general chug all around."

"Chug-a-lug."

"Are you all really doctors, like your friend says?" the other asked. "You look a bit young to be doctors."

"Doctors . . . doctors . . . you bet!" said Fergie. "Plastic surgeons. That's how we manage to look young. What else would we be?"

"Here, here, Dr. Fergie, plastic surgeon, my good man, let's show these gals how we operate," and they raised their glasses once more.

So that was the end of the conversation—no one said a word as I slid quietly from the booth.

When I got back to my room, I picked up *Principles of Biochemistry,* but I couldn't concentrate. This was hardly the sort of situation I'd expected to be getting myself into—picking up strange women with oversexed Lotharios. When I'd been out here for the interviews, it was the first time I'd ever seen the East Coast, and it had all seemed much subtler then—more variegated, more promising. I'd come out to visit two schools, Columbia and Yale. It was a vacation, of sorts, a look at a new life: Eating pretzels on the streets of New York. Emergency rooms in the busiest city in the world. Amtraking along the steel rails of Connecticut. A whole new world, there for the taking. I'd thought, if I came here, that I might begin to find the things I wanted, whatever they might be.

Interviews. My temporary home base for the weekend was on 158th Street, in the perpetually gray, south side of Harlem, and after a round of torture at the College of Physicians and Surgeons, I'd taken the train to New Haven, for round two.

The first person I'd met at Yale was Bill, a student. After fifteen minutes of waiting for him in the lobby, he popped out from a hallway and introduced himself. We shook hands. There were only two applicants, me and this other fellow, Eric. We both looked young for our age, a potential disadvantage for getting into medical school. Bill was tall and gangly, well over six feet, and as we talked, he had a way of moving his basketball-sized hands as though he were actually going to grab you and mold your body into some shape, some physical representation, that would better communicate what he was thinking. For some reason, I took this as a sign that he would one day be an outstanding doctor. This and his tallness.

We ate lunch in the cafeteria. I squeezed packets of mayonnaise onto my sandwich, while Bill explained why there were no grades at Yale.

"You're on your own. You're an adult now. They assume every-one here is a dedicated student, a real book hound, or else you wouldn't be here in the first place." Reasonable. He held out an open palm at me, then at Eric, then back at me. His eyes were a bright blue, an ocean blue, sincere. His eyes were inviting you to trust him—another ploy he must have picked up in medical school. He talked about medicine as if it were a tropical holiday. "No one notices if you go to class. You could spend two years in Bermuda. Just so long as when you come back, you pass the Boards." He reached down and grabbed a quick bite of his sandwich. Both Eric and I were halfway done and he hadn't even started eating yet. "That's the Yale System," he said, his mouth full.

"Has anyone ever done that?" Eric asked, somewhat astonished by the premise. No tests? No grades? It sounded too good to be true, a gimmick that the administration must have thought up to lure students. Columbia had grades. Harvard had grades. Johns Hopkins not only had grades, but class rankings posted every two weeks. There had to be a catch. We were cross-examining him, looking for the truth behind the sales pitch.

"Done what?"

"Spent two years in Bermuda. Or wherever."

"Not that I know of. But that's not the point." He put down his sandwich. "The point is, you make your own rules. Sure, they offer practice tests, and you take them because you want to do well on the Boards. But no one says you *have* to study. No one here says you *have* to do anything."

We stared at him.

"Look, okay, it's not like there isn't work to do. But you do it at your own pace. You study during the week and get drunk on the weekends. Instead of spending Spring Break in the library, you go skiing." He grinned, a goofy, self-satisfied smile, as if one of those drunk weekends or skiing trips had just come to mind. "Face it, guys, the place is *human*."

So that's when I decided on Yale. Call me cynical—who'd want grades if you didn't have to have them?—but there was more to it than just the lax attitude. It was *Yale,* the name, the prestige. Here was the purpose to those endless years of physics, chemistry, biology... knowledge that had been building in me, bit by bit, like the slow accumulation of power, almost electrical in its surge and flow, and which I could for one blindingly clear moment anticipate what it would be like to master, discharge, control. Two plus two. Oxaloacetic acid dehydrogenase. Blam—a cure. Oh, what joy! *The knowledge of life and death itself, the universe in all its human manifestations, the power to* heal. The medical fraternity: Just thinking about it gave me palpitations. Besides, they had fewer tests than the College of P & S.

Bill took us on a tour around the campus. He showed us the hospital, the classrooms, the deformed fetuses kept in jars outside the anatomy lab, like rows of pickles. "Poor kids," he said. He tapped lightly on the glass, as if the preserved stillborns behind it might wave back.

"So what should we do in the interview?" Eric asked. He never did return in the fall.

"This *is* the interview," Bill replied.

"I mean the next one. The one with the doctor."

He patted Eric's shoulder. "Don't worry. They're pretty mellow. They might ask you something like 'What do you expect to be doing in ten years?' Just tell them you expect to be doing research for Yale."

The doctor I met next was just as serene as Bill had promised— he'd gone to Yale, too. He showed me the wards, the kidney unit, the three-hundred-year-old medical instruments on display in front of the library. He bought me dinner, too, at a famous old hamburger stand. No surprise questions about photosynthesis.

"Hope you're as impressed with this place as I am, Paul," he said afterward, and shook my hand before going back to work.

I finished by eight o'clock, then took the train back to Manhattan, simply looking out the window, satisfied with the day's progress, admiring the shapes of things as they passed by: a gas pump, a bridge, a burned-out car, a stack of tires. Each item, as it framed itself in the train's window, presented itself as a symbol— although of what, I wasn't sure. I sensed it had to do with surfaces, decay, transmogrification. But the indecipherability vexed and dismayed me—my scientific training had taught me to read things, to see one thing as a sign of another, and it made me nervous if their meanings remained elusive.

But that ride back to New York was my first opportunity to relax, and as I did so, an idea crept unwittingly into my head: When I got off the train at Grand Central Station, I would walk down Forty-second Street to New York's infamous mecca of pornography, where I would buy a magazine, a shiny book plastered cover to cover with pictures of naked men. It was something I'd always wanted to do. The idea sounded incredibly sleazy and exciting. I was twenty-one then, and this would be the first time in my life that I'd have the opportunity to debase myself in the total obscurity of a major metropolis. My plan was to take the magazine back to my empty dorm room in Harlem, where I would look at it in private.

No sooner had I made up my mind to do this—no chickening out—when my palms began to sweat, and I held my hands under my thighs. All throughout my high-school and college careers, I'd had these disturbing dreams and sexual fantasies that my waking mind would deny, but never before had I dared to acquire evidence, printed matter (except for an underwear ad—involving a sweaty weight lifter—that I had clipped out of *Time* magazine and kept hidden in the back of an old chemistry book) that I could hold in my hand. The dreams could get pretty randy sometimes, but I myself had always been meek, playing trumpet instead of sports, avoiding the heated political squabbles in my fraternity, wanting the world to mind its own business and leave me out of it. I had a girlfriend—a feminist, who seemed more interested in debate than sex (which was fine with me, and perhaps the reason I'd decided to go out with her in the first place)—a group of fraternity freshmen who for some reason idolized me, and a made-up knee injury that kept me off the soccer field. There didn't seem to me any reason why I couldn't get along reasonably this way, being academic during the day and lascivious after midnight, forever.

I listened to the metronomic Dopplering of the train, imagining what reading that magazine would be like.

By the time we pulled into Grand Central Station, it was after ten o'clock. I walked out onto Forty-second Street with my jacket over my arm. Flashing neon ... Blimpies, Fast Photos, skyscrapers: New York at night was electric. The air had the crisp smell of pavement, bus fumes, and roasted peanuts, and I thought how strange it was that this smell seemed so familiar to me, so much like the smell of someplace you'd call home, even though I'd never been in New York before. Maybe every man, woman, and child born in America had a blueprint of New York City odors stored in his or her collective memory. The wind blew leaflets and leaves into eddies, whisking them off into the dark corners, where you wouldn't want to follow.

Past Seventh Avenue, I picked a store and started out in the front room—the straight porn, long rows of crates filled with back issues of *Club, Oui, Playboy,* the store's display window lit up with enough neon for a carnival booth. A swarm of men filed through the rooms, in and out of doorways and then back outside to crowd the street. Toward the back, over one of the side rooms, a sign in black Magic Marker said, GAY. It seemed more private back there, but the surface anonymity was a small reassurance: The sign designated not only what was in the room, for purchase, but the sort of people who could enter—GAY (faggot, wimp, sissy, queer, pervert, introvert, narcissist, security risk, etc.)—the one epitaph I most scrupulously avoided, like a bad grade, and just walking in meant having to admit my essence in terms of someone else's predetermined identity. I'd have rather had people know me as an M.D. Or Paul Levinson. Or just about anything else. Strands of variegated beads hung in the doorway. I made a couple of tentative passes. Then I pushed aside the beads and walked in.

At first, the sight of so many pictures of men having sex with each other struck me as a bit repulsive. It was so blatant. But I wasn't sure if my reaction was natural (a kind of *defense mechanism*), or something I'd conditioned myself to feel, since all my friends professed to be disgusted by even the idea of two guys and a phallus (as if anything outside the mainstream could even possibly *be* sensual), let alone a picture of it. What was I doing here? I didn't want to be GAY. I wanted to be NORMAL. I wanted to want women, to be able to sort through the collection and pick the most appropriate one. If I was gay, how would I ever be successful (article in print in the *New England Journal of Medicine*), happy (wife to cook my dinner and the proper fraction of kids to carry on my name), free (able to purchase stereo/TV/car/condo on credit and at the optimal interest rates)? Gradually, however, I started getting an erection. (You know, despite what you think you want, there are some things you just can't help.) And so I picked a row of magazines and started leafing through.

I soon found something interesting. *Fraternity Romp.* The most unthinkable of tableaux, in handsome eight-by-eleven photos. Fifteen bucks. I brought the magazine to the counter, paid the cashier, and he put it in a sack and handed it back to me. My hands were shaking—I stuck the magazine under my arm and put my hands in my pockets. Then I walked out.

I was horny as hell now—that room had finally done it to me—and all I wanted to do was get back to my room at P & S, ASAP.

"Hey. Hey, you."

Someone put a hand on my shoulder.

"I saw you buy that magazine."

The man who'd stopped me wore an ugly, olive-green overcoat. One of his front teeth, crooked and streaked gray, overlapped its neighbor. Had someone hit him in the mouth or was he just falling apart? He lowered his voice and ducked his head a little. "Give me twenty bucks, and I'll let you suck my cock."

I didn't know what to do. All I could think was, what sort of deal was that? Who'd want to suck his horrible cock and *pay* him for it? "I don't have any money," I said, which was a lie. I still had eighty dollars.

"Give me a twenty or I'll tell that cop you propositioned me." We looked over together at the corner, the one that held the entrance to the subway—my escape route—and sure enough, a cop was standing there, pacing back and forth, keeping tabs on the porno crowds. "Ya got that magazine in your hands. He'll know you're a fag."

I couldn't think. This guy was going to kill me and toss me in the Hudson, wrapped in the magazine, and then everyone would find out I was gay. He was going to follow me for the rest of my life, popping out at my graduation ceremony, pointing his bony finger in accusation, like some anonymous Grim Reaper. He was going to keep me out of medical school. Hell, just pay the man.

I took out my wallet and removed a twenty, glancing in the process at my driver's license in its little window. Shit, I thought, identification. Why hadn't I taken it out? I gave him the bill, his gnarled hand closing around it. "Here," I said. "That's all I've got." I walked away from him as fast as I could, stuffing the magazine in a trash can as I went by. My plan was to walk past the policeman without flinching and then disappear down the subway. But behind me I could hear the guy calling, distant, laughing, almost a voice in my head, "Hey, you didn't have to throw it out. . . ."

When I got back to Harlem, the guard buzzed me into the dorm, and I went straight upstairs, turned out the light, and crawled into bed. Lying there under the freshly changed sheets, I could feel the city outside, waiting, spreading its malevolent embrace over the building, over the neighborhood. That man out there in it, somewhere. I couldn't fall asleep, couldn't stop this thought from circling my brain all night: *This is the most intense experience I've ever had. And I'm going to go through my entire life without ever mentioning it to anyone.*

But really, when you thought about it, it was too good a story to simply forget. After two full hours of lying there, I decided I wasn't sleepy. Instead, I got back out of bed and looked for a scrap of paper. I wrote down, word for word, what had happened to me on Forty-second Street. I re-saw it in my mind's eye, recording each event objectively, empirically, trying to get some grip on what had happened. I thought: At least this way, even if I can't ever tell anyone, I'll have something for posterity.

*   *   *

That had been my only adventure with New York, with the East, and it had put a fright in me, for sure, but now that I was back here, I was starting to regain my confidence—I was starting to think about those magazines, and how I might get at them. The thing I regretted most about that night on Forty-second Street wasn't having been suckered out of twenty bucks, but having thrown away what I was sure would turn out to be the world's only existing copy of *Fraternity Romp*. All I wanted was a little contraband to keep me occupied, to keep my fantasy life alive. Now, stuck in New Haven—no car, no friends, in the company of hustlers—I didn't know what my next move should be.

Eventually, I *was* able to concentrate on my text, my studies, despite knowing that Pete and Fergie were carrying on where I'd left them. I fell asleep reading, and dreamt that I read the entire book, that I woke up the next morning knowing everything there was to know about biochemistry.

I woke up in the middle of the night on page three.

That was the Yale *System.*

□   □   □

The following morning, I opened my door in time to catch a flying Pop-Tart.

"Here," Pete said. "Breakfast."

He continued down the hall, tossing out pastries right and left like a deranged paperboy, until the box was empty and he crumpled it up and lobbed it toward the wastebasket. People were emerging from their rooms, looking startled. I ate off the strawberry-flavored sugar coating while Pete walked back to get his books, so pleased with himself, with his own generosity and the attention it generated. It was an exhibition of the special something that had qualified him as "Yale material."

"I didn't expect to see you back here this morning."

"Oh, Paul, dream on, man. Those girls were just having a good time. I told you, wait for the weekend."

Then about ten of us headed off together across the courtyard for the wonderful world of carbohydrate metabolism.

When we got there, Pete, Fergie, Julie, the whole crowd I'd walked over with—they shuffled into the back row, where they could talk among themselves, but they didn't leave a seat for me. Was this intentional, a signal? Who cared; I wasn't even trying to break into their clique anymore. I sat next to George Yan Su, the only other person I really knew.

This lecture hall had a hidden vortex to it: Every day the walls drew closer together. The paneling was reminiscent of some Reform synagogue, a modern design meant to elicit, in symbolic fashion, certain values. Sprays of light flowed in diffraction-grating patterns from the top of the walls. I imagined organ music accompanying the phosphorylation pathways. Once she got to the podium, Dr. Sylvie singsonged with her standard rhetorical questions . . . *turns into what? Is the metabolite of what?* Oh, do tell us, Dr. Sylvie. My nonmedical friends thought we were supposed to revere all this stuff with something like a rapt punctiliousness (but . . . what if that was the one bit of obscure information that would have saved someone's life, and you'd missed it?). I started doing the daily crossword puzzle. George asked me to name a synonym for *intractable*. Someone passed around a list for a softball team being formed against the law school. I didn't sign. People started dropping off to sleep around me, heads lolling forward and back, as if someone had put barbiturates in the coffee.

When the lecture was half over, I told George I was ready to bolt.

"Where?"

"I want to check out Daniel's locker. Before it gets too late. I'm sure there's something in it."

"What for?"

"George—have you no sense of adventure? No unbridled curiosity? No urge to brave the unknown?"

He shook his head. "Nope."

I waved away his negative attitude. I shoved Stryer under my arm and, crouching, made for the rear exit. When Pete and Fergie saw me go by, they got up also. I'd started the daily exodus.

Just outside the door, there stood Veronique, staring out the pane windows that overlooked Cedar Drive and taking a long, refreshing drag off a Salem. She smiled at me, and I at her. They were smiles that said, *Aren't* we *the smart ones?*

In our whole class, she was the only person who smoked.

The halls around the anatomy lab were completely empty, undramatically gray, and just waiting to have their substance drained by the daily ritual of the wan, descending afternoon light. Daniel's locker was next to mine; I'd never used mine, but I had a feeling, just a hunch, that he'd found a use for his. Maybe he'd stuffed it full of stolen merchandise. Maybe a final message, a will of sorts, the impersonator's version of a suicide note, *if in the event of my untimely unmasking.*

There was no lock on it or anything. I simply pulled it open.

At first it looked empty, and my heart sank—although who knew why, what I'd been hoping to discover. Then I noticed the slip of paper at the bottom.

It was a torn-out page from the Clemente atlas: Figure #10, Superficial Thoracic and Abdominal Muscles. Beautifully drawn torso of a man, every muscle labeled, arms outstretched and missing, like the *Venus de Milo* without skin. To me, these drawings weren't just meant to be instructions, they were art. They were elegant. They even came on heavy-stock paper. How infrequently people recognized their other use. But Daniel—imagine—actually dismembering Clemente! That wasn't the Daniel I knew. On the other hand, I could see him carrying this paper around with him, using it as a crib sheet, trying to memorize enough quick essentials so he could talk his way through class. Maybe he *had* appreciated it, as I did, as a visual design—maybe that's why he'd taken it.

I slipped the page inside my biochemistry text, where it'd stay fresh. I couldn't believe I'd actually salvaged something, a memento of Daniel, some indicator of his person, his presence, something to remember him by, before the authorities had come along with their pencils and protractors and wastepaper baskets, and put everything in order again.

I tacked up the picture to the bulletin board over my desk. I wanted to be able to look at it, have it there staring back at me, even though I had the identical picture in my own text. I put it next to some snapshots of my sister, the park by my house in Indianapolis, a postcard of Pink Floyd. I didn't have it there as a reference: I was thinking of it as memorabilia.

Pete, I said, Fergie, Julie, George. This is what you've missed. This is the thing about him you never saw. Daniel's vulnerability. His crutch. The man in the picture was ideal in mass, shape, outline—what an alien from another planet might make of a man—so that there was nothing whatsoever intended to be sexual about him. It was merely someone's outline. But there was still an irrational appeal, the appeal of blunt objects, which were sexy just in their mass, their solidity, the fact that you could pick them up and hold them in your hand—and they *had* used a rather studly model.

And I thought about how you could strip away each layer of skin, fat, muscle, tissue, and when you got to the true inside, there would be no inside, there would only be your desire to know, driving you on. Certainly a body and its person weren't the same; yet where could you articulate the difference? Not here, not in this place—these books...I spent the rest of the afternoon reviewing class notes, my schedules, my homework. It was so clear and yet so hard to simply admit that medicine was about science, not humanity, about knowing, not experiencing. (Oh, they were offering optional classes in literature, all right, that were supposed to humanize you like piano-playing or charity fund-raising, but that wasn't the real metal, that wasn't what the twenty-five-thousand-dollar-a-year tuition was for.) When I studied the textbooks, I was as hungry for the bright, hard clarity of scientific knowledge as I'd ever desired another actual person or image, no matter how mind-rattling that clarity could sometimes be. I was fascinated by the revelations, entranced by the diagrams: immunoglobulins, DNA, receptor proteins, carboxylic acids, inclusion bodies, bacilli—all rotating in the imagination like computer-generated models of ships docking, airplanes landing, fractal thunderclouds expanding. It was all so amazing: stick-figure molecules coursing through the blood and lymph, zillions of microscopic Erector sets gathering as patiently as the weather, getting ready at any moment to assemble or disassemble a particular human being—you, your doctor, your mother. Oh, the structural beauty of it, this elaborate creation of human consciousness we call modern medicine, so breathtaking and awe-inspiring, the way the great Renaissance cathedrals were magnificent in their endless, majestic detail.

And you could actually even keep someone from dying with all of this. Improve the breathing, unclog the arteries, clarify the thinking, sew back on severed limbs.

What more did I want?

Back in the anatomy lab, they'd already replaced Daniel with a physician's assistant: Nathan. Julie and John introduced themselves, and thereafter said not one word about it. We went right back to work. Cut, cut, cut. Snip, snip, snip. Daniel and I had bought a Clemente for the lab, which we all continued to use as if it'd come along with the instructors and the cadaver; this was the one with the missing Figure #10. It dawned on me: That atlas, that was thirty more bucks Daniel owed me.

"Did you see the story in the paper?" Julie asked.

"Story?"

"Yeah," Nathan said. "It even had Mr. Cash's picture." And he posed for us, in profile, cheeks puffed out, even though he looked nothing like Daniel.

"Hey, folks. Let's get back to the dissection. We're fifteen minutes behind."

"Sorry," Julie said.

"Yeah. Sorry."

"Did the paper say where he is now? Where they've taken him?"

"Paul. Turn the page, please."

No one answered my question. We just cut, cut, cut. I couldn't believe we were just going to let all this blow over. Not even Pete or Fergie wanted to discuss it anymore. Not even George. They were too busy with other things. They said the topic was getting boring.

Maybe it was.

But nevertheless, two nights after the arrest, I went into the anatomy lab with my camera, to take pictures. How could we just let him slip away like that? Once again, there was an event here that I didn't want to just forget, that I needed to record, preserve, if for no other reason than to ensure the fragile truth of it, whatever that might be. The lab was always unlocked until midnight, but this early in the semester, no one wanted or needed to come in and study. At that point, we still had a sense of the anatomy lab as an exceptional place, like a cemetery or church, that was supposed to frighten you or at least earn your respect. So it didn't occur to most people to go there alone. Although it wouldn't be long until we thought of it as just another laboratory, a place to conduct experiments, and would pooh-pooh all that sentimentality as mere astrology and superstition.

At nine o'clock at night, the room was silent and empty, completely uninhabited. Except for the dead, row upon row of them, like a grocery store. And somehow, I felt strangely comfortable among them. As if the dead posed less of a threat than the living.

I put on plastic gloves, pulled the sheet off our cadaver, unwrapped the moisturizing gauze. Then I removed the soiled gloves and took snapshots with my thirty-five-millimeter SLR. It was like being a forensic detective or a Third World spy. I took pictures of the cadaver's head (still mummified), his inte￢ ￢ines, his gray chest skin, like a mildewed piece of carpeting. I tilted the camera and looked for interesting angles. I took a snap of Zorba's hand, the one that Daniel had shaken as a joke. I had in mind that I was going to make a montage. I was going to put all the pictures together, give them captions, and add them to a collection I was making. If no one else cared to look at them, that was fine by me. *I'd* look at them. I didn't know exactly why else I was doing it.

I was going to call it *Daniel C. Anderson: Medical Student*. It'd be, along with Figure #10, part of the continuing record of my life, something to preserve, but rendered differently, as a translation, as schemata of images and suggestions, much as Daniel himself had been able to translate whole characters, whole histories, personalities. Perhaps it'd be an impression of Daniel that would ectoplasmically emerge, half-finished, haunting, and luminescent. Or would it be an expression of Lyle? And I wondered what he'd think of me doing all this, if he'd find it foolish, juvenile, or if he'd approve. I wondered if there might be some way to signal him, to tell him—here, Daniel, what do you think, confide in me, I won't give you away. What's your story, why do you do it, who will you be next? Tell me, Daniel. Tell me the secret of your identities. Tell me how do you create them, how do you escape?

2

Cells

———————

Once Daniel was well out of the picture, so to speak, the excitation that was Yale started to ebb. I didn't find the place quite so fascinating anymore. We started pulling up the covers and snuggling in with our textbooks. We started getting ready for our long, endless hibernation. Here they come to tell us our bedtime stories—oh, tell us the one about phenylketonuria. Tell us about monoclonal antibodies. Tell us about the dangers of overempathizing. Maybe you've got some slides.

But the day I'd first arrived at Yale Medical School, parents in tow, an official Yale Medical Student, it hadn't mattered that I had no desire to tuck myself into this particular bed, that I'd rather stay awake and explore the world—for this *was* the world, and just being there, a newly arrived Ivy Leaguer, was exploration enough. That first day was probably the sunniest ever in New Haven. Blue water sparkled in the Sound—not gray, not late-fall slime green, as would become typical—the sun glinted off treetops, the ivy-studded college stood grandiose and monumental like some picture postcard, while Dad drove our Ford through the ghetto streets (and even they looked friendly), hauling an orange U-Haul, taking all my possessions—the tennis racquet, trumpet, computer, toaster oven, stereo—to what turned out to be a fourteen-story dormitory, made of brick and tiny unopenable windows, that looked like a women's prison—Harkness Dorm, which the students fondly renamed Darkness.

After we'd managed a complex series of maneuvers down one-way streets, we were finally able to drive past the dorm, park illegally, and unload. Dad took the lock off the U-Haul, flipped

open the doors—unleashing the musty odor of a two-day drive—
and started handing me my stuff, which I took inside, loaded into
an elevator that we'd commandeered for the purpose (my mother
holding open the door, dusting things and rearranging them as I
set them down in the elevator), and then brought up to the eighth
floor. My room was stark, what with only a thin, soggy wafer of
a mattress, a wood desk that smelled of eggs, and a dusty tile floor.
It looked even starker once I got all my boxes, bags, and bed sheets
inside.

"Nice, Paul," my sister Jenny said. "Look—it comes with your
own Roach Motel and everything." She held up an old box she'd
found under the sink, something I probably would never have
touched.

"My, this really brings back the memories." Dad stood with his
arms folded, gazing around the room, seeing gold veneer on the
tattered venetian blinds, no doubt. "Don't tell your mother, but
when I was in dental school . . . ," and he proceeded to recite some
outrageous odontoid adventure that I'd heard a thousand times
before, something about how he and his buddies had substituted
a professor's mouth model with a set of chattering teeth.

"Don't listen to your father," Mom had told me once after I'd
heard this tale. "That wasn't the way it happened at all." And she
proceeded to set the story straight, making it a lot less funny. But
still, I knew there was something, some essence, that was revealed
more thoroughly in the way Dad told it—some truthfulness about
himself that was lost in Mom's stubborn accuracy. Already, Mom
had slid my college graduation photo into her wallet, and she'd
pull it out and show it to people whenever she saw the opportunity
coming, saying, "This is my son, Paul. He graduated with a three-
point-eight average and he's going to Yale Medical School."

"Why don't you help your mother find the pop machine," Dad
suggested to my sister. "I think she's lost. We don't want her
wandering into any strange rooms." So Jenny put the roaches back
under the sink and took off down the hall. While I opened one
of the boxes, Dad slipped quietly away after her.

That's when Pete first appeared—who had then seemed
friendly enough, despite his intimidating air, that anything might
be possible.

"Hey, a tennis player," came a voice from across the hall. He
walked into my room, picked up my racquet, and started twirling

it in his hands. "We'll have to get together for a game. There're some courts behind the medical school, but I hear you have to sign up on a list somewhere."

He had oversized thighs, obviously a player of some sort of varsity sport. Already I was attracted and intimidated.

"You're lucky, you know." He put down the racquet and looked out my window. Short. Smooth brown hair. Vague, West Coast accent, something between Ventura and Newport Beach. Blue nylon running shorts with a tear in one leg, along the hem, complementing the line defining the muscles from his hip to his knee (*quadriceps*, we'd learn later), the line of desire over which I dared not step. "You've got the good view here. I'm stuck looking out at the parking garage."

"Yeah, well, it still isn't the Ritz." I stood next to him, looking out at the courtyard, where some students were having a makeshift picnic. Beyond this little enclave of the medical school was one of the poorer neighborhoods of New Haven. I was thinking of my uncle Sammy, who was something of a world traveler—he was reputed to have actually stayed at a "Ritz," the one in Paris. What would he think of all this squalor? I had tried to talk Uncle Sammy into coming with us (it'd been at Sammy's urging, partially, that I'd even conceded to come here), but he and Aunt Kate had been packing for a week in St. Petersburg, FLA, when we'd made the grand Levinson exodus for the Delivery to Medical School of the Firstborn. Sammy had never needed a doctorate to make his fortune. I don't think he'd even finished college.

Looking south beyond the courtyard, you could see the street—Cedar Drive—across which was yet another hospital. Then some trees, some tenements, smokestacks here and there, some smoke. I remembered the parking garage across the street on the other side of the building. It was ten stories of concrete, had sodium-vapor lights, and medical students weren't allowed to park in it.

"Well, maybe we can play this afternoon," Pete said. "It can be our first assignment at Club Med. Find the tennis courts."

I wasn't a great tennis fan—the racquet was mostly for decoration, a remnant of tennis lessons taken here and there to placate my parents. I liked the idea of doing something with Pete, but I hoped, by lunch, he'd forget about tennis.

When he saw that I hadn't answered him right away, he scrunched his eyes. "Unless you're going to be studying, that is."

"Studying? Now? Classes haven't even started yet."

"Well, McEnroe, that's what the guy down the hall is doing. Studying. With his door locked."

"No shit."

We went next door, stared at it a moment, then knocked. There wasn't an answer, but there had to be someone inside; we could sense it. We knocked again.

"Can't you read?" came a muffled voice from inside.

"What?" Pete with his thighs said, a belligerent *what,* as if he'd heard him fine.

"I said, can't you read? 'Do not disturb.' I'll be done in a minute."

Sure enough, a sign hung on his doorknob—DO NOT DISTURB, with a picture of a maid holding a finger to her mouth. I had a flash of being in some Florida hotel, then realized where I was, the absurd incongruity of not just this pitiful attempt at privacy but the whole collective urge to combine dormitory, scientific, and professional life, to make everything fit together in one concrete building. ZANE OBERSON, said the nameplate on the door.

"See what I mean?"

"My God, what could he be studying the day before classes start?"

"Biochemistry," came Zane's voice from behind the door.

We went back into my room. I opened another box and started dumping supplies into my desk. "Well, not me."

"Maybe you'll be studying the medical students on the seventh floor instead, eh?" He wiggled his eyebrows, beautiful brown eyebrows, an endearing gesture. "That's the all-girls floor. This, I just unfortunately found out, is all guys." He stuck out his hand. "I'm Pete, by the way. Pete DuPree."

"Hi. Paul Levinson."

"Great. Now all we need to do is find Mary and we can start up a band." He shook my hand like a professional, just forceful enough to be firm, but not overly affectionate, like someone who's become adept at handshaking. Pete wasn't the type of person I'd normally fall in with—a person with a perfect handshake—and I suspected he felt the same way about me, but we were new, and

we were in some sense forming a coalition against the Zane Oberson types. At that moment, it was conceivable that we were the
two closest-to-normal people in the whole freshman class.

My father walked back in the room, carrying a trunk, which
he set at our feet. "That was sure an armful. Oh, hello. I'm Paul's
father."

"Pete DuPree," Pete said, and they shook hands. "I was just
telling your son here about the tennis courts."

"Oh?" Dad tossed some rope on my bed. He wiped his brow
with the back of his hand, sweat dripping down his shirt (I sweat,
but I don't drench my shirts, so it looked as though I hadn't been
doing any work at all, in comparison)—he standing there out of
breath and Pete looking like the cat that ate the canary. "Well,"
Dad said, "what about them?"

"You have to sign up. We're going to play this afternoon. Then
we're going to check the place out, see what sort of scenery it has
to offer. You know." He winked at my father, almost lewdly—
none of my friends had ever winked at my father before.

Dad smiled. He actually liked it, this Pete, his brashness and
swashbuckling chumminess.

"Hey," Pete said. "Need a hand with the rest?"

"Sure. Follow me down."

There was more? Maybe I'd forgotten about the load of stuff
in the backseat.

They stopped in the doorway. "Hey, Paul," my father called.
"You want to come along?" They both chuckled, and I could see
I was going to be stuck playing second fiddle to Pete DuPree until
my parents were on their way back to Indiana.

Before I could follow, Zane caught me, coming out of his room.

"Well, hello, neighbor," he said. He had a beard like an Amish
minister, a thin melon slice swinging under his chin, and I couldn't
stop staring at it. It looked totally fake. He seemed unsure what
to do next, just shifted from foot to foot and looked around inside
my room, without stepping in. He told me about biochemistry for
a while. "Well," he said finally, "if you don't need anything, I'm
off to start the next chapter."

He disappeared back into his room and closed the door. My
father and Pete were probably on their way back up by now, or
having a good old time down below. So I went back to putting,
one by one, my pens in my new desk drawer.

□   □   □

Pete stayed around for lunch, for tennis, for dinner—I thought he was going to become part of the family. "Oh, yes, Mrs. Levinson, it's so *picturesque*," he'd say in his most polite voice, when asked if he liked it here, while my mom nodded solemnly at this effusive bit of wisdom—Pete unfolding his napkin with a snap, always looking at me with a smirk on his face.

"I hear the Vitello Tonnato here is wonderful. You really have to order it." He was even holding the menu upside down. But I was the only one who noticed it.

"The what?" Jenny said.

"The Vital Tomato, honey," my mother told her. "It's a juice."

"Or maybe the scallops. After all, this is New England, and you have to try the seafood. . . ."

He looked over at me, trying his darndest not to laugh—he knew that I was on to him, and that, for some reason, I wasn't going to give him away. Who knew why he did it, this snow job? It seemed autonomic, just something he did, like breathing. I watched him constantly, never before having had the opportunity to examine up close one of these great salesmen/athletes for any extended time, for they usually simply acknowledged me and went on their way, selling themselves, engaging people in athletic conversations. But I sat there and smiled along, for some reason secretly siding with him, wanting only that he should like me.

When my parents finally said their good-byes, they acted as broken up to leave him as me.

"*Pete DuPree,*" my mother said, taking out her purse and writing it down in her address book. "You'll have to give us your parents' phone number."

The next day, Pete and I walked together to see the campus, to the co-op to buy books, to the gym to sign up for a locker and towel. It was conceivable that we could become best friends, brought together by the simple caprice of a situation. I'd always wanted something like that to happen. With someone as *hurrah* as Pete, it had always been impossible. So why now? I tried not to get my hopes up. We spent our day simply adjusting to the Gothic Yale architecture and busy New Haven streets, amazed that we were actually here, among the Ivy League: Harvard, Yale, Princeton, Columbia, Cornell, Dartmouth, Pennsylvania, Brown . . . their insignias reproduced endlessly on every shirt, beer stein, and car window, floating among us, icons authenticating our newfound existence, an achievement we could barely comprehend.

I tried to think of something illuminating to say. "Most of these buildings look like they were built around the same time, don't they? A Germanic influence or something. How old do you think that one is over there?"

"What, that church?"

"Yeah."

"It's just a church, I guess. Not too old."

"Uh-huh. I thought so."

It wasn't until two P.M. on Tuesday afternoon that we queued up for the first official activity, to take place outside the dean's office, second floor, in the vestibule around the library lobby: picture taking for ID cards. Identification before anything else— before socialization, before ceremony. We had to be made official. On the second floor of the medical school, the hall opened up into a circular balcony, from which you had a view of the library below, built in the shape of a Y, for Yale. The little round logo on the library's floor was a map of the library, a small Y, encoding the building's structure like a gene segment or some mystic medieval rune. We stood in a line, waiting for the voice inside to call our names.

"Daniel C. Anderson," we heard, and Daniel, who was standing in line ahead of me, ducked to get his Afro under the door as he went into the room, from which proceeded a tiny flash of light, and then emerged a stunned-looking boy with Oriental eyes and a punk haircut—the velveteen black hairs standing straight up like bristles on a whisk broom—concentrating so hard on the card in his hand, he almost bumped into me.

"Excuse me," he said. "Sorry."

"How'd it turn out?" Pete asked.

"I look like a convict." He showed us the picture. He did. Someone just busted for PCP. His name was George Yan Su, which I read from the card. "I've got to live with this picture for four years? It's not even me. I was holding back a sneeze when they snapped it. If they want to see what I look like trying not to sneeze, then okay. Otherwise . . ." He shrugged. He told us his name was George Yan Su, which we already knew. Someone in the room called my name. "Don't look directly into the light," George advised as I walked away.

When it came my turn to be photographed, Pete stood behind the cameraman, making faces. "Turn your head," said the cameraman, holding up his light meter like a maraca. "Smile. Sit up straight. Chest out. Show a little teeth. No—don't guffaw. That's better."

I realized that I was squinting, that I could wind up with a picture like George Yan Su's. My portraits always came out so different that I could never get a stable image of myself in my mind. Did I even know what I looked like? Only in photographs.

"His name really isn't Levinson," Pete said as the camera was about to snap. His voice was conspiratorial, affectionate, as if he realized the implications of pinning you down to a little two-by-three card that you had to carry with you everywhere you went, that you were lucky if it even *remotely* bore a resemblance to that idea of yourself that you carried in your head. "He's really an undercover cop. Looking to make a few benzedrine busts."

I laughed, the camera flashed, and Pete slapped his hand on my shoulder. It felt good; his hand, what he'd said to me, or rather, the chummy way he'd said it, saving me from the fate of a bad photograph—and then he took his hand off. When they gave me my picture, my face reduced to the size of a thumb, it didn't look bad, but it didn't look as good as I'd hoped either. I looked strange, a stranger—this guy with too-long hair and an out-of-fashion shirt—and I had the bizarre sensation of being attracted to myself (which I ignored).

I waited for Pete to get his ID, then we walked out of the room together, this Daniel C. Anderson person staring suspiciously at us as we went. At the time, I couldn't decide if he was black or not (later he told me "it didn't matter")—he was sort of taffy colored, not really any specific color at all, which unnerved me. It was the Afro that made him look black more than anything. Maybe he was Colombian. He stood there, watching us and not saying anything, as if he didn't speak English.

"Hey, man," Pete said to him as we walked by. "Don't look so glum. We're Yale Med students now. Yale Club Med. We're gonna get some books, some financial aid, some fabulous babes, some brewskis. Hey, we're gonna be *doctors.*"

Dean Kowalsky began the *official* orientation.

"Hello," he said, his voice echoing off the walls. He tapped on the microphone. "Welcome to Yale Medical School." And then he proceeded to talk about the vibrant, illustrious, industrious, noble history of scientific research. "You couldn't choose a more trenchant occupation...."

Already, I spotted someone's eyes beginning to close.

Kowalsky told us that he was greatly encouraged by the amount of research we'd done collectively as undergraduates (enough to fill three volumes of the *New England Journal of Medicine,* he said), about how, although it was true that a small minority of us might become nothing more than mere practicing physicians, he had hopes. He introduced doctors Flavin, Grant, Sylvie, and so on, all of whom would walk us from the islets of Langerhans to the optic chiasm.

Here we were, all 103 of us, in this lecture hall, inhabiting a name, the name *Yale,* which obscured our vision of the actual walls and carpeting and ceiling around us. Maybe it was the very terror of the place that I was fascinated with. Kowalsky was worried about how much research we'd be doing once we graduated, and I was wondering if I could make it through the next four years. Sitting next to Pete, Mr. Confident, I felt especially guilty about having violated some unspoken moral imperative: If I wasn't absolutely sure I wanted to be a doctor, I should have stepped aside and given the highly coveted place to someone else, the way you were supposed to either eat all your vegetables or send them to the children in Africa. But I was a selfish bastard. Who'd refuse a ticket to the nifty, cachet-laden world of upper-class education? Yale meant never having to say, "No, sir, I'm not familiar with WordPerfect, but I'm a quick learner."

But Dean Kowalsky was beyond all that. He was pointing out how, now that these days medical knowledge was expanding at such an exponential rate, even if we studied twenty-four hours a day, we'd only be able to learn a tenth of what was considered absolutely necessary, and half of that would be obsolete by the time we graduated. He said it jokingly, aware that this had become something of a medical cliché, a standard gripe with the students; but in fact, the idea of an impossibly large and paradoxically expanding body of knowledge seemed to give him some sort of perverse pride, as if all the student activism and bleeding-heart liberalism in the world wasn't going to change this simple fact, as solid as a proton and as sure as the speed of light.

"Of course, there are plenty of on-campus organizations that could use your help. If you get tired of the lab."

But he got off that topic quickly. Apparently he'd only mentioned it at the behest of the student chapter of Physicians for Social Responsibility, who were waiting in their jeans and sarongs to take the floor next. Kowalsky came to the end of his talk—he took off his glasses to emphasize the point—and returned to his theme of research, of our taking up the mantle of all this technology. "And even if you do go into private practice," he admonished, "remember, nothing says you can't publish on the side."

Next and last on our schedule was the pièce de résistance—a benediction from Henry O'Benny, the dean of Yale. We went back to the dorm, where I brushed my teeth and washed my face. Then I put on my suit, which I hadn't worn since the interviews, picking off the lint. If all they were going to do was give us speeches and ceremony, I could handle it. There was something soothing about letting all these bureaucracies carve out a space to belong, a home and society and way of belief that you could easily slide yourself into—and the rewards and security they promised, like the simple pleasure of turning on a computer or six-chamber CD player or some other labyrinthine technical machine, and being assured of its initiating electronic glissando. Just be happy that it worked. Just don't look at the machinery too closely. That seemed to be what everyone was always telling you.

As soon as Pete and Zane were dressed and ready, we locked our doors and marched ourselves over to main campus.

"For the next few years," O'Benny announced from his pulpit, "you will be entering into a specific field of study, a very tiny field, like a room. And in this room, all the doors and windows will be shut tight." He gripped the sides of the podium and spoke with the furor of an evangelist. We were in Woolsy Hall, the cathedral where famous harmonica bands played on their tours through the continental U.S., where popes dropped by occasionally for Sunday Mass. The Most Impressive Pipe Organ in the World (it had some official title like that) stood in amber and golden array like a corona behind O'Benny's head, while all along the sides above us were balconies and second balconies and pyramiding epi-balconies, all with centuries-old uncomfortable wood seats. A thousand sweating graduate students clothed in dresses and ties filled the floor, waiting to be awed. O'Benny's body was small and distant—since we sat toward the back—but his voice echoed clearly over the invisible loudspeakers. "For a time, you will concentrate on your chosen area of study to the exclusion of all else. You will submit yourselves to the whim and fury of temperamental advisers. You will work night and day on their petty projects, participate in their back-biting politics, lick the very spittle from their boots. Your lives will be their insignificant playthings. But rest assured, one day those doors will open again, and you will be let loose from the dim desk-lighting of graduate study and out into the bright neon of the real world. And maybe even get a job."

"Sounds promising," whispered Pete.

"Lovely." I concentrated on a fly crawling up Zane's collar: It crawled over the top and then down the back of his neck.

"Pete. Hey, it's Pete DuPree."

Pete turned around. A highly tanned guy sat in back of him— cheekbones you could ski down—and he was startled as hell to see Pete. He slapped him on the shoulder. "Dude, don't tell me you're going to be a Yalie too?"

"Hey, Ferguson. What brings you to the Great White North?"

That was my first meeting with Fergie. But his wasn't a face that you could easily get out of your mind. I'd soon learn that all too well.

"Can't take sunshine forever, dude. Melanin cells need a rest. Didn't Diane tell you I was here? Diane Veldt? Or haven't you seen her?"

They began an intense conversation about people and places I'd never heard of, most of the names having the word *beach* in them—Pimple Beach, Venus, Dismal. *Now we're going to take out your appendix, dude. Then we're hitting the waves.* Not exactly the GP for me. But then, GP, I suppose, was the farthest thing from Ferguson's intentions. They hung their arms over the pews and talked like cowboys at a fence. Pete—I'd lost him. He'd found one of his own.

Right then I had a vision: ten years later, Pete and Fergie as sports orthopedists, Porsches in the parking lot and buxom sec-retaries in the lobby, binding broken surfing arms. It was inevi-table. They already had it in them, growing, this embryo of their future capacious selves.

"Shhhh," warned Zane, but Pete and Ferguson didn't hear him. "Shhh," he said again, tapping Pete lightly on the shoulder.

"That's Ambassador Vladimir Petrivov. He's giving the closing remarks."

Pete and Ferguson sat back in their seats. But they both kept smiling, and wouldn't stop, so happy with themselves, so happy to have found each other.

We walked back to the medical school as a group of four, rather than three, and in the intervening period there'd been a definite shift in group dynamics. Pete and Ferguson stayed close to each other, walking ahead at a pace that required genuine concentration to follow, but was just short of running away. Sometimes they jostled over the rough pavement, and their arms touched, and sometimes they bumped into each other on purpose. I didn't want to watch this, the deceptive innocence with which they communicated what I couldn't help but interpret as an almost erotic intimacy. (Almost erotic . . . almost erotic . . . How could there be eroticism, purely in the abstract, if the participants weren't aware of it? Was eroticism a quality, as the metaphors claimed, like chemical transport or electricity, some absolute physical principle independent of the bodies through which it flowed? Something to be observed and verified by an independent objective eye? Like myself? Or was eroticism something completely idiosyncratic, something I could design and apply however I saw fit?) They'd formed an instant fraternity; Zane and I were the remains.

"So Zane, where're you from?"

"Minneapolis, actually." He walked with a shuffle, deep in thought. You could practically see the wheels of the Krebs cycle spinning above his head. We passed a bookstore, a bagel shop, a druggist, three or four ice cream stores, but he didn't notice any of them. I made mental notes—where to come back to in the future, which ice cream stores had the best specials, the most colorful chalkboards. Zane shuffled along. "How about you, Paul? What'd you get on your MCATs?"

I invented some number, something outrageously high, but Zane only nodded, deep in thought. The subject was dropped. By the time we got back to the dorm, Pete and his friend had disappeared, and it didn't take much effort to lose Zane.

The next day, we got our cadavers. Human dissection was supposed to be the most notorious ordeal of the year, but I was actually looking forward to it. I thought it would be the most interesting thing going on: learning about the body, not abstractly, but actually taking one apart. A chance to push back the white lantern of rational understanding, to exorcise all the dark childhood ghosts in the machine. And in some oblique way, I felt that the completion of a physical cartography might secure the moorings of my wandering sense of self, might give me something solid to hold on to. I had two parents, a sister, a home in the Midwest, a 3.8 grade point, a ticket to medical school. Ordinary enough statistics. Yet was that all there was to me? Did anything remain when you took all those facts away? Maybe something revealing would be there, encrypted, lurking in those formerly human slabs of meat we were getting ready to dissect.

It was like a bargain basement sale; we were given between ten A.M. and noon to grab the cadaver we wanted for the semester.

I'd assumed that Pete and I would be lab partners (I'd already scripted out the development of our relationship, and that was the natural next step), but that morning, I couldn't find him. I stood knocking on his door, waiting for some response. I covered every floor of the dorm. He wasn't anywhere. So I went over to the anatomy lab alone.

It was okay. Why should anything happen the way I wanted? I couldn't be lucky forever. He was in the lab, of course, already teamed up with Ferguson and two women. They were inspecting their body, lifting up the sheet and being careful not to touch it, as if this would give them some sort of head start on their homework.

"Hi, Pete. Nice body."

He looked up. None of the others did, though; they were too engrossed with the cadaver. He started to reply, but I held up my hand to stop him.

"It's okay, *dude*. I need to start meeting different people here anyway." I walked away before he could respond.

I was upset, but at least I had a chance to pick the cadaver I wanted, by myself. I chose the first one that looked healthy—#34, sixty-two-year-old male—then checked under the sheet to make sure everything was there. The face was wrapped in gauze, like a mummy. It reminded me of the pig from high school—bigger, hairier, but I could wait to find out the details. It was ten o'clock, and already more than half of the bodies had been claimed by people who'd arrived early. I signed up on one of the spaces by #34, where there was already one name: John Vettori. Then I went back to the body and planted myself, waiting for potential partners to come to me.

A woman wandered by, lifting the sheets of nearby cadavers, looking for the numbers on the tabletops, then looking around the room.

"What's this one like?" She seemed tired, frazzled, her hair undone.

"Male. Kind of fat. You should be able to see everything." At this point, we hadn't looked too closely at the corpses, just glanced quickly at them, at their shriveled, gray torsos, like huge dried fish in a delicatessen.

"Hmmm," she said. She came over, pulled down the sheet, squeezed and prodded the dead man's belly. Then she made a noise, a little whimper. "Ick," she said, and pulled away her hand. "Cover it up."

"Well?" I pulled the sheet back over his head. I didn't know why the face was the only part they didn't want us seeing right away. Maybe they thought it'd be the most disturbing thing to look at. Maybe they didn't want any students freaking out on their first day.

"Fine, yes, I'll take it."

"Did you see there was already a name on our list?"

She didn't answer, just looked once more around the room. She had the smallest chin I've ever seen on a person—it came to a point, like a triangle—and a tan as deep as Ferguson's. I'd been surprised by how little the people here looked like medical students (whatever they were supposed to look like), but here was someone who didn't resemble any sort of student at all. She could have wandered in accidentally from some island vacation. Maybe it was her dress. Who'd wear a dress in an anatomy lab? "I wonder where they get all these bodies. Don't you?" She introduced herself as Julie Tishman, from East Lansing, Michigan, and boy, could she use a happy-hour margarita, did I know of a good place to get one? It was only ten o'clock in the morning; after two days, no one had yet mentioned the name of a bar.

"I don't know about this anatomy business," she said. "It's kind of gruesome, don't you think? Maybe it's too much of a hurdle, their putting in hurdles like this. I've been thinking of psychiatry, myself. Anyway, aren't they supposed to have computers to do this for you now?"

Finally, a woman who didn't fit the preconceptions I'd hastily concocted of this place. What a relief. Everyone else I'd met so far seemed so together—so conscious of keeping up appearances, quoting medical scripture, making sure that everyone knew they really *deserved* their acceptance—I'd thought I was the only idiot around. *Oh, you've heard of Dr. Clawson's work? I found him marvelous to work with. He's simply a tiger with the Southern Blot.* My nagging doubts about medical school weren't that I wouldn't ever become a doctor, but that I might. And then what would become of me? I'd go around babbling about pneumoroentgenography. And after all the money my father would have spent. "It's what we've been saving it for, Paul." Such liquid funds were never available when I mentioned things like an English major, sabbaticals abroad, classes in photography. Why did our family have to be so practical? To me, their investment in my education was no more than that— they were dumping assets into Yale Club Med just as surely as they'd purchase undeveloped real estate or a money-market fund, hoping for fantastically high yields. But I wasn't so sure. Money...parents...guilt...the three were inextricably linked, drawing my life into this insurmountable conundrum. Okay. So maybe the people at Yale weren't all the snooty eggheads that I'd first thought, that we all wanted one another to believe. Maybe I was, sometimes, just as guilty of it as anyone else.

Just then I spotted the guy with the Afro, Daniel, standing in the doorway, looking as lost as I felt. "Hey, Daniel!" I called, surprised I remembered his name, him looking surprised that I knew it. "You need some partners?"

After lunch, we had the afternoon free, so I wandered around taking pictures: my dorm room, the logo on the floor of the library, the facade on Cedar Drive. It was becoming a habit of mine— every time I arrived someplace new, I wanted to make an album, a record of my presence. I traipsed through the corridors with the camera around my neck, every so often sending off the strobe. I did it with such deliberateness and concentration, I knew no one would mistake me for a tourist.

I didn't go into the hospital itself, probably out of respect, out of concern for my potential academic obligation. But I knew that was where the really gritty photo-ops would be—that if I was ever going to take the quest for the truthful image seriously, as something more than a hobby, I wouldn't be able to coddle the niceties of my "occupation." I knew, too, that it was bound to catch up with me eventually: One day, years from now, some spectacularly brutal, purple otolaryngial laceration would enter my ER, and all my carefully learned anatomical and biochemical knowledge would fly out the window. I'd just want to take a picture of it. But I couldn't help it—I'd taken up photography, poetry writing, in college, and it was the only fun around here I could have.

I got so involved with my camera, I forgot that classes were going to start the next morning, that by now not only Zane, but just about everyone else was studying, reviewing, memorizing, cramming tiny biochemical arrows into their poor, overstuffed heads. So I picked up Anatomy Lesson #1 and read the most I could in the remaining hour. But the scribblings just sat there, being scribblings. I'd already spent my daily allotment of transcendence.

I didn't think it was destined to get much better.

That night they'd scheduled a party, with alcohol and dancing and everything. So at seven o'clock, I shelved my books. The party would be in the lobby, sponsored by the second-year class, with plenty of faculty invited. Our big chance to start earning brownie points. I looked through my wardrobe and decided to wear a sport coat. I dressed with my door open, and Pete dressed across the hall, his door open, and down at the other end of the hall, it turned out, lived Ferguson, who rushed down every few seconds to lend Pete his mousse, or borrow his comb, or fart into his socks, or whatever else fraternity ex-presidents do to avoid seeming to actually like each other.

"Hey, Levs. What kind of party do you think this will be?"

"No clue. If it's too boring, maybe we can dig up something else."

"Yeah. I hear they have keggers at the colleges. But you need to know people to get in."

"Don't worry," Ferguson said, walking past. "In a week, old Peter here will be getting into every girl on campus." He hit Pete on the shoulder, then whispered something in his ear, intended for me to hear also—although I couldn't quite make it out—*faggot,* something like that, while jerking his thumb toward Zane's door and shaking his head. That was the thing—these Fergie types were always getting it wrong. It didn't raise my hopes for the medical profession. But then, Fergie didn't raise my hopes generally.

Pete came into my room, patted me on the cheek. "Now come along, son. Let's meet the people who've made all of this possible." He knocked on Zane's door. "Hey, Zane, babes, I heard the women are having this strike. They refuse to go to class tomorrow unless you come to the party."

"Coming!" Zane called from behind his door.

Ferguson giggled, then changed his mind and stopped, as though Zane's condition was beyond even humor. He took his sunglasses out of his pocket and put them on. And with his collar up and his hair gelled, he looked ready to intercept any level of chic this party could possibly offer.

In the "piano room" off the lobby (which had no piano), the furniture had been pushed back, and someone had set up a home stereo surrounded by two Radio Shack speakers, a bowl of M&M's, and a dish of guacamole. The tape deck played Madonna, but no one was dancing. About twenty people filled the room. To my relief, I recognized one of them: Bill, the guy who'd interviewed me the year before. He had on a Hawaiian shirt, too small for his chest, even with an extra button undone. He was the most casual of anyone there, but it was definitely him. His jaw muscles clenched smartly as he chewed the ice in his Dixie cup.

"Hello," I said. He'd just finished talking to some older man, some professor, and now I stood in front of Bill, waiting for him to recognize me. I could tell when he did—his eyes went round.

"Oh, hi. Glad to see you made it. What's your name again?"

"Paul Levinson."

"Right. Wow. I didn't think anyone I talked to would actually end up coming here."

"Well, you sold the school pretty well."

"Thanks."

We stood.

Pete tapped me on the shoulder. "Who's this?" He pointed at Bill. Pete and Ferguson must have followed me.

"Bill . . . ?"

"Mack," he said. "Bill Mack." He shook hands with both of them.

"He was my tour guide when I interviewed here last year."

"Nice shirt, dude," Ferguson said.

"Thanks." Bill looked down at his shirt and smiled, satisfied.

"Hey," said Pete. "Know of any parties? This thing's kind of a dud."

"None tonight. Wait around—last year this turned out to be the best event of the year. I know, that's not saying much yet. But it'll improve, trust me." He stared at Ferguson's sunglasses. He was about to become thick with the two of them, I could tell. He was the second-year version, but essentially the same model. "Hey, guys, we're having a scene out at our beach house in October. Small, but it'll be fun. It's something of a ritual around here." He fished around in his shirt pocket. "Have an invite. You too, Paul."

The cover was a palm tree. Inside was the address, directions, a picture of a beach ball by the ocean. It was all drawn to perfection, detailed indentations on the palm leaves, as if contracted out to a graphic artist. It was the sort of obsessive party invitation that only a medical student would create. "Thanks," I said, and put it inside my jacket.

"Excuse me, guys. Have to hit the john." He sucked on his straw as he walked away.

The three of us stood there, drinking our drinks. Madonna segued into her next pop single, and still no one danced. They called this a party? I remembered the days of college: sliding through beer puddles, dancing all night, serenading the library at three in the morning. There'd been so many people to do things with, you hadn't needed to get emotionally attached to any particular one of them; they'd all had a place for you. How I wished I were back there. I guess the days of science and dignity had finally arrived. Okay, so maybe I was being nostalgic. But you needn't rationalize a lifetime of solitude, of being the perfect student; you needn't ever have to reveal the real reason for it (that you had nothing better, such as romance, to spend your time on)— people just assumed that's what dedication entailed. People just assumed that if you got one exceptional grade, all they need ever expect from you was more and better analysis. And what people assumed, people generally got. I phased out and talked to no one, just stared at the party, at the way it was taking place. Watching these things was more interesting to me than actually participating in them ever could be.

Both Pete and Ferguson mouthed the words to "Material Girl," neither one aware that the other was singing too.

Except for a brief conversation with Julie Tishman ("Anatomy starts tomorrow?" "Yep." "This drink tastes like shit."), the party stayed dull, so I took my daiquiri and headed out into the night air. Here I was, wandering around an empty medical school court-yard, which could have been Hawaii, Acapulco, Florida—except that there were no palms, no resorts (Yale Club Med, they called this place!), only hospitals. But there was that ocean feeling, know-ing there's an ocean nearby and sea gulls at your feet. So was this place paradise or was it hell? Uncle Sammy would have known. Sammy, right away, would have been out investigating everything New Haven had to offer, out on the streets, out collecting stories and adventures to bring home to us kids (including Dad). That's how he'd made his reputation.

"Don't remember much about the war," Sammy had said once, when I'd asked him about Korea. "But Seoul, Paul—that was phenomenal. Did you know that I made fifty thousand bucks there importing prophylactics?"

And here I was, sticking to my obedient itinerary. The thing was, they were going to inundate you with so much information, you weren't going to have time to figure out *where* you were. Already we had a schedule that would have overwhelmed Eleanor Roosevelt. I wandered aimlessly for almost an hour, then decoded my way through the heavy glass dorm doors and rode up to my room on an empty elevator, puddles of Kool-Aid and flecks of cake spilled haphazardly on the tile floor.

There was a crowd in Zane's room. I unlocked my door. People had overflowed into the hall, so I went over to take a look. The tableau: Julie Tishman, deep in the room, wearing that same lamé dress, as if it were the only costume she owned. And hovering all around were Pete and Fergie and their lab partners and Daniel and George Yan Su and a few more I didn't recognize or couldn't see, with Zane in the middle like some Arabian shah distributing salutations and vodka. Julie was trying to trim his beard with a scissors, but kept poking him in the cheek. "Ow," Zane protested. "Quit moving." It was like some surrealistic performance piece. I called out to them ("Julie!" I called, then, "Hey, Daniel!"), but the room was noisy and they didn't notice me. I could have forced my way in with them, but with the inattention and the cumulative effect of the daiquiris, I was overwhelmed by inertia. So I went back to my room.

As I rested my head on the cheap plastic pillow, the noise of the party pulsed through the wall and the room spun around me in the dark. It was as if I had washed up on some tropical archipelago, midnight coming, natives thundering off in the distance. But before I could change my mind about joining them, I fell asleep.

When I woke up, I found myself buried under the flag of the State of New York. At first I didn't know what it was, but the flag slid off me and I saw its clever blue insignia. At the same time, I discovered that I was still dressed in my suit from last night, although someone had removed my shoes. My door was open; across the hall, Pete sat at his desk, writing a letter, the morning sunshine spilling across the parking garage and through his window.

"Hey," I called. Then, again, "Hey!" I didn't think that he was necessarily going to answer me. My mouth was glued together with that cornstarch, morning-mouth taste.

Pete walked over. "Well, what happened to you? You missed all the fun."

"Fun? Did you find a party?"

"Nah, I'm talking about next door. Zane lost some money."

"Money?"

"Yeah. Someone stole some cash from his dresser. And a blank check from the middle of his checkbook. At least that's what he says. Never saw any money myself." He picked the flag off the floor and started wrapping it up, folding it over his arms, end over end. "You were sleeping with your mouth open. Like one of those cadavers. Thought you'd preserve better covered up."

"Someone stole his money? When?"

"Last night. He had a bunch of people in his room."

"Yeah, I saw."

Pete sat on the corner of my bed, holding his flag. I sat up and crossed my legs. Mr. Athletic, Mr. Enthusiasm, Mr. Friendly. First he'd be distant, then close—why couldn't he make up his mind? I'd always gone out of my way to avoid these friendships, afraid of the emotional seesaw they created. Somehow, I had to make my feelings become more Platonic, more stoic. Then I wouldn't have to bother with the oscillations.

"It's creepy, I tell you. What's going on."

"Creepy?"

"Well, you know, everyone there last night was a first-year medical student." He arched his eyebrows and spoke with sinister overtones.

"So?"

"So." He stood up, triumphant. He snapped out his freshly folded flag and wrapped it around his neck like a scarf. "So that means...someone in our class is a thief." He let the suspense hang, as though the words had transformed him slightly, and he wanted me to notice it. As if they'd made him, by association, potentially mysterious, now that today was the first day of medical school, we were both hung over, someone in our class had kleptomania, and Pete had been the first to deduce it. But he wasn't any different—he was just plain old Pete DuPree, someone I knew well even though I'd only known him for three days; someone I felt as though I'd known forever, his whole life, as though I knew everything that he'd ever done or could ever possibly do. He stood there, flag in his hand, and wiggled his eyebrows dramatically. Then he went back to his room.

My phone rang. It was Mom and Dad.

"Honey, how are you? It's so nice to hear your voice."

"Hi, Mom."

"Paul, how's everything? We thought we'd call to see how you're doing. How's medical school?"

"How's medical school?" I coiled the cord around a finger, then started taking off my wrinkled clothes, crumpling them up and tossing them in the hamper. "I don't know. It's all right I guess. It's a lot like summer camp."

Our first class of the year was anatomy lab—an appropriate way to begin, I thought, since anatomy wasn't really so much about facts as it was about becoming intimate with a body, the centerpiece of this whole profession. As I looked out the window of the dorm, preparing myself for class, the plan of my life came for a few moments into focus, and I saw myself as a participant, looking down on the medical school from on high, from the vantage point of the impartial, the window where I stood. It was all so automatic. And I didn't know if it was me who was watching this scene, or my parents.

As if answering a religious call, clusters of students started coming out of the dorm, walking across the courtyard in their fresh smocks. With those smocks on, they didn't look like the people I knew anymore, like the rowdy and amiable partyers from the night before. They looked like professionals. It was spooky. Then I put on my own smock, and I looked like one myself.

Julie and Daniel and I—we gathered in a group around our cadaver like an Indy 500 pit crew ready to change tires. Before we were allowed to touch anything, the instructors showed us a videotape of what we were going to do. The bars flickered on the television screens, and then we saw a hand slipping a scalpel through the best (plumpest, smoothest, chunkiest) cadaver of the bunch, parting integument as smoothly as a hostess carving a slice of Brie, then pointing a finger at the each of today's illustrated muscles and tissues, brightly yellow or red or purple, while some anonymous, monotone voiceover catalogued each part. The message of the tape seemed to be: See how easy—the body not only comes apart, but explains itself in the process. On the TV, you couldn't tell that the dissection was human (it might have been plastic, a special effect), so it wasn't too bothersome; besides, you were used to seeing things get cut up on TV. It had an air of inevitability. Like everything else about this place. The hand on the tape (Dr. Grant's, the anatomy faculty team leader) sliced through our entire two-hour dissection in less than fifteen minutes. "Got that?" the voice asked in the end, as the screen went to snow. Then the instructors turned on the lights and snapped on their gloves. The show was over.

"Begin," they announced simultaneously, one placed in each corner of the lab. Did they actually expect us to just start doing this ourselves? Our own cadaver wasn't half as photogenic. He even had what I thought was a patch of mold, right above his left hip.

Daniel grabbed a scalpel and held it up, poised over the body like a boy waving a tiny American flag. We could tell that he genuinely wanted to start cutting, to make that first intrusive incision, and yet he didn't want to disturb that perfect integument of flesh. Who could blame him? The body below him was real, no pixilated image: gaunt, flattened, vaguely fishy, the skin waxen and yellow as a parchment made from whale bones and rawhide. Only the chest showed, greeting us in all its bared glory with two hardened nipples on a broad, gray surface speckled with wisps of hair. Julie Tishman had opted herself out of the running—"I'm not carving that thing"—but she stared at the cadaver from a safe distance, waiting, perhaps, for it to take the scalpel from out of Daniel's hands and cut open its own chest, part the ribs, and display its marvelous innards like a traveling salesman unveiling his suit-case.

The last person in our foursome, the alacritous John Vettori, stood off to the side, calmly observing. Since no one was making a move to begin, Daniel, Julie, and I were starting to turn it into a joke. "Just think of it as hemming a garment," Julie suggested when Daniel still wouldn't move. "It's not going to bite," I added, then became quiet, afraid he might decide to make *me* do it. This John person didn't say anything—he had remained unknown to the rest of us until this very moment, yet here he was, sneaking into our group: square-jawed, wire-rimmed, with the look of a sea captain and also the air of a man who would never captain any-thing; he had that type of vague, undefined personality so for-gettable you forgot what he looked like even as you stared at him. He stood half-reading his anatomy text, half-watching the cadaver and Daniel's waiting scalpel. Along the side of the room, our in-structors wandered up and down, hands behind their backs, look-ing for teams who needed help.

It was then that I realized they'd lied when they said that there'd be no tests here.

"Okay. Why don't I do it," John said into his book, and still not looking at Dan or Julie or me, he took the scalpel from out of Daniel's hands and cut a fourteen-inch line from sternum to navel. He moved with the precision of a sewing machine, in this little playacting of surgery, giving a stylish flick of the wrist when he was through.

"So now what?" Julie asked. The incision had changed nothing about the cadaverous cadaver except make it seem all the more daunting. There was an irremediable fact here: This thing before us wasn't a frog, or a pig, or a shark, as we'd all seen in high school, but a human being. A human being who had once had a wife and kids and—who knew, a house in the Hamptons?—and whom we were about to take apart into cords and globules like so much sliced pastrami. It was both this physical representation of death, in the shape of a two-hundred-and-thirty-pound man with a face wrapped in gauze, and the absence of any discernible sign of life in its greasy corpus and formaldehyde stench, that so unnerved us. We were used to grease and formaldehyde and death, but we weren't used to the Dead, or their messengers, the Dissected. As for myself, I concluded that the deadness and humanity of the sample before us was only a concept, an idea, in our minds— a projection of our own fear of death and humanity. The obvious trick to getting through the class would be to learn to think of a cadaver as nothing more than another interesting hunk of meat.

So I did just that. I selected one of my own brand-new scalpels and finished the "I"-shaped cut that John had begun (carving our "I" onto this other man's body). Then I started pulling back the flap of skin to reveal the muscles, interstitium, and fat underneath. Julie, John, and Daniel each pulled their fair share and then we all leaned in closer.

"What are we looking for?" asked Daniel. "Something called the intercostals?"

"Yes." John consulted the pictures in the anatomy book, more colorful and clear than the human specimen before us. We had three atlases in the lab with us, and we looked at them constantly, hoping to navigate this strange new territory; we were like a group of tourists let loose with Michelin maps and a Berlitz dictionary. If you wanted to find anything, you weren't going to locate it by looking at the deceased, who were never organized enough to present themselves in complete body systems and color-coding (although the injected acrylic dye did help). "These are them. Here and here." He pointed with his scissors at some vague tissues.

"Ah . . ." said Daniel. "Yes, quite interesting."

"Looks like ribs to me," Julie said. She was rubbing grease into a circle along the cadaver's thigh. Her nails stretched her plastic gloves almost to the snapping point; the spot below her fingertip was shiny and discolored. "What next?"

"We haven't gotten to the fat yet." I glanced quickly at the rest of the assignment. "All around the stomach. It looks like we just spend today scraping away fat."

"That's going to take a while."

"Yeah, this guy has a lot of it. No Scarsdale diet for him."

We scraped lobules of yellow fat, like little daffodil petals, into a metal bowl. As the room heated up, the lobules melted, turning into a clumpy sauce.

"It's too bad they can't do this to you when you're alive," Julie said, carefully transporting a teaspoon-sized lump of fat over the body and into the bowl. "Isn't it?" She said it with obvious distaste, curling up her nose as the spoon moved past her eyes.

"They can, you know," John replied.

Afterward, we looked for a sink.

"Well, that's it." I threw my gloves in the trash and washed my hands with pumice soup. Daniel stood next to me, copying my movements exactly. "Our first day of anatomy."

"I . . ." Daniel began. "You think we did okay, huh?"

"Sure. Except for when Julie knocked the fat on the floor. Besides, who cares how we did, as long as we learned something. We don't get grades anyway."

"We don't get what?"

"Grades. We don't get grades."

"Really?"

I stared at him, and he must have noticed, because he immediately changed his expression. "Oh, you mean *grades*," he said.

"Oh, come on. You know. . . ."

He didn't say anything more, just copied my movements exactly. Apparently he was going to stick close by while he figured this out. I wiped my hands, and he wiped his, and then we walked out of the lab, passing the rows of horror-babies-in-jars along the way: this one spina bifida, that one cyclops, over there Siamese twins joined at the face. They mimicked real humans like a Sears Catalog of Cosmic Misery, harbingers of all the horrors and terrors human beings could contain—criminality, fear, barbarism, mutation, hunger, blindness, pain, intelligence. I hated them, their miniature reproaches, their sick, unformed pig faces, yet they entranced me—and I could have stared at them for hours.

As we left the building, Daniel seemed to be bursting to say something, but he wasn't speaking. He kept watching me as we walked, watching my feet. I tried to act as if I didn't notice. We were already in the courtyard. So was everyone else; we had all ended class at the same time. The shower was going to be packed.

"That Dr. Grant," he said finally, and shook his head, as if he'd finally figured out the appropriate remark, extrapolated from previous moves and errors like an algorithm for learning chess. "He isn't very good. His demonstration tape left out all the essentials."

"Essentials?"

"You know, why the body part has that name, what it's supposed to do. How can you learn anatomy if all you do is memorize Latin?"

"Well..." I felt exactly the same way, of course, but I didn't let on. I thought maybe Daniel's honesty was some sort of trick. Maybe he just wanted me to admit my doubts, information he'd find some way to use against me. Besides, who were we to reproach our teachers? I sniffed my hands, which still smelled of formaldehyde, even after all that scrubbing. The air outside was heavy, cool...rain coming. Someone in the dorm was hanging a rebel flag in one of the windows, while on a picnic table, someone else was fitting the carpals and tarsals we'd been given into what looked like a house of cards. Less than a day had gone by and we were already papering the skull-boxes with our personal artifacts, attempting to imitate life. I needed that shower badly; I felt as if I'd been rolling in cadaver juice.

"He just talks and talks.... I don't think he even knows what he's saying."

"I wouldn't quite go that far."

"Dr. Grant is not the type of quality instructor they should have at Yale. But the other one, the woman with the glasses, I think she knew what to do."

He was getting bolder, more confident of his opinions. The algorithm was working. He'd followed me up the elevator. Now we stood in front of my door. I had to end the conversation and go in, even though talking to him was fascinating, oddly obscure, unlike anything I'd yet encountered at Yale. I wanted to know more. I thought maybe he was brave or something, brave enough to see things honestly.

He put his hand on my door. "Uh...by the way," he said, "I was wondering if I might borrow some money. The computer made a mistake with my account. And you know, I need my books right away." He stood close to me—too close, it seemed, so that I could feel his breath on my face.

I opened the door with my key. "Sure." I shrugged. "How much do you need?"

He walked into my room, started looking around at my stuff. "How about fifty dollars?"

"Fifty dollars?" To me it was a lot of money, but not so much, really, that I'd miss it. I didn't need to ask what name to write on the check.

"Here you go."

He sat on my bed, smiling as he took it from me. He folded it in two, stuffed it in his pocket, then looked back up and smiled at me again. He seemed so happy, sitting there on my bed with my check in his pocket... and at the time, I thought it was because we were about to become friends.

That afternoon, we had our first cell biology lecture. Half an hour before it began, a crowd lined up outside the room, talking to one another, speculating about our lecturer, Dr. Flavin, the most famous of the famous at Yale. Biographers had written books about him. *Time* magazine had done an interview. Legend had it that he kept the article taped to the wall by his office, above an electron micrograph of a cheese sandwich (chosen because of its resemblance to an endoplasmic reticulum). At the moment, someone else was lecturing to the second-year class, and we couldn't yet go in. A postcard from Hawaii taped to the door said, "Aloha, everybody," the words written next to a picture of ripe coconuts, the whole thing addressed to the physiology department and signed "Dr. Alain Bernardo."

I spotted Daniel talking to Veronique, who was wearing a flowing orange caftan, the ubiquitous cigarette dangling from her lips. "Yes," Daniel said, "I was in Angola, too, last year and the suffering there is terrible." Veronique had braided hair, and she wore a necklace of seashells. Daniel stared into her eyes, his pullover shirt looking more and more African as he talked (perhaps it was the design along the collar), taking on as he watched her the characteristics of his listener as if he were a B-movie robot. He stood with his weight on one leg, as she did, and asked for a drag off her smoke. Had he bought his books yet? No, but he'd bought a doughnut, which he stuffed in his mouth between puffs as he talked.

I shouldn't be watching him, I thought. I shouldn't be worried now about what he's going to do next, about his opinion of things. But I was.

So much noise and conversation. I wondered what all these people could possibly have to talk about. Medicine? Had to be— it was all we had in common.

When we finally got inside, two hundred pounds of lecture notes sat ready for us on the stage, photocopied, collated, and stapled, next to the podium. Dr. Flavin had yet to arrive. I took a packet and stood for a moment, looking for a seat. I felt seasick. It occurred to me, for a moment, that my whole situation might have been a mistake, the result of turning left instead of right long ago at some now forgotten intersection. But there was no way to retrace my steps. On the first page of notes: multi-labeled pictures and triple-axis graphs. I flipped through. Today's lecture was eighty pages long.

I scanned the room for people I knew, to see where they were sitting, where I might intrude. In the front: John Vettori and Daniel, side by side, looking at each other's notes. A little farther back was Veronique. Then there was Zane, talking to some good-looking African-American guy in a Polo jacket, and then George Yan Su, doing a crossword puzzle. Pete, Fergie, Julie, and the lab women were all in the back row, leaning in and telling jokes and laughing. The back row was the place you sat if you didn't want to pay attention. (I'd read medical-school jokebooks that had informed me of this.) Julie's being there disappointed me, but I supposed it was only natural. I suppose I would have been there myself, if I could have.

I sat next to George.

When Dr. Flavin walked onstage, the lights dimmed, everyone hushed, and the slide show began. Here was the most respected cellular biologist alive today. The man who'd identified three quarters of the working parts of the mitochondrion, not to mention the granular and agranular endoplasmic reticula. He tapped his pointer against his leg, looking slightly ridiculous carrying a stick twice his height, and his head was as bald as a newly hatched egg. A small, white carnation was pinned to his lapel.

"Theese . . . ees a cell," the doctor finally said, slamming his pointer against the screen with a great swack. He pronounced the word *cell* with particular accent and relish, as if it were full of strange consonants we'd never heard before. "Now, you must remember, ven you get to the vards, you von't treat people—you treat . . . cells."

The audience sat rapt at attention. Dr. Flavin asked for the next slide. A picture of a cell nucleus. "Theese ... is a cell nucleus."

Three rows down, Zane Oberson wrote in his notebook, *cell nucleus.*

It went like that for two and a half hours straight. By the time Flavin finished, half the class was asleep.

After cell bio it was raining, the drops falling in patient cartoon lines over the buildings. The streets were prematurely dark, car headlights glinting in red, white, and yellow off the pavement. I rubbed dust from my eyes. The whole day was shot.

"How about we skip the rain and just head to the library," George suggested. He'd followed me out of the lecture hall.

I shrugged. I'd been sedulously avoiding the issue of where to study, but it had to be faced sooner or later. "Sure. Let's do it."

We pushed through the library doors, a whole crowd of us, pausing for a moment at the fork of the Y, then turning left and filing into the Antique Book Room. The room itself turned out to be an antique: overstuffed leather chairs, Oriental rugs, and refinished oak tables. "Wow," George said. "Nifty room." It was. There was even a fireplace, and someone had lit a fire. It was such a grand room, like something from a hotel, we were prepared to stay there quite a while; and in fact that's just what we did, studying anatomy and cell biology under lights with the glow of oil lamps, talking in hushed tones and whispers until well after midnight, until George and I took a quick break for a dinner of fish sandwiches and Cokes bought from the vending machines in the basement.

While we slid quarters into the machines, I stared at George's hair, at the bristles—how did he get it to do that?

"So, you like punk music?" It seemed like an affrontive question, but I couldn't think of anything else to ask. His head was daring me to ask it.

"Yeah, I like Lab Report. But I didn't cut my hair for them."

"Maybe there was a subliminal message on the album—'cut your hair/go to medical school. . . .'"

"Maybe. It would explain a lot."

We stood under the phosphorescent lamps and talked by the microwave, until it pinged. Then we swallowed our fish and headed back upstairs.

After a few hours of biology notes, I decided that studying in this library wasn't necessarily so bad—actually, it was better than any other place I'd ever studied. I got up to wander around the room, picking books off the shelves, books from the eighteenth century about outbreaks of cholera, their pages yellow and brittle. I liked it here, with these books, this fireplace, the dust motes twirling in the light from the windows. Here, finally, was an official inauguration of my Yaledom, more so than any welcoming lecture. Holding these old books, I felt not just a spectator of History, but also, for the first time, a participant in it, headed toward my reserved place in the technocracy. Think of all the stories here, the doctors' tales, and me, as possibly another of them. It was an anecdote, an appraisal, that I could relate one day to Uncle Sammy, to my father. They'd be overjoyed that I'd found something to like about the campus so quickly.

Of course, what I really had was three hundred pages of science to memorize. And there wasn't much to like about that.

That week I studied so much, I forgot all about my life before. It didn't matter anymore. I forgot having conversations with people; instead, I had conversations with Clemente, Stryer, and Moore. Did you really feel a tinge of anaesthesia around the umbilicus just before an acute case of appendicitis? Yes, you really did. And Daniel himself told me one day over the cadaver: how easily we were all beginning to lose touch with the outside world, to get mixed up in the head, to think that the elaborate structures we were studying were real.

"I hear everyone talking as if what's in these books is so great. Sure, the books are interesting and all, like some sort of crossword puzzle. But they're not so great, they're just a bunch of names made up by some dead people. Why get so uptight about them? Ever notice how this picture would be so much more interesting if you just looked at it, I mean just looked at the shape?" And he held up Figure #196: Musculature of the Trunk, Axilla, and Neck. Only he held it upside down.

It was a revelation to me. A new synapse connected in my brain, creating alternative dimensions. Daniel was becoming more interesting, and I tried to encourage him, but he still wasn't saying very much. I hoped for more of a clue.

As for myself, I felt simply lost, trapped in the urgency of simply figuring out what everything was called, of surviving the assault, a mixed-up gale of enzymes and ligaments and cells that were now whirring about forever in my head, even in my sleep. I'd doze through class all day and have visions about Dr. Flavin lecturing all night. The boundary between sleep and waking life disappeared. The water mark on the ceiling became an elaborate map of cell anatomy; the menus at breakfast became indexes of biochemical reactions. At lunch I picked vein-artery-nerves out of the chicken.

"What's this one?" I showed my chicken wing to Pete.

"Looks like the peroneal nerve. What's that one over there?"

"Stop it, you guys," Julie said, putting down her fork in protest. "I'm trying to eat."

"Peroneal nerve ... peroneal nerve ... peroneal nerve," Pete squawked, like Norman Bates in *Psycho*, making the wing flap about the table.

But as it was now, meals were just about the only time I ever saw anybody. I didn't have a moment free the whole week. I didn't think I ever would again.

Finally, fed up with classes and notes, on Thursday I turned on my computer. I *had* to get away, if only for a few moments. I thought I'd write a computer game, a program to quiz me on anatomy.

WELCOME TO: ANATOMY QUIZ!

-> How many competitors? (Answer 1 or 2)

-> 1

-> Enter player's name: _____

-> *Paul*

-> For how long do you want to torture yourself, Paul? (Answer 1 thru 10)

-> 2

-> Paul, you've chosen to answer *2* questions about last week's anatomy lesson. You are now at the level of "intern." You must an-swer correctly 67% or greater in order to advance to the level of "resident." Good luck.

-> What plane is situated midway between the jugular notch and the pubic symphysis?

-> *Transpyloric*
-> Yes, correct!

On-screen, a little cartoon showed a picture that I'd drawn of the peritoneum (roughly outlined) flashing on and off, until it dissolved, to be replaced by the next question.

I played a few times, but it turned out that playing the game wasn't as fun as creating it had been. In having to write up all those questions, I'd noticed the poetry in the Latin: axilla, cutaneous, omentalis. I enjoyed the sound of the taxonomy, the shapes of the organs. Daniel was right—the annoying thing about medicine was that everything had to have an exact meaning, a one-to-one correspondence between the name, which some old quack had made up in the first place and which changed or modified daily as medical science progressed, and its object, which varied from person to person and was never so ideal as it appeared in the anatomy and cell biology atlases. And I didn't think such a correspondence was possible to maintain. In fact, I thought what was wonderful about the world was its rich ambiguity, that you didn't always have to know where the road was leading, or what the words meant, or what was the exact right thing to say.

Maybe that's why I'd liked the library so much. There was no need to have the information be "precise," "empirical," "reproducible," all just to create a more elaborate system. Dusty medieval roads; barren stone houses; physicians and clerics wandering about in the dead of night—those stories could be populated any way you might imagine. How much more fascinating that was than studying for a choice between A, B, C, both B and C, or none of the above.

I went over to my closet and fished out the notes from that night I'd come back from Forty-second Street. Thinking about the library, and Daniel's comments, had given me the idea that I might try looking at all these notes and pictures and memories differently, try seeing what sort of form I could give to them, if I couldn't get them to tell me something else, something beyond their surface suggestions. I'd just gotten back my first roll of film, the pictures of the medical school. I laid out everything across my bed. I thought I'd make some sort of photo essay, a story from the random snapshots, and type the captions into my computer. I cut the pictures into curved and jagged shapes and pasted them into an empty scrapbook. It was much more fun than any real work, the formulae of biostatistics. I sat at the console and tried to think of what these images represented: The objects in the pictures— Harkness Dorm, my desk, the front of 333 Cedar Drive, a NO PARKING sign—had become unrecognizable, simply colors and lines (and the crooked letters O PAR, from the sign). They'd some- how become exotic, erotic, released from their everyday duties.

I typed a few words....

The boy takes off his shirt and looks at the jagged shapes of himself in the mirror.

I stopped typing. I felt pretty stupid—and guilty about wasting time. What was I ever going to use this for? This was simply playing with toys, all these words, cameras, electronics; it didn't generate data or cure anyone—it wasn't purposeful or productive. And I wasn't very good at it. But I was involved beyond the stopping point. There was a flood inside me, and this destruction of the order of things—it was a stopgap that let me ease the pressure, ever so slightly. It was like rising up to a higher plane and catching a glimpse of the crystal reality that Daniel had spoken of, that stratosphere where there was no space between things and the idea of things; but only temporarily, without the terrifying pros- pect of having to leave solid ground completely. As I wrote, when- ever I felt guilty, I'd save the sentences to floppy and insert Anatomy Quiz, tinkering with the programming—which, being science, at least had a justification. A use. Then I'd get to day- dreaming and I'd switch back. But every now and then, I'd be taken out of both activities and notice the machine itself—I mean the computer monitor, with its green neon glow, the alphanumeric letters composed of minuscule luminescent lines—and how, as I typed, my words—thoughts, ideas, selves—became almost magi- cally inscribed on the body-machine-brain of the computer.

2150 DATA WHAT MUSCLE MESHES LATERALLY WITH THE EXTERNAL OBLIQUE

Looking in the mirror, he traces the outline of his ~~external oblique~~ *stomach muscles, slowly running his finger under the elastic of his shorts.*

2300 DATA WHAT VEIN IS LOCATED BETWEEN THE DELTOID AND PEC-
TORALIS MAJOR

*Today he's met a boy exactly like himself, with the same gaze, and he
pretends it's this other boy whose pulse he feels.* . . .

Veins, eyes, mirrors, muscles. The more I wrote about this
boy—the more I searched the cutouts for his outline to emerge—
the more aroused I made myself, until I couldn't concentrate on
the questions anymore, or the typing, or the language—until I
had to pull off my pants, lie back on my bed, close my eyes, and
let my hand reach down. It was an all-consuming fantasy. Jaded
with the physical world, I launched into my mind completely,
sailing the geometrical mental landscapes of my imaginary animation. I had nothing real to hold on to, no solid shore on which
to land, but the picture, the fantasy, could be anything I wanted,
and I could sail there, undisturbed, for hours.

Although it didn't make up for being stuck alone amongst the
crowd in Darkness Dorm.

The next day they arrested Daniel. And so the progress of our
evolving intimacy was cut short. No more would he turn flax into
gold, anatomy lessons into art. It was as if he had died, and all
my memories of him had been replaced with those of a sinister
replicant, Lyle, whose every word was suspect and had to be turned
over in the mind, like counterfeit currency. The money I'd lent
him was foolishly gone now, as if in a night's entertainment at jai
alai. And I wondered why a petty resentment over fifty dollars
(along with the pilfered page of the Clemente atlas) was the only
thing that Daniel had left for me. I wondered why I still thought
of him as Daniel. Was there really a difference between the names?
Or was the difference all in me, in the way I looked at it? Could
a name really mean so much?

I didn't know. Maybe it was all academic, anyway. Daniel
wouldn't be around anymore to keep me occupied, to get me
thinking. I was on my own.

*   *   *

"Look, George, what about capturing contemporary science in
a new art form? Computer programs of quarks or something. A

fusion of two different systems. It could even lead to more ideas, more inventions. Someone could be like a contemporary Vesalius or da Vinci—back when empiricism and perspective used to mean the same thing."

"I never did see what was so artistic about all that: *Gödel Escher Bach.* Mandelbrot sets. That's just mathematics being spastic. Give me good old Andy Warhol. The Sex Pistols. When I'm taking a mental vacation, I want culture, not science."

At least, though, we were having a conversation. It made me realize the extent of the mental interaction that I'd been missing—things like judgment, rhetoric, opinion. That's what talking with Uncle Sammy had always been like: the push and pull of verbal boxing. He was the only one in my family who really understood me.

"George, I just don't know about this place anymore. I think I'm going crazy here. I think I'm ready to leave. Thank God you're here. Thank God I've finally found someone to talk to."

"You're just bored without Lyle Montgomery Cash around to pick your pockets. Look, according to this schedule I've devised, I've got forty-five minutes to practice my keyboards." He unfolded a scrap of notebook paper and showed me his to-do list. "Why don't you follow me upstairs. Then, afterward, you can spend twenty-two minutes with me while I eat dinner, fifteen while I walk to the library—and we can spend the last four hours and thirty minutes of the day studying cell biology."

George lived on the fifth floor, directly over my room. For about a week, I'd noticing that the chords of "Wachet auf!" came drifting through my ceiling early every evening. On one of those occasions, I'd gone upstairs and knocked on the door—and it had turned out to be him. I'd shown him the photo-story I made, the one called *Daniel C. Anderson,* and he'd liked it, despite his earlier reluctance to do any locker raiding. He'd flipped through, page by page, and gave an explanation for each picture, as if the scrapbook were designed as a photographic Rorschach test—although his interpretations had little to do with what I'd intended: supernatural auras, dancing clarinets, planetary incendiaries. But I appreciated his viewpoint nonetheless.

His room was starting to become my regular hangout—it was the most comfortable one in the dorm. It completed a style, a coordination of colors and themes, what with the carpets, the plants, the posters of Ken Russell's *Lair of the White Worm* and *The Rocky Horror Picture Show*. A whole second home.

"You know, George, I don't think that I was meant to be a doctor. Don't tell anyone I told you this. I just feel out of place. What am I going to do when I graduate, pretend to go into practice?"

"Well, if you're not going to be a doctor, what are you going to be? You have to be something. So why not medicine? It's better than being a secretary." With his foot, while he played his keyboards, he opened the refrigerator under his bed. "Want a banana?"

I broke one off for each of us.

My father had once made the very same argument. I wish I knew how to refute it. For a moment it felt as though Dad was in the room with us, flipping through a dictionary and choosing the words we could say. Weren't there any other practicable options at all?

"So tell me. Where'd you learn to play like that?"

George concentrated on a particularly difficult sixteenth-note diatonic while he peeled the banana, held under his shoulder, in between key changes. Then he segued into "The Peanuts Theme," took a quick bite, and smiled back at me. All this was his means of reply. He wore glasses whenever he read or played music: He reminded me of Rocky and Bullwinkle, Mr. Professor, but in other ways he tried so hard to overcome that image. His clothes and hair and music were part of his attempt to be "hip," something you could schedule as a five-minute exercise between classes. He achieved a very different look from Pete's raw masculinity. It was the appeal of sizzle over steak. Yet as I'd followed him up to his room, I'd thought—there's a *person* walking in front of me. In full regalia. Not just his hair, but an impressive list of after-school activities and hobbies shined about him like sequins.

As for myself, I imagined I looked nondescript. Teachers always acted exasperated when, three quarters of the way through the year, I'd ask them a question and have to repeat my name three or four times.

George's music made me sad. "The Peanuts Theme" always made me miss my younger self, my cartoon childhood where I'd always been happy simply pleasing everyone—parents and teachers—and which had inadvertently brought me here. I didn't want him to stop that haunting, deceptively cheerful melody, but he did; he went back to running his scales.

"I'm getting a roll of film back tomorrow," I told him. "But with those tests on Friday and Tuesday, I'm not even going to have a chance to look at it. And I haven't written a thing in my notebook all week."

"Someone told me about a punk bar downtown. Want to go?"

"When? Tonight?" He didn't reply. "What about cell bio? What about that schedule of yours?" How easily we gave up our plans, when pressed.

He unplugged his keyboard, folded it up, and stuck it in his closet. "Screw it. Can't study all the time, Paul. Besides, it's the . . ."

Yale System, we said simultaneously.

I went downstairs to get my jacket.

The bar was downtown, near the Green, in a neighborhood of boarded-up department stores. George had managed to slip into a black turtleneck and a pair of black Levi's, leaving me as the oddball still dressed in a shirt and slacks. But then, I wouldn't have had anything different to wear anyway. I'd never done this before.

As soon as we were inside, we bought beers and watched the goings-on from a corner. Some of the customers wore leather arm bands, safety pins in their nostrils, things of this sort. Jungle finches, deep-sea lampreys, desert lizards. They barked and brayed and rammed into one another on purpose. I'd never known that a place like this existed. We sank further into the corner. The people were certainly interesting, but more so from a distance. They were minstrels. They were sculptors. They'd carved themselves from their bodies, their exoskeletons, their clothes.

A woman looked at us as she walked by, her eyes red and dark with liner, her hair bright magenta and in strings. Her expression was shell-shocked, as if any emotional response was beyond her. It was obviously well into a typical Wednesday evening for her. She might have been thinking any number of things about us, but her attitude conveyed complete apathy. Her gaze rested on something else, something presumably more interesting, and she walked away.

George, still standing in place, started dancing, or rather, swaying. I was worried we'd have to pick up a pair of girls, to dance, and this was a charade I'd become increasingly bored with. But the advantage to a punk club, apparently, was that the exigencies of The Dance were given primacy over such suburban distractions as heterosociality. There wasn't a defined dance floor, like in most clubs. Dancing happened like a strain of contagious fever, wherever it broke out, and with whatever "partners." All definitions were left intentionally vague.

Someone bumped me, hard, and didn't apologize. He was with two other guys and the woman we'd seen earlier—they were dancing in some sort of magic circle. I wiped the beer off my shirt as I watched them. I stared at the one guy—the one who'd bumped me—for minutes, before I realized that it was more than just the wild way he was dancing that enthralled me. He had slick hair, a religious medallion resting on his chest between the open leaves of his shirt, sleeves draped over his arms like the peel of an orange. There was a singular aesthetic to him; and not just to the startling masculinity of his body, or his Sixties-retro, self-mocking uniform, but also in the way he complemented the surroundings, the way he put himself and his background in motion. But as soon as I realized that I was interested in a less than innocent way, I looked away. I tried to make it seem as though I'd been staring at the girl the whole time. George hadn't noticed any of it. He'd been reading the label on his beer.

But now, I was starting to have fun. How many different people there were here—people with charge! People in motion! Something in me strained to join them, or rather, un-join those things with which I was enjoined. I tried not to glimpse any further at that notion for fear of the limitless decimation it might unleash.

The music stopped for a moment, and George put his beer on a ledge. "Hey—you know who you ought to meet, Paul?"

"Who?"

"Dr. Sparrow."

I shrugged—Dr. who?—and the music came back on. George forgot the conversation and started swaying. He really did enjoy this music, it seemed. I could discern a rhythm and pattern to it, sure—something vaguely human, something primitive and deeply felt, what with those screaming hydraulic guitars—but I'd always assumed that pain was something to be avoided.

I read some graffiti on the wall: BORN IN HELL, in red crayon.

There were other things etched near the ceiling. The words were easy to read, but too high to have been written without a ladder. So it must have been the work of the management, to give the place an atmosphere.

And that's when I realized that there was a whole economy associated with this *culture*, an entire system of life. That New Haven had to be a multifaceted, if small, city, with several intersecting and lurid histories, of which my own medical-school community was just one small component. It didn't seem as if I could ever really find out about any of the other fragments of this town, the dark, chaotic ones, that for the first time exposed the security of my own medical-student existence as merely one of their supercilious and arrogant antipodes—and not the extent, as I'd thought, of the world. There weren't any college students in *this* bar; or, if there were, they were here, like George and I, undercover. They were "slumming." They were "in costume." They couldn't really be living this life, taking these chances, high on whatever intoxicant that you could quite plainly see on each punk's battle-weary face.

We didn't try to talk over the music. Even without standing three feet from the speakers, it was too noisy to carry on a conversation. George just kept dancing, and so I started dancing too. We were the only people in our corner, and I worried that others might misinterpret and think we were dancing together. But no one else looked at us. There was no need to "ask" someone to dance here. Such form and function were *not cool*. That was certainly a relief, yet I was afraid that without rules, I'd simply make a fool of myself. But I was sensitized now, feeling the mechanical transfer of energy, and willing to let the fools fall where they may. And the more I danced, the more I realized that self-consciousness was not only inappropriate, but irrelevant. Dancing here was both completely narcissistic and completely social; the difference simply didn't exist—the idea was to delve into your own private sector, and then explode outward, carry your awareness to the far ends of the room, in return for which you were able to disappear, *become* the energy the communis so fervently generated. And so that's the way I did it, even better than George (if I may say so). It wasn't so much a dance as a form of aggression, a physical assertion and obliteration, the closest thing to a community ritual in a community defined by anarchy.

For the first time in a while, I'd genuinely understood something new.

"Interesting place," I said as we left, taking one last look around as we walked out the door. "Certainly had an . . . interestingness to it. Inspiring, in a way. I wonder if they'd let you bring a camera."

"You wouldn't get a chance to use it. Not with the way you were dancing."

"I was just trying to get the hang of it, George. I thought you'd be proud of me."

But George was already concentrating on something else. "Dr. Sparrow, the guy on TV," he said again. "Haven't you heard of him? He does a weekly medical report on cable. He's on the staff here. Internist, I think. You should get in touch with him. Your type of guy."

"Dr. Sparrow?"

"Yeah. He's even won some sort of Emmy. I'm sure he'd be fascinating to talk to. You know, especially if you've got some questions about alternative careers."

It was a possibility. But I couldn't really focus right now on something as vague as the future. "I wonder if the library's still open, George. We must have preempted at least three hours of your schedule."

"It was worth it, though—watching you dance."

Dance? No, that wasn't me. That must have been someone else.

But on Thursday, I went into the student lounge to watch Dr. Sparrow's TV show. Nine-thirty P.M., Channel 23, just after "The Weekly Business Report."

The episode began with a whirl of double-helixes and caducei that eventually scintillated into a stable icon in the corner of the screen. Pretty impressive effects, for cable. I wondered: What did those snakes on sticks have to do with medicine anyway—the venom? A philter? Did they really connect to DNA? I was remiss on my mythology; it went beyond me. But I was intrigued.

The scene cut to an older gentleman (Sparrow, presumably) seated at a relatively conservative desk, its mahogany recalling a past era—the 1950s, say, a time when medicine was unquestionably respected, established, taken at its word—yet with enough pastels (on the recursive television screens in the background), enough sleek angles (the contemporary chrome edge and rounded corners of the desk), to suggest also the modern era: image making, persuasion, heterodoxy. The podium upon which the desk rested—mutely carpeted, with several recessed levels—also indicated that the position from which Sparrow spoke was somehow no longer the "ground," somehow suspended in a network of other transections. To me, the whole idea was an explosive, chimerical hybrid—medicine meets television—some sort of post-nuclear mutation, and I was held rapt to the screen.

"WELCOME TO 'HEALTH BEAT,' WITH YOUR HOST, DR. CARLIN SPARROW, YALE SCHOOL OF MEDICINE."

Dr. Carlin Sparrow
Yale School of Medicine

were the letters that flashed for thirty seconds under his picture.

"Interleukin-2. GM-CSF. Erythropoietin. In the next series of shows we will be investigating the products yielded by monoclonal antibody cloning techniques. What are the potentials for cancer, transplants, AIDS, acne, and Hershey's candy bars?"

Sparrow was calm and stately, seated comfortably at his desk, like royalty talking idly to the press.

"What, you might ask, is a hemopoietin? Well, watch closely...."

I watched closely.

He talked about interleukins, colony-stimulating factors, as he'd promised, in a more interesting and entertaining way than any of our lectures. He flashed slides, animation. More interesting, I think, because he left out all the facts—the data we were routinely required to memorize.

"Okay. Let's look at the life cycle of a blood cell." He pulled down something like a weather map, a diagramed chart of red blood cells and all their cousins. Then he plucked a pointer from his pocket and elongated it (so that it became longer and more impressive than even Dr. Flavin's), and identified everything that went into making big blood cells out of little ones. "And this little ditty right here is what we're interested in. It's because of our ability to genetically clone response modifiers such as these that, for the first time, medicine has a plan—and the body's mechanisms are under our control."

He clasped his hands together and smiled into the camera. He sounded so happy about it. Especially for someone who looked ready for retirement. Apparently, this was the first episode of the season: just an introduction to the diseases in store. Before long, his half hour was up, and the show ended with the same orgy of computerized graphics and special effects, as digital and captivating as the cloning techniques Sparrow had been talking about, as if this whole world had been regurgitated out of the same binary and infinite mind.

Afterward, I went back to my room and drafted a letter.

"Dr. Sparrow," I wrote, *"I'm a first-year medical student who's seen your work. I too am interested in doing something different with my medical career. I would like it very much if we could get together sometime to discuss things, things such as photography, essays, television, reporting, whatever you might suggest. . . ."*

I sealed the envelope and walked it over to his campus mail box. It happened to be in the admissions office, and the secretary assured me that he picked up his mail every day, even though he wasn't teaching any classes this semester. Maybe he just liked going for the walk. I gave it to her and she slipped it in.

I didn't leave the office right away. I stood there, staring at the letter in his box, as if it were something he'd been waiting to receive for twenty-two years. God only knew what he'd make of it.

I was thinking—this is it. TV medicine. The Sparrow Residency. The solution to all my problems. I'd even enclosed some of my photographs.

But another part of me remembered the punk bar, and that boy, and the energy, and everything that I wanted *really*: It was a nagging voice in the back of my head. And it was this voice that said, *Jesus, Paul, if it ain't one fantasy, it's another. What kind of an asshole are you? What kind of an incorrigible dope?*

3

Heart

"**H**e let himself get rather out of shape, didn't he," Julie said. We were spending our afternoon cutting up the cadaver, our favorite routine. She talked and talked while we kept pumping the scissors. "A real couch potato," she said. "A real slobbola."

More and more, she was making comments about Zorba's personal life. "He must have been having an affair." "How many kids do you think he had?" "I bet he voted for Nixon." It was an infectious habit. We spoke about him now as if he were a favorite relative or absent friend, the fifth member of our team. (There was one team whom everyone referred to as "The Bobs." Four guys, all with the first name Bob—they'd named their cadaver Bob, too.) Every nook and cranny of Zorba's slowly decaying hide had become completely familiar, old carpeting. We dissected him with increasing nonchalance. Nathan pushed Zorba's intestines to the side while John cut away some annoying tissues. There wasn't much talking going on among the three guys anymore; we were doing our science.

"Pizzas, gyros, you can be sure. Television and Schlitz. Just look at all this sclerosis."

Julie was the one who'd named him Zorba, and "Greeks, Italians, you know, they all eat a lot of greasy food." John was Italian himself, and thin, but he didn't stop her oratory. "I bet he had ten kids—ten kids and an affair with the souvlaki waitress on the side. I bet he was about to develop pancreatitis too, with tissue like that."

"Here, Julie," John said. "Hold tighter. You're letting go of the rib cage."

It always embarrassed me when we got into these discussions about Zorba, as if there was still the possibility that we might help him, rather than simply take him apart. We were well into the abdomen now, getting to all those familiar, picture-book organs. The purpose of the acrylic dye was to dehydrate his blood—the greatest pool of it had collected around his heart: pink, pasty, and granular. Once we cleaned it away, I cut open the heart with a scissors, and after peeling away layers of blood, found a whole universe of trabeculae, a jewel box of secret passageways. I stuck my finger in an auricle, searched for an opening, and watched as it wiggled out of the aorta, like a worm.

"Neat, huh?" The heart had always been my favorite organ.

"Wow," Julie said when she saw my finger poking out at her. "Let me try that."

She stuck her finger in there, too; she was getting more daring every day. Then she laughed, easily amused. I had to admit, she made the thing—this human heart—seem like a pretty ordinary sack of flesh.

"It really is so fragile, isn't it?"

Afterward, we drained the cadaver juice from the plastic sheet, as usual. We wrapped everything in preservative-soaked cheese-cloth, then covered up Zorba for the night, organs and flaps of skin all folded into place. I went back to the dorm and took a shower. My hair was wet, my skin tingling. Still smelling the formaldehyde, I felt slightly ill as I walked back to my room, walking down the hall in only a robe. I unlocked my door, kicked off my sandals (you didn't want to step on any shower-roaches in your bare feet), put on clean clothes, then tossed my smock under the sink—a smock soaked with oil, bits of skin and fat and hair, like something from a back-street Chinese restaurant. That's when the phone rang.

"Paul, I'm glad you're home." My father's voice sounded hollow; right away I knew something was wrong.

"Hi, Dad. What's up?"

"It's Uncle Sammy. He's had a stroke."

My mother came on the line. "Honey, honey? Are you all right?"

They didn't tell me everything, just that things didn't look good, but somehow I knew he was dead, I sensed it. I couldn't move. My parents' voices echoed in my ear. Uncle Sammy? *My* uncle Sammy?

"Paul, can you miss classes this week? Could you book a flight home?"

I said I would. After I hung up, I paced the room. I picked my anatomy book off the floor. I couldn't breathe. I felt guilty, irreverent—all that cutting up I'd just finished, it had to be related. Maybe I was just jumping to conclusions. But all my decisions, my plans: How could you rely on them if the people who you made them for died?

My parents called back, told me Sammy was "gone" after all.

"He didn't feel a thing. It happened so suddenly, there was no warning. That's the way he would have wanted to go."

They told me they'd booked me a flight. They told me Dad would meet me at the airport. I hung up the phone and, without even thinking, too numb to feel anything, took a suitcase from under my bed.

*   *   *

The night before the funeral, I went to see my father in his study. We were supposed to stay at home and sit shiva for seven days, but I could only afford to miss classes for three. Dad opened envelopes with a letter opener he'd gotten from the Jewish War Vets, the handle in the shape of a mezuza. Sammy had had one just like it. They'd always been like brothers.

Dad was disconsolate, silent—I didn't know how I should act around him. Even over a period of weeks, his hair seemed grayer, although he still had the square jaw and stern good looks of an I.U. undergrad—I was surprised because every time I saw him again, I rediscovered this. Dad. What if something ever happened to *him*? I remembered how when I was seven or eight, Mom would bring home Dad's shirts in starched packages of five, and when he held me, there was always the scent of pine. He used to plant trees and vegetables in the yard before he took to watching television. On the weekend we'd drive down to see the Hoosiers, and on the way I'd explain to him my theory of cosmology, black holes, time travel. He'd debate it seriously with me as if we were engineers scheduling the next expedition to Mars. That was years ago, when

I was a child. Now we rarely talked anymore, unless I needed money or he needed to convince me of my role in life.

But sitting in that room back in Indianapolis, Uncle Sammy newly dead and all, the only thing that came to me was—what's the biochemical profile of a stroke? Are strokes going to be on the next exam? I just couldn't conceive of this event in any other terms. So the stupid thing I said to my father was, "He had a stroke, huh? Do you know what kind?" The idea scared me; I wondered what it'd feel like to have a stroke, if you could sense the lack of oxygen, the paralysis, if you began losing your concentration and willpower along with your autonomic activity.

"It was an embolism, I think." Dad read another letter, then pinned it to the corkboard above his desk. He didn't say anything else. I fidgeted with the knob under my chair. I didn't know if he was supposed to be consoling me, or I him. It was eleven o'clock. The rest of the house had gone to bed.

"The reason I ask is, see, we've just finished dissecting the heart, in anatomy lab." Dad didn't look up, so I went on. "There's a pericardial pouch around the heart, you know, and in our cadaver, when he had his heart attack, all this blood was stuck in it. Dried-up blood. I wonder if that can happen in the brain. I mean, if he had an embolism, maybe Sammy's blood could have been trapped in the meninges." *Meninges*, I thought. What a strange word.

Finally, I had Dad's attention. He stared at me. "Clinical son of a bitch, aren't you?" He slammed the desk drawer and walked out of the room.

Wow. I stood up and went to look out the window. Why had I said that? Maybe Dad was right, maybe there was something inhuman taking control of me, something that gave me a perverse pleasure at seeing how undetached and emotional the rest of the world could be, and making them suffer for it. A revenge, of sorts. But wasn't Dad sending me to medical school for the very purpose of becoming a *clinical son of a bitch*? That was the thing about Dad— he could be as irrational as he wanted, whereas I was always supposed to present myself logically. Hell, I was just as confused and upset about Sammy's dying as he was.

I stood in the room alone, perplexed. It didn't occur to me to apologize. I thought, simply, that it was typical—that my parents had always pictured me as the ever-cool scientist, the rational experimenter. Maybe they knew nothing more about me. I should have realized that before. I should have known that my parents had always thought of me as the next Louis Pasteur or some such. They probably thought I had no use for emotions at all.

Their assumptions could have even begun as far back as third grade. I remembered that year—the year of in-class reports; I'd decided to give a presentation on the heart. I could see, now, the added significance my parents must have attached to that. Maybe *that* was the moment of the mysterious, fatal divergence in my life. Ever diligent, even then, I'd decided that I needed not just a poster, diagraming atriums, ventricles, and valves, or a plastic model, opening up to reveal a web of fine, white plastic trabeculae that twanged through your fingers like the strings of a piano, but a flesh-and-blood Heart, donated by an authentic member of the animal kingdom. I had wanted something impressive. Uncle Sammy, in fact, had put the idea into my head. I was talking about it at dinner one evening when he said, "Hey, Paul, I bet you your father could get you a *real* one."

So it was settled. The day before that eventful Tuesday, my mother cleaned house more vigorously than ever, vacuuming be- hind my bed, ironing shirts buried so long in the heap of laundry in our basement that I never knew I owned them, even polishing the little gold medallion that was my first-grade math award— rubbing it carefully and precisely—while, probably, fantasizing about sending out invitations to my medical-school graduation. "My God, Paul, is that really you?" she teased as she dressed me for school, licking a long, sharp finger to paste down one of my uncooperative cowlicks—familiar, darting fingers that I habitually ducked to avoid. Perhaps even then she had me arriving in Stock- holm for the Nobel Prize. "If God only knew what *nachas* . . ." she said as she stood up. I could tell that she was particularly satisfied with what she'd made of me; she only used the Yiddish on special occasions.

That Tuesday, my father closed the Office of Periodontics (a word that I loved to say—periodontics, periodontics, like the name of a great, lumbering dinosaur—always having to explain to the other kids the distinction between a periodontist and a dentist) and drove with Uncle Sammy twenty miles outside Indianapolis to the stockyards. I'd asked for things before: a pony, a speed bike, a guitar, a six-foot-by-seven-foot map of Africa. All had been refused. But for some mysterious reason, they'd granted my ghoulish request for a heart.

I couldn't know what really occurred in that car, of course, but from the stories Dad told later, I knew the mood between Dad and Sammy must have been light, celebratory. After all, they were two proud Jewish American males on an errand for the *bu-oy*— proud because, to Jewish males, machismo is a vague, rabbinical intelligence, mixed with a street-smart business savvy, and at that time they must have had no doubt that in me, this testosteronic miracle was on full course.

"Back to goddamn nature," Sammy supposedly said as they pulled into the stockyards. "Look at all this horse shit." He was overweight and smoked too much; his cigars came smuggled straight from Cuba—his most expensive vice—and he rested his fat arm out the window while blowing puffy strands of smoke throughout the car. The hair on Sammy's arm had turned gray, so that it always reminded me of our dog, Skippy, a schnauzer, and whenever we gave Skippy his bath, we always commented on how he looked just like Uncle Sammy.

"Cow shit," Dad corrected. "That's cow shit, not horse shit. You of all people should know the difference." He laughed and nudged Sammy in the arm as he pulled up in front of the office, the front end of the Ford sinking down in the mud with a sigh. "Okay, Mr. Cow Heart. Bring the bowl."

The butcher, in a blood-soaked apron and fatter than Uncle Sammy even, had been expecting them. He came right out to the car. "Hiya, boys," he said. "Dr. Levinson, right? Excuse me if I don't shake hands." But he went right ahead and put his paw-print on the Ford's handle.

Sammy mumbled something as they got out of the car, trying to knock the mud from his shoes but only accumulating more as he walked. "I didn't expect the kid to take me seriously, you know. But who knows. Maybe you'll be voted the PTA Father of the Year. Maybe Paul will get a scholarship out of all of this. Maybe he'll become Surgeon General. A lot of possibilities here, you have to admit."

My father didn't speak. *Possibilities* was not the best choice of words. Before Dad had become a periodontist, he and Sammy had gone on a spree of recondite investments, none of which had gone anywhere for Dad, but which, each time, had managed to net

Sammy a little cash. (This was well-known family lore, by the way, although I'd never been privy to the details.) Finally—the lore went—as Dad perceived he had a family to raise and a real life to pursue, he'd given up his dreams of entrepreneurship and gone into gums, which held the promise of not only the independence of his own business but, more important, the security of a regular income. After graduation, Dad had found himself going to Sammy for the money for his office—money that Sammy now seemed to have plenty of. Sammy'd given it to him, gladly. But the loan, Sammy seemed to feel, entitled him to make suggestions about Dad's business, his investments, the hygienists and receptionists he hired. And even though the money had been paid back years before, Sammy's suggestions had become a habit. We kids thought of him as something like Dad's business agent. For a while Sammy even pressed Dad about getting into periodontistry himself, if not through an accredited dental school, then through my father. The idea of owning part of his own business became a beacon to him. But like everything else with Sammy, his attention eventually waned. Even so, Dad could never do anything without first getting Sammy's tacit approval. He loved Sammy, we knew, but this meddlesomeness . . . it was like a wet blanket over everything he did. We heard him complaining about it nightly at the dinner table. Walking into the entrails room, Dad must have seen the rest of his life with Sammy hanging over him, as blank and two-dimensional as the gray, Midwest horizon.

The butcher slid open the door to the parts room with a clatter, letting out the stench of a massive road kill. The room lacked windows and, from the smell, air conditioning as well. "Cow parts, kidneys, spleens, livers, hearts," the guy told them. "Whatever you want."

Once inside, Sammy handed the bowl to my father and scraped the sole of a shoe with his cigar. "Goddamn nature, all right."

Dad gave the bowl back to Sammy. "You want to help, or you want to criticize?" They waited a minute, then the butcher brought them a heart—red, mulchy, and nondescript as a blob of ectoplasm, which came as a small surprise to Sammy, who had expected something more valentine-shaped and spectacular, but not to my father, who, having once worked in a delicatessen, was used to the fleshy indeterminacy of animal organs. The butcher placed the heart like a lump of pizza dough into Sammy's bowl (which Dad had taken from Mom's kitchen—without telling her), where it sank sadly, then Dad and Sammy covered it up with a kitchen towel and paraded it back through the mud to the Ford, Sammy carrying it before him like a docent carrying a crown, cigar stub in his mouth and mud splattered up the sides of his bell-bottom slacks. Dad got in the driver's seat and they rocked a few times to get dislodged from the mud, then waddled the car on out the gate, rumbling over bumps, lumps, and potholes.

Meanwhile, the heart sat between them, enigmatic as a bowling ball.

"Let's stop," Sammy said as they drove past Barnaby Downs, which fortunately hadn't been along the route to the stockyards, but coincidentally appeared through Sammy's window as they drove toward the elementary school.

"I don't think so," Dad said. "We're on a schedule."

"Let's stop," Sammy repeated, like a mantra. "One race only."

So stop they did, at the moldy but Soon-to-Be-Renovated Barnaby Downs, where somehow Sammy managed to convince Dad to blow eighty dollars and an hour and a half on two "lucky" horses (an event that Dad never told my mother about, but which he'd confessed to me at my bar mitzvah, empty liquor bottles and drunken uncles all around, the feel of backslapping, the heady aroma of the Torah and conferred, clandestine masculinity) until the realization that they were running late overtook them and Dad rushed to Pinewood Elementary faster than a high-school speed demon, swerving around cars, old ladies, stop signs—mumbling, *"Let's stop, let's stop"*—with Sammy uncharacteristically silent (and characteristically richer) beside him.

Meanwhile, a freshly harvested cow organ had been sitting in a ninety-five-degree car for over an hour, and the windows were open, this time, out of strict necessity.

*   *   *

So this was the picture I had of Sammy and Dad zooming toward my elementary school. The problem was, I'd never before reconciled it with the picture of myself, eight years old, waiting for them to arrive. I'd never seen how I was merely one small actor in a larger design, caught in a nexus of children and teachers, brothers and sisters, fathers and mothers, and all their confused and assorted dreams. I'd always thought only of my own.

And in my own, I dreamt of escape. God, how I'd longed to get out of the confines of Pinewood Elementary. How I thought I never would. The place was built like a mental hospital—a one-story ranch house, basically a long corridor, narrow as a dungeon, that turned here, and then there, and then again later, rounding in on itself like a shell. You entered at the mouth, and there were twin classrooms for each grade, each one opposite the other, going down the hall—two kindergartens, two first grades, two second grades, and so on. As a third-grader looking ahead, it was possible to see the future extending out before me, *clat, clat, clat,* infinite and even-spaced and color-coded, until it veered away into the distance. Every day, we lined up and marched past it, onto the playground for recess.

On occasion, to be sure, Pinewood Elementary could also be an as-yet uncharted wilderness, effervescing with intrigue. We had carnivals for the kids at Pinewood twice every year, and for weeks afterward, some random object—a large coat hanging in the coatroom, a colorful piece of tape that hadn't been pulled off the wall—would remind me of the carnival nights, the nights of transformation when the school building, the whole lumbering apparatus that surrounded us, seemingly disappeared, and our everyday desks and classrooms would take on the resplendence of distant stars and galaxies. Then I'd stare at that coat or piece of tape, lost, as though I had no idea what I was looking at. This was the feeling that I had as Dad and Sammy showed up at Mrs. Pepperdine's door, carrying Mom's mixing bowl, with that thing—the heart. I waved from the back row. Sammy smiled and waved back, pointing redundantly at the bowl carried like a football under my father's arm.

There they were, my relatives.

As I walked up to the door, the girl at the podium interrupted her oratory to flash a glance at Sammy and Dad. Now that my prize exhibit had finally arrived, on time and apparently in one piece, I was both relieved and, for the first time, nervous. I suppose that I'd never fully believed they would actually turn up with it, that I would actually get to show the kids something so amazing, so true-to-life, that only adult surgeons (almost) ever got to see. I'd been preparing myself to be satisfied with the models.

I lifted the cloth and looked at the organ that I was about to display for my classmates. I just stared at it. It was meat-colored, striated with lines of fat, and completely spherical: You couldn't see any of the infamous chambers. I was a little disappointed. You couldn't tell *what* it was, exactly; the kids might think it was just a pot roast. It was even in a mixing bowl.

"Good luck, Paul," Sammy said.

But I wasn't listening. I dropped the cloth and went back to my desk, where I sat with a cow heart in a plastic, yellow bowl on my lap. Somewhere in the other world was the rest of this animal, as big as a car. And I could hear my own heart, beating inside, impossible to look at, really. And for the first time I felt made of removable bits of machinery, parts over which I might not have any conscious control.

I thought Dad and Sammy might leave now, but they didn't; they drifted toward the back of the classroom, trying to look inconspicuous.

When it came my turn, I took my poster boards, my intricate models, and my cow's heart up to the front of the room, while the students around me quieted. I set up all my posters in a semicircle. I stood behind the podium. I couldn't see the bowl from back there, but the smell of blood was unmistakable, so I knew it was okay. I looked out at the class. They shifted around in their seats, already getting bored. "I'd like to present . . . the Heart," I began stupidly. But my voice gradually improved. I talked about the chambers— frog chambers, fish chambers, mammals. I had the words CIR-CULATION and OXYGENATION printed on my poster, and pointed to them in the places where Sammy had advised me to. . . .

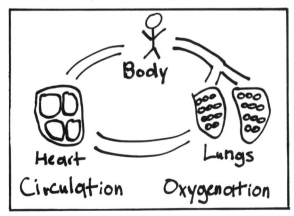

The body, as I'd drawn it, was spatially inaccurate (it didn't belong in the middle), but I had no other means of representing it the way I'd come to understand it—as an indivisible entity, a separate and pure object, ordering about its components: units that I might build a model of, and bring to class. I showed the other children a panoply of atriums and ventricles, arteries and valves, each plastic piece labeled delicately with its own musty letter. It wasn't my accuracy that was wonderful so much as the smell of glue—and the slab of meat that sealed the illusion, that made it all irrefutable, a miracle. And this purity of explanation was something, over the years, that would eventually be lost to me, as I was compelled to take the diagrams seriously—to answer tests, memorize details, and to stake my future on getting the answers right.

I read my notes off of index cards, picking them off the podium with a sharp *flick*. Fourteen years later, I would dissect a human heart, I would study elaborate pictures in a textbook of clinical anatomy, but I would never know more than I knew on that day.

After I was done, I let the kids come around and touch the heart if they wanted. They formed a small line, coming one by one, each poking it with a cautious and curious finger, leaving small indentations like oceans on the surface of a planet.

My dad was at the end of the line.

"My boy, the cardiologist," he said, somewhat jokingly, but still too seriously for me. He put his fatherly hand on my shoulder, and I smelled the cool in his suit, which reminded me of downtown, his office, but today also smelled of straw. He rarely touched me that way; this seemed his way of claiming me, of taking a small amount of credit—credit he deserved, I felt, for all the encouragement he'd given—and it made me feel good that we'd done this favor for each other.

Meanwhile, Sammy talked to Mrs. Pepperdine in a nearby corner, and I craned my head to see what she might jot in her grade book. He smoked his stogie and laughed crudely at something she'd said, short bursts too loud for the classroom, and I hoped that his presence wasn't going to influence my grade. Smoke curled up in the sunlight streaming through Mrs. Pepperdine's big third-grade windows—unwanted smoke, dirty and beautiful.

The adults surrounded me. The class was over, the day was over, the other kids had gone home.

"That was an excellent report, Paul." Mrs. Pepperdine scribbled in her book. "You ought to thank your father and uncle for bringing you the...uh, display." She lifted up the towel and peeked into the bowl, confirming for all of us that by now the smell had gotten too rancid to permit any further close examination. She dropped it quickly.

"Thank you, Dad. Thank you, Uncle Sammy."

"Great kid, huh?"

"He's okay." Dad smiled at me and ran his hand through my hair.

"Come on, Fred, let's take him for some ice cream." He nudged my father in the arm. I could tell from Dad's stiffness that he wasn't keen on it. I didn't know if that was because he was anti–ice cream, or because it was a suggestion that he'd wanted to make himself. "Hey, my treat," Sammy said, and winked at Dad.

"Dad?" I didn't want to say "Daddy" in front of Mrs. Pepperdine. But the clipped, mature word still felt strange to me.

Dad picked up the bowl and put it back under his arm, thinking about it, then turned to Mrs. Pepperdine. "It was a pleasure meeting you, Mrs. Pepperdine." He shook her hand.

"Yeah," Sammy added. "A pleasure."

Mrs. Pepperdine laughed, Sammy's hand lingering in hers, while Dad turned to look out the window at the schoolyard, where some of the kids from the junior high next door hung around after school every day to play basketball. I followed his gaze to see what, exactly, he was looking at: six shirtless, shining bodies, different shapes and colors, dancing around the pavement. I saw those same boys every day, whenever I walked home, and afterward, as I walked, I'd continue to see them, choreographing their steps in my mind. They always brought up in me this vague, undefined yearning, so vague that sometimes I had to stop walking just to figure out what it might be—which I never could. (Later, of course, I knew what that yearning was: not just desiring their beauty, but wanting somehow to *be* them, to have their skill, their confidence.) When I watched them, I didn't care who they were, in terms of personality; they were probably troublemakers whom I wouldn't like very much. But like the pictures that I'd started seeing in health class, advancing one by one from a shapeless child to a well-defined, curvilinear hominid, I wanted my body to grow up just as solid.

It all flooded me with something warm: the muscles of the heart, the muscles of the basketball players, the muscular notes on the index cards—they were all exciting, they all exuded a similar quality of seduction that I'd not been able to isolate or name at that time. Certain things about the world just made me bristle with expectancy. But I didn't tell people this—not exactly. Already, I was learning to differentiate among the types of allure—learning which I'd be rewarded for, which no one had names for, which I wasn't supposed to have.

So I was nervous about Dad spotting these basketball players of mine, even though I was certain he had no idea what I was thinking of when I watched them. But he didn't say anything about it. His thoughts were probably along a totally different path: He was probably thinking about wanting to join them. He was probably thinking about all the reasons he couldn't anymore.

"Fred, let's go, huh?" Sammy winked at Mrs. Pepperdine, then looked at me. "So how's a banana split sound, Paul?"

"Sounds great, Uncle Sammy."

"Do something with that thing, Fred," Sammy told Dad, pointing at the bowl. "Dump it somewhere."

Throw away the heart? Weren't they going to save it, preserve it, like my math awards? But no—that's what the ice cream was for, a diversion. They were already one step ahead of me.

"Hey, guys, let's get a move on." Sammy dropped his cigar butt on the floor, rubbed it with the heel of his shoe, then picked it up like an insect and tossed it in the wastebasket. Then he walked out of the room, waving at my teacher as he went. Dad followed behind, and I brought up the rear, carrying the heart. And what with Dad's staring and Sammy's cigar, I felt that we were like a bunch of kids running around in the basement of Temple Tov Torah, indulging our urges, ignorant of authority, disrespectful of the Commandments. A marvelous, intergenerational conspiracy.

*   *   *

Fourteen years later, when I got my acceptance to Yale Med, it was the first time I'd ever stop to think: So I'm going to medical school. Medical school. How'd that happen? It was the most ambivalent night of my life. The letter came in the mail over Winter

Break: my family congratulated me, I said thank you, and then I
went upstairs to stare out the window. It was a great feeling to be
accepted—which was all I'd ever wanted to be. But I was still, after
fourteen years, looking for an escape. Over all that time, I'd grown
up, graduated high school, graduated college, and nothing in our
family had ever changed. I was still going to Uncle Sammy for
advice.

"Uncle Sammy," I said when I got home for summer vacation.
"What do you think, should I go to Yale, or shouldn't I?"

It was June, and we sat on the porch in our backyard, eating
leftover hamburgers. The rest of the family had gone back inside,
the screen door rustling closed behind them, one after the other.

"Hmmm," Sammy said. He wiped a blotch of ketchup off his
mouth with a napkin. "Don't you want to go?"

"I don't know. Maybe." That was the truth, and the extent of
it—besides, I didn't want to prejudice him by saying anything
more. He thought for a moment, wrinkling his brow, giving the
problem serious consideration. He finished the last of his hamburger, stuffing it in his mouth all in one bite, chewing it slowly.

"Well, Paul, it's hard to turn down Yale," was all he finally
said. Like everyone else in my family, Sammy had gone to I.U.

I was disappointed that that was the extent of his response.
My parents had promised to send me Eurailing through the Alps
over the rest of summer vacation, and I knew the real reason was
to keep my mind off school (to keep these doubts from surfacing).
It was a gift-horse I couldn't refuse. They were still, after all these
years, one step ahead of me. I'd been hoping that Sammy, at least,
would have been more willing to suggest heresy. "Yeah," I replied,
looking at the ground.

"Paul, what else do you want me to say? 'Don't go'? Your
parents would kill me. They already think I'm undermining your
future every time I talk to you."

"Just because I pledged your fraternity instead of Dad's."

"I think it maybe has to do with the two weeks of Spring Break
someone spent anonymously in my condo in Florida perhaps?
When they were supposed to be studying for admissions tests?"

I almost smiled, but held it back. When he saw that I still wasn't
convinced, he shrugged. "How bad can it be? You can do a lot
with an M.D., I hear. Maybe you should talk about it with your
father."

"Yeah." I knew what he really thought—just like my parents, that I'd be an idiot not to go. Sammy was a gambling man: I was his horse, and for years, he'd only listened to my father's predictions about me. Some things even Sammy saw as too much of a self-indulgent risk to take.

So the next night, before bed, I knocked on the door of Dad's study.

"Come in." Already he sounded ominous.

I sat down on his couch. When we'd gotten new furniture for the living room, Dad had brought the old couch up here—this orange monstrosity with green and gold vines on the print. He was always salvaging things. I sat there, feeling like a patient in his waiting room.

"Yes, Paul?" He didn't look at me. He was reading his mail.

"Dad . . . I was just wondering . . . about medical school. You know, just about . . . why I'm going. See, I thought I knew, why I was going—before—but now, it escapes me . . . exactly. And I thought you might—"

"You're going because you've always wanted to be a doctor. Haven't you?" He turned around, twirling that letter opener between his hands. He'd just gotten home from work, and there was a stain on his shirt, a slight discoloration of spittle near his shoulder.

"Well . . . I guess."

"Besides, what else would you do?" He poked me in the chest with the opener, the blunt end. "Clean toilets?"

"I don't know what I'd do," I said, and rubbed the spot where he'd poked me. "But I don't feel old enough to do this yet, spend the rest of my life just doing one specific thing, forever."

"You're twenty-two."

"Yeah, but I'm thinking I'll be ready for it, I don't know, like when I'm seventy."

He shook his head. "Are you worried about it, is that it? Look, Paul, I know it's not going to be easy. I know from experience. But we've got all the confidence in the world in you."

I shrugged. "No. I'm not worried."

He slapped my arm. "Paul, you'll do fine. It's okay to worry about these things. How do you know it isn't just a case of cold feet?"

How did I know I didn't have cold feet? He was already a better doctor than I.

"It's your decision, Paul. Be a garbageman if you want. But what about happiness? You think garbage will make you happy? You want to be a hippie? Look at them, they tried being poor and decided they didn't like it. They hung up their tie-dyed T-shirts for jogging shorts years ago. There's nothing wrong with medicine. It's the most honorable profession in the world." Dad rarely made a speech, but there were certain points of principle with him, and my going to medical school was, apparently, one of them. He was twenty-five years older than me; he had a right to know these things. He poked me again, in the same place. "Look, Paul, how could you turn it down? It's like winning the lottery. God forbid, people will think you're not grateful. I know you, Paul, it's just nerves. You're like your mother."

"Uh-huh." I stood up. "Yeah, I guess you're right." So the decision was reduced, like everything else, to a dichotomy: medicine or garbage, success or failure, Dentyne or halitosis. He was right: How could I not want to go? It didn't make sense. God forbid I should do something there was no explanation for.

If I stayed in that room any longer, I'd be black and blue.

"So serious—my son," my father said to himself, and opened another envelope.

*   *   *

The morning of Sammy's funeral, Dad and I put on our suits and ties, Jenny and Mom their best dresses. It was so quiet, you could hear the house settle. We went downstairs and drank orange juice as we waited to drive to the funeral parlor. We looked so formal, so proper, like a family portrait. We left the house without saying three words among the four of us.

Even the car itself was quiet.

As we walked inside the funeral parlor, all the men put on yarmulkes, the women veils. The family had to wait in the antechamber, to shake everybody's hand. My parents still weren't their normal talkative selves. This was the physically closest the four of us had been in years. Jenny took Mom's hand. I looked at Dad. He was staring at a wall, absently, not like the dad I knew at all. I was afraid to touch him.

"Just like Sammy to go owing payments on three sedans."

"Yeah," I said, and shook my head, even though I had no idea what he was talking about.

We shuffled into the temple across the hall, where the coffin was, where the rabbi gave a speech about Sammy—he talked about immigration, tradition, the number of times Sammy had come to temple—but all I could think about was how Jewish the speech was, how remote. He threw in words like *kreplach* and *schmaltz*. Was this all your life amounted to, how much kreplach you've eaten, the number of times you'd shown up in shul? This wasn't the Sammy *I* knew; the Uncle Sammy I wanted to remember would have been eulogized with racing forms, a trip abroad, a party at that Florida condo.

I looked at Mom and Dad. They were somber, but also, I think, comforted by the rabbi's words. They didn't see any irony in his eulogy at all. At that moment, I felt that what separated me most from all these people, from my family, was Judaism. It was something they all had in common. So easy: a set of rules, a way of life, something they just expected me to accept. Maybe my failure to think of myself that way was part of the reason they didn't understand me. As the only Jewish son, it was my duty to go to medical school, to take a Jewish wife, to produce more Jewish sons, who would go out into the world and continue the process. How could I even think of breaking the chain? It was very *Fiddler on the Roof*. To me, though, that was just another play—and there were a hundred other scripts out there I related to more.

And the funny thing was, they weren't devout Jews, or anything like that. Then, maybe, I could have understood—I could have engaged them in a philosophical or religious debate. I could have countered Rabbi Ezekiel with St. John or Wang Yang-ming. But they were Jewish out of reflex. They'd simply swallowed the whole Jewish smoked salmon, from *their* parents. They rarely went to temple, they worked on Saturdays, but still, they *thought* of themselves as *Jews,* as if it was some essential attribute, when to me, my ethnicity was merely incidental, like my hair color, or the fact that people from Indiana were known as "Hoosiers." My parents hated politics, but whenever Jews were on the news, they'd perk up, they'd get interested. They subscribed to Jewish-interest magazines. They'd talk about America and Jews, American Jews, The Jews in America, Jews in the news.

Personally, I doubted that I thought myself any more Jewish than George felt especially Buddhist.

After the service, we went to the cemetery. Mom and Dad sat in the hearse; Jenny and I followed in our Oldsmobile. I drove, taking my father's place there behind his brand-new steering wheel, listening to the car talk to me with all of its insistent reminders.

"So are you going back to Yale tomorrow?" Jenny asked, looking out the window.

"Yep."

"You know, Elizabeth has a brother who's going to Yale Law School next year."

She was watching me—I could feel it—but I wasn't taking my eyes off the road. "Good for him," I said.

Jenny—she was only trying to be upbeat, trying to strike up conversation. She was at that age when it was important to prove to people that you had social skills. I was at that age—ten A.M. on the day of Sammy's funeral—when I just wanted to be morose.

She finally gave up with me and turned on the radio. Top Forty station. Outside the car windows, leaves fell on the road, then swirled as the cars drove by; the fall colors were spectacular, but nearing their end, the trees being reduced to limbs. How impertinent it seemed, that the world could just go on like this on the day of a funeral, the deejays talking and the leaves falling, as if everyone was still around.

At the cemetery, they lowered Sammy into the ground while the rabbi read more prayers, from a chapbook. How would Sammy walk around stamping out his cigars in that tight little excavation? At least he had neighbors. The rabbi finished, and Dad picked up the shovel and threw in a cluster of dirt. That was the end of the service, the end of Sammy. We milled about the grave.

One of my aunts put her hand on my shoulder and gave me her condolences. She asked me about school.

Oh, yes, Aunt Edith, I said. I surely do love Yale Med. I surely do think it's wonderful. Oh, yes, Aunt Edith, all the girls there are smart, all the girls there are beautiful.

A breeze blew leaves past our legs, and Aunt Edith grabbed her hat.

And I thought, of all things, of Daniel—of how he would have said to my aunt exactly the same thing. Of how the illusions he perpetuated were merely the recirculation of our fantasies—what we called "the real world"—and the perspective he must have had on the rest of us, so caught up in our daily insignificant games.

That evening, after all the relatives and guests had gone home, my father and I drove out to a pizza parlor, despite shiva, to pick up dinner for the family. Friends had brought by a week's worth of meals, but it was Sunday, the day Sammy and Kate always ate over, so Mom didn't want to turn on the oven, put service-ware on the table, do anything in our routine that would remind us of Sammy's absence. "It's . . . it's got to be different, if he's gone. Or what's the point?" She stayed upstairs in her bedroom, putting away clothes. She didn't want to talk to Dad, Jen, anyone, but just be alone with her thoughts.

"Thank you, honey. Thank you all for understanding."

It was kind of awe-inspiring, the way she had so suddenly and completely filled with dignity.

In the car, Dad was still silent. Perhaps he was scared, wondering what was going to happen to him now. Or maybe he felt a bit guilty, that secretly all this time he'd been hoping for Sammy to disappear, and now that he had his wish—his independence—he regretted it. Whatever he was feeling, he didn't tell me.

This time, I worked up the courage to put my hand on his shoulder. He let it stay—he didn't say a thing. It was I who eventually became self-conscious, and pulled it away.

When we got to the restaurant, we had a discussion about the pizza: Dad wanted to order it with pepperoni, the way I liked it, but I wasn't too interested in pepperoni, or even pizza, for that matter. I wanted them to make it with mushrooms—the way Dad liked it. Jenny and Mom never cared what was on it. Dad said to the clerk, "Just make it with pepperoni, okay?" He watched to make sure this suspicious-looking boy with earphones wrote it down, then he walked over to the men's room. After he was gone, I grabbed the pad and changed the order. I called out to the pizza boy, "Hey, make it with mushrooms, would you?"

When we got home and opened the box, it was smothered in pepperoni.

We ate the pizza in silence—Jen, Dad, and I—just staring at one another. We could hear Mom upstairs, walking around in the bedroom. She was going to be up there all night. She was going to make us feel inadequate.

Afterward, I managed to corner Dad as he went into his office. I sat down on that stupid couch. After all this time, the couch was still there, I still took my same old position.

"Dad, I know this isn't a good time to bring it up, but I have to tell you, I don't think medical school is working out."

"Oh?" he said, noncommittally.

"Well..." I faltered; I knew that he'd think I was being selfish, that I had no consideration for Sammy, that I was just being spiteful, a *clinical son of a bitch*. But I was leaving for Yale the next morning—I had to get it out now. "I just don't seem to be that interested in it. But don't think I'm complaining. I'm just saying, that's just the way I feel. I'm always thinking that I'd rather be doing something else."

"Like what?"

Now I had him; for the first time, I had a reply, I had an alternative that had popped into my head. "Photography, for example. I've been taking a lot of pictures lately."

Dad looked at me as if still waiting for me to answer the question.

"Or, you know, film. Something that has to do with recording things. That's what I like to do. Record the design of things, but...not necessarily as people see them. Or see them at first. It's hard to explain. Like...anatomy lab. Now, this is a really interesting class, in itself—I mean, the corpses are interesting, but I don't care much for the way they teach it. Except for one thing: Each day they show a video of the dissection you're about to do, and what's interesting to me is the way that after you watch the video, and then look at the cadaver, you see the cadaver differently than you had before; you see it the way they'd shown you on TV, the way they'd structured it. I mean, even if you didn't pay attention to what they called everything exactly, you somehow picked up a sense of the anatomy from the television."

"Uh-huh. Well, that does sound interesting."

"And?"

"And...Well, like you say, Paul, medicine has a lot of design to it. A lot of, uh, picture-taking. There's...radiology, for instance." He became more animated with this inspiration, and held out his palm. "There you go. That's a whole field devoted to imaging."

"I've been making cutouts from my pictures. And writing scripts for them. I keep them pasted in a book. I want to do a whole portfolio."

He thought about it for a moment, rubbing his chin, like Solomon. "Well," he said finally. "There's nothing wrong with being interested in photography. I'm sure you could do that and be a doctor, too."

"No, Dad. How can you do both? I mean, no one else at Yale is interested in those things. All they're interested in is medicine."

"It's a medical school, Paul. What do you want them to be interested in?"

"But that's my point. I'm bored."

"I go to work every day; you think I don't get bored? But I've got a family to support. I've got a son in medical school. So when you graduate, you buy a camera. You can take pictures on the weekend."

"Dad . . ."

"Paul, what—you want to leave school because you like to take pictures? Because you're bored? Think about it. Think what you're saying. Think how ludicrous it sounds." Then his mood broke; he smiled at me. "Honey, this feeling won't last. It's, you know . . . I think it's just the situation. You've just got a crazy notion in your head. Go back to New Haven."

I let out a sigh. My chest felt tight as a glove.

"Paul . . . okay, fine. We can't discuss this now. You're not being rational. Sammy's dead. Your mother's upset. At a time like this, let's not add to the *tsuris*."

Oh, God, I thought. Now with the Yiddish.

Dad opened his desk drawer and pulled out a slip of paper. He studied it for a moment, then handed it to me. "Okay. I want you to take this with you. Look at it every day. Put it up on your wall. Look, over twenty-five thousand dollars a year. For four years. Plus four years of college. You don't think that means we love you?"

I looked at it. I could barely focus.

"It's a sacrifice we're making—I won't burden you with the things your mother and I have had to give up. But the Lord has managed it so we can afford it. And Jenny will have the same. It's what we've saved all our lives for. But honey, the money means nothing to us; not like the two of you do."

"But if I don't go, you won't have to pay anything."

"But we *want* to give you the money, Paul. How can you not go to Yale? We love you. Don't you think that's why we're doing this?"

I couldn't see the receipt anymore. I was ready to cry.

"One day you'll have bills like that for your own kids. Only they'll have more digits, believe me. Then you'll know what I mean."

So good-bye, Sammy, I said. Good-bye, Indiana. Good-bye, good-bye. The next morning, Mom, Jen, and I drove over to Aunt Kate's; she'd insisted we come over to see if there was anything of Sammy's that we'd want to have. I found some postcards of Paris in his desk drawer: L'Arc de Triomphe; Eiffel Tower; Champs-Élysées; woman in a bathing suit; woman in a fur coat, walking a poodle. All stereotypical, touristy, but odd, too, in their Art Deco, 1940s stylization. Sammy's infamous trip to Paris? What had these pictures meant to him? Too late to ever find out for sure. Mom took one of Sammy's hats, some clothes, a brass barometer that I thought was just an ugly piece of junk, but that she saw something more in. She wrapped up the Cuban cigars for Dad. Jenny took his I.U. pennant, the deck of cards he'd used to teach us pinochle, an old stuffed bear that Kate hadn't even known about. I searched for racing forms or old lottery tickets, but couldn't find any. So I took only the postcards.

Before we left, I looked around Aunt Kate's bedroom, at the curtains, the big double bed. Kate sat in a chair, watching us. How lonely she must have felt. But she didn't cry. She just watched. She looked solid as a rock—she'd always been exceptionally stoic and stable. What would happen to her now? Maybe nothing. Sammy had been just as irresponsible in dying as he had in living. I admired her for having been able to love him for all these years— it took fortitude. We'd all need some of that fortitude now, to fill Sammy's absence, all of us. Things would change, our family would change; it would have to.

And for some reason, I wasn't as upset about that prospect as I thought I should be.

□   □   □

On the plane, I took my anatomy text out of my carry-on luggage. I found a highlighter, took off the cap, and opened to a random page. I'd missed the entire forearm dissection. I didn't think there'd be time to catch up. I just hoped none of my patients ever got carpal tunnel syndrome or tennis elbow.

The upper limb (extremity) or "arm" in lay language is the **organ of manual activity***.* . . .

I hated this stuff. I really did. But I didn't stop reading the whole trip, even after we'd landed on the tarmac.

4

Eyes

_____━━━━━_____

As soon as I got back, I called up Dr. Sparrow. I didn't even bother to unpack. I couldn't wait anymore for a reply. He was listed as an instructor in internal medicine in the departmental handbook. I wanted to start rectifying my life as quickly as possible.

"Dr. Sparrow. It's Paul Levinson. I wrote you a letter a couple of weeks ago? I thought we could get together and have a cup of coffee."

There was a silence while he moved the phone from his ear; I could hear the hospital PA in the background, mumbling mechanically, calling people to their rounds. "Sure," he said finally, this voice just barely resembling the one I already knew, the one from the TV. "That sounds doable. Why don't we meet at the hospital?"

Finally, things were starting to look up. I walked myself over to the hospital, anticipating this meeting with Dr. Carlin Sparrow, TV star, medical bigshot, with whom I'd have to pretend to be familiar. I went through all the scenarios in my mind. His life seemed to me a series of Nielsen ratings and ECG readouts rendered simultaneously, and the more I contemplated it, the more I admitted that being a doctor could, after all, be exciting, maybe even exciting for _me_. My mind was where the problem was; I just had to change it. Even if my life were never televised, there would still be the crises to resolve, the halls to walk down, the lives to save, the sense of urgency. There'd be the emergency-pulse of the city and the million-dollar machines to play with, new biologic territories to discover and the secrets of human existence to reveal.

It'd be tele-*like*. It'd be magnificent, magnified, magnetic. A projection of the imagination. Like "St. Elsewhere" or "Health Beat," only better, if you thought about it: With the right editing and sound track, I could actually live a life-and-death, half-hour scenario twenty-four hours every day. Dr. Levinson to surgery, please. Dr. Levinson to the art gallery. Dr. Levinson to his NEA fundraiser and Barbara Walters interview.

After all, Dad was right; medical *school* wasn't supposed to be fun. That was just the boring, everyday reality to the dream-image. I was just being impatient; it was the dream-image I had to keep in my mind. If I suffered through the interminable present, I could eat my cake later. If I gave up my twenties, I'd wake up in my thirties: I'd comb my never-graying hair and have a home in the San Fernando Valley and a byline in some cardiothoracic journal, reap international fame and recognition for my amazing compassion and monoclonal techniques. I wouldn't even *need* a camera. I'd simply be the ubiquitous subject of other people's documentaries.

I waited for Sparrow in the cafeteria, sipping coffee out of a Styrofoam cup.

A man came down the hall, and at first I didn't recognize him, although he couldn't be anyone but Sparrow, what with that long, woodlike face; yet he seemed smaller than on TV, farther away. The TV Sparrow would be as well conglomerated as a block of granite, and this Sparrow was more washed out and diffuse. But he still had that TV aura, a nimbus, more vivid than the people around him. He matched his televisual as though each feature had been rigorously copied from the tube—tallness, lankiness, male-pattern baldness. Pens in his pocket and stethoscope around his neck. With each step he covered nearly the space of a gurney, like a mechanical cop.

I wondered briefly what I was getting myself into. It was as if, in my desperation, I'd summoned a golem from the depths.

"Mr. Levinson," he said as he arrived. He shook my hand perfunctorily as I half stood up. "You've got coffee?"

"There's a pot by the cash register."

He nodded, and I waited while he bounded over and then back. These awkward introductory moments were always so difficult to negotiate. I picked flecks of Styrofoam off my cup, reviewing the mental list of questions I'd prepared to ask.

"Ah, so there was." He set his cup on the table and pulled up a chair. Then, slowly, methodically, he began stirring in three packets of sugar. He had a mole by his thumb . . . a mole, a mole, dark and deformed, and I wondered how he lived with this absurd growth of flesh, this disturbance in a hand that was surely no perfect representation of divine form. How could he stand it, this mole, dark and distorted as it was? He seemed entranced by the movement of the swizzle stick; he just kept stirring. "We creative types must keep up our glucose levels, mustn't we?"

"Uh . . ." I didn't know about that. It was one thing to fantasize, another to be teased. He was disparaging himself (presumably) and assuming that I'd want to be included in that sentiment. But I certainly didn't think the few photographs I'd sent him in the letter qualified me as "creative," with all the self-importance that word entailed; he could only be interested in what I had to say as some form of diversion. And so his insinuations were completely beyond me.

"Well, now. So what did you want to talk about?"

About me, Dr. Sparrow! About you! About the representations of us, and how they delimit boundaries that we can only escape through careful and diligent re-creations of our ontic paradigms. About technology, medicine, science, silicon. About whether this intricate Latin anatomy and its concomitant biochemical pharma-analysis is all there really is to us, all there is to hope for, the most we can ever know. About how you manage it, what your line is, how I can become famous like you and get out of here. About how you learned to be seen, Dr. Sparrow, through the variegated eyes of a tripartite camera crew.

"Uh . . ." I took a deep breath. "Well, Dr. Sparrow. I'm thrilled we were able to meet in person. As I said in the letter, there doesn't seem to be a lot of people here with whom I can just talk about things. I've been getting quite involved with cameras recently, but I've always been interested in other ways of expressing myself. . . ."

I . . . I . . . I. I was all I had to talk about. I didn't have anything but a bagful of outdated artistic clichés. I detailed the short, pathetic chronicle of my dabbling; mysterious as my own history was to me, I was able to describe it in a succinct and thorough narrative. I painted myself as an artistic ingenue, a panchromatic Mr. Hyde, navigating the shores of my personal introversions. Sparrow didn't seem to be paying much attention anyway; it was more as if he was listening to his coffee. It was saying to him, *Do you believe this bozo? Just who does he think he is?* He just nodded like he agreed with it.

When Sparrow finally answered my questions, I was on another plane altogether. I'd become so used to watching his mouth on TV that its mere movement in person simply mesmerized me. "Well, Paul," he started to say, and the sounds coming out—my name—were so amazing, I could barely follow what came next. He really did have those televised attributes and mannerisms, I hadn't just imagined them, they weren't just creations of Channel 23—that upper-class wispiness, a seafaring New England accent, nice shirt, pens and pencils, a degree from some Ivy League college. He was amazing, a real gem. The person who would sympathize completely with my plight.

"Paul, there's nothing to say you can't practice medicine and do your scrapbook, too."

"Oh, I know that. It's just that, who has the time?"

"You have to make time. But you can do that here—that's why you came to Yale, isn't it?"

I shrugged. He had me there.

"Do you keep a diary?"

"A what?"

"That's what I do. Keep a diary. Every day. It's the only way. If you're really serious, you need to establish a routine."

I shrugged again. I'd always thought diaries were for teenage girls. But I was becoming more open-minded.

"Look, I have an idea. Why don't you do a project? You could do something for 'Health Beat.' I'm always on the lookout for material."

"What kind of material?"

"Whatever you want. Take some pictures and write something to go with it. Develop some concept—the perspective of today's student, that sort of thing."

"Don't you want to see some more of my work first?"

"What for?" He waved his hand, which trembled slightly, a bit Parkinsonian. "I'm sure it's all good. No, this is just something to give you a goal."

I didn't answer him right away; I think he could tell that he'd hooked me, but I didn't want to seem desperate. "I don't know," I hedged. "I've never done something like this."

"Well, Paul, there's no guarantee. We'd give it a review. And we'd probably rescript it, of course, to fit the format. But we're always in search of new ideas."

"How long would I have? I mean, with classes and all . . ."

"Oh, take your time, definitely. We couldn't use it for a few months anyway. We've already finished taping the fall season. But the point is to get busy on something right away."

"Hmmm . . ." It sounded too convenient, too set up. I wasn't really interested in "Health Beat"; I just wanted to take pictures of whatever—experiment, expand. But I knew an opportunity when I saw one.

I asked if I could borrow his pen. I wrote on a napkin: *diary; Health Beat. Idea for episode.*

"Okay," I said. "I'll do it."

I bought a hardbound book of blank pages at the bookstore and wrote in it twice each day, morning and night. Dr. Sparrow's prescription for artistic health. Up, down, up, down . . . scrub, scrub, scrub . . . scratch, scratch, scratch. Page 1. Page 2. Page 3. The lines filled slowly. I could use up more room by making doodles, drawing cartoons. I didn't have much to say, but I figured some inspiration would come eventually. I had months to come up with something, so I wasn't going to rush it.

Soon it was Monday, then Tuesday, then Wednesday. I got up every morning, gobbled down a cafeteria breakfast of orange drink, scrambled-egg substitute, and toast, then went to class—anatomy, biochemistry, histology, cell biology. After a while, the project for Sparrow lost prominence—I had so much to do for class. Sometimes the lessons were interesting, sometimes they weren't. But cell bio riled me the most.

"Not this snooze-ola lecture again," I said to George as Flavin took the podium. " 'Theese . . . is a toupee.' "

Out of all of them, that class had become the most insipid—it was a symbol of all that I hated most about modern medicine: human beings reduced to the cell, from Websters, *cell (sel) n. [ME. < OE. < OFr. celle < L. cella, small room, hut, in LL. (Ec.), monastic cell, < IE. base *kel-, to conceal, whence Goth. halja, HALL, HELL, HULL],* **celled-in, cellar, concealed,** the Basic Building Block itself further reduced to a collection of esoteric and fetishistic names that added up to who knew what, but certainly not, as Flavin constantly claimed, "the patient." And not me—not me sitting here, thinking about all this mumbo jumbo.

"We forgot our crossword puzzle."

"Sure. Hold on."

I ran back out to get the paper. Then we found a seat in the back row.

"Okay, George. We're all set. Now, what's a word for 'extreme lassitude'?" And after class—another eighty pages of notes to read.

Our other homework was generally more interesting. In neuropsychology, for instance, we'd been assigned an oral report: twenty minutes devoted to whatever intriguing brain phenomenon we chose. That, I thought, had potential.

The good topics went quickly: Alzheimer's, schizophrenia. Everyone else had to improvise—Huntington's chorea, alcoholism, sexual dysfunction. I was determined that my project was going to be different, unique—it was going to have more general application. Then it came to me: I'd do mine on the human soul. That was supposedly a brain phenomenon. Plus, it had to be good for the requisite twenty pages. And it could serve as the project for Sparrow, too, if only I could come up with some pictures to go with it, some idea for a visual. So it would kill two birds with one stone, and I'd have enough time to do it all.

I researched my paper on main campus, where I'd go after dinner, pulling books off the shelves and reading them in the stacks. The soul wasn't that easy to find, but I was hot on its trail. I knew it was in that library somewhere. I'd be there every night until after midnight, reading, taking notes, drafting paragraphs.

THE MIND/BRAIN PROBLEM

Topics in Neuropsychology   by Paul Levinson
Drs. Eversol and Pink

The mind/brain problem has been attacked by nearly everyone. What is the problem? Simply, it is the interface of one (or two) of the most elusive and puzzling phenomena in the universe: mind and brain. The mind has been variously known as "the soul," "consciousness," "self-consciousness," or "psyche." The brain is usually referred to as "the brain."

The approaches to the mind/brain problem can be divided into two basic approaches: those who divide the mind from the brain (dualists), and those who do not (monists).

Most famous for being a dualist is Descartes, who said that the mind and brain interact through the pineal gland. Of course, we now know that the pineal gland is a mere vestigial photoreceptor, used not for being the seat of the soul, but secretion.

Dualisms, though, are most frequently given a problem by the homunculus; this is the person supposedly somewhere inside the brain who watches "a procession of memories and thoughts projected on the neocortex," the way a popcorn-munching customer might watch a film at a drive-in movie. By reading the inputs from neuronal impulses and electrochemical signals, the homunculus translates the thoughts of the "brain" into those of the "mind." The problem, though, is who watches the homunculus? Who translates his thoughts? Another homunculus?

Monism, on the other hand, dates back to Democritus and his theory of atoms. This person, Democritus, had a theory that everything, including mental processes, was made of atomic elements. People who look for the smallest characteristic shared by a class of things, by which those things can be grouped, are called reductionists. By reducing the brain to its smallest element—neurons—and neurons to their smallest element—neurotransmitters—and so on, until the smallest characteristic has been named (although there's no reason that this process should ever end), an elaborate map of the "mind" can be made. Modern research scientists are generally descendant from this idea.

For this reason, the research of modern scientists has come to be known as "Neuroreductionism." Much progress has been made this way. For instance, it may be possible, one day, for machines to imitate all mental processes. However, these machines would have to be composed of living tissues . . .

The class was a round table of fifteen students and two instructors. After I read my paper, no one had anything to say. The soul? Where were the lab values? The intracellular mechanisms? They stared at me as if I were an escapee of the Dark Ages. Twenty dumb faces. I should have worn my cassock.

I had to admit, I was disappointed. That wasn't the way they'd greeted last week's report, the one on Sudden Infant Death Syndrome. They'd asked questions for an hour. But Sudden Infant Death Syndrome—that had everything these people loved: Action! Romance! Drama! Technical Hardware! Doomed Dying Babies! Measurable Human Time Frames! But since I hadn't mentioned any statistics or drug therapy, there didn't seem to be anything to debate. They just didn't seem to find the soul a controversial topic.

"Thank you, Paul," my instructor said, and gave me a check in his book (since we didn't get grades). Then he let out class early.

Sparrow, though, would *have* to be receptive. He seemed the type to be interested in controversy. Especially if it came with pictures.

Pictures of the soul? It wasn't going to be that easy. I went into the neuro lab—got out some gray matter. Most of our brains weren't too photogenic, but I found a nice one: plump, fresh, unblemished, like a prize-winning cauliflower. As for "mind," I figured: Some of the best minds in the business were right here in this building. I went to wait outside Flavin's office while he was talking to another student. Through the window in the door I could see Flavin's face, the other student's head, a blackboard in the background (with some equations, and a drawing of something round and hairy—cell nucleus, I think).

I'd intended to go in and ask his permission. But he just talked, and talked, and talked, and it looked as if he was going to be there for hours. I had high-speed film in the camera (no need anymore for intrusive flashing), so I just shot his photo through the window without asking him. I figured that he had to be willing to represent, for the world, the image of "mind." That seemed somehow just, after all the people he'd relegated to "cells."

I met Sparrow in the same cafeteria, this time over lunch.

"Uh-huh," he said. "So what's all this?"

My roll of photos was spread before him, and I'd reprinted my report on blue steno paper, to give it a sort of Hollywood veneer.

"The Mind/Brain Problem, Dr. Sparrow. See, this one's the 'mind.' And this one over here—Dr. Flavin—he's the 'brain.' No. Wait; I mean that the other way around."

"Okay...Paul. First, the pictures are very nice. This one of

Flavin, especially." He held up Flavin's photo and laughed, like some sort of voodoo, as though he were laughing right through the emulsion and into Flavin's face. Maybe he knew these things. Then he put the picture down and stabbed his salad. "But this isn't what I wanted you to do."

I should have guessed. Why did I even bother? I started gathering up the photos.

"I mean, this report, Paul. Doctors Eversol and Pink. You wrote this for class, didn't you?" He chomped on the lettuce, little rabbitlike Sparrow, in that long, lanky body, taking orders from his little homunculus. How easy it would be to crush his skull with my fist.

"Yeah," I admitted. Okay—I knew I'd forgotten about something.

"Well, that defeats the whole purpose, doesn't it? Isn't the point to come up with something on your own?"

He made it all seem so reasonable. My excuse—that I didn't have time—was just what he didn't want to hear.

"If you don't have the time, maybe you should give up trying to do something creative."

I sulked, toying with my French fries, these little rectangular chunks of congealed cafeteria fat, dragging them through the pool of ketchup. Sparrow kept his eyes down, on his salad, but I could sense him watching me.

"Look—it really isn't the type of thing we do anyway, Paul. We need something more . . . concrete. Something that people can grasp immediately."

"You want me to do something of my own, right?"

"Right."

"And that's the point—that I think of it myself, and write it up for you, start to finish."

"You got it."

"Okay. I'll try it again. As soon as I can."

Back to square one. So I'd made *no one* happy. Except perhaps me, for a while—but that counted for zero, especially in the great scheme of career advancement. I didn't know if Sparrow had truly disliked the work or if he was just being difficult, just putting obstacles in my path, to boost my endurance, to make me more concrete. That seemed like something he might do. If it was the latter, I wanted to warn him about the danger of going too far. At this point, I was easy to discourage.

And I really *didn't* have any free time. I tried snatching creative moments between classes—being a roving eye, there to record. I'd just be aware of it all, come up with a metaphor later. I kept watch of the school from overhead, out of body, recounting it all in a notebook at night: Here we all are, going to the anatomy lab to do our dissections, to peel away skins, peritonea, epithelia. We were all just a bunch of skin, weren't we? Even the people I knew. What could you ever "know" about skin-people? You are not Julie Tishman today, but a quivering mass of follicles and ganglia. Even you, Pete, proportionate as you are, are simply a collection of molecules. This mortal coil. This outbreak of psoriasis.

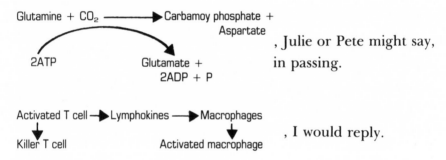

Glutamine + CO_2 ⟶ Carbamoy phosphate + Aspartate

2ATP   Glutamate + 2ADP + P

, Julie or Pete might say, in passing.

Activated T cell → Lymphokines → Macrophages

Killer T cell   Activated macrophage

, I would reply.

It went this way for months.

Late one night, as I walked past the rumpus room on the way to the Coke machine, I caught the closing melody of "My Three Sons"—ya-da, ya-da/ya-da, ya-da, the plaintive clarinets. And I realized—the primordial familiarity of it all, the ideal adolescent vision . . . it was all ending, I'd missed the episode. All that remained was the theme song. It was how my life was now; I had only the theme song—*you're gonna be a doctor/you're gonna be a doctor*—and I had to keep in mind what it was supposed to encapsule: a TV show, playing all night, telling you there's a light on somewhere; we're in transition, we're going into the next half hour, and even if you should expire, the network will stay on the air, the world will survive, time will progress. My mind had been filled at that moment with pages of leprotic arms and legs, human decay, and it all seemed so clear to me, that TV wasn't about the images they broadcast, but someone always being there, awake, to watch over you and make you alert to your own pulse. And I understood why the most important instrument in a hospital room was the television.

I wrote all this in my notebook. Maybe, finally, I was on to something. I just had to think about it, make it more concrete. . . .

"Paul, wake up . . . snap out of it."

George snapped his fingers under my nose. "Jesus, if you're not studying anatomy, these days you're plugged into your word processor. Give it a rest. We'll be late for the party."

"Party?"

"The Bill Mack party. The one you've been waiting for all year."

"Is that tonight?"

He rolled his eyes and tossed me my jacket. "Paul, sometimes you're on a more distant planet than I am."

I had to admit, though, that the twenty-minute drive through the country refreshed me—I'd been imprisoned in the dorm so long, I'd forgotten about birds and trees and things like that, yellow leaves fluttering down on the road, twilight on the farmhouses, and the smell of pine wafting in through the windows. Connecticut could actually be beautiful, the sun setting on the Sound like a travel poster. From what I'd seen so far, I'd thought it was merely a repository for waste, concrete, and winos.

Once we got to the beach, finding Bill's house was simple. At least twenty cars lined the street, and the distant sound of Billy Idol could only be coming from one place. The music seemed to emanate from some USO-type flotilla out in the Sound, amplifiers spreading the voice thinner and thinner over the water, over the whole goddamned community. Something about the distant voice made me nostalgic, but it was an odd nostalgia, because I didn't know what it was for. Maybe "My Three Sons." The house had a string of nostalgic-looking lights, too, colored ones, in a row along the gutter and hanging down from an awning, the place lit up so much it looked like the Connecticut State Fair.

We stepped out of the car. George slammed the door, looked around, picked a flower off a nearby bush, and started gnawing on the stem. "Scary tunes, Paul," he said, chewing his flower and evaluating the surrounding beach property like some West Coast manager come to buy out the place. "Nothing close to Skinny Puppy. You say there's beer at this party?"

"That's what they told me."

We went in the back door and looked around. The house was run down but cozy, like a fraternity house, bedspreads and mattresses lying around here and there, and a brick fireplace. The living room overflowed with people wearing dresses and ties—too dressed up for the decor of the house—only a few of whom I recognized.

"Well, it *looks* like fun," I said to George, hoping he might be more discriminating. He merely picked up a pretzel and nodded his head. A woman walked by, and he put his flower in her hair, without her noticing it. We looked at each other and smiled. I understood perfectly the impulse to do something so ludicrous, and for a moment I felt a kinship with George, a mutual perspective on people, something that I'd never shared with someone before. I searched his face for some kind of discontentment, some inner turmoil, some further isomorphic representation of my own mental state, but he only stuck out his tongue.

Veronique floated up to us, smoking, and handed us each a seashell. "Hello, beautiful people," she breathed. She beckoned with her finger, and after we'd leaned in closer, she told us her name was really "Veronique Maria Sebastian Contessina Lake," and that "We're all good friends of the host." She took a long, meaningful drag, then walked away before we could think of a response. George's eyes were unblinking, his face round. He was probably thinking about all the fun we were supposed to be having.

I myself was ready to look for the exit.

Then I spotted Julie Tishman, waved at her, and the three of us navigated toward the center of the room.

"Paul, have you looked at Monday's dissection? Pretty hairy. We've got three different neck glands to find."

"Let's not talk shop. Not right now."

Julie was drinking and eating a potato chip, and some of the dip fell on the floor. She wasn't paying attention to herself.

"You dropped some dip," George told her.

"Oh." She jumped back and brushed at her dress, about three or four seconds too late.

"I'm George, by the way. George Yan Su."

"Sorry—I thought everyone knew each other by now. George, this is Julie Tishman, one of my lab partners."

Julie finished her chip, and they shook hands. "I know your name," she said, chewing. "You're in a band, aren't you? Malignant Neoplasm?"

"Uh-huh."

I hadn't known George was in a band.

"Your mother writes fashion pieces for *Mademoiselle,* doesn't she," he replied.

"That's right."

I hadn't known that about Julie's mother. Where'd they get all this info?

"Would you like a refill? I'm headed over to the bar."

"No, I'm set for now." To demonstrate, she took a sip.

George nodded knowingly and headed off. "I'll get you a beer, Paul," he called, disappearing into the crowd.

Alone, Julie and I didn't have anything more to say. We variously smiled at each other or stared at the rug.

"People really let loose at these parties, don't they?"

I shrugged. "Sure. That's what they're for. Look at her, for instance." I pointed at Veronique-Maria-Sebastian-etc., who now was out alone on the porch, blowing smoke rings and twirling in circles, her dress billowing out from her legs like an umbrella.

Julie's gaze followed my arm. As she adjusted her sights along my finger, she swayed slightly, lost in her high heels, and just then I realized she was drunk. Without warning, I suddenly liked Julie Tishman. It was almost like love, this liking Julie Tishman, a wave of it, washing over me. I was in love with the fact that she was a human being.

Julie lost her balance and fell forward, her hand on my shoulder—or maybe she put her hand on my shoulder and then lost her balance. It was hard to tell.

"Oops," she said.

I maneuvered her to a nearby couch. Meanwhile, George returned with the drinks.

"So, Julie, what's your neuropsych report going to be about?" He handed her the drink meant for me.

"Alcoholism," she said and took a sip of my beer. "And you?"

"I've already given mine," I told them, but they weren't interested. They were too busy establishing communications.

I listened to their badinage, and launched other attempts to
break in, but they were too self-involved—they talked like Yin and
Yang, Bip and Bop, two porcelain figurines facing each other on
a carousel. I had mixed emotions about their getting along so well
together; sure, I was glad to have been the instrument of their
meeting, glad to engender any new set of interactions, yet I was
afraid I was losing them, both in a single stroke. What could I do
besides be jealous? I left them like that and went to look for hors
d'oeuvres.

Hours later, the party was in full swing and I was still on my
own, when a crashing noise came from the porch—someone
yelled, voices came from the beach. Everyone rushed outside, leaving behind coats and drinks, like an evacuation. You would have
thought people were coming out to look at the stars, the beach at
night was so peaceful, romantic, the water lapping slowly against
the shore. But they weren't interested in the scenery. They rushed
down porch steps to where a crowd had gathered, in a circle. A
plastic cup of beer sat on the porch rail above the crowd, and
nearby was a tipped-over patio chair. I didn't bother to run down
the steps. I simply moved the cup of beer and looked down at the
scene from above.

It was Pete. He was laid out on the ground in the center of
everyone, one arm twisted slightly behind his back. "He's fallen,"
some people were saying, or so I made out. Down in the circle,
Pete tried to move, then winced. He grabbed his shoulder with
his left hand. His right arm didn't move at all; it just hung limp,
a limb, as if it wasn't even part of his body.

He spoke up at the crowd. "Ha. What're all you people looking
at? Where's my drink?"

"Can you move? . . . Don't move it . . . It's probably a glenoid
dislocation. . . ." They speculated about the injury, twenty or
twenty-five of them, as if taking bets. How could they just stand
there and talk like that? All our endless textbooks had told us just
what to do in this situation: *Emphasize that the main stability of the
shoulder joint and the normal relationship of the head of the humerus to
the glenoid cavity is maintained by the rotator cuff muscle tendons which
fuse, etc.* Still, we all just stood there, stupefied, as if medicine had

nothing to do with people actually getting hurt. Eventually someone got the bright idea to call an ambulance. Julie and George
walked out from the house and stood next to me, arm in arm, as
if out for a stroll.

"What happened?"

"Pete fell off the ledge. Now twenty-five amateur doctors are
trying to fix his shoulder."

She laughed. "They won't do any good. We don't start the
shoulder till next week."

George didn't say anything about how he and Julie had been
able to hit it off so suddenly. Arm in arm already, as if they'd
spent their whole lives together. He just watched the scene below,
evaluating it, while I focused on his eyes, on how he was looking
through them, these two balls of gelatin with apertures in the
middle. Sight was such a strange phenomenon. Where did it come
from? Where did it go? The whole world digitized and transmitted
through some animate, two-inch remote, something you could
squash in your hand like a ball of Jell-O.

I was maybe starting to feel a bit drunk myself. "That Pete.
Always showing off. I wonder what he was up to. . . ."

The ambulance arrived ten minutes later. Two medics came
down to the beach. They scooped Pete into a stretcher, handed
him his beer, and carried him up the stairs to the porch, then back
through the house and out the kitchen door. The crowd followed,
drinks in hand, like patrons wandering from room to room at a
gallery opening. After the ambulance drove off, everyone got in
their cars, following in procession. I reached George's car just as
Bill appeared at the door of his house, to watch everyone leave.
It was the first we'd seen of him all night. "Hey!" he called, hands
cupped to his mouth. "Where's everybody going?"

Fergie had asked us for a ride, so he climbed in the back with
me. Julie sat in front with George.

"What a klutz, huh?" Fergie said, nudging me in the ribs.
Meanwhile, George started the car and shifted into gear. "He left
his date down on the beach." Fergie wiped a circle in the fog of
the car window and put his nose to it as we pulled away. "Want
her phone number?"

"No thanks."

"Another nurse, I bet." He sat back, folded a slip of paper, put it in his shirt pocket. "I'd better save it for Peter. It'll probably be the first thing he asks for when he comes out of his month-long diencephalic coma."

"Probably."

Meanwhile, Julie and George, in the front seat, tickled each other and giggled. The party was over. We were all going to the hospital to watch a dislocated shoulder.

The whole crowd was there, plastic cups in hand, as though they'd all been lifted up and transferred verbatim from the beach. A cocktail party in an ER. We hadn't been allowed to see the residents put on the cast, but they let us into Pete's room, to gather round, Pete sitting on the bed with his doctor standing beside him, ready to lecture to us about the shoulder joint. He ran his hands over Pete's shoulder as he talked—big surgeon's hands—but he caressed his work gently, intimately, the way a lover would. Pete sat peaceably, immobilized by the shoulder contraption, beaming. He was the center of attention.

"In the meantime, the pads here"—*slap*—"and here"—*slap*—"will keep the arm stabilized while the cartilage heals." The doctor's face was haggard and a bit unshaven—this was the Friday-night shift, after all—and I wondered if he had a wife, a family, or if this hospital was his devotion, as it seemed with so many of the residents.

He addressed us as fellow professionals, avoiding lay terminology. He wanted to make it clear that we weren't to empathize with Pete, get all mushy and emotional, but to *understand*. We'd been in this hospital once already this week. Maybe even the very same room—they all looked alike. It had been for a class called *Introduction to Clinical Practice*, which involved asking a heart patient personal questions about her disease. Since it was our first week, we'd been allowed to ask just about anything we liked—we had no idea what the information might mean anyway. She'd been huge, folds of skin drooping over her legs, a woman who slapped her thighs when she laughed and told us we looked "so young for doctors." She sat in a chair with her mother and aunt and two daughters—the whole clan—gathered around her. The five medical students, all in white coats, had also squeezed into the room, with our adviser, her "primary care physician," standing in the back, arms across his chest, watching all of us with a smile.

"But I guess y'all know more about it than I do," she said, while one of my classmates stood over her with a stethoscope, afraid to touch her.

Now we were doing the same thing to Pete—investigating his body, his mechanics, hooking them up, turning them into a structure of bricks and mortar, levers and pulleys. Yet how could someone be both a patient and a medical student? Patients were meant to be the raw material, the unread texts, the objective data; doctors the machines, the readers, the interpreters. You couldn't just flip the polarities like this. With this cast on his arm, Pete was unfamiliar, contradictory. Until it was removed, he could no longer be one of us. He'd be, like the woman in our class, another specimen.

And it began even before we left the hospital. His doctor spoke to us as if he were lecturing from a textbook, absently caressing Pete's shoulder—that perfectly muscled shoulder, with all its bruises and disjointedness, wrapped in its casing. The gesture infuriated me. I didn't think Pete had the greatest of personalities, but it still seemed a bit sleazy, this medical caress, like the swagger of a cheap prostitute, and I wanted him to take his hand away.

"So now that you've seen all this great anatomy up close and personal, what do you think? Who wants to run the saw when it comes off?"

Pete spent the night in the hospital room. The rest of us went back to the dorm, where I accompanied Julie up to George's room, up on the fifth floor. They'd insisted I come. Perhaps they wanted a chaperon. Or maybe they were just nervous, that what was happening to them might not last the evening, and they wanted someone to witness it, a linchpin.

Julie wandered around George's room, picking up ornaments or reading the credits at the bottom of his movie posters. "Did you really see all these films? Look here—Orson Welles." She picked up one of his tureens and nodded her head. She was either agreeing with the sentiment in the object, or the gesture implied by George's having placed it there. I couldn't tell. His Rocky Horror lips, his volumes of Lawrence Ferlinghetti poems, his Skinny Puppy CDs. Much of George's room was set up to make unambiguous political statements.

"You know, I'd do it," I said.

"Do what?"

"Take off Pete's cast. When it's time. Think how much you

can learn from that. I've never removed a cast before." It'd be a good test for me, to see just how clinical I could really be.

"Oh, Paul, don't be a geek." Julie hit me on the arm. She'd sobered up a bit, and she wanted to prove it to us by taking something seriously. "Fergie should do it. You hardly know Pete."

"Paul has a point, though. Pete's shoulder could be a real learning experience for someone."

It was already starting. For the next few weeks, no one would talk about Pete as Pete. We'd talk only about "Pete's shoulder."

"I *do* think I have a point, George. Why waste a good opportunity? Pete won't mind. Anyway, why would Fergie want to do it more than anyone else? It's just taking off a cast. It's just medicine."

"Don't you guys have any sense of propriety?"

"Of what?" George sat down on the bed, and Julie sat down next to him, close, holding his hand. They were divided on the issue, it seemed, but not over how to allot the space between them.

"Respect for the person involved. Maybe he wants some privacy. Maybe he's got feelings about the matter."

"It's professional curiosity," I said.

"Maybe you're just trying to take a woman's position," George added.

"And what's that supposed to mean?" She raised an eyebrow. "Are you implying that there's something *wrong* with a woman's position?"

"No, I didn't say—"

"If I'd known you were a chauvinist, I wouldn't have come up here." But she didn't take her hand from his. So this was all just intellectual calisthenics, a game of sorts.

"I just mean that you were using . . . that people expect women to be . . . that . . ."

"Forget it, George," I advised from my position cross-legged on the floor. "You're just making it worse."

"No, let him answer. I think it's cute, watching him squirm."

"You know, being oversympathetic with the patient—you're taking refuge in that posture, that's what I mean. . . ." He squeezed her hand tighter as he said that, and put it in his lap.

"But I think the point that Julie's trying to make is that a more sympathetic position isn't necessarily a *woman's* position."

They both looked down at me.

"I mean, if it was a position a man took, then it'd be a man's position, wouldn't it? I don't think you can prove that no men have ever taken that position."

"Yeah. That's right." She looked at George.

"Better to say that it's a nonfactual position, if indeed that's what you wanted to say."

"That's what I mean," George said, picking up the cue. "Nonfactual."

Julie glowered at me. "Paul..."

"Nonfactual," he said again. "That's what I meant."

"Debate team. Pinewood High School." I slapped my thighs and stood up. "Well," I said. "I think now's as good a time as any to leave you two lovebirds alone."

I went back to my room. After the night's excitement, I felt as though I could just pass out, but I couldn't make myself fall asleep. I was too wound up—Julie and George, Pete, Sparrow, Sammy, Dad. Everything gusted around me, people lived and died, fell off ledges, and meanwhile I just stood around watching the bodies land.

Julie and George would have forgiven each other by now and were probably getting around to some serious hanky-panky. It was hard for me to imagine. I couldn't see them exchanging fluids— I could more readily envision them swapping chemical equations. Medical students were supposed to be so busy with our studies, we weren't expected to *have* sex, so much as simply imagine the possibilities. Of course that wasn't true, completely, but it'd been a while since I'd even imagined. So, seeing as I was drunk, and unable to sleep, I decided to head out into the bleak New Haven night in search of porno, or some other degradation. It'd been a year since I'd been out on the streets. It was high time that I did something irresponsible. I couldn't stand to think of all this making out going on without me.

It was after one in the morning—few people in the dorm were awake. Chances were good that no one would see me when I returned, so I could bring back whatever I liked. I exited out the back door, holding the lock, then slipped it back into its frame. I walked past the Green, to the center of town. It was the weekend— you could tell there was action going on somewhere, just from the feel, the energy, even though hardly anyone was out. I stopped in front of a bookstore, one I'd passed several times before, one I'd remembered would be open at this hour. The bell on the door jangled sharply as I walked in.

For a while I pretended to look at the newsmagazines. Then I worked my way over to *Playboy,* to *Penthouse.* I had a routine. When no one was looking, I slipped over to the gay mags, picked one up, and flipped through. I found a picture I liked and stared for a while, trying to decide if it made the magazine worth buying. When I glanced up, I noticed a man across the room, staring back at me. He had his hands in his coat pockets. For a moment, we looked at each other, eye to eye. He was young, dark-haired, wearing one of those trench coats popular with the undergraduates. I thought I recognized him from somewhere; he had that punk look—I'd seen it before—but the clothes were slightly different, not punk, but scholastic, Ivy League. Could it be the guy from George's bar, the dancer? He walked around a corner, picked up a paperback and ruffled through it, but he wasn't looking at the book, he was looking at me. I knew he could tell what I had in my hand. It was obvious in his slight smile, the cockeyed way he stood. Something could have happened, right then—I felt in tune with him—but I got scared. I broke the eye contact and took the magazine to the clerk. I bought it as fast as I could and pushed out through the door.

I was almost to the end of the block, when I stopped. I mustered my courage and turned around. There he was, standing in the doorway, looking out into the dark. His hands were in his coat pockets. He smiled again, as if to acknowledge the game—the slight absurdity in what we were doing. Was he going to talk to me? I started to take a step forward, but halted. His eyes—as though I recognized them—and his face, empty and eager . . . and yet, he was a person, not just a face, and what excuse did I have to talk to him? What would I have possibly said? Nothing in my twenty-three years of playacting had taught me how to handle the etiquette of this situation.

"Jeff!" someone called from down the street. "Hey, yo!"

Three college boys, and they walked up from seemingly out of nowhere. He recognized them, said something to the one who'd called his name. Another of them gestured with his head—they were going somewhere. They talked for a while, then he walked off with them, not once looking my way.

I decided to follow. What the hell. Maybe that's what I was *supposed* to do. Tail them. Maybe that's what he would have suggested, if he could have signaled somehow.

They turned the corner, and so did I, staying a good block behind. Their voices echoed faintly, in staccato, off the buildings. All I could see were four broad backs, one in a trench coat. No one else was about. I still carried the porno mag, under my jacket. What if I got stopped? I held it closer to my chest. We kept walking, and I lost track of time—I was watching the boy, "Jeff," the way he walked, the bob in his step, his coat as it swept along the ground. I felt fueled, thoughtless, driven by total instinct.

They turned another corner, and I hoped we were nearing their destination; I was less and less familiar with these roads. The New Haven architecture circled us—I could easily have been anywhere, even the other side of town, and it would have been turning up much the same. I rounded the corner after them, but they were gone—vanished, apparently, into one of the million old row houses along this street.

I stopped. Where was I? REPORT CRIME, said a street sign in front of me. NEIGHBORS AGAINST DRUGS, someone had flypapered on a lamppost, and someone had crossed out the AGAINST and written DO.

Had he led me here intentionally? Had he hoped for me to follow? Had the whole thing just been my imagination?

It was dark out, and late, and I was wandering the dream/nightmare labyrinth of New Haven, alone, with a gay porn mag hidden under my coat.

I pointed myself toward a Yalish-looking spire and started looking for a familiar name. I came to Chapel Street, then followed street signs until I made my way back to the dorm. I could see my breath, the smoke, but I wasn't cold at all. I was warm as hell. I was wired, just like the time in New York. Only this time, it wasn't fear—it was lust. I replayed the journey through town in my mind, over and over, trying to hold on to its power, its magic, the sequence of the city, "Jeff's" figure in its labyrinth. I didn't even have a clear picture of what he'd looked like, just his eyes, the way he'd turned, the afterimage of his clothes. But there'd been no mistake. I'd always made such a conscious habit of hiding from everyone; now that I'd been caught, exposed, it rang through me.

Once I was in my room, I took out the magazine to fantasize, but I found that I didn't need the pictures at all—all I needed was to remember Jeff, his gaze.

It lasted me for weeks.

I began going to the bookstore almost every night, hanging out on the edge of campus. I didn't keep going just in hopes of seeing Jeff again (although I admit the idea occurred to me), but because I'd somehow crossed a line in my mind, the line separating "medical students" from "riffraff," and when I'd crossed it, the line had dissolved: I could see a whole potential landscape waiting for me on the other side. In this light, Pete, his braggadocio, they paled—this was something else, a real possibility, a whole world of validated desires. Meanwhile, I could buy the magazines now without effort, without worry. I already had a whole collection, which I kept in my bottom drawer, underneath my sweaters.

I was buying homosexual magazines every week, but I still didn't think of myself as "gay." Of course I was—I just wasn't ready for a commitment. I didn't think I needed to come to any hasty conclusions. I was maybe, just . . . interested.

On one of my forays into town, I noticed the New Haven Art Gallery. What was it doing here? Why hadn't anyone ever mentioned it? Instead of browsing the bookstore, I spent the day looking at exhibits. I studied the Man Rays, the O'Keeffes, the Social Realists. The photographs in the art gallery—I didn't see how they were that much different from those in the porno 'zines. I felt pretty much the same attraction to both of them: one with my mind, abstractly, the other with that familiar stab of respiratory desire. But they both, in a way, made me dizzy. If anything, the two were different only from the photos in my textbooks, which I found simply dull.

I spent a whole Saturday perusing the gallery. There was a picture that reminded me of the REPORT CRIME street sign and one that reminded me of my own pictures, in the way it played with the messages inside the frame. I saw a mural of the HIV virus, in vivid blue and red, and it gave me ideas—the alternative ways of processing the world's information, the different uses for it, maybe more than I knew of even then. On the third floor, I encountered some neon signs re-displaying their messages, re-echoing each other, blinking red and black. I liked those particularly. They could drive you into a tonic/clonic fit.

I stayed until closing, at five-thirty. I had to run home and read biostatistics notes until three A.M. to make up for the time I'd wasted.

But I was getting to know this new neighborhood well now, these farther reaches of the Yale campus—the art gallery, the bookstores, record shops, libraries, all far from what I increasingly saw as the provincial world of the medical school. It was a carnivalesque city that I'd been overlooking, filled with lights, street vendors, music, invention, season tickets to the Repertory Theater. Still, in the expansion of my horizons, something had been lost as well as gained: I no longer felt that aura of mystery. I had, in its place, a new and flatter sense of competence.

*   *   *

"Hello, Paul. Any progress?"

"Progress?"

"How's the project?"

"Oh . . . oh, the *project*. . . . This is Dr. Sparrow, isn't it?"

What was he doing calling me? Was I running that much behind? I checked my watch. It'd only been, well . . . a month? Two? I hadn't been following "Health Beat" very regularly. Had I overlooked something? No, he just wanted to check up on me, see how my thought process was evolving. If he only knew about my thought process. I gave him all the reassurances I could think of—I ended up promising that I'd have him something in a month. I was lying through my teeth.

"You know, Dr. Sparrow, I think this project is one of the most useful things for my work that I've ever done."

"That's good, Paul. I'm flattered, too, that you came to me for advice. I enjoy giving advice to students. It makes an old man feel useful."

"I'm sure you've got plenty of uses left in you yet."

He laughed. "Well. Just thought I'd check in."

After we hung up, I searched through the pile of magazines and class notes in my closet. I was looking for my scrapbook. I had no idea what was going to satisfy him now, but I had to come up with something quick. Soon papers were scattered everywhere, but I had what I needed: the few photos and stories I'd compiled when I'd first arrived at Yale. My obscure history. My rudimentary visions. It was a start. These, at least, I could claim were entirely my own idea. And they were more concrete than twenty pages on neuroreductionism. It was nine-fifteen on Thursday, and "Health Beat" was on in fifteen minutes, so I went downstairs to watch it and take notes. It was time to get serious.

It was time to close my eyes, to focus on Sparrow's desk—lifting off, levitating from its runway, headed for me like a bird of prey. He swooped and lofted, dashed around the room . . . then chased me down, coming in for a strafing run. . . .

Will colonies of modified bacteria produce enough human growth hormone to enlarge the Pygmy population of central Africa?

I covered my head. He turned and tried for another swoop.

Have scientists in Princeton found a genetic marker for the trait commonly known as "recalcitrance"?

While at night, a thousand pictures of Dr. Sparrow circled my bed, flickering tenuously like the midnight light from the television. Their mouths moved, they all spoke the same thing: "Where's the progress . . . where's the progress . . . where's the progress," as if echoing the sentiments of a hamburger merchandising campaign.

In the morning, I pushed through the cobwebs; I gathered myself together. I strapped on my camera and took it across the hall to Pete's room.

"Paul, buddy, what's up?"

He stood before me in just jeans, no shirt or socks, and his cast—a smaller one now, with a strap across the chest securing his arm to his side. With the other hand, he munched on an apple.

"I've figured it out, Pete. What I'm going to do for my project. I'm going to do you."

"Me, huh?"

"That's right. You."

He shrugged and let me in his room.

I told Pete about the idea that had come to me: I was going to take pictures of him working over the cadaver, while wearing his cast. The medical-student perspective. I didn't know where, exactly, it would go from there, but it was getting more concrete all the time. I was in charge, and Pete would be my designee.

"Sounds great, Paul. A real photo session. So you lead."

He went to put on a shirt, but I told him I wanted to take a picture topless, at first. "To get the details. Like an anatomy book." I hoped he believed this explanation at least as much as I did.

I took the apple core from his hand and tossed it in the trash.

He sat down on his bed, and as I looked through the viewfinder, I focused on Pete's cast, the hair on his chest fuzzy in the background. The object in my camera was anonymous, sterile, subdued, yet there was enough curvature in the frame that it was, perhaps, suggestive of the possibility that you didn't have to look at it that way; the centering and focus might guide you to alternative conclusions—at least, with the way *I* was directing it, it might. It was halfway between Man Ray and *Gray's Anatomy*. There was writing on his cast, part of which I got into the photo—*ast time you'll ever*—and a drawing of the uric acid pathway. And his bare chest above it, of course.

I didn't know what these pictures were exactly, pornography... or merely the objective recording of data. How could you establish the difference?

Either way, I was going to keep an extra copy for myself.

"Okay, Pete. Now to the labs."

A few people were in there studying, but they ignored us when we came in. No one was working by Zorba, so we took our pictures there.

"First, I think, I want you to lie on a gurney, and I'll roll it up next to the cadaver."

Pete looked at me as though he hadn't heard me right.

"No, really. This will be good. Trust me."

After a while, even someone as primitive as Pete went along with the plan. All I had to do was sound sure of myself.

He turned out to be the perfect model, staying absolutely still in whatever position I placed him. I snapped three or four shots of each pose, some with his cast in the air, some posed just like the cadaver, arms by his side, lying next to it. In another room, a couple of students were practicing their optical examinations on each other—Veronique and some guy. I had a few shots left over, so I finished the roll with some pictures of the two medical students facing each other, each using an ophthalmoscope to look into the eye of the other.

"The Student Examines," I would call this piece.

Before I let Pete go, I wanted to do an interview (for the text, the captions). I asked him the questions I'd written out beforehand, jotting the answers in my notebook. How does it feel to be a patient yourself? What do you think about everybody's curiosity?

What were your feelings when Dr. Grant used you as our exhibit last week? Do you think you became a doctor because of a fear of death? Is there something new to your patient perspective now, is it all that much more complicated?

"Well, Paul, I'd say that there's quite a tendency to put a lot of faith in the doctor. Even if you know what's going on. You still want to have someone else take the responsibility for telling you it's all right. You still want to believe that the doctor's infallible—that his word is golden."

"That if he knows enough about it, nothing bad can happen?"

"Yeah. And even if you know exactly the same amount as he does, you still believe the doctor knows something more, some extra fraction, because of his M.D."

"And because it isn't happening to him."

"Presumably." And he laughed, and held up his cast.

I transcribed his words furiously. I was surprised at his articulateness, the way he'd confirmed my own suspicions. Maybe I'd confused him too much with Fergie. Maybe people were never quite entirely the way we thought of them. Or maybe he simply knew the answers I'd been fishing for. After all, I'd set up this closeness artificially—intentionally—as part of the whole artistic experience, and I shouldn't have been all that surprised to have gotten the results I'd wanted to see.

That same afternoon, in our psych class, we began screening films, as if they could sense that we'd all reached the point where we were saturated with data and just wanted to hear a story. The first was called *Infant/Nurturer Bonding and Dysfunction.* Not quite *Raiders of the Lost Ark,* but we all brought a bag of microwave popcorn and passed it down the aisles. It was the medical-school version of entertainment.

In the film, Marty is a two-year-old boy, left by his parents to be cared for at a nursery, while his mother has a baby. We were told by the narrator that we were about to witness an objectively recorded situation, which would have happened precisely the same "had the camera not been there." "Under the conditions of 'isolation' and 'afamiliarity,'" the narrator said dramatically, "we will document Marty's progress from a normal, well-adjusted two-year-old into a traumatized, asocial child."

Day 1. His parents first leave Marty at the care center. He

whines and cries, but after finding that this strategy elicits no guaranteed response from the nurses (who are distracted by at least thirty other children), he eventually segues into a steady, pathetic whimper.

Day 2. Marty is more sullen. One nurse tries to spoon-feed him, but he won't eat. "Objective" long take on the full bowl of oatmeal.

And so on. Essentially, the film shows how no one pays any attention to this boy, except our narrator, of course, who maintains an anonymous position behind the camera, always watching, always talking about him, telling us how isolated and ignored he is.

I just didn't buy it. It was like in a horror movie, when the teenagers go off into the woods to have sex, and you want to yell at the characters for being so dumb—haven't they ever seen a horror movie? Why pretend they haven't? At one point, Marty even reaches plaintively for the camera (toward the psychiatrist), but at this decisive moment she (and we) don't . . . can't . . . respond, for we don't want to ruin the experiment, do we? The narrator placidly continues her catalog of the different socialization stages the child is going through—stages one, two, three, four, five, six, and seven. We all take notes as she enumerates them. Eventually the kid gives up any attempt at communication at all. He sits quietly in the corner while other children bump into him with their toy trucks. After two days of it, his father comes to take him home. Marty's shy at first, unsure who this person is, but eventually responds to his father's embrace.

The whole auditorium sniffled.

We saw a bunch of these sorts of films. Each time, I identified with the characters, not the camera. I was the seventeen-year-old psychotic who plastered his parents' stocks to the wall. I was the thirteen-year-old anorexic who tore IVs out of her arm, afraid of the sucrose. It was hell being all these people. Each time, as their pain was made into a medical condition, something sterile and scientific, something to be analyzed rather than overcome, I was left feeling drained and frustrated. I knew I was just reacting to a film, and most of the time I could calm myself. But more than any other, the movie about Marty got under my skin. I couldn't explain to people exactly why. I didn't want it to become yet another explanation. I just fumed, to make sure everyone knew I was upset.

"I know," George said, trying to soothe me, "it's pretty callous, if you think about it. You just have to look at it from a different point of view. You have to think about what was learned by this, the good that can come from it. Like Third World babies, what their lives are like, how this might help. That sort of thing."

"Well, George, I like to look at it as just plain callous."

By week's end, I'd gotten back the pictures from the developers. I selected the four best ones, wrote the commentary, and met Sparrow in the hospital to hand him the finished product. The year was in full swing—and even so, things were coming together for me. A real accomplishment.

"All my own idea, from start to finish."

"Great!" He seemed distracted, about to bound off to his next important function.

"And it's all about a medical student—easy to grasp."

"Uh-huh, uh-huh," he said, shuffling through the photos.

"So you really might use it on the show?"

"Of course. Sure. Give me a chance to look through them first."

We stood in the middle of the corridor, patients and nurses rushing back and forth around us.

"Wish I could chat more, Paul, but I'm running behind."

"Of course."

He slipped the pictures under his coat, we shook hands awkwardly, and he headed off toward Intensive Care. So I'd finally gotten it right. Now all there was to do was wait.

And wait. And wait. I knew this collage was only a first, small step. I had too much else to do than to spend my life worrying about Sparrow and his quaint little show. But worry I did. How long had it taken me to do this simple thing—four pictures and a narrative? Two months? Three? At this rate, I might put together a portfolio by the time I was sixty. Maybe by then, I'd have achieved one small portion of one small goal that I cared one little bit about. But what would my life amount to in the meantime? Why was I wasting my time, piddling away my valuable years? Why couldn't I just spend my time doing the things I liked? If there was some psychiatrist monitoring me, watching this film of my miserable life, I wanted her to step in and stop the experiment right now.

In our *Introduction to Clinical Practice*, we'd been assigned a permanent patient, whom we were supposed to visit once every week. Just visit, like a social worker, to get a sense of what it was like to talk to someone with a serious illness. No diagnosis or medicine involved—this was only about social skills. My patient was on dialysis: end-stage renal disease, waiting for a donor. He could be waiting the rest of his life. Carlos was Hispanic, tough, twenty-one. Of course this made it all the more difficult for me, since I could so easily identify with him, his youth, his attitude. I spent most of the time imagining what it'd be like to be in his shoes. For his part, he seemed to like talking to me: He never let on if he was bothered by my being such an amateur.

"You have a girlfriend?" he asked one day while his blood ran circles through the filter. I sat next to him in a metal chair, in my pressed oxford shirt. Tubes and wires, needles in his veins—he had to go through this drainage process three times a week. Whenever he first came into the ward, he'd be oblivious; nothing he said made very much sense. But toward the end of it, he'd start getting more outspoken, even wistful, full of remembrances for all the sports and practical joking he couldn't perform anymore.

"No," I told him, as honestly as I could. "I'm single." Sometimes I thought to myself—here's someone I could really open up to. What would he do with the information, anyway? He wasn't going anywhere. But I didn't want to overshadow his problems with mine. That didn't seem to be the right protocol.

"I wish I still had a girlfriend, man. You don't know what you're missing. You're healthy, man—you should be out there having a good time."

"Can I get you anything the next time I come? You want some books?"

"Nah. No books. But...you got some video games, maybe?"

He was so classically handsome, strong-willed, it pained me to think of his body in such ruins. Sometimes his family came to spend the afternoon with him, an attempt to dispel the impersonality of all that chrome and machinery. On those days, I wouldn't talk to him so much, but chat a little with his mother and aunt, talking about him, evaluating him, while he lay there with his eyes closed. Some days, when his family wasn't with him, he wouldn't say anything to me at all—it seemed as though he just hated me, for all the things I could do that he couldn't.

All this went on weekly, until the class ended and we were given something else to take its place in the schedule. At the last visit, I brought Carlos a cheap, hand-held video toy, but he was having a bad day—he didn't have the energy to thank me, or respond much at all. I simply set it beside him on the night table. Afterward, I wrote up the required twenty-page paper. "CL has successfully learned to integrate his illness into his daily matrix," I typed, in conclusion. "He takes each day in stride." And I submitted it to my professor, who gave me "an A equivalent." And I never saw Carlos again.

But it was during this time, at night, that I began to once again see Daniel, for he began to visit my bedside. Daniel was perhaps not so bizarre as I'd first thought. He had a pretty good take on the world. He wasn't so uptight about his one, little persona, his one little role in life: He had a million of them; he could perform them whenever he liked. He was a projectionist, throwing his image up on our collective screens.

Daniel, you are so intriguing.

Thank you, Paul.

May I touch your hair?

Yes, please. Go ahead.

I ran my hand through his Afro, so fine, so frilled.

I've always wanted to do that. I've always wanted to forget about whether it was racist or liberal, to have such a desire, or rather, to be so curious. I've just wanted to be able to touch your hair.

Thank you.

No, thank *you*. You can touch mine too, if you like.

Certainly. Why not?

Dr. Grant had warned us that the dissections we were coming up to—the face, hands, and genitals—would be the most emotionally difficult of the year. They were the parts of the body supposedly most human. Human? That hadn't ever bothered any of us before. I breezed through the face and hands—no problem—but when we got to the urogenital system, I understood, finally, what he meant by "difficult." Who wanted to dissect a dead penis? We drew straws to see which one of us would "do it." ("Do it" had become our euphemism for cutting—"I'm not going to do it, you do it." "Uh-uh . . . it's your turn to *do it*.") The three guys all thought Julie ought to have been the one to do it, by default.

"Come on," Nathan said to her. "I'm sure it doesn't mean as much to you as it does to us."

"Chauvinists."

So we had to draw straws. Naturally I got the short one.

Just then, the radiators halted and crunched, as if wounded, giving off steam. The anatomy lab really didn't smell so bad in winter, as long as the room stayed cold. But when it was cold, you shivered, which you were prone to do anyway, in this room with so many dead bodies. By now, though, we were pretty well used to it—most of the time.

I picked up a scalpel and ran it straight down the center of Zorba's penis. Then I started peeling back the layers, one by one, circumcision with a vengeance. It hurt to do this, but I wouldn't let myself quit—I wasn't going to be beaten by a cadaver.

"Ugh..." Julie said, watching, or "Oooh...," hardly helping matters.

Right in the middle of all this, a delivery boy walked in the room. UPS—he had on the uniform, and a package in his hands. When he saw us he stopped dead, just stood in the doorway, staring. At that point, I reached an impasse, and the dissection started getting sweaty, with lots of squinting and yanking. The guy in the doorway was only a teenager, greasy looking, obviously a kid from town. What was he doing here? I cut some tissue away from the urogenital diaphragm, with a scissors, so I could get underneath. The delivery boy's jaw dropped open—literally. I'd never seen anyone actually do that before.

"Are those real?" He stared at us as though we'd murdered the cadavers ourselves, us grave robbers. His astonishment distracted me, and for a brief moment I saw the horror contained in our actions, in this room, in myself for being here, as when someone slaps you and, for a second, things crystallize. My own uncle had died only a few...however long ago it was. Yet at the same time, I failed to grasp the boy's astonishment. Of course they weren't real—it was just an anatomy lab.

"Can I help you with something?" John asked.

I went back to my cutting. By now, my scissors were pretty dull. I was tired. And I wanted to take revenge on this guy, for the brief glimpse he'd given me of myself. He thought he'd seen gross? I grabbed a strand of penis and started ripping it off with my hands.

"Just what *is* a penis?" I asked loudly. "Huh? Just which of these bits of tissue?" I held up some skin for the UPS boy. "Is it this? This? How far do I have to go? Do you even recognize it anymore? Do you even know what one is in the first place?"

I was being watched by everyone in the immediate vicinity. I didn't care.

"Oh..." the boy said, waving his free hand in front of him. "I didn't mean to bother... I'd just delivered something down the hall... and I thought you might..." He backed slowly out of the room, not taking his eyes off me. "I thought... I... never mind."

And then he disappeared.

After he was gone, the rest of my team laughed nervously. "Jesus, Paul," Julie said. "I think you're getting a bit loopy. Maybe you should have asked me to do this dissection."

I wiped sweat off my brow, careful to avoid touching the plastic gloves to my face. "It's just a little stuffy in here." I was breathing heavier than I should have been, feeling even more tired. The thing was, that boy would never understand how long it'd taken me, taken all of us, to be able to do that to a cadaver so calmly. He'd never understand our accomplishment.

Zorba's penis was now in three long strands, strung all over the legs and halfway up his abdomen, in ropy pieces so we could hardly make out what anything was. It was a terrible dissection.

"Well, then. How about some help here?" I said. "How about a little relief?"

That night, in my diary/notebook, I wrote:

I don't know why this is so important—this meaningless incident and that stupid delivery boy. I don't know why I blew up like that. I just can't get this episode out of my mind.

But I had some suspicions. Things here were getting to me—why was I still here, anyway?—and in a moment, I found myself pacing back and forth like a caged animal, turning over chairs and throwing books at the wall, for no reason at all. I kicked my closet door so hard I hurt my foot. I was hyperventilating, feeling as if I were about to pass out. I didn't know what was wrong with me. I thought I was going crazy.

It was a Thursday night, already February—I knew the month only because of Valentine's Day. I remembered every Valentine's Day as it passed, this sentimental, meaningless holiday that chugged by me every year like an empty subway car. There was snow in the streets, black mounds of ice and soot piled up on the sidewalks, icicles hanging from the buildings. I hadn't been out of the library in days. I hadn't seen the sun in weeks. But the worst thing was that my mind was . . . what? Pickled, tattered—dry, dried out like one of those dried-out brains in the neuroanatomy lab. I'd seen a movie once where a guy just crushed a brain in his hands and washed it down the sink. And the thing was, I couldn't think anymore, I couldn't even study.

I was losing track of my chronology, my academic record. In the time since Sammy's death, I'd taken twenty tests, I'd read five anatomy books, gone home for winter holidays, made friends with George and Julie—yet it seemed like nothing. Since the first days of school, my mind had become a blur of Latin nouns and chemical equations. My past had become a blur. I had another supposedly "optional" test tomorrow, but I couldn't stay in this room a minute longer. So I put on my coat and left.

I was going out looking for Jeff. No self-deceiving games this time. Jeff would be my debaucher, my savior. He would correct all my imbalances, rectify all my systems. "Jeff . . . Jeff," was that even his name? Maybe it was just a schema that I was using— collecting the associations, to give me direction, to get me off my duff and out of the dorm. Jeff was a goal, a destination, maybe also a person. I had to use it; whether it was true—accurate—or not, who knew?

I walked toward the Green, passing the drugstores, the bagel stores. I stood at the window of Richter's and looked in. There were undergraduates in there, so confident of who they were, bright with drink and sure of the future. You could hear the laughter. The room was lit with soft incandescence, like firelight, a Kodachrome orange. It looked so warm, all those people in sweaters. But I couldn't go in there. It would have been a lie to go in there—I would have had to wear some sort of mask, a disguise of false laughter, and after twenty-three years, I was weary of it. I preferred the outside—the tumble of buses, the cold, where I could walk with the wind in my coat. I turned toward the street lamps ahead, leaving behind the Green, the bar.

I was haunting New Haven, wandering the streets and peering in the windows. Public ones and private ones, too, just to see what was going on, the insides of things. I didn't feel especially old or perverted or lonely doing this, just in another dimension. A ghost. What I wanted was a body, something to surround and inhabit. Not that I'd actually look at people through their windows. Just imagine them. Like when I'd done the Millikan Oil-Drop experiment in physics lab—looking through the slit, watching an electron levitate in the dark, wondering about the invisible forces that supported it. I started humming a theme song to myself as I walked, a made-up tune, something pleasantly sci-fi.

"Jeff!" I called out at three A.M., the dead of morning, when no one could hear me. Eventually, the night ended, I found myself back at the dorm.

In the morning, I went to classes with my eyes red, half shut, to doze uncomfortably in my chair. In the afternoon, I went to the reserve room of the library, to sleep there, too.

I let my work slide. I started skipping classes more often, more deliberately. Instead, I took rolls of photographs, spent time gazing through photo albums and card catalogs, spent evenings watching TV. I took advantage of the Yale System. I was more relieved, and more tired, than I'd been in months.

I spent a whole morning lying on my bed, daydreaming. I stared at my hands—the veins, like road maps, like the charts in the anatomy books. I had a poster of facial nerves on my wall. I'd been studying anatomy for so long now that I couldn't look at anyone's flesh anymore and not see it as a collection of muscle, nerve, tissue. I would watch people eating in the cafeteria and notice the way their throats moved when they swallowed, the masticator muscles pulsing in their temples. Now I was watching myself, and I felt like both the cadaver and student in one. Yet there *was* a difference, between my flesh and the flesh of the cadaver. I never thought of the muscle men in the magazines in terms of their anatomical design—they weren't objects, and I wasn't the originator of an objective gaze, objectifying them. I'd been learning something from the pornography, the artwork, my midnight wanderings, even if I couldn't name what exactly. And that morning in bed, those two different visions of bodies became one, and my hands became *my hands*—soft, fleshy, alive. I ran fingers down my arm, to feel my aliveness. Slowly, I took off my shirt, my pants. I lay flat on the bed, naked, and lightly touched my arms, my legs, outlining the muscles. It was as though I were outside myself, watching. I watched my body as though I'd never seen it before, and it *was* strange to me, the patterns the hairs made, the way it excited me. I wanted to tell someone: My body was coming to life.

By the time Sparrow got back to me, I was already studying for finals, if you could call it studying anymore.

"Hello, Paul?" he said over the phone, and immediately I knew who it was. He had the news I'd been waiting for. My heart raced.

"Well, first I want to say that it was a very interesting piece. We really must get together and discuss all of its merits and so forth."

"Okay." I fished for a pencil on my desk. I thought maybe he was going to schedule a conference.

"But really, the reason I'm calling you has to do with the show. We want to use some of your pictures."

"That's great!" Success—so quickly. I dropped the pencil.

"But...we can't use your project exactly as you have it. It's not quite...the sort of thing we can fit neatly into the schedule...the way you've done it. But watch the show this Thursday. You'll see part of it."

"What part?"

"I can't really talk now, Paul. Watch on Thursday." And without explaining further, he hung up.

So on Thursday, Julie, George, Pete, Fergie, Veronique-Maria-etc., and a few others joined me in the lounge. At nine-thirty, the familiar jingle of "Health Beat" came on, with the synthesizers and cardiovascularlike blooping sounds. Then, through an elaborate wipe, Dr. Sparrow appeared at his desk, that heavily guarded fortress from which he prepared his coming assault, shuffling his stack of papers.

Pete passed around a bowl of popcorn.

"Tonight—allogenic bone marrow transplants. How far have we come with this lifesaving technique?"

"What's that got to do with Pete's cast?"

"Shhh," I said. "It's just supposed to be a segment. He didn't say how he's going to work it in." By now, Pete's shoulder was fine—the whole cast episode was just a memory. Everyone crunched loudly, asked for the bowl, and I could hardly hear the TV. I hadn't wanted a whole crowd of people watching the show with me. I hadn't wanted anyone, actually, but Pete had told them all about it, and it would have been impossible to have forbidden them to come.

I tried to think what Sparrow could possibly have in mind.

He started his talk about the bone marrows and their treatments: cartoons of granulocytes falling dead from heatstroke, close-ups of the various chemotoxic agents and radiotherapy machines, smiling nurses and unconscious patients. All entertaining, but nothing that remotely resembled the material I'd given him. I wondered if he'd told me the wrong day.

Halfway through, they cut to a Listerine commercial—statistics about gingivitis.

"Well, Paul?"

"Yeah, Paul, we're waiting for this great debut. I know, I bet that's Pete's mouth right there."

"It's big enough."

"Hey—you don't have to stay if you don't want." I said it offhandedly, but they could tell I was peeved. They stopped joking around.

After the commercial, Sparrow segued into a specific patient narrative—Alfred Lund's—and he showed some photos of the Lund family: the happy twins (Alfred and Larry), the backyard, the dog, all very "Leave It to Beaver" until tragedy struck, and this beautiful, healthy, twenty-two-year-old boy, Alfred, was rendered horizontal by a galloping non-Hodgkin's lymphoma.

We all grew quiet. We were all just about twenty-two years old.

"Before the procedure can be scheduled, the donor undergoes a complete physical . . ."

Another picture appeared, and at first I didn't recognize my own photograph. But then I realized I was seeing only half of it: a doctor looking through an ophthalmoscope. I realized who it was, too—Veronique, although you would have had a hard time recognizing her without the cigarette.

"Hey, Veronique, that's you," someone said.

The other half of the photo—the guy looking back—had been cropped. Now, presumably, it was supposed to be a *patient* that she was looking at, *Alfred Lund.* In the context of Sparrow's narrative, you'd have no reason to think it was anyone else.

"I can't believe this. People are going to think I'm some sort of hematologist."

"Don't sweat it, Vera," Fergie said, slapping her knee. "It's exposure."

"Paul—is that all?"

Sparrow didn't show any other photos, any of the ones with Pete in them. He just finished his story about the Lunds: Alfred survived, was cured, returned to his job as an air-traffic controller. Later, his brother Larry died, a victim of a terrorist explosion over Italy. But Sparrow gave that only a footnote.

The theme song played over the credits, so that was it. After the names of Dr. Carlin Sparrow, Host, Marvin T. Wassermann, Producer, and Linda Grolnick and Charles Frank, Cameras, the roll call of "technical assistants" scrolled across the screen. My name was up there—Paul Levinson—buried in a speeding blur with about fifteen others. But it wasn't true; he hadn't used my ideas, he hadn't even used *my* pictures. I hadn't contributed a thing at all.

"At least you got your name up there," George said softly, as if speaking only to me. "At least that counts for something."

"Oh, who cares." And I walked out before anyone else had a chance to move.

I went back to my room, threw myself on the bed, and made a list.

Photography	Medicine
Pleasure	Money
Child	Parents
Insight	Knowledge
Self-Respect	Respect of Others
Empathy	Access
—	Power

This was it. No more games. I had to boil it down to a simple dialectic. I had to make it into a clear choice of options. No more murkiness. No more wishy-washiness. I was taking the bull by the horns.

I couldn't come up with the word I wanted opposite "power"— I tried "criticism," "magic," "flexibility," "illusion," but none of them had the encompassing quality I was searching for. So I left it blank, and gave up trying to make the columns come out even.

These divisions were always so arbitrary, always so impossible to explain.

And besides, I'd already decided which side of the sheet it was time to cross off.

*   *   *

The year was nearly over anyway. All we had left was our anatomy practical. We lined up outside the labs, waiting for the teachers, quizzing one another with last-minute stumpers.

At ten A.M., Dr. Grant and the other doctors arrived to unlock the door. We could begin at any table we wanted, and then we were to continue on in numerical order (they'd all been numbered), going from gurney to gurney, examining each cadaver, all arranged to exhibit a different muscle, tissue, or nerve. I got to Zorba—he had been arranged to exhibit, of all things, the corpus spongiosum of his penis, the one organ I'd thoroughly demolished. Why not his abdomen or cranium, which had been neatly dissected into picture-perfect striata? I guess they were trying to be tricky. What I'd left looked more like chopped liver than a male organ. I only spent a second at my own cadaver—by now, I knew exactly what I was looking at, and having a tiny red flag pinned to my cadaver's private parts embarrassed me, to say nothing about what it implied of my skill at dissection.

At the last cadaver I came to—a small, shriveled woman— someone had shaved off the pubic hair and replaced it with some white, curly substance. There was a red flag planted in the middle of it, and a sheet of paper taped to the cadaver's thigh, where people had written

> *Enterobius vermicularis*
> *E coli*
> *spaghetti*
> *gonorrhea*
> *AIDS*
> *dental floss*
> *vermicelli with a clam sauce*
> *Lyle Montgomery Cash's last deposit at Yale*

Pete, Fergie, and their lab partners stood chuckling in a corner. Maybe I was taking the whole thing a little more seriously than

was necessary. Why should it matter how many penises I muti-
lated? There were a million of them out there, a million replace-
ments waiting in the wings.

Besides, it wasn't even a test I cared about.

In a few hours, everyone finished, and the answers were posted
in the hall. We graded our own exams. So I'd passed, if I wanted.

Afterward, I went to knock on George's door, to tell him the
news.

Julie answered. "Malignant Neoplasm's playing in half an
hour," she told me, pulling a sweater over her head. "The Graduate Student Lounge. Want to come?"

"Sure." So we headed out together, in search of George, in
search of our last celebration. On the way, we joined up with
Veronique, Pete, Fergie, Zane, a few others, so by the time we got
out of the dorm, we had a whole crowd.

The sun was setting, the air was warm—an early-summer evening—and we all expanded and eased a bit with the encounter
with the outside.

"I can't believe it's over," Veronique said, smoking cloves today,
sending the smell of spice down our familiar hospital streets.
"What a year."

"It's only just starting, folks," Pete said. "Three more years.
Then internship. Then residency. *Then* the megabucks."

It took a while for someone to think of a good retort.

"Then Africa, you mean," Veronique finally corrected, matter-
of-factly. "Then kwashiorkor and AIDS and the World Health
Organization."

"You're so noble, Vera. You know that? We'll have an audit
done on you ten years from now. We'll interview your accountant.
Then we'll find out just how charitable you turn out to be."

"Come on, people," Julie said. "Be nice. There are plenty of
diseases to go around. Besides, we're almost there."

Julie. She'd really grown up in the last few months. She'd been
performing an alchemy with both the science and her humanity,
turning it into an even more potent mixture, an increased awareness of the world around her. And I realized—for some people,
Yale was just the sort of place where they could thrive.

Once in the lounge, we got drinks and snacks from the bar
and then sat down, all in a row, to listen to the band begin their
first set. Julie sat in one of the leather chairs, and I sat next to

her, sipping a Sea Breeze and listening to George play the riffs, fingers skipping madly over the keys, playing as intensely for a crowd of hundreds as he'd ever played for Julie and me alone.

"He's good, isn't he?" Julie leaned toward me as she spoke. "I know that's just my opinion, but I really think it's true. They could do a record if they wanted. They could go on David Letterman—Medical Student Band."

"Play 'Sympathy for the Devil'!" Fergie yelled, hands cupped over his mouth.

Julie closed her eyes, listening to her Malignant Neoplasm—or rather, George's harmony in it—entering a world of compassion and fullness that I could only imagine. And up onstage, George tapped his keyboards, absorbed in the music, the jazz. He was reaching some sort of peak. He seemed so relaxed, so unconcerned about where the music might take us, or, for that matter, where it might not. He closed his eyes, just like Julie. I watched them. It was something they shared—they were connected. They were complete. They already had all that they might ever need, right here, a future that was ready to unfurl all the happiness and tragedy they could ever possibly plan.

And I knew then that anything I might ever want wasn't here, but out there, and had been all this time. I only had to have the courage to go out and find it. I didn't have Sammy to give me advice anymore. I didn't have Daniel. Only me. I only had to take, finally, some adult and decisive action.

And so I listened to George's music, and vowed that I would act.

The next morning I was hung over. I stood at the sink and stared at my bloodshot eyes, thinking about everything I wanted to pack. When Sparrow called, I was ready for him. It was as if I'd sensed he'd call just then, just as I was about to open my suitcase, about to say good-bye for good.

"Paul, I've got your pictures, if you want them back. We still need to get together. You should know that I . . . thought they were . . . quite interesting. But we can talk more in detail later. Maybe you could work some more on the idea?"

"Maybe," I said. I wasn't in the mood for a discussion of aesthetics, especially after he hadn't even used them right. "I think you should know—I'm taking a leave of absence. I'm going to be working on another project. Something big. It's not going to be for 'Health Beat.' "

"Uh-huh. Well, Paul, now, what do you mean by a leave of absence?" He sounded as if it was still all his idea, what I did with my life, rather than mine.

"I mean, I'm leaving. I'm sick of this place. Not Yale—just medicine. I'd love to stay at Yale if I could." I hadn't intended to tell him all that. My feelings had just overtaken me.

"Well, Paul, that's quite a big step. Have you thought it through carefully?"

"Yes."

"Because, you know, this may not be the best time to take time off from your studies. You should be starting your research project this summer." He paused for a moment, thinking further. "After all, photography is exciting, but it isn't going to do anything for your career."

"Well, Dr. Sparrow, that's just the thing. I'm tired of thinking about my career. I think, instead, I'm just going to live my life."

And then I hung up.

5

Teeth

"**P**aul, thanks for the visit," my father said as he hugged me, same old guy after all this time. "It's always good to see you."

"Of course, Dad." Where else did I have to go? But I wasn't looking forward to what I had to tell him, or what I knew would be his reaction.

We sat in the car for a moment, listening to the oak trees in our driveway, their liquid green leaves rustling in the evening breeze. Just a brief, peaceful moment. Then Dad opened his door, and I opened mine, and I was home once again.

The cat rubbed my leg as I walked in the house, then sped down the stairs to the basement. A sign across the foyer said WELCOME HOME, DR. LEVINSON, OUR HERO. This was going to be even harder to do than I'd thought.

I took my luggage to my room and changed my shirt. The house was too hot—Dad never turned on the air conditioning till midway through July—and I wanted to feel as comfortable here as I could. I came back downstairs to see what was up; whenever I came home, something was always up, in the way of a fuss over me, and I had come to accept it. I went into the living room and my mother offered me a beer.

"No thanks, Mom."

"Oh, Paul, you have to have a beer. Who else is going to drink it? Dad, you too. You guys...you're both such workaholics, it's time to relax."

Workaholics. She must have gotten that from some talk show.

Mom went into the kitchen, the place she always seemed happiest. Dad and I stared at each other. We tended to get stuck like this, unable to start a conversation. Maybe we were both just awkward at it. My family and I were alike in so many trivial ways, and different in so many substantial ones, that coming home was always awkward.

"Hi, Paul," my sister said.

"Hi, Jen."

She stood, peering into the room, hands behind her back. Why didn't she come inside? Jenny, my sister. It was as though she were hiding something: a bad report card, a wedding ring. Already she was sixteen, and I didn't know a thing about her love life. Jenny never talked about boyfriends. I thought she'd gotten the habit from me. I was curious about her, but didn't feel it possible to ask her about her life, one person to another. We'd lived like strangers, shipwreck victims floating on two separate rafts, signaling each other every now and then, but having no real procedure to help each other. She shuffled back and forth, as if unsure whether she was invited.

"Come on in, Jenny, come in." Mom shooed her into the living room, carrying two beers in her hands. "Dad, you've got the gifts?"

"Right here, Mom." Dad pulled two gift-wrapped boxes from under the coffee table, a large one and a small one. "We got you something, Paul. It's a congratulations gift, for finishing your first year of medical school." He set the boxes on the table. Mom put my beer next to it. So this was it, the fuss. The gifts had red bows, white ribbons, four-dollar wrapping paper.

"Open them, Paul," Mom said. "Go ahead."

The three of them pulled up their chairs and moved in closer, to watch. Only Jen seemed to give me any look of sympathy about this, rolling her eyes when Mom and Dad weren't looking. I smiled back, the only way I had to thank her.

"I have a hunch you'll like this, Paul," Dad said. "Just a hunch."

"They've been talking about this for weeks."

I read the card—"Congratulations"—then put it on the coffee table. I ripped the paper off the large package. A cardboard box. On the side, in block roman letters, it said:

VCR

"Oh, Dad, you shouldn't have . . . ," but *wow,* I thought to myself. I was hooked, if only by the seduction of gift opening, like reading the surprise ending of a tantalizing mystery novel. *Technology!* this one announced. Without even unpacking the first box, I tore the paper off the second. I couldn't understand how they'd suddenly learned to read me so completely. A camcorder.

"I can't believe this. This is too much. Really. It's not even my birthday. . . ." They'd never given me something half this nice even when it *was* my birthday. It was an occasion without date. They were *making* an occasion. I couldn't express the overwhelming magnanimity I felt toward them at that moment. But they knew. It was on my face. Maybe that was the one gift they'd always been waiting for from *me*.

They all beamed, pleased as punch.

"We figured you could take some pretty good pictures with that."

"You really like it," Jenny said. "Don't you?" She seemed amazed; for once my folks had guessed right.

I folded up the wrapping paper and placed it on the floor. "I can't accept it."

"Right, Paul." Dad rubbed his knuckle in my arm. "Like hell you can't."

"No . . . no, really. I shouldn't have been so excited." I held out the camcorder box. "Take it back. You shouldn't be spending money on me. For what? It's not right."

"Oh, now, Paul, who else are we going to spend it on?" My mother's impeccable logic. "Just say, 'Thank you, Mom and Dad.' And we'll say, 'You're welcome, honey.' "

"Thank you, of course, but really, there's more to this than you—"

"You're welcome, honey." She hugged me, tightly, and I couldn't say anything; I could barely breathe. "We're so glad you like it."

My father hugged me, too, big burly arms that he didn't feel ashamed to put around me. "You deserve it, Paul," Dad said. "After all that hard work. See—take some time now, enjoy it. We know you can't work all the time. Just, come fall, don't let it interfere with your studies."

"Fred," Mom said.

"He knows I'm joking." He let go and squeezed my arm. "Hey—you want to set up the VCR?"

So what was I to do? It was overwhelming. And I had to admit—I was curious.

"Okay. Sure."

Mom collected the paper from the couch. "First Jenny gets a hug," she said as she crumpled up the paper and threw it in the trash. "Go on." She nudged her. "Hug your brother."

Jenny didn't surround me like my parents had, just held me a little. All this hugging . . . I was grateful Jen was there, as a diversion. She'd have understood my ambivalence. I wished I could have told her about it. All I did was squeeze her tighter.

"Well, I've got homework, you know." She wiggled out of my grasp and inched backward.

"Homework?" Dad said. "Noooo. . . . You're kidding."

"Nope. Talk to you later, Paul." She jogged around the corner, her ponytail in a sway. Her feet echoed on the stairs, then up above us. Her door closed—a door which she'd probably lock, then guard with the noise from the stereo, the way I used to do. I could see it all clearly, as if I were once again that age, as if being around your parents made you always that age.

Mom brought in some freshly chilled beer steins from the kitchen. "Here you go. You'll have to teach me about the VCR, Paul. I never know how to work those mechanical things."

But I didn't believe her protestations anymore. Mom knew more than she gave herself credit for; I knew now that her innocence was an elaborately played game, a conceit whose rules and rewards remained vague to me. Why did she always efface herself from our conversations? Why did she always take refuge in the kitchen? Why couldn't she be more like Julie, or Veronique, or the other women I knew, who were out and about in the world? I'd always thought that if my parents had something else to focus on—a hobby or something—they'd spend a little less scrutiny on me. My mom had her hair done every Saturday, and in twenty years she'd never altered the Jewish sandwich-roll style. Even sitcoms updated occasionally.

"Okay. Paul, Dad, I'm going downstairs to do some laundry. I'll be able to hear your conversation from there. I wouldn't want to interrupt, though."

She left the room, to conduct her surveillance, as if going to watch her favorite soap opera.

"She can hear us from down there?"

"Sure."

"I never knew that."

Dad and I drank the beers in silence. He seemed to be waiting for me, offering me the initiative, but I wasn't up to it at the moment, seeing as I felt like a thief. I sipped from my mug. The beer was fine, chilled and all, but it wasn't as relaxing as I'd hoped it would have been—drinking cold beer at home, with my father, after just having seen my sister and a brand-new VCR and Video8 Handycam Camcorder (with a bonus pack of three blank tapes and a head cleaner) sitting in front of me on the floor.

That's when it dawned on me, that what my parents really wanted was for me to be a DOCTOR, that what they needed most was the title—and perhaps to see their son in a lab coat and stethoscope. They had an image they wanted to complete. A word they wanted to spell. They'd been spelling it since their own child-hoods; they'd keep stuttering along until they could finish it. The only obstacle in their way was me. Why couldn't I just *say* I was a doctor, and skip the school, the practice, the office, the whole preplanned routine? I'd be a doctor of video; doctor of arts; doctor of mystery. Daniel had had the right idea. Just pass yourself off, be what people wanted.

Dad was looking at the VCR, too, drinking his beer, thinking perhaps that this was an elaborate experiment, a last-ditch reverse-psychology effort, and he just prayed to God that it worked. The thing was, now that I was home, all my resolve was quickly leaving—he was my father, and I was his son. And we really did love each other. What right did I have to so thoroughly disap-point him?

"Okay," Dad said finally. "Let's do her up."

I opened the box and removed the VCR. Gently, I touched the machine. It was so electrical, so metallic. This was what my parents had bequeathed me: VIDEO IN and VIDEO OUT. Now *I* owned the hardware; it was mine to use. I hooked it up to the television. All these cables, feeding information, feeding signals—electronic blood, lymph, conduction, digitized particulates linking up to high-res Omnivision. The machine was a being; there was no fine line.

Dad offered to help, but I told him I could do it myself. He unwrapped the cellophane, crunching it in his hands.

"What should we record? What's on?"

"You got me." Dad handed me the blank tape and flipped through the *TV Guide*. "Sitcoms probably. What's this? 'The Cosby Show'?"

"Please, nothing popular."

I turned on the TV and what came on was the news: specifically, Dan Rather, and behind him, a picture of some punk-looking demonstrators outside a basilica. The insert zoomed in for a full-shot of two men embracing, one from the back, disturbed looks on their faces, apparently conducting some sort of vigil. The only reason for their presentation was the sensational value, apparently, or perhaps the cursory use of their image as a shorthand visual icon or dictionary reference (*faggots*, see also *lesbians*), but to me the pair seemed impossibly romantic—the way the taller one embraced his cohort, shared his expression without needing to see it for himself; the way the man in front leaned slightly backward into the security of his lover. They were handsome, too, like International Males (was this, perhaps, another part of the mixed message?). A soft voice-over explained the situation, unintelligibly. Meanwhile, Dad fiddled with the VCR, trying to tape the show, recording and rewinding, playing and recording....

"*Homosexuals in / homosexuals in New / homosexuals in New York today* ..." the tape repeated with each rewind, and the noisy snow in between, but I tuned out the rest. I couldn't stand it. I had to hold my breath. It was like being stabbed unexpectedly from the darkness; I couldn't believe this was coming so unobstructed into our home, right there in front of me, in front of my father. I could tell that the story wasn't really anything that might actually be called an "experience," an "event"—that it was just "news." That is, that it wasn't, really, about homosexuals. Whatever those were.

They cut to a commercial for diapers.

"Grrgle grrgle grrgle," the baby said on TV, crawling across a white floor. And the voice-over: "*Incredibly, the incredibly absorbent secret ingredient absorbs five hundred times its weight....*"

"Humph," my father replied, and crossed his arms. Then he went back to fiddling with the VCR.

What had it meant, that inarticulate grunt and that posture? I couldn't tell if he disapproved of the homos, the newscasters, or the machine. I wanted to fall through the floor. Who knew—

maybe he hadn't even noticed. It wasn't as though it would be something naturally on his mind. It was so odd, how no one I knew personally had ever even used that word, *homosexual,* let alone held a discussion about it, yet in the media you heard it constantly: Phil Donahue, *The New York Times,* "Nightline." It was ever present, like terrorism or nuclear disarmament—something impersonal and political to take a position on, or have a scientific diagnosis about, rather than an attempt to describe an aspect of my own unvocalized and vague experience. *How many of you for or against the homosexuals? Let's hear from our viewers.* A year ago, I wouldn't have jumped like I had; I would have been more sure of my abilities to ignore it. But so many things were happening to me recently—intangible mutations—and I hadn't had a chance to reconcile them; I hadn't yet perfected my new act.

"Well," Dad said finally. "It seems to be working. Now, what about the camcorder?"

I read the instructions and set it up. I was off the hook, apparently. He wasn't going to think about his own unmarried, mysterious, inexplicably moody son. I slipped in a blank tape and pointed the camera at the television.

"What, are you taping now?"

"Uh-huh." The red light blinked soothingly in my viewfinder. The camera—my baby—it fit so perfectly in my hand. It had such weight, such solidity, as though it'd always been there, in my palm. It was another extended apparatus of my being, another limb and aperture, plugged right in. The news was over; I was filming some nighttime soap opera, or sitcom, or game show, or commercial. *Send your boy to medical school,* the TV program said. *Send him to Yale. Send your daughter, too. Send everyone you know. Make out your check to Squish Pharmaceuticals.*

Dad walked over to stand behind me. He bent down. He was apparently trying to estimate what, exactly, was in the shot, since I was concentrating so hard.

"What are you filming the television for? What's it going to do, walk away? Why don't you film something more sensible? Film your family. Film something you're supposed to film."

"The television's 'sensible.' "

"What's so interesting about the television?"

"It's not the television itself, really. It's what's *on* television."

"So—you need a camera to tape that? That's what the VCR is for."

"No, Dad . . . this is different. I want to tape what's on television *in your house.* I want it . . . implicated. Understand?"

"Just forget it. Put the camera away."

I removed the tape and put the camcorder back in its box.

"Filming the television. Only you, Paul. My brilliant *meshugana* son."

Forget it. All you could do in this house was watch television, not criticize it.

Dad sat down to read the camcorder instruction manual. I stared at him until he looked at me. "I didn't mean to yell, Paul. You can do whatever you want with this thing. It's your gift, honey. I'm sure you've got better uses for it than I can think of."

"That's okay."

He looked back down at the manual. "Did you know it's got full-range digital autofocus, five lux light sensitivity, and a single-page digital superimposer?"

"Uh-huh."

He looked up at me again. "Do you know what any of that stuff is?"

"No."

"Hmmm." He tossed the manual on the coffee table.

"Look: *Planet of the Apes,*" I said. "Dad, it's *Planet of the Apes.* Why don't we record this?" Okay, so there were things about which I was an unreconstructed TV addict myself. It was nearly over, anyway—the scene where Charlton Heston stumbles upon a half-buried Statue of Liberty (*My God, my God, no . . .* , my favorite re-membered image, but now I could see the seams between the sand and the Lady, the simulated nature of the special effects). We watched mindlessly, drinking beer until everything was relaxed, until it was just like the old days, the days before I'd left home, father and son lounging around the house, watching TV.

"Dad, by the way, there *is* uh . . . something I need to talk to you about."

"What's that?" He put his beer down, as if he already knew what I was about to say, was just waiting for me to say it so he could make the reply he had in his mind. He must have known all along, I thought; he knew everything (practically) about me.

But the thing I wanted to tell him, the words as I'd rehearsed them, were so impossible—especially here, now, with this brand-new machine and my mother, who had chilled the glasses for me, listening to us from the basement. My head was awash just thinking about it. How could I? How dare I? I blanked for a moment—I didn't know whether I had already said what I was about to say, or if my mouth might yet speak of its own accord. I forced myself to say something, anything, just to get it over with.

"I need my teeth cleaned."

*　　*　　*

I'd never been in the Hoosier Tower before, where Dad's new office was. The city was changing too fast to keep up with it. Dad gave me detailed directions, to make sure I wouldn't get lost. The elaborate elevator rose like an I-beam through the lobby, yet it was close enough to the glass facade so that you could look out and see the Indianapolis skyline rise up and shrink before you as you rode to the top levels of the building, rising up and up and up like the imagination of Sigmund Freud. Finally, the elevator chimed, the doors opened, and I walked off onto a floor that looked just like every other faceless, carpeted hall in every other building in the world.

"Paul Levinson," I told the receptionist.

"Of course. I know who you are, Paul."

The reverse wasn't true, however. Dad never spoke about his office personnel at home. Yet these women always knew about me in advance, as if they'd been warned. "Just a minute. You're early. Why don't you read a magazine?"

A few minutes later she opened her window again. "Go right in, Paul." So there was some advantage, after all, in being the Doctor's Son. She smiled a mouthful of perfectly straight, perfectly bright, dental-receptionist teeth.

I sat complacently in the dental chair while Cathy, the hygienist, set me up.

"Well, Paul, have you been brushing like I showed you? The uppy-ups and the downy-downs? Too busy studying to remember to brush your teeth properly, I bet. Tsk, tsk, tsk."

I always wondered how my father picked them. Did he have completely objective criteria, or were they here for their clean hair and bland, inoffensive demeanors? This particular hygienist had always known me well—she'd known about me before I was born, an omniscience she had no inclination to abnegate—so she always had a lot of facts about me to dredge up in conversation, while I had to strain just to remember her name. As she cleaned my teeth, she asked me questions about school, about medicine, about my love life.

I drooled as I answered her. "Mmmm...ahh...mmdcl brrds...uhht thhh mmai ee, unhll I et out ahh oooll...."

"Well, you certainly are diligent. Is that going to take a lot of work?" She sat so close, her perfume overwhelmed me. Sweet-smelling skin, the skin of a baby-sitter.

"Uht I nnt innk ee ohs aaht einn ooing oo ooh."

Cathy picked up a corner of the bib and wiped my chin.

"That's the right spirit. I'm sure your parents will approve." She smiled at me, awfully pale under the X-ray light of the dentist room, pinned-up hairdo vibrating ever so slightly with her movements. "Your dad will be in shortly," she said, inserting a set of Styrofoam dentures over my teeth. The dentures held a fluorine gel that tasted like cold motor oil. Her fingers danced in my mouth. "Now hold that still for a minute. That's the new strawberry flavor."

"Mmmmm," I said, the gel freezing my gums and giving me chills.

Cathy left the room. I looked at my watch and tried not to spit. I looked at my watch, looked at my watch, looked at my watch.

She came back a minute and thirty-two seconds later and removed the gunk.

"There," she said, throwing the Styrofoam in the trash.

"Ah," I said. And then—"Nnnnn," moving my tongue around the edges.

"No food or water for an hour."

I saluted.

She didn't smile, just snapped off her rubber gloves and threw them in the trash. A moment later my father walked in the room. He wore his dentist smock, the short-sleeve one, which looked something like a bowling shirt, only white, exposing his hairy forearms. "So let's see what we've got, eh, Paul?" My father looked so masculine dressed as a periodontist. He pulled up a stool and picked a dental instrument from the tray that glided next to the chair, a probe with a hook on the end. He held it up over my mouth, poised, ready to enter, and gave me a smile. I thought briefly of Daniel C. Anderson poised over the cadaver, waiting for us to tell him what to do. Where was he—who was he—now?

"Open," he said.

I opened.

"Uh-huh...uh...mmm-hmm...looks like she missed something here." He started pulling on my teeth with his hook.

"Uh, D'ad, d'ers 'omething I really have to d'ell you."

"Yes?" He pulled away his tools. This was my father now—interrupting his work to listen to his son.

"Actually, I've been wanting to tell you this for a while."

"Uh-huh. Go ahead. I'm listening."

"Well..." I paused only for a moment, but that moment contained all the trepidation that had been building up inside me for weeks, all the sweaty palms and attacks of nausea—at just the thought of saying this. I closed my eyes. I forced them open. There was my father, and all those dental tools, and myself lying before him in a plastic bib, drool running down my shirt. I clenched the side of the chair. I couldn't look; it took all my strength just to talk.

"I've decided to leave medical school."

THE GREAT VOID

This void represented above opened up for me at that moment—I saw it gaping in front of me. Down went the whores, the gamblers, the movie extras, the Golden Calf, with Moses and Aaron smirking self-righteously on the sidelines. A second later—which seemed like an eternity—the swirling, twirling room resolved, and I knew that with those words, I'd killed not my father, but my Father, just as surely as if Isaac had done a Back Reverse Flip on Abraham and told him, "Sorry, Pop, no." But Dad, the actual one, must have been a bit put off by it also. Those words I'd spoken had stopped the very movement of the air, hanging there in front of us as if on ticker tape—PAUL LEVINSON IS LEAVING MEDICAL SCHOOL—imposing a looming silence as Dad sat up and sat back, the pick and the mirror still in his hands, as though he'd forgotten about them. For the first time, he didn't seem prepared, he didn't have anything to say. And I, I had no more to add. I hadn't wanted to do that to him, not intentionally, not after all the nice things they'd done for me, but what other choice did I have?

"Open," he said finally.

"Dad, I've been thinking about it for a while and—"

"Open," he said again—not harshly, but steadily, the way one recites a fact. The fact of a mouth, a tooth, a cavity.

I opened. He put the tool back in my mouth, back to the tooth he'd been playing with before. He started yanking on it, hard, pulling my jaw with him, until a little piece of plaque chipped away and I felt his hook scrape along my tooth.

"Dad, let me explain."

He sat back again. "Explain what? You've already made up your mind, so do whatever you want."

"Right," I said. I'd expected an argument, prepared a list of my reasons, the practicality and frugality of my decision, but he didn't seem to want to hear about it. "And you're not angry?"

He wiped his tools and set them down on the tray. "Your teeth are fine." He stood up, flicked off the arc light that had been shining into my eyes. "Angry? You're only making the biggest mistake of your life. Why should I be angry?"

I tried to measure my response. "Maybe it is a mistake," I said. "But it's my mistake to make, isn't it?"

He turned away from me, to write something on my chart. While he did, I explained it to him, everything—why I had to leave, how this wasn't meant to be a reflection on him, or Mom, that I loved them just as much as always, that this decision had nothing to do with love, or devotion, or my willingness to take care of them in their retirement years. He actually seemed to be listening to me, with his back turned, listening to what I had to say, and considering. "Yes," he said finally, taking off his smock. "Well, I suppose you're right. You've got to make your own mistakes."

As he turned around to hang up the jacket, he looked at me.

And seeing him against the wall like that—without his coat, hair a mess, going gray at the temples—well, I'd never seen my father in that way before: as just a man, getting older. It practically destroyed my resolve. I wanted to cry. I got out of the chair, still wearing the bib. I didn't know what I was going to do. I just wanted to walk over to him, to say something more, comfort him somehow.

But it wasn't my place to comfort a man whose hopes I'd just dashed.

I left the building and walked out into the city—Indianapolis, Indiana, so whitewashed, Midwestern, clean. I had a picture of it in my mind, as I walked out of that building: an aerial view, like a map...a thriving nestle of buildings in the middle of a plane. All around were its major arteries, its nerve centers, its corpuscles and congestion and plaque—and here I was, another of its millions of molecules, coming out from my father's office, waiting for the bus. I didn't necessarily like what I'd done, but I felt great.

I thought—well, this is it. For the first time, I'm on my own, for better or worse. I could go right out now and walk into any building I wanted, go anywhere, do anything; there were no more restrictions. I was my own man. My future was a slate wiped suddenly clean. The whole world was out there, with the sun going round and the moon in its orbit and the ozone slowly depleting— it was all waiting for me.

That afternoon, I packed my car, the clanky Honda Civic: In went the television, the golf clubs, my album collection, my old books in boxes, clothes in plastic bags. I hadn't taken my car to New Haven before, but now I wanted it. Everything was coming with me: these objects, these possessions—it was all of my old self that would remain. They'd be the mortar of a new existence.

I told my father that I was leaving behind the VCR and camera: "I said before that I couldn't accept it, and I meant it. You bought it for a reason, and now that reason doesn't exist anymore."

"So you want to insult us as well as ruin your life?"

We stood staring at each other.

"I think what your father means is that it's not right to take back a gift, even if the reason you gave it in the first place was out of a good heart, but not one hundred percent out of altruism, right, honey?" And she gave Dad a look that I could only say that I sympathized with. So they weren't, apparently, the solid and unified front that I'd always perceived them to be.

"Okay," I said. "But I'll keep it just so as not to be insulting."

"Humph," Dad said, and left to watch his Saturday-afternoon football. After he was out of view, Mom gave me a stern look, as if to say, *I might have stuck up for you, but we don't have to feel good about it.*

"Have you got the apples and sandwiches?"

"Yep."

"And the strudel?"

"Yep."

"The one with the raisins, not the other, the sour cream that Jenny likes?"

"Uh-huh."

"Okay, then."

Then she gave me a peck on the cheek. It wasn't the typical *Honey, when are you coming home again?* good-bye.

"It's my opinion, young man, just my opinion, mind you, that your father isn't happy."

"I know. I offered to return the gifts. I apologized. What more?"

"I'm just saying. I won't get in the middle."

"Mom—we've been all through this. My mind's made up. What else can I say?"

She tried to think of something. "You'll call us when you get there?"

"Sure, Mom. Don't worry." I gave her a hug. It seemed to make things okay, at least for the moment.

"Well—drive safely," she said, wiping her eyes, the first time she'd been at a loss since I'd known her.

I packed the VCR in the trunk. The camcorder I let sit in the passenger seat, next to Mom's food, in case I found an immediate occasion for it. I had actually been hoping that they wouldn't let me give it back. I was still, basically, a selfish bastard. Besides, there was a lot of countryside to cover between Indiana and New Haven, a lot of photogenic opportunities. And once you got away from your family, out on the open road, you never knew when you'd get the urge to record something.

PART II

Mechanism

6

Circulation

I was going to move in with George. We'd agreed before the end of the year: out of Darkness and into some apartment in the suburbs of New Haven. He knew all about my designs, and if he had any skepticism, he kept it to himself. We'd finish out the summer together, maybe beyond. For me, I had more invested in New Haven than in Indianapolis. For George, I think he was looking forward to the idea of having our own place, our own alternative lives, as much as I was.

It'd be an adventure for both of us.

Yet our lives wouldn't overlap greatly. George would be heading into his tunnel, piling up his books, his charts and diagrams, while I'd be restructuring my life—whole days without schedule, without boredom. The prospect was glorious. On that day I left Indianapolis, I had no worries about mundane, day-to-day cares: cleaning, cooking, paying the rent. I was too involved in my dream of freedom. Freedom—free—anything I wanted. The sky was overcast for my drive east, but the highway shimmered ahead of me. All the way out, the road was laced with weeping willows and early-summer flowers; I imagined what they would look like in my viewfinder, in what network of patterns and shades they might present themselves, how I might arrange them. I felt like a part of the countryside, part of the scenery. My car hugged the curves, purring in rhythm.

Mainly, I was looking forward to the idea of living on my own, in my own place. I remembered how as a teenager, I used to fantasize about having my own apartment, where I could stock the shelves with spaghetti and crank up adolescent rock songs without anybody telling me different. I'd taken an obsessive interest in other people's furniture. I was about fifteen then. My fantasies always involved only me, getting away from my parents, no significant others. When Mom and Dad went shopping at furniture stores, I'd pick out my own future couches, end tables, dish racks—I told my nerdy adolescent self that I'd come back ten years later and purchase the stuff. Whatever I wanted.

Now I was living with George Yan Su in a run-down Victorian student ghetto. Our only furniture was what the four or five former tenants had grown too weary to remove when they'd left.

"So, George. When do I get my first private Neoplasm concert?"

"The other guys in the band don't want to rehearse here." He tested the door on the bathroom, which squeaked as he opened and closed it.

"Why not? What's wrong with this place? It's got running water. Hardwood floors. Genuine cracked tile in the bathroom." I pointed around like a real-estate broker.

"They don't want to rehearse anywhere. They say they're too busy."

"That's terrible."

"Yeah. Terrible that they're right." He sat back on a suitcase and turned on his TV, the first thing we'd plugged in. We hadn't even hung our clothes in the closets. "We can't even find a night that we're all free anymore."

Maybe George was willing to room with me because he saw it as a chance to experiment with his own repressed fantasies of leaving school. As I encountered obstacles, he'd be able to congratulate himself about having made the right decision; as I enjoyed myself, he'd enjoy himself vicariously. He wasn't, apparently, going to have that many more opportunities to keep playing with the band.

I left him in his sullenness and went to call my parents, as I'd promised, to tell them I'd made it back to New Haven safely.

"It's not too late to change your mind, Paul," was the first thing out of my father's mouth. "Maybe the adviser you talked to is around for the summer?"

Couldn't we talk about something else, even for a moment? "I think my mind is pretty well made up."

A pause.

"Well," my mother interrupted, judiciously. "Maybe we shouldn't discuss this right now."

So we didn't. We made some idiotic pleasantries. Then we said good-bye, as if I hadn't even called. So that was that. I was on my own.

On Monday, as George went to work on his summer thesis, I slept till eleven A.M. What a change. I skipped my shower; just threw on a sweatshirt, sat on the couch, and turned on the TV with the remote. Finding a job was going to be a job in itself.

"Train for a career at New Haven Technical College . . . auto mechanic, secretary, the exciting world of home electrical repair. . . ."

Here it was—my wonderful freedom. No two-week training courses for people who leave medical school. I alternately stared at the tube and read the morning paper, head in my hands. Soap operas, beer commercials, "Love Connection." Two years' experience wanted, five years required, telecommunication professionals earning $8.50 an hour. *"Joseph Gianelli, age thirty-four, market researcher, meet Jane Williams, age twenty-one, cosmetic technician."* Where could I fit myself into this elaborate, second-tier network? I'd never survive as an auto mechanic, I could barely change a light bulb. I was having a crisis of faith. Maybe the conventional wisdom was right—God loved Republicans, socialized medicine was an evil, and people who did well on standardized tests could become anything they wanted, as long as it was a doctor. But it'd been less than four hours, and I wasn't going back.

The phone rang.

It was Fergie, of all people. He'd heard about my situation through Pete, who'd heard through Julie (who knew through George), and he had an idea for me. For the past few months he'd been tending bar on the weekends at a Cajun restaurant. This, in itself, would have been surprising, if it weren't that anything Fergie did didn't surprise me. He was quitting his job to start his research project, and the restaurant was looking for a full-time bartender.

"Won't I have to answer some quiz? Recite drink ingredients?"

"Nah—just tell them you have experience. That'll be good enough."

"What if they want me to soothe customers with my potential bar psychology?"

"It's a back bar. You don't meet the customers. Besides, you're a medical student. It's not like you need credentials."

When I still didn't get it, he lowered his voice, as if we were planning a conspiracy.

"Who do you think works in these places, anyway?"

"Who?"

There was a pause. "Just tell them you know me. If that doesn't get you in, I don't know what will."

He was giving me this information as one medical student to another (they called it a medical *fraternity*, after all), not necessarily because he felt he owed me anything personally. But that was the way with medical students: You never had to work for anything, it was handed to you. All you needed was to know someone. And I did.

The restaurant was overflowing with people when I got there, waitresses and busboys rushing about, a madhouse. The lady who interviewed me was black; a large chromium earring dangled from each ear. She said that she'd squeeze two minutes out of the bedlam to talk to me. We sat next to each other on a bench beside the bar. Already I liked the place, liked the turgid sound of the name—*Big Moe's*—the drama of the blue-neon lights shining down from the corners, the posters of tumescent body parts and scenes of the bayou. I felt light, buoyant, sitting in this restaurant, doing for once whatever I wanted with my life— which was, at the moment, to get some sort of impractical but exciting job, like this one. I was in a dangerous frame of mind, and this place had potential for danger: neon menus, art cuisine, healthily priced popular creole. It was five o'clock on a Wednesday; the place was jammed.

The manager's name was Angela. She'd been brought in from a restaurant in New York not more than a month ago. The previous manager, two busboys, and a bartender had all quit within the space of a week, she told me, frankly. Her earrings tinkled politely with each small motion of her head. She was the only one in the restaurant dressed with any sort of élan.

"I need someone who can start immediately. Immediately," she emphasized, attempting to be businesslike, but barely concealing her desperation.

"Is today immediate enough?"

Angela glanced hurriedly at my application, asked me a few random questions, the answers to which she didn't pay attention to, and that's when I put to work Fergie's lie. Sure, I told her. I've tended bar. Parties, weddings, you name it (in truth: one fraternity party). And I really came to believe that I had some supernatural ability to tend bar—some nascent, mystical talent that only needed to be nurtured.

"Yep, yep, yep," she said, nodding along. Meanwhile, her sweaty arm was soiling the resumé I'd typed that morning on my creaky Smith-Corona. When she saw she was getting my vita dirty, she folded it, leaned past me, and stuffed it in a corner by the cash register.

In the meantime, waitresses and customers flew past; you couldn't tell who was supposed to be going where. The building itself was a mishmash—brick, concrete, scraps of carpet stuffed under the coatracks, the smell of fresh-cut pine drifting from where they'd just put up cabinets; it was as if it'd been built intentionally to look like someone's half-finished basement. It even had paneling. But there also lingered smells of seafood, cayenne pepper, and some sort of bittersweet chocolate terrine (seven slices of which sat deliciously in the dessert case across the room). The smells were so luscious and distinctive, I was instantly hungry. Steam billowed from the kitchen, along with noises of pots clattering, knives chomping, customers chattering, cooks calling out the names of food (jambalaya! catfish! creole!—creole!—creole!). Three plates of shrimp creole sat steaming in the kitchen window, waiting for someone to pick them up.

"Dax! Order up! Where the hell are you?"

Someone—Dax, presumably—rushed past, glaring at Angela as if he wanted to do her in with a blunt instrument. Maybe he'd had his own bid in for manager. Maybe all the people here had. Dax's haircut—it looked as though someone had superimposed the Purina checkerboard on his scalp. He rushed back the other way, with a salad and a head like a badly mown football field, not saying a word.

"Fine," Angela said to me again, "you're hired." She was already walking away, chasing Dax, who was now rushing back again, for the shrimp. "Be back by seven!" she called.

□   □   □

Once home, I emptied out seven liquor bottles (they were years old, and almost finished anyway), filled them with water and various food colorings, and placed them on the kitchen table. This may have been a bartending job, but I was going to be just as methodical and quick about learning it as if it were organic chemistry. I had with me the *Instant Home Bartender's Guide,* which I'd bought in a bookstore I'd passed on the way home.

First, you must learn how to pour.

Beneath were instructions for the bartender's count. I memorized—*one, two, three, hup*—the hup the upstroke upon which you were supposed to raise the bottle. One bottle stood for whiskey, another vodka, another vermouth, and so on, although they had all once been tequila (George's favorite). You were supposed to hold the bottle by the neck and give it a quick flick of the wrist. I turned the bottle upside down and let the water run out. "One...two...three...hup," I said, flicked my wrist, and it worked. Nothing spilled, so I did it again, faster. It just came naturally. It was like marching-band camp all over again—doing this wrist-flicking to a rhythm, a count, a natural musical motion— only this time I was yanking on bottlenecks. I one-two-three-hupped all over the place, with all sorts of bottles representing all sorts of liquors, spilling water everywhere, pools of blue and red swirling indiscriminately on the floor.

At a quarter to seven, I rummaged through my closet for a white shirt (lab coat?...nah, maybe wait for Halloween...) and black pants. I left the bottles and the mess—I didn't have time to clean it, and besides, it was a shorthand way of telling George I'd found a job. I locked the door and ran back to Big Moe's, up Whitney Avenue and along the lake into the suburbs of Hamden, reciting in my head the recipe for martinis, Manhattans, hot buttered rum.

Five parts whiskey and one part vermouth.

And as the lights of New Haven lit themselves in a row down the sidewalk, I thought: I've done it—I'm employed; life's great; it's summer.

When I showed up at the restaurant, everyone was too busy to acknowledge me, so I put my book underneath the bar, next to the napkins (a cheat book, although I didn't know if I'd get a chance to refer to it). I tied on an apron, picked up a menu, then went over to the cash register, to memorize keys. I thought it'd be simple, but it was like washing up on some foreign shore, signs all around in an unknown language. Every item had its own key, every wine its own number. Meanwhile, I kept getting interrupted by the waitrons (*waitrons,* they were called, like some sort of robot), who each had his or her own special request.

"You don't have to use that measuring glass," Dax told me, attempting to pin his order to the stand. "Don't listen to anything Angela says. She doesn't know anything about the Moe."

Obviously not. She didn't know half of what was going on around here. Ten minutes later, another bartender appeared. Angela hadn't told me I'd get training. Jill introduced herself as an actress-in-training, bartender on the side. She showed me everything, then went to business perfecting her act, pouring six glasses of wine. She wore a tight sequin dress, like a disco sparkle-ball, and every now and then the sequins caught the red neon and flashed enchantingly. I was mesmerized by her: Bottles tumbled from her hands, each glass filled itself to just the right height. A real professional. Here I was, behind this bar with Jill, looking at it from the inside, at all the secret cubbyholes and compartments, at the thirty different brands of alcohol at my fingertips, and for the first time I was scared that maybe I really didn't belong here. But I was still willing to give it a shot, as we bartenders liked to say.

"You going to be okay back there?" Angela asked finally, pausing in her circumference around the restaurant to rest her clipboard on the beer taps. She didn't seem to have any specific purpose for the clipboard, but carried it around, apparently, because it gave her a more definitive managerial air. She was too stiff, too formal, still trying to get the feel of the place. I knew that because I'd just done the same thing myself, at Yale. Her copious analysis of everyone's job didn't seem to be making the service go any faster. Already I could tell that no one was paying one iota of attention to what she said—instead, they did their jobs.

I nodded, smiling. I'd worked in a Burger King during high school—I knew the one imperative of any restaurant: Keep Smiling. Even when you feel like shit.

Angela scrunched her eyes. "Good—don't call me unless something explodes." She turned around.

"Dax!" she shouted. "Dax!"

A lull in drink orders arrived. The few checks that came in Jill rang up with one hand, while gazing absently at the two-year-old restaurant reviews tacked to the wall beside her. So there wasn't much for me to do except memorize entries.

"I'm only staying for an hour," she said between checks. "I've got a date. Is Angela going to take over the register for you? Or can you do it yourself?"

"I think I can handle it."

Then I thought: mistake . . . and I looked around for an escape. Angela was debriefing one of the cooks. "I *know* it's supposed to taste like fish, Marlou—the guy's a jerk. Just do something about it, okay? Throw some more cayenne pepper on it." While Marlou or whoever banged around pots and pans like a kid throwing a temper tantrum.

"Maybe I can get some practice in before you go?" I didn't think Jill knew that I'd written "experienced" on my application.

She clicked her tongue, as though she were my mother, which I found bizarre, since she had to be younger than me. "Okay. But I've got to leave soon. It's a date—you know, a *date*."

"Yeah, a date. Sure, I know. Don't worry."

It took me fifteen minutes to ring up an order of jambalaya and two Coors Lights. Meanwhile, ten different waitrons (or maybe they were only two or three in several incarnations) told me they needed this or that "yesterday." Jill and I bumped into each other as we rushed to pour drinks. It was like Laurel and Hardy. Then fifteen orders came into the bin in less than thirty seconds, and we were too busy to squabble. We lost track of the time. Angela herself was the worst continual interruption. She stood at the counter and quizzed us. "*Where* are the napkins? There are *supposed* to be napkins here, we've *got* to have the napkins." And when we finally got them out, "Not like this, Jill, you're supposed to fan them, Jill, are you watching, they have to be nicely *fanned*, they have to make a *pattern*. What's the matter, kids, haven't you read your manuals?"

While I worked on that first check, nine more orders came in.

"Here," Jill said when the drawer finally clattered open. "Let me do the rest." She grabbed the pile of checks that had accumulated and took control of the keys. "I think Dax needs a glass of white wine. It's under the garnish rack."

"What about your date?"

"Forget it. He'll wait. He owes me one, anyway."

And with that, I was relegated back to pouring wine for the rest of the rush. So ringing up checks was going to take me a little longer to learn than, say, cell mitosis.

Around ten o'clock, the rush slowed enough (*rush* was the name for it all right, not just a flurry of activity but a head rush, so busy spinning around in circles that I felt high) for me to notice that Jill had left. I was behind the bar alone, while Angela rang up checks and picked up for neglected tables, now seemingly everywhere at once. I'd been spinning in circles so fast, I hadn't even noticed Jill walk out the door.

"Here," Angela said, unclipping her earrings and slipping them behind the bar, then coming around and accosting me from the front. "I need a Remy, pronto." She hit the bar with her hand, with enough emphasis to make it clear that she was ordering me around. It was slow enough now that I could take a good look at her—I couldn't decide her age, but there seemed to be a youthfulness to her that belied her hyperadult authority. She'd been prematurely forced into being forceful—that was the only way she was going to insinuate herself into the society here.

"Okay, okay. Don't have a coronary." It was risky to tease her. Jill had told me that Angela was facing an uphill battle and not to count on her "being around for long." Jill didn't seem all that reliable herself, but what other resources did I have?

"Come on. Where's that drink?" Angela asked again, not missing a beat. She lifted her chin. "I thought I was hiring an expert." Then she smiled, giving her deadpan away.

I poured the whiskey in front of her eyes. I wondered if any of the awkwardness between Angela and the others was subtly racial, or if it was all purely the result of her newness. A black woman running a Cajun restaurant in New England? I had a theory, that obstreperous people were obnoxious as a test. You had to measure up to their standards, not be too wishy-washy or equivocal, to be acceptable, because that was their greatest fear about themselves.

"Well, where's the check?" I asked. "I can't give you the drink without a check. You taught me that."

"Here." She waved it in front of my face. "Now give me my drink."

"Where? I didn't see it."

"Come on. Seriously. This is for Oleg."

"Who?"

"Oleg, the owner." For a moment the alliteration stopped her. "He's Russian. I can't explain *now*." She grabbed the snifter from my hands. "God, just what I need, another clown." She strutted off, swinging her arms and muttering, but I sensed that once she was out of my vision, she was grinning, satisfied. Whether this had been a test for her or me, we'd both passed.

Once in the dining room, Angela put the drink on the table and sat down, commiserating face-to-face with this Oleg person. It was a table for eight, the best in the house, smack in the center of the restaurant, and they were going to ignore the rest of the customers while they enjoyed themselves. They probably had some serious business to take care of. What was a Russian doing owning a restaurant in New Haven? He certainly had the Ivy-League look down pat—tweed jacket and bulging college ring. He snapped up the snifter and gulped. What a pig, I thought, that innocent piece of glassware being used so irreverently, no check, no inventory— even if he *was* a revolutionary, that was just how businesses sank. Angela leaned her elbows on the table as she talked to him. She looked so intense and romantic, staring at him. As if she was about to fall in love. Now why in the world would a woman like Angela be attracted to a poseur like Oleg? Then it occurred to me that she might be putting on an act, faking this look the way she was faking being the manager, trying to keep everyone spellbound, trying to keep enough balls in the air to climb up on top of them, make something out of nothing. Then I liked her *more*, once I considered that, for the guts that took. Oleg had an air of unreality about him. He *owned* this place, as if descending from some lapsed Tsarist epic. But still, how could Angela sit there with a man so obviously suspect and ogle him like that, even as an act? Could I be jealous? Just the thought that I might be confused me. Why would I possibly be jealous of Angela?

Or was it simply that I disagreed with her taste in men?

An hour later, Angela started letting people go home. "The rush is over," she said simply, when I asked why she was letting people leave before closing time. And she was right. Only six of the eighteen tables were occupied, including Oleg's. It was the first time I'd really been aware of anything here beyond my keyboards and beer taps. I thought—what an insane job. But exhilarating, an accomplishment to survive, like boot camp. *Survival, success*—the words took on a whole new meaning here.

Angela, Angela, let me go home . . . let me . . . let me. The early-shift waitrons and bus people crowded in a circle around her, begging to be chosen. Angela had a smile a mile wide—she seemed to love this act of dispensation more than anything else. Maybe manager was something she'd always dreamed of becoming. I, myself, couldn't see getting such satisfaction running some self-styled, Cajun, college-town eatery. I had an ironic outlook about it all, just like I'd had in medical school. Maybe it was my background, or my experience, but here I was, already spoiled for work.

Meanwhile, I wiped down the bar with a towel. When that was finished, I started the mirrors. No need to tell *me* what to clean. What was cleaning to me? It wasn't even something that needed to be figured out. I got interested in the ammonia and forgot Angela was there.

"Okay," she said to me finally. "If you've got the tap under control, I'll show you the inventory."

I picked up her clipboard and followed her in that well-traveled circle about the restaurant. She showed me the white wines in the cooler behind the bar, then the red wines in the wine rack. "Here's the bourgeoisie, the marmot, the bangladesh, the baccalaureate. . . ."

What was she saying? I knew nothing about wine; I just followed along, writing down the numbers, nodding as she pointed with a pencil. If she thought I knew what she was talking about, so be it. Back in fifth grade, all those kids who couldn't even do the multiplication tables, let alone fractions—my friends and I used to completely dismiss them. I wondered what had ever happened to them, the average and below. Apparently they'd gone on with their lives, as had I, and now, as if by dint of some cosmic irony, here I was, a sort of freshman, cleaning mirrors and counting bottles of wine. When you started over, you had to start at the bottom. It was strenuous, boring, more demanding than calculus. We finished the wine, then went back behind the bar and did the beer, the cherries, the lemons, the oranges, the olives, the stemware, the matches—everything in a jar we counted. Nine. Fifteen.

Twelve. Twenty. How boring, how unchimerical, things like integers could be.

"Get it all? Okay, now the basement."

Downstairs, she had enough liquor for a warehouse, plus huge tubs of cornmeal, boxes overflowing with napkins, paper towels, toilet paper, aprons, giant jars of Dijon mustard . . . and crates and crates of wine, lining the walls, four rows deep.

She walked me around, showing me everything. I stooped when she stooped, peered over boxes as she peered. Angela—she was naming wines and whiskeys by the hundreds, and I'd never heard of any of them, and I wasn't about to remember a single thing she said.

"Okay, come back up when you've counted it all. Then we'll z-out and do the drawer."

"Z-out?"

"The register. The ticker tape. The little computer program inside the thing that does the thing with the thing."

A blank look.

"You'll see. I'll show you."

She closed the door behind her, the tumbler falling as she locked it (she'd explained that this time of night and with this much wine, the neighborhood wasn't "what you'd call safe"). I tossed the clipboard on the desk and sank into the swivel chair. So now what? Well—if I could memorize the twelve cranial nerves, I could remember the names of a few wines. Although both tasks seemed equally pointless. It took so much useless information to function as an adult—everything from knowing the noises a car can make to the amount to tip a bellhop—and for all that I'd learned, I still didn't know anything useful. I considered putting myself at Angela's mercy. I imagined confessing all of it: *Not only don't I know a Velvet Hammer from an Irish Rickey, I'm a complete pushover—I couldn't bounce a drunken midget out of a rocking chair.* She was desperate; she wouldn't fire me. But it was the end of the night; everyone's tempers were frazzled.

It was a short-tempered crowd. But I liked these people. They were obnoxious, rude, vulgar, and sincere. Just what I'd been looking for.

For a moment, I just sat. Relaxed. Contemplated the silence. Then something rang, and I jumped. It was Angela on the office phone, her voice never ceasing, even when teleported and transistorized—she wanted to tell me about some wines she'd forgotten.

I counted everything, then called her back, fumbling with the phone lines till I figured out how to use them. She sent down one of the dishwashers to unlock me. "Later, man," he said as I stood at the door, then disappeared like a shadow into the night. Back upstairs, finished with the inventory, Angela and Oleg were the only people left in the restaurant. The chairs sat upside-down on the tables; the lights atop the I-beams were turned off. No more hard edges and glare. The walls had a softer hue now. The place was lit from the deli cases in the kitchen. All the liquor had been locked away, except for a bottle of Stolichnaya, and they were drinking it out of highballs, on the rocks.

"You will have a drink," Oleg said—to me apparently—while Angela sat on the bar. She reached up above her for another glass, grabbed the Stoli by the neck and poured, like Jill, like an experienced bartender. Better than me.

"Oleg, have you met Paul? He's the new bartender."

Oleg held out his hand. He had a vivid masculinity, a fake preppy smile, and patches on the elbows of his jacket. It was a shock to actually touch him; the warmth, the fatherly envelopment. But I didn't think he was particularly interesting physically, especially under that weirdly skewed costume. Angela gave me the vodka, and then I was drinking Oleg's profits along with him and his new manager. Oleg continued saying whatever it was I'd walked in on—something about stewardesses, whom he apparently knew in profusion, but despite that fact had failed to persuade one to take off with him for the evening. Angela refilled my glass every time it started to look half empty.

"Yalie, Yalie, drinking tight," Oleg intoned, and I smiled as he continued his display of literary allusions gauged, apparently, for my delight, even if the Yale reference wasn't completely accurate anymore. Angela must have told him all about me. "And you are happy in this environment, no? I hope so." It made me feel welcome—his attempt, based on a single obscure fact of my history (albeit misunderstood), to outflank and engage my interests; yet it disturbed me, too, since I wasn't sure how much about me I wanted all these new people to know.

It looked as if they might make me one of the *in* people, the group who stayed late and drank with the owner. But I didn't know if that was because I was the new bartender, and that was the status that came with the job, or because I was a "Yalie," and they felt I would have been offended otherwise. Other than someone who came from Yale, I didn't know exactly who they thought I was, or who they wanted me to be. And a Yalie was the last thing I'd ever considered myself.

Mostly, though, they talked amongst themselves. Neither of them ever told me *why* I'd been invited to stay, or made much more of an effort to include me in the conversation, and after about fifteen minutes, Angela suggested that it was time for me to go.

When I got back to the apartment, I unbuttoned my shirt and tossed it on the couch. Then I sank down on the floor, spread-eagle, in front of the television—Dave Letterman trading witticisms with Paul Shaffer: hip New York nightlife piped into your living room at all hours, so you could realize just how unexciting your own life was. The restaurant had had some of that late-night glamour, though—in measured doses: Jill the actress; Oleg the Russian capitalist; all exaggerating their characteristics, being extreme like some sort of street mime or crazy bedroom comedy. But the restaurant was more glamorous to me than even the most glamorous of TV shows, which were alluring only by means of an elaborately crafted illusion; at least it was more exciting than the libraries that my life had consisted of until then.

"Find a job?" George called from his room. "You left a mess in the sink."

I stood up, grabbed my shirt, went in to talk to George.

"Yep, tending bar. Actually," I told him, standing in his doorway, "it's kind of fun. All sorts of people come into the restaurant. And some pretty interesting characters work there. This one guy has this haircut that looks like . . . I don't know, a checkerboard or something."

"Uh-huh."

"And they gave me some free drinks before I left. I mean, the drinks alone were worth ten dollars. Oh—and I made twenty dollars in tips." I took out the cash and held it in front of him.

"And that's only half what I'll make next week, when I work the bar on my own. Pretty good for a Wednesday, huh?"

"Pretty good," George said. His biochemistry book sat open on his desk; he was still reading it as we talked. His research project wasn't biochemistry, so he must have been brushing up on some esoteric reactions. I knew better than to bug a medical student when he was studying.

I put the cash back in my pocket. "Well, I'm bushed. I never realized how much a job can take out of you. All I want to do right now is sit in front of the TV, not think, not move, nothing. Now I know how people can live like that, just come home and not want anything but food and cheap, mindless entertainment. It's not that they're not interested; it's just that it's all they can handle, these people. Working people."

"Working people..." George echoed, reading his textbook. Then he thought for a moment, and registered, in that brain of his, what I'd been talking about. "Okay, Paul. Forget the books." He slammed it closed. "Tell me all about it."

"You have time?"

His glasses, his face like an owl's—so serious all of a sudden. "Sure. You don't think I'm just going to ignore you for however long we live together?"

"No. I don't think...."

"So then talk—I always like to hear what you have to say."

So we went into the kitchen and talked until three in the morning, laughing, telling jokes, forgetting about our daily routines, until George fell asleep at the table, and I tapped him on the shoulder and made him walk to bed.

The next day, I woke up at ten-thirty, and George was long gone. Maybe he was sleepwalking. I didn't, of course, get to see him all day. In the evening, I called home to tell my parents I'd gotten a job. "Good news," I began. They didn't seem overwhelmed. I mentioned, offhandedly, how good it felt to be done with medicine forever. Beamed by satellite, my father's voice said, "Don't kid yourself, you're going to end up on welfare."

"Dad..."

"Medical school, that I can maybe understand. But tending bar? Is this what you want to do with your life?"

"Come on, Dad. It's a good job. It's not forever. What do you want? I have to make a living somehow."

"You could tell your adviser you're going back to school in the fall."

My mother chimed in. "Could you try just one more year, Paul? Maybe it'll get better. I think the first year, baby, it's just to weed people out."

"They do their gardening in college, Mom. One more year isn't going to make any difference."

"Paul..."

"Dad..."

Mom started crying. Dad hung up without saying good-bye. Why couldn't we get away from this sordid topic and move on to something more pleasant? They had me feeling like a complete loser; I was ready to agree with them. The phone conversation was a catastrophe.

Okay, so maybe leaving YMS wasn't exactly an upwardly mobile career move. I'd had in mind that I could leave behind libraries and equations and do something poetic, like something out of a French New Wave movie. I'd write notes in cafés and one of my customers would turn out to be an art dealer. New Haven wasn't Paris, but that was the way I saw Big Moe's.

But my parents maybe had a point. By not being firm, I'd given them a weapon, so it wasn't their fault that the whole thing was getting sloppy. Before the end of the year, I'd gone to see Dr. Howitzer, Dean of Student Affairs, in order to make my departure official, and he'd talked me into being more squeamish about it than I would have liked. I'd made an appointment with his secretary. Howitzer was a formidable dean. You could almost call it a regimen, the affinity he shared with his select student-friends: Pete had become one of his protégés—taking trains with him to Manhattan, meeting for weekly discussions at dinner, attending the Yale Rep. Others—Fergie, Julie, or George, for instance— had failed to elicit his attention. Neither, needless to say, had I.

I'd shown up early, so the secretary had me wait in his office. Scuttlebutt had it that he'd set up the office as a test, by which he was able to judge your personality and temperament within the first ten seconds of a meeting, just by noticing where your eyes fell. Bric-a-brac littered the room: pictures of the wife and three kids, friends, two white ceramic ponies, a pile of *JAMA* on the floor. This was my chance to look around without caring what it said about me, so I picked up one of the ponies and turned it over, to see what it was made of. In the center, where the stomach should be, was a hole.

Behind his chair, on the bookshelves—Clinical Gastrology, Endocrinology, three volumes of pathology, interspersed with some Hemingway (*The Sun . . .*), Chekhov (*The Cherry . . .*), and Allen (Woody). Why didn't he read something more definitive, Rilke perhaps, or Dostoyevsky? But I suspected that as with everything else in the room, the books had been chosen for something other than their content.

"Paul Levinson," Howitzer boomed as he came through the door, taking a racquet glove off his hand. "What's on your mind? Hurry up, I'm playing squash with DuPree at four." He winked at me, making fun of the stereotype of the golfing doctor, but the wink didn't mitigate the fact that he really did have a game of squash on his schedule.

"I, well, Dr. Howitzer, I came to talk about school."

At that, his chin fell long and drawn, and he stroked it seriously a few times without saying anything. Then he sat down behind his desk and pulled out a few forms, pens, manila envelopes, readying himself for my onslaught. "Okay, Paul. Tell me about it."

"Okay." And I told him about all of my outside interests, starting with how Sparrow had been encouraging my photography.

"Oh, Sparrow," he said, "he's behind this?" And for the first time, I realized that one doctor might disagree so principally with another.

"It's not his fault. This is something—it just goes way back."

Howitzer eventually convinced me not to resign, exactly, but to take an extended absence. To not *say* that I was resigning, in so many words, but take refuge in some institutionalized loophole. A bureaucrat's way. Anything was fine with me, as long as I was out of there.

He nodded at me, in sympathy with my feelings. "Well, then I think we understand each other." He started filling out the first page. "Now, what should we say you're going to do?"

"We can say I'm working on something for Dr. Sparrow. Yeah . . . that's it . . . a project. Something related to the human form. How's that?"

The irony was wonderful. We were creating a fable, Dr. Howitzer and I, a fiction for the records. I hadn't told Sparrow about any of this, but that was all right—he didn't need to know.

"Sparrow," Howitzer said again. "I should have guessed right away." He shook his head. It was futile to argue Sparrow's innocence once more. All this time, I'd thought that all physicians hung together, that they were something like a monolithic entity, whose mouth was the *NEJ of M* and whose mind was the AMA. Of course, this was untrue. None of the potential physicians I knew—George, Julie, Pete—none of them were like that. That was only some nonexistent, abstract average. But if there was no such thing as the physician lifestyle, then what was I leaving behind? What was I rebelling against? I didn't want to pursue it.

"We could call it, say, a study of doctor versus not-doctor."

I got, perhaps, a bit carried away. Howitzer would think I was an idiot. It was the last official room I ever inhabited at Yale Med, and while arguing on the phone with my parents, I remembered the scene with Howitzer as an ordeal, a rite of passage; if I uttered the correct words, I'd be allowed to leave, transformed into a new animal with powers of speech and flight that would carry me far beyond my immediate torments. I'd been searching for those words, the ideas with which to form them, the courage to say them. But in that moment of make-believe with Dr. Howitzer, in that moment of fabulation, I could also foresee how the spell could lose power over time, could slowly erode, until it at last became its own form of speech, its own trap; I'd be telling people how clever I was to have left medical school, until I'd become known as "the person who left medical school"—and I foresaw how you'd need a new spell to get out of the old one, and a new one, ad infinitum. And the revelation that I'd had that moment when I looked into Daniel's eyes was for a second understandable to me: I'd been looking into the vicissitudinous hub of life.

*   *   *

But as soon as I hung up the phone, I forgot about my folks and all their arguments. I forgot about medical school altogether. These days, I couldn't think upsetting thoughts for long. I was too busy enjoying my independence, my self-creation. For the first time, I was free to be anything I wanted: account executive, banjo player, adman, computer programmer, porno star. Anything but a doctor. I wondered if I wasn't burning my bridges too thoroughly, but they were sure fun to burn. It was the first time I'd ever been so inflammatory, and I was simply enchanted with the flames, with my power to make them.

Every day, I went through the same routine:

A. Get dressed to go in to work (select tie).
B. Open up.
    1) Set up bar.
    2) Banter with waitrons.
C. Dinner rush.
    1) Make drinks.
    2) Ring out checks.
    3) Help Angela make origami dragons and horses out of the napkins.
D. After-dinner lull.
    1) Banter with waitrons.
    2) Make more horses.
    3) Ignore dishwasher performing nightly drug deal behind restaurant.
E. Z-out.
F. Do inventory.
    1) Count upstairs liquor.
    2) Count downstairs liquor.
    3) Readjust inventory for after-hours drinking with Oleg.

Behind the bar, I poured beer, wine, everything. Whenever I had a doubt about how to make a cocktail, I looked it up in one of my books. I was a naive bartender; I thought all you needed to do to make a drink was follow a recipe. I never got a chance to find what I was looking for, anyway; Angela would rush over with instant advice—*put lime juice in the margaritas, float the Galliano with a spoon, add a shot of Tia Maria, what the hell.* She didn't trust my knowledge of drinks. She'd snap off her earrings and slip them behind the bar whenever things got hectic, giving her plenty of opportunity to peer over my shoulder. "There's a good head," she said after it looked like I was getting the hang of the beer taps.

She was constantly playing with her earrings, turning them over in her hands and putting them on—she had perhaps thirty different pairs, all chrome, all some wierd musical shape. "You like these, Paul?" She held out an earlobe. "Generally, I go with the hoops over the studs. And Napier, not Trifari." I wondered if she wasn't lonely here, new from New York, no one else around with whom she could discuss the attitude, the fashion. I got the sense she was learning to discuss it with me.

After a week of initiation, I was feeling confident enough myself to work on my own, ready to pull in forty, maybe fifty dollars a night. My first night alone behind the bar, Dax came up to talk to me. "She's relentless, isn't she? Make my order first, all right? I know she's reordering the checks."

"I doubt it."

"You've probably missed it. Here, I'll put mine in front so you can see it better."

After he left, I put his check back where it belonged and made the other orders. I knew, at least subconsciously, that Dax was gay—at least, in a stereotypically gay way: He'd figured out a way to tell everyone his orientation by acting and dressing in a way that they all would expect a person like that to act and dress, since there was no other way to do it, short of wearing a sign around your neck. How dumb could you be? I was surprised to find myself aroused by this discovery—not attracted to Dax, who struck me as impolite, but excited by the knowledge of him, by my seemingly new ability to decipher his code.

You simply had to run him through an extended lattice, understand that his actions *were contained and took on meaning only within a larger context of social preconceptions and expectations,* as one of my books on the subject would later explain to me. You had to see him with a new organon of perception.

I was developing new organons.

When things at the restaurant got slow, I made camera frames with my hands and imagined potential tableaux, various combinations of customers and food. I recontextualized things to make them more interesting: I imagined Dax walking imperiously through a crowd of starving medical students, Oleg dressed as the pope and handing out gold necklaces and crawdads, or Table Four as a podium under the lights of Times Square. Everything became artificially poignant, in my viewfinder. Now that I had a camcorder, and not just a camera, there was a third dimension that I needed to integrate into my representational universe: motion as well as contrast and design. It multiplied the variables. Sometimes I jotted notes on the cocktail napkins. Sometimes I simply looked around for things to read, for ideas. Someone had left a lingerie catalog on the bar, and as I flipped through it, bored, looking at the underwear, one of the waitresses spoke up.

"What do you think?" Her question startled me, coming from out of nowhere so quickly, and I slapped the magazine closed and stuffed it away—I was so used to reading things I felt guilty about.

"Of what?"

"The women in the pictures. You don't have to hide the magazine. I just want your opinion. As a man." She was carrying a tray full of food, about to go out to a table.

I rubbed my chin, trying to look as though I was seriously considering it, the aesthetics. "I don't know. They're . . . shapely, certainly." I looked at her, for a reaction, and nodded slowly when she didn't have one. "Yes—shapely, that's it. It must be hard work."

She nodded. "That's me, on page three."

"Really?"

"Yep. I went to school for six entire months to learn how to do that. We had to know how to stand perfectly still, tummies tucked and chins out, for hours at a time. Hard work is right. You're the first man who's ever pointed that out first thing."

And then, "I'm a professional beauty contestant, too. By the way, my name's Leona. I have a competition in a month."

"Uh-huh." She made me want to disappear. Her slinkiness, her immodest sensuality, it all seemed so suddenly intrusive. It was impossible to be completely sure of what was under the uniform, which made everyone look orchestral. But she was tall, with thin cheeks, dark brown skin, and perfectly plucked eyebrows. So I believed her.

She spun around and walked away, satisfied with her demonstration. For about twenty minutes, I resented her for having pointed out so plainly to me my own absent-minded queerness, then I decided I liked her, precisely because of the ease with which she handled her sexuality.

By the end of a night, the counter was a mess, the restaurant a wreck, and me a mental meatball. Angela took me to do the closing rounds, which were getting easier...I simply followed what I'd done the first night with a sleepwalker's unthinking familiarity. The basement seemed smaller now, more manageable in its disaster of restaurant paraphernalia. After the inventory was finished, I slumped in a chair, dropping the pen and clipboard on the floor. No energy, not even a reserve. I didn't know if I was having the time of my life, working at this job, or killing myself, or what.

The lock in the door started jiggling, and I jumped out of the chair. Angela was back to take a cigarette break. She sat on top of the desk, dangling her legs over the side.

She offered me a cigarette. I shook my head.

"You probably think smoking's bad for you, huh, being an ex-pre-med and all." She lit her cigarette with one of the restaurant matches: They came in a black-and-blue box that said *Big Moe's* overtop a headless chicken, fried pork rinds in a halo all around. "It sure ain't the healthiest thing in the world."

I wanted to tell her that there was a difference between a medical student and a pre-med, but decided that the distinction would seem trivial to her; I didn't know if she'd even finished high school. I would have said that my not smoking had nothing to do with medicine, that I simply had never known anyone who smoked. The act of smoking/not smoking established a line, a class division: I didn't do it, and everybody else here did. But some lines I had no desire to cross.

"Doctors," Angela said, shaking her head. "They're the worst. They come in during the middle of rush, the line's an hour long, they want a table right away, no excuses. 'I'm a doctor, you understand? I spend half the night sewing together people's organs and you expect me to wait like an asshole in your overpriced restaurant? Build another room.' Then they tip five percent."

This animosity was common, not restricted to restaurants. Her comment made me feel, defensively, in the position of the doctor. If I'd have finished the other three plus three plus three plus (?) years of the medical ordeal, racking up financial and emotional debt, I'd have been short-tempered in hour-long lines, too. Of course, when she made the remark, I said nothing. I was used to that.

"I tell you, this whole setup sucks." She grimaced, inhaling shrewdly, putting her feet on a chair so hard they made a noise, a *plunk*. "I can't believe that Russian jerk left me here alone. Till goddamn midnight. What am I supposed to do with Sarah?"

"Who's Sarah?"

"My kid. She's really great. Want to see a picture?" She took her purse from the desk, fished out a Kmart picture in a plasti-coated red book and showed it to me, still holding her cigarette absently between her fingers, dropping ash. "I was sixteen when I had her. Too young to raise a kid, that's for sure."

The picture looked recent: Angela behind her Sarah, arms around shoulders, the girl maybe three (which meant the mother was maybe nineteen, my first real indication of her age), standing by a fireplace, blurry. In person, Angela was much thinner, more frazzled than she was in the picture, which had her primped up as sort of a young Cicely Tyson. It was the worst photograph I'd seen in a long time, yet there was an artistry, a nostalgia, achieved precisely *because* of the lack of technical sophistication. I made a note of that. I didn't know what caused the effect, but I thought that it might be something to remember, something I could use. But then, Angela wouldn't have seen any of that. To her, the photo wasn't a meshing of technology and expression, of perception and conscious experience, but a simple message, one saying, basically: *I'm a mother.* She put it back in her purse. "My husband skipped out when Sarah was born. But you know—life goes on."

I nodded. What was there to say to that? Besides, she didn't give me a chance.

"Her grandmother's helping me with her. She and I moved up here together. But Mom's got to be at the train station by five A.M. She can't be staying up this late with her. You know?" The way she was telling me this, it made it sound as if she was complaining more than she deserved, which wasn't the case. Here was a nineteen-year-old black, single mother, single-handedly running the trendiest new restaurant in New Haven, about to keel over right in front of me from exhaustion. Who else could have made me feel so shitty about all the opportunities I'd just thrown away? She took an extra-long drag off her cigarette.

"The train station?" I asked. "Where does she go?"

She looked at me for a second, as if I'd spoken in a foreign language. "Nowhere," she said finally. She took the picture from me and put it back in her wallet. "She works there."

"Oh . . ."

"But what about you, Paul Levinson?" She became more animated, with this change of subject. "What's your story? You're a mysterious fellow, aren't you, leaving Yale and all?"

"Just strange, I guess."

"Like hell. You're too normal to be strange. You're Mister Normal America, that's what you are."

"I have my eccentricities." I'd torn a paper cup into sixteen different strands—a daisy wheel of paper—and I held it up for her and spun it.

She crushed the cigarette in the ashtray.

"You know, Paul . . . I knew you didn't know a good goddamn about tending bar when I first saw you. But I hired you anyway. Want to know why? I don't know. I don't know why. I'd like to know myself. There were three bartenders scheduled to see me that afternoon. Why would someone like you want to leave Yale? That's what I don't understand."

"I was never meant to be a doctor," I told her, flipping my cup-ribbons into the trash. "I'm going to make a video."

But I hadn't gotten as much taping as I wanted done yet. Most of my time lately had been taken up by simply trying to pay the rent. Even during my sleep—I'd started having dreams about work, always with something slightly altered—I'd be at Big Moe's cooking, instead of tending bar, or else I'd be behind the bar, drinking Stoli and dissecting a giant lobster. Then a thousand checks would appear, and I'd have to ring them up on the register one by one. I'd wake up from those dreams distraught and disoriented, regretting that I hadn't dreamt of something more relaxing.

Still, no matter how busy the Moe kept me, it wasn't half as bad as medical school had been. I had the mornings free, and the time was there to work on my art—within a month, I had collected a whole roomful of pictures, sketches, ideas for projects. My investigations involved everything—television, countrysides, people, books—although sometimes it seemed that I was goofing off more than anything else. How to tell the difference? Maybe there wasn't any, really. I was concentrating on cutting up some photos, their scraps falling into a pile, when I heard this noise—*wham wham wham*—a high-pitched siren, plus an ominous obscure voice-over, like Satan doing "The Price Is Right," and someone screaming. It was coming from George's room.

"What the hell?" I stood in his open doorway—I had to yell to get his attention. George was sitting in front of his stereo, lotus position, isometrically placed between the speakers, listening.

"Sorry. I was just taking a study break. Does it bother you?"

"What's this now?" I picked the CD box off his stereo. Something of a revolutionary group: "Fuck Politics," "Fear of Fear," "Puke on Your Mother." "Well ... maybe you could borrow my headphones?"

"Actually, I probably should get back to work."

"No, George—don't do any work because of me...."

He smiled and flipped off the stereo. "No. I'm really too busy to relax. I don't know what I was thinking of."

So George studied his neuroanatomy until late at night, in relative quiet, and I stayed home alone during the day, becoming familiar with the game shows, with the commercials, with anything that might lead to a project. So much life went on during the day, so much that was normally overlooked. I made time to read the morning paper in doughnut shops. I took my car in for needed but non-acute repairs. I waited in service garages and Sears tire stores. I started taking trips out to Sleeping Giant, East Rock, West Haven Beach, the library.

"What should we do today, George?" I'd ask, whenever he wasn't busy studying, or visiting one of the faculty, or spending the day with Julie—an increasingly rare event indeed. Since he'd started using headphones, for his piano too, most of the time now I didn't even know when he was home.

"Why don't we go for a drive? Take in the atmosphere of the city. It'll make us feel better about not ever getting to see anything."

So drive—aimlessly—we would. I noticed how everything in the area was named "Haven"; there was East Haven and West Haven and North Haven (south was the Sound). On the road signs around town, North Haven was abbreviated NO. HAVEN.

"No haven," George said. "That's this place exactly."

We liked to fancy ourselves oppressed, deprived. Maybe our fancies were real, in a way. But where there was really no haven was across the invisible line on the west end of Broadway, an imprecise boundary separating the college from the slum. Burned-out tenements, barbed-wire fences, four-doors without wheels. It wasn't but a few blocks from the campus. And I knew that it wasn't just this underside of New Haven—it was Indianapolis, it was every city I'd been in. So how did I get so lucky? Why wasn't I a nineteen-year-old mother? A thirty-five-year-old busboy? What had put me on the right side of the tracks? And what, after all, made me think that my side was the "right" one?

I was on surer ground with my art. I took up fingerpainting. I'd lay huge canvases across the living-room floor, dribble globs of pink and blue and yellow, and then mush my fingers through it and smear it around. Sometimes I made pictures that looked like the food at Big Moe's. The paint was cold and gelatinous and oozed between my fingers. Occasionally I'd take off my shirt and get paint on my back, my stomach. I made prints of hands, feet, arms—repeated over and over until they produced schizoid, formalistic patterns. George would come home and I'd explain to him what each painting meant, then when they were dry, hang them on the refrigerator. At dinner, he'd translate them for Julie. "This one represents movement. Mass times velocity. Action painting."

"I told him all that."

George reaching for another helping of green beans: "Yeah, but it's true. It's great. Can't you see it?"

"Jeez," Julie would say. "It's like he's our kid or something."

After dinner, we'd all wash the dishes, then the two of them would go into George's room and close the door. I'd hear them laughing, although I had no idea over what—I'd be left with just the paintings, my books, the TV.

But my best companion was the camcorder. I made an effort to increase my work with it. I read the manual from cover to cover. I shot a six-pack of practice tape, keeping a record of shutter speeds, zoom reduction-ratios. The tape's surface became a re-production in miniature of the city around me, an electromagnetic model, magnesium filings aligned and arrayed like stalactites pointing out the arcades and cloisters in the cave called "New Haven."

I'd film the local repair shops, the various architectural embellishments of our apartment, or go out on the porch and shoot the charcoal grills and bug lamps on the neighbors' patios, books and flowerpots in the neighbors' windows. Then I'd change clothes and go to work.

It was in this semi-ghetto of students, grandmothers, fraternities, and blue-collar families who worked at Universal Illumination and parked their Chevrolets on blocks, that I'd finally come home at two, three in the morning—neighbors still awake, their voices carrying in the darkness, the sign that said DRUGS casting its hippie-ish reflection down the street. And if I wasn't filming my neighborhood, I was picturing filming it; I'd have a script of myself playing atop my actual movements, these images running through my mind as I rounded the corner onto my block.

And I carried the camera into my most intimate fantasies, as well. It was like receiving an injection, a cryogenic substitution: photons for blood, magnesium for sperm. Electronic reproduction. Even when I had a different tool in my hands, I'd have a vision in my mind, a series of perspectives, my point of view receding through various vanishing points. Sometimes I masturbated to earlier pictures of myself masturbating. I accumulated a whole collection of videos—some of myself, some of the pros, copied from rentals. It was all material, all circulating, and I would insert myself, naked, within it. I had set up a continuous loop, with myself—the camera eye—in the nodes, in the interstices.

The TV sat in the middle of my bedroom, a Sony Trinitron on a tripod, like some Egyptian god: legs of a man, head of a TV. And across the room was the displaced eye of the camcorder, its tiny, pterodactyl-like cousin. The TV could preview the scene in the camera viewfinder. Stand between them, and you'd multiply to infinity, you'd be a series of mathematically reduced images, like Zeno and his Tortoises. Move your hand, and a cascade of hands would move after you. Special effect: short circuit of desire.

I filmed a continual tossing in bed, filmed looking at porn, filmed flipping through magazines. I spread the magazines on the bed and sprawled between them, camera aimed. All this glossy paper, photos of dicks, chests, legs—when it was humid, I stuck to them, the camcorder rattling in the background. When I was finished, the TV screen had absorbed all the space in my bedroom, had expanded beyond my visual horizon, and I was trapped upon it, trapped within it, a film on the surface of the tube, reproduced in ever-receding processions—my flesh, my skin, constructed into the images of my fantasies. But I was outside it as well—the two places simultaneously—and it was this duality of position that captured me most.

Meanwhile, I wrote regularly, daily, as Sparrow had once instructed me to.

Cell Bio

So this is life: livers, pancreas, kidneys, spleen? Basophil, neutrophil, leukocyte, phage? Do all the parts add up to a whole? Some primitive virus learns to replicate itself half a billion years ago, and now here we are making artificial organs and right-to-die laws. So if I knew the sequence of every gene in my body, how to repair the mutations and keep myself alive forever, would that mean I knew how to live? If I knew every detail of the camcorder mechanism, would that give me a better idea about what sort of pictures to take?

I'll say one thing, you go into that neuroanatomy class and look at those slides of the cerebral cortex and no one ever asks, is that Fred, was that Fred, is that the brain molecule that was the essence of Fred? Descartes might have asked, but these people—never. They'd laugh you right out of the lab, they'd call you a religious fanatic: this is neuroBIOLOGY.

Sketch for a potential video:

Uncle Sammy arrives in Paris. The accordions play and the Seine flows. He's only twenty-three, a soldier with papers, headed home, fresh from surviving Korea and awed by life. Girls with parasols jump onto gondolas and old ladies sell Brie and fresh bread in cheese shops along the streets. Sammy greets them all with a tip of his hat and tells them about the stockyards of Indianapolis. He's thin and handsome, but well built, being played by Tom Cruise or Robert Downey, Jr. Maybe I could get Pete. He walks down the street with a bounce, ripping off chunks of bread and chewing them.

Cut to a scene of a picnic, near Versailles—Sammy and some pretty young thing eating water crackers and drinking Lambrusco.

"Monsieur, isn't ze country magnifique?"

"Truly it is, my lady."

They recline on a blanket, birds chirping overhead, trees in bloom and hanging down with their fecund limbs, like a Walt Disney cartoon.

"I could never have been here," Sammy says, "if I had listened to my father."

Books

I'm reading Carlos Castaneda. Interesting. I think it might be a way to get into other lives. He gives detailed instructions, and I tried following them. I found my power-spot—the northwest corner of the front patio—sat cross-legged on the floor, and willed lizards to come to me. When they didn't, I went out on foot to search the neighborhood. No lizards in New England, but I found a bullfrog. I painted the frog's head with mystic ashes (no mystic ashes handy, so I substituted baking soda), and sent him on his way. I closed my eyes to see through his. It was like a fiber-optic connection: I thought I saw something, a sort of orange circle—and in the center, Daniel, reading a magazine. He looked up, as though he could sense that I was watching him, but then it went black, and I wasn't sure about what I'd seen at all. Had he been in a cell? Had he been free? Had it only been my imagination? I started feeling stupid sitting out here in public with my fingers on my temples, so I went back inside.

I lay down on my bed, to try to leave my body. I wanted to float over myself and look down. This mysticism was so different from science, so silly. But it was something you could believe in. It explained things that science didn't. Now that that super-rational stopper wasn't there, it was all flowing out of me, a regurgitation of the ineffable. I concentrated on a single spot on the wall, until my eyesight blurred. All this thinking about leaving my body started me thinking about my body, which started getting me horny. My body wasn't so bad, why would I want to leave it? I absently rubbed my nipples. Then I realized what I was doing. So I jacked off and went to sleep.

Animals

And so I think: Libidinal energy causes some of our actions, but not all. In a repressed individual, however, it can become so strong as to take over. The person becomes an animal.

But neither can we deny our animal nature. Rather, we must recognize it and understand the animal that we are. In some mythos, human beings have a certain animal, their alter ego or also known as a familiar. A panther, say, or a wolf, or bird. This animal is different from the animality of libidinal forces. It is a visual—a mythic—representation of human spirit.

And so it seems clear to me now that scientists who search for the spirit in the brain are destined to come up empty-handed. Just as they'd never find it in a plant or an earthworm. It's because they must give it a name—spirit—that they think it is an entity to be found. This desire to name and find stems from the libidinal animal's motivation. It is not part of the spirit animal's motivation. This spirit animal is here for a purpose, which is not a naming and finding purpose. The libidinal animal distracts the spirit animal from its ultimate purpose.

Video Number Two—

A character named Paul is wandering the streets of New Haven. He's in search of his alter ego, a certain animal or a familiar. Also known as Jeff, or not Jeff, but Lyle . . . or whatever. . . .

Voice-over:

Stage One . . . the infant must first learn to recognize. . . .

When George saw me writing in my notebook—reading it over my shoulder while brushing his teeth—he asked if I wanted to do mushrooms with him. He said that he'd noticed my increasing involvement in things abstract and otherworldly—my reading material, my psychic experiments. "So if you're really interested in being mystical, Paul, they're it. I'll show you how to do them right." He walked into the bathroom and spit in the sink, as if this was the first stage in the process of doing shrooms—learning how to spit out toothpaste all in one glob.

Why not? I wasn't a medical student anymore; he had more to lose than I did. Besides, it wasn't only Castaneda—I'd just finished reading Huxley.

George got the shrooms through the mail from a friend; I didn't know where. As soon as the weather turned exceptional, we wrapped them in a plastic bag, then stuffed them in a knapsack along with some peaches, granola bars, a Frisbee, a quart of orange juice, and two hats. "Have to have the right equipment," he said. We dressed up in tie-dyed shirts (George had an extra one that he lent me) and walked to a nearby park. "The right attire, too. It's all in the atmosphere."

I was a bit nervous about it, but I trusted him. He'd done them before; plus, he was a medical student. *I* never reassured myself when *I* was a medical student, so I knew my feelings were unfounded, but they were hard to disabuse. Besides, I needed this opportunity to do something with George. He'd been spending all his time with Julie lately, and I needed to see someone, needed human time with something more than a two-dimensional male model or some faceless customer's check. I think he sensed that he was just about my only routine contact, now that I wasn't connected to the world of Yale Med, and only barely connected to Big Moe's. Barely connected to anything at all. I couldn't spend my whole life in the netherworld of my cameras.

Besides, the shrooms would have to be good for my creativity.

We ate them as soon as we got to the park. We each picked up a stick, to be our staves. We walked, tossed the Frisbee, waited for the meltdown. "It'll be like a wave of alternative reality, washing over you, dripping in front of you. Nothing really changes, nothing in the world *out there,* but you perceive it more intensely. You see the real nature of things."

"You mean like an optical wipe?"

"Yeah, kind of. Only it happens to *you,* not just your eyes."

I was certainly anxious. I made myself alert to every change . . . was this it? Was this it? For a moment, I thought I saw the trees in front of me start to sway. George ambled down the path, leaning on his staff, like some sort of guru—my own personal Great Pumpkin, coming into my life with music, shrooms, and simple wisdom. I felt overwhelmed with good feelings toward him. He was my mentor and confidant, my *friend,* the way he'd so selflessly shared his drugs, without qualification, without reserve, and there were volumes of personal trouble that I wanted to tell him of, a whole loquacious confession that I wanted to unload. But the words got in the way. It was like the writings in my notebook—if only he could read them all and understand, perceive their true meanings, the meanings of their meanings. It was all so intricate and inter-twined. There was no end and no beginning. I watched the trees start to dance before me, like when heat rises from asphalt in the dead of summer.

"I think they're here," George said.

They were. The trees struck me as being so treelike, and the flowers—they were PURPLE or RED, like an idea come to life. This wasn't normal. It was *better* than normal. The whole forest trembled with the forces of life, of goodwill and peace, all rendered visible, all in a rainbow-colored spectrum. And I, too, felt atremble with variegated impulses. I was good—my thoughts were good—there was no need to separate myself from them. "Hey," I said, and touched George on the shoulder. "I love you, George...."

"I love you too, man."

"No—like, I really love you. It's a feeling I've never let myself express before. It's like I've got so much love inside for *everything*."

"Yeah. They're pretty good shrooms, aren't they?"

And I started crying—at how beautiful the world was. How natural...birds, trees, flowers, George, love...all that human emotion. And Sammy—God, he was gone now, wasn't he? And I'd never told him how I really felt about him, I'd never even realized it myself. It was all so sad, that for all these years, I'd never let myself appreciate anything. What had been my problem? What had I been so scared of?

"You all right, Paul?"

I nodded and rubbed my eyes.

"These must be weird drugs. I've never seen anyone react quite that way."

But I was hearing him through a filter. I walked off down the trail to say hello to all the plant life around me: Hello old tree, hello Mr. Fern. Hello world. It was billions of years old. How remarkable. Me too—I was simply another part of it. We were gathering patiently. We could wait hundreds of years more. We wandered for hours through this Lewis Carroll landscape, George and I, staring at the shapes, the colors. After a while, the psilocybin didn't end so much as slowly dissipate. The objective world sta-bilized, the colors toned themselves down, but I felt refreshed and clear, like after a vigorous massage, a brain rub, all prickly and tingling. We hung around the park, tossing the Frisbee. We wanted to prolong our belonging. We were there for hours. When the sun started to set, a cop came by.

"Hey! You kids can't be in the park after dark."

We stared at him. He was sending out bad vibes: uptightness and repression. Then I remembered the clothes. He must have thought that we wore them all the time. He must have thought we were hippies, not medical-student types. We shrugged and packed our knapsack. "Hey, dude, that's cool," George told him, trying not to laugh and give us away. I wondered how the cop would have reacted had George showed him his Yale/New Haven ID. And I remembered that I still had mine, which no one would have had any reason to question. This cop, he was making a real mistake. We could reenter his world in an instant, George and I. We could walk between the two—his world and ours. We had ghosts of ourselves in our pockets, images ready for transport, proof of our alternative existences. He watched us leave, staring steadily and not once diminishing his angry glower, tapping his dummy stick against his thigh until we were out of his field of view.

The next day at the restaurant, Angela announced that she had started seeing the landlord's nephew, a fellow named Gray (she'd never publicly indicated a genuine interest in Oleg, but I still suspected otherwise, despite this Gray development). Not long before, Gray'd been given a job by his uncle bussing tables. There he was—one hundred and forty pounds of long blond hair and a skateboard. Everyone was on a "busboy alert," making jokes about loose wheels when his back was turned. It was hard for me to readjust to such a trivial social scene, the effort of relating with people, after my day of shroom-induced clarity. Their treatment seemed to me unfair. I thought there was an aphorism—don't date people who work for you—that Angela was in danger of violating. Gray had a pleasant roughness to his features when they became visible from beneath his coiffure—cleft chin and nose slightly askew—a low-income ruggedness that actually made him more attractive than people like Fergie or Joe, whose well-refined beauty always had an air of artificiality. He rode the skateboard to work every day, dodging pedestrians, hopping up the front curb and right into the lobby, despite all the warnings. *Cool, huh?* seemed to be his permanent expression. I didn't know what Angela

saw in him, either, but he did have a certain naive charm that
worked wonders, especially with old ladies and small, domesticated
animals. He was absorbed by Angela's every word. All night, he
followed her, grinding his pepper mill at her customers' demand
and cleaning her tables. Periodically he'd come up to me, lean on
the bar, and talk aimlessly, a way of reasserting his presence.

"You know, she's pretty keen, for a manager lady. She loaned
me her 'Boyz II Men' tape."

"Gray," Angela would snap, "quit jabbering and clear Table
Four." She was in a rotten mood these days. Rumor had it that
Oleg was threatening to have himself bought out.

Without looking behind him, Gray would twirl his towel over
his head in a mock helicopter, then head back to work.

As for me, I was taking in two hundred dollars a week in tips
alone, with no one to spend it on. The waitrons and I started going
out on the town after closing: a piano bar rebuilt from an old
diner, the cocktail lounge of a nearby Mexican restaurant, a
crowded disco popular with the Yalies. I'd try out new drinks—
Godmothers, B-52s, Yale Cocktails—with the excuse that I was
looking to increase my repertoire. I'd offer Leona a sip (she didn't
drink; she was on a permanent diet) and we'd play Question Mark
and the Mysterians' "Ninety-Six Tears" over and over on the juke-
box, allemanding in the aisles and creating a scene. I thought I
was the only Mysterians fan in the world until Leona told me she'd
once had a roommate whose aunt had dated the Mysterians' drum-
mer.

"Don't you wonder whatever happened to them?" she asked
me, sober, serious, while the rest of us were getting drunk around
her. "Don't you think they could have a reunion?"

We held philosophical conversations across Formica-topped
tables; I overtipped the bartenders, came home at night and threw
the leftover cash on my nightstand in wadded-up fifty-dollar bills.
It was a romance of my own creation, a romance with life. Why
sacrifice your youth, I thought, when the best time to enjoy it is
when you're young? I'd never had so much fun. Compared to my
life before, I'd never had fun at all. And yet, underneath all the
good times, something was still missing, and I was in some ways
just as miserable as ever.

My camcorder, or Carlos or Rainer or Fyodor, or the irra-
diating late-night TV—that was all that was waiting for me at Rue

de la Wasteland, a carousel of fantasy worlds. A classmate from high school was getting married in September; the beautifully scripted announcement followed me around the room, pinned helplessly to my corkboard. I sent a card but never planned to go to the wedding. "Have fun," I'd written, "if you can," and signed my name. I was becoming . . . extreme. Not totally. But it was how those things began.

Some nights I'd jack off in my bedroom, some nights it was the bathroom, where there were no blinds, and I had to rely on my knowledge of physics: I didn't think the neighbors could see, across that grimy precipice, if I kept the light out. Watching Mr. Doe scratching his rump while I whacked my meat in the darkness wasn't necessarily pleasant. But it was a distraction.

And it wasn't that I had a predisposition for exhibitionism. The bathroom was simply cooler, the bedroom being this blocked-in arrangement that didn't get the breeze. I looked at myself in the mirror; I wasn't yet satisfied by my body—I wished some parts bigger and other parts smaller—but I'd lost some weight, and it was a start. I looked at my body as though it were a new uniform I wasn't sure I liked—perhaps too rumpled, didn't fit properly, but still, it could have alterations. Actually, the way I was scrutinizing it, without feeling guilty about it anymore, that's the thing that was new.

Increasingly, I had trouble sustaining an erection. The videotapes, the porno mags, they had no substance, of course, but they were all I had, all I could turn to. My own skin was interesting, yet more and more, touching myself left me feeling plastic. It just wasn't as much fun anymore. But there was nothing else, really, to look forward to. Late at night, frustrated with/by/about sex, I spent my time watching black-and-white sitcoms, popping popcorn, calling dial-a-party and listening to the other lost souls in the area code. When morning came, I managed to drag myself out of bed, jog, clean house, put on a tie, and tend bar.

I was somehow losing all the motivation I'd assembled when I'd decided to leave Yale, my original determination to straighten myself out. I knew now that there were important corrections in my life that I still had failed to make. I wasn't just a lump of biological substance, a collection of assorted enzymes, neurotransmitters, digestive juices, floating atop an undifferentiated experiential sea. I had to end this ameboid existence, give myself motion and direction. I had to start making a plan. Otherwise, I really would be pathetic, and debauched, no matter how much fun it was.

And Item A on the plan was to be more daring about my sexual realities.

Letter dated July 2, to Horace Leviathan, author of A Boy Among Boys—

Dear Mr. Leviathan,

I used to be a medical student—you probably say so what, it has nothing to do with what I'm writing about. I just don't know how else to introduce myself. . . .

I found your novel fascinating, it's giving me the courage to do something more definitive about my "sexual orientation"—I suppose you get letters like these all the time, but maybe not, maybe you'd like to read one, it'd give you a thrill, I don't know how you get your thrills . . . what happened in chapter two seemed pretty thrilling to me.

Actually, I'm a self-styled artist myself. I'm thinking of filming a video. I don't know why you should care about that either. Just thought I'd tell you.

Does everyone go through such a period of "reckless sexual abandon" as you describe upon ending the "years of denial"? Other than high school, when even my straight friends had never been laid, my years of denial have been approximately six (if you don't count heterosexual sex, which was for me a contradiction in terms). So perhaps there's a more fundamental reason for this phenomenon of abandon having to do with society's long repression of gay sex and Sigmund Freud. But this is a philosophical issue.

Well, no need to reply to this letter, I just wanted you to know you had a fan. I didn't know gay love could be so . . . commercially successful.

Sincerely,
—Paul J. Levinson

P.S.—By the way, your jacket photo is very becoming.
P.P.S.—I hope that comment doesn't make me sound, you know, too queer.

The letter was horrible, but after six or seven rereadings, I decided it contained just the right mixture of innocence and enthusiasm, and that the FBI would never be interested in tracing my correspondence. And I'd used the word *gay* right in the middle of a sentence. So that was another accomplishment.

It was a Sunday afternoon; I jogged to the corner mailbox, pulled open the lid, dropped the letter down. I felt a twinge of anxiety as the envelope fell from my hand. It was my first confession to another human being, irrevocable now in the FEDERAL OFFENSE TO TAMPER with U.S. MAIL. But it really meant nothing. If I wanted to get anywhere, I was going to have to do something more courageous than write a fan letter.

To calm down from my derring-do, I went for a jog. Since moving in with George, I'd taken up exercise: jogging, weights—how typical—but it really did make me feel better, more alive, more in touch with the solid earth around me. I put on shorts, laced my seventy-dollar (pre-bartending) sneakers, and headed out the front door. I needed time to adjust to this new way of thinking, to what I knew would have to come next.

After about ten minutes of this homeostatic jog, I discovered that I was being chased by a dog. The dog had perseverance—he kept a steady five feet behind, pacing me. A black Lab, his tongue hanging out of his mouth and swinging back and forth like the clapper on a bell. He watched me as though I were about to fall into several pieces of steak at any moment. That patient look in the eyes: a real killer.

All right, I had an imagination. But the dog was real, he was really behind me. I'd heard dog stories; I was scared. I rounded a corner, and he rounded it behind me. Maybe he was lost. I ran faster. Just a little. Don't panic, I told myself. The dog was still there, like a shadow.

We ran like that for minutes, the two of us. I was unable to shake him.

So I headed up the nearest driveway, toward a stranger's house. I'd just read Sartre's *The Flies*, so this was an even larger gesture for me. God, I said, let it work. I jogged up the wooden stairs of the porch, stopped in front of the door, turned around. The dog had stopped in the yard. We looked at each other.

"Go away!" I said. "My house. This is my house." I pointed at myself, the house, the dog, far away. I put my hands on my thighs, drops of sweat dripping on the porch. I had an erection, from the thrill, the idea of being eaten. The fucking dog was so muscular, he was practically obscene.

The dog looked at me—no expression—then turned and trotted away, his little snub tail bobbing along like an insult.

I stayed a few minutes, to get my nerve back. I might have died in that encounter—maybe it had been a warning, but my number hadn't been up after all. It was one of those moments; I thought about the incredible impossibility of human consciousness, its frailty. I thought: What about this body of mine, that can be mauled by an animal? How can such elusive forces such as "wants" and "hopes" really circulate through such a machine? How had they—those forces which I'd thought to be the most intimate of feelings—come to be directed and controlled by others? For I knew that that was what had happened to me, that I'd only *thought* I'd wanted to go to Yale, a brainwashing, conducted by everything and everyone I'd ever met. And I wondered: What could have happened to me all that time—my whole life—that I could have been led to have desires that were not my own? And in that case, what could anyone mean by "I," by "my," by "own"?

Starting back home, I glanced over my shoulder—a pair of eyes were watching me from behind the curtains, which closed as I turned. I didn't feel better, knowing those eyes had been there, watching, documenting my absurd encounter with this animal. In fact, I felt embarrassed, as though I'd been caught doing something pornographic.

But I wasn't going to let it bother me. I'd reached a turning point: It was as if those eyes had been there always, always watching every move I made, always aware. But now, I realized that all this time, they'd belonged to no one but me.

7

Biochemistry

It wasn't too long after the dog business that I discovered two women kissing behind the restaurant. Exactly the sort of opportunity I'd been waiting for.

One of them was Marlou, the cook, a tall, thin gourmet with spiky lobster-red hair, who kept the hands of hungry busboys and dishwashers out of the pot with the swift swipes of a spatula. I admired Marlou from afar. The cooks generally kept to themselves, but whenever Marlou was on duty, she communicated between their world and ours, and the restaurant achieved a greater vibrancy because of it; she buzzed through the kitchen like someone possessed . . . *cook, cook, cook*—shouting out orders and ingredients—and the other cooks and waitrons fell in line behind her. She knew her sauces—the special timing each dish required, what gave it its character—even if she did nothing more than concoct the thirteen Big Moe's creations that were based solely on the dictates of Oleg's mélange of recipes. But she ran the restaurant in all the ways that Angela didn't.

I'd never thought very thoroughly about Marlou, except for her gumbo origins, and whether that had given her any natural advantage when it came to learning Oleg's upscale imitations of Southern-style sauces. I'd gone outside to toss some crates into the Dumpster. On my way back, that's when I spotted her embrace. They were both in white: white shirts, white pants, sterilized. And Marlou with those eccentric punk ear cuffs. Another cook, perhaps? I didn't recognize the other woman. I wanted to know— the atmosphere at the Moe was one of continual gossip, and I'd learned not to be shy about my curiosity.

So I stared a bit longer than was probably right. It *seemed* as though she was kissing another woman, but I wasn't *sure* it was a woman, and I wanted to make sure. Her girlfriend's head came up only to her chest. Marlou glanced over long enough to flash me a frown. She probably thought I was some conservative yahoo so shocked by their behavior that it'd stopped me in my tracks, but there was no way to convey that that wasn't the case at all. I smiled, but I don't think she quite got the message. The whole episode lasted only a second or two; Marlou and her friend went back to their smooch, and I went inside.

I started stocking up the liquor rack, dusting each bottle as I pulled it from the crate and placed it on the bar. Maybe the woman had been a relative—a mother, or sister. Like a good-bye kiss. It seemed a little passionate for relations, but I hadn't stared long enough to tell. I dusted another bottle as Marlou walked inside. She gave me a look that said, *You're no friend of mine, so keep your trap shut,* then went into the kitchen. I knew then that I'd seen what I'd seen.

After that, I thought Marlou had it in for me. It was hard enough to make friends with the cooks as it was. And she and Angela were inseparable. Angela was always looking after some emergency, always in a rush, but when Marlou had something to tell her, she managed to set her clipboard on the nearest ledge and make time to chat. Marlou, however, even when gossiping, never quit working. She'd pour oil into pans, sending up great clouds of smoke, always stirring around juicy lumps of chicken, or pork, or shrimp. So skinny, for a cook, she was the most visible feature of the restaurant—you could always find her by that flame of hair. She had a toughness much different than Angela's, too— I knew if I tried to cross her, divulge her secrets, she might not say anything . . . I'd have my kneecaps broken.

I listened in, at the first opportunity, on one of Angela and Marlou's conversations. They were discussing *Marlou's new friend.* Those were the words, but the implications were vague. Intentionally, it seemed. Her new friend was "more anxious to do things" than her last one, but not "responsive enough to her interests." They were only half-aware that I stood there, sipping my end-of-the-evening beer and listening.

"I know about friends," I said. "Friends are something everyone needs."

They both looked at me as though I were speaking in tongues. I finished the beer and walked away, wondering why the hell I'd said that. What had I possibly meant? Why couldn't I just come out and tell it to them in English?

But I had an in now, and it was only a matter of time.

The situation I longed for (and dreaded) soon came, in the form of an after-work party at Marlou's apartment, where I was sure to get some time with her alone. Beforehand I prepared myself: I reread *A Boy Among Boys*. I reread Carlos Castaneda. I watched some videos. Hours before the party, Angela, Gray, and I went for drinks at the Mexican restaurant. We clambered into a booth near the bar, where the walking time for liquor would be shorter. We wanted to be good and ready by midnight.

"God, if Kirk calls me 'sugar baby' one more time, I'm going to plow him in the nuts." Angela shifted uncomfortably in her seat, downing her vodka (which she'd complained about having to pay too much for). "Where'd this punk come from anyway? The guy can't even add."

"Chill out, baby." Gray turned to me. "She's threatened by those abusive macho attitudes."

"Mister Wonderful." She clunked some extra ice cubes into her drink and rolled her eyes. "At least you're smart, aren't you, Paul? I can tell—you smart kids, you have that brainy look. The smart kids in my school used to have this group they hung with. I was almost smart. I got B pluses in high school, you know? I bet that surprises you. But where are the semi-smart kids from Elmhurst going to go? ..." She finished her sentence with a shrug.

"It's funny," I told her. "I used to think that there was this group of kids—the ordinary kids, who went to parties and had fun and such—and I could never hang out with *them*, because I was supposed to be a nerd." And I shrugged, too.

But she wasn't impressed; she had other things on her mind. "God, don't you just remember high school, though? In high school, we used to go up to Flushing Bay to drink beer. We couldn't hang out in school, we couldn't hang out at home, so at least we had this one getaway to go to. Lawrence, my husband, he loved horses; he worked at the track. Then something happened—I don't know—he got hooked with the wrong crowd, he got started on crack. It's everywhere, I tell you. You know that dishwasher selling drugs out of the back of the restaurant? He was so coked, he left a rolled-up hundred-dollar bill in the bathroom."

"Nice income for a dishwasher, huh?" Crack, coke—what would it be like to have a life like that? It seemed so dangerous, luminous, like TV.

"But me, it was horrible in New York, having a two-week-old kid and all. Guess Lawrence couldn't handle fatherhood. The guy was nineteen and he thought his life was over—having a family, working at a garage, never been out of the city except for that week in the Catskills when he knocked me up in the first place. So he decided to be a statistic. Look at me, I'm nineteen now myself and you think I'm afraid of a little hard work? But with guys it's different. Some guys just freak, I guess, having a kid. Must be their stunted sense of mortality." (Mortality? Morality? I hadn't heard her exactly.) She glanced over at Gray, but he didn't notice, he was busy drinking his Brown Cow. "But like I say, I got over it. When it happened, I was so mad, I might have actually killed him; Mom had a Remington. But he knew better than to show his ugly face. He sent me a hundred dollars last week, the first money I've seen since he left, so maybe he's developing a conscience after all.

"I guess everything works out somehow. I pray to Mary, not Jesus—Jesus was a man even if he is God. You're Jewish, do you pray? Oh, you pray, everybody prays. Gray prays, I make him. Gray's great with Sarah. They're pals. I guess it's like, some guys have it in them, and some guys don't. It's funny. Gray's already dropping these hints that he wants to propose. It's so Spike Lee." She nudged Gray in the arm.

"What?"

"Hinting, Gray. That you want to propose."

"Yeah. That's right." He sucked noisily on his straw.

"Paul, have you seen my new Mazda? It's great. A real beauty. Here, we'll take it to the party. I'll put the top down." She picked up her purse, paid the check, and in a moment, we were piling into her car, Gray squeezing in on my lap between us.

"You and your sports cars," he grumbled.

But I was having a great time; Angela was the most interesting person I'd ever met. She made all the tragedy in her life into one great escapade—I wondered if anything could get her down.

"Wheeeee!" she yelled as she threw the car into reverse. She shifted gears again and we roared out of the parking lot, breeze in our hair, top down and radio on, and in no time we were driving down the streets of New Haven—not Yale's native New Haven but Angela's adopted one, which wasn't a cosmopolitan mini-opolis of tertiary hospitals and high-powered medical schools, gymnasiums the size of Kiev and library collections that rivaled the Smithsonian's, but Small Town, a place where up-and-coming young enterprisers came to start out on their own, came to find jobs and families and lifestyles, and could only see as fodder for their dreams the strange fashionable students who came to town every semester like a seasonal migration of tax attorneys. That's the way I saw this town from Angela's car: a city of several worlds, planes, all existing in the same physical space and each invisible to the others—with me, for some reason, able to move indiscriminately between them.

Marlou handed each of us a plastic cup as we walked in the door. She'd put a keg in the bathtub and Pee-wee Herman on TV. "Heh heh heh," he laughed, in signature, but no one was watching. It was just background noise. We mingled with the other employees, who showed up one by one as the restaurant closed for the night.

A bari bassoon stood in the living room, and I asked Marlou about it, a way of breaking the ice. "Used to play in high school. Haven't touched it in ages."

"Funny. I used to play trumpet."

Baritone → cook. Trumpet → bartender. The more I drank, the more I felt there had to be some sort of fate involved. Marlou stood in the center of the room, surveying the props of her life, the people. She looked around until she found someone else to talk to. What the hell—the night was still young; I'd get my chance yet.

I mingled, talked to everyone, although I felt surrounded by a blanket, protected by a screen, the minutes clunking by. Maybe it was the alcohol. Maybe it was my nerves. Or both. After a while, Oleg showed up, and that's when the party really got going. He made it official. He sat on the living-room floor, holding his beer with both hands. A good five or six of us had gathered in a circle around him.

"Marlou's the best cook in the state," he said, "but her alligator sauce needs work. Doesn't it, dear?"

"Like hell."

"Honey," Dax said with a Julia Child—like hand on his hips, "if you can't take the heat, stay out of the kitchen." He laughed at his pun, hands fluttering. He went on to do some impressions: jogging through the Yellow Pages, a fly drowning in olive oil, whatever.

Meanwhile, Oleg was taking an origami-sized square of paper out of his pocket and unfolding it. He worked carefully under a desk lamp someone had placed on the coffee table. Inside the envelope was that reliable old fine white powder. Despite his flippancy, Dax leaned in closer to watch. Marlou did the same. Hell, so did I. Sure, I was leery about adding another abuse to my repertoire, but I didn't want to be impolite. Besides, cocaine seemed a logical drug of choice for the ratty, go-go environment of haute cuisine, and if I truly wanted to be part of it, I couldn't nerd out on them now.

Oleg chopped the coke with a razor blade—sideways, upways, downways; he divided it so many times, with such concentration, I thought he had a nervous disorder. Then he cut six lines, and I watched as he and then a few suddenly friendly party guests each in turn picked up the gold-plated straw and inhaled. I studied their techniques: one carefully dividing a line between each nostril, then rubbing her nose; another inhaling his whole portion in one big elephant snort; a third one inhaling each particle in a series of careful inspirations, then slowly massaging his membranes, as if testing the temperature of a swimming pool. Why was Oleg being so generous with his stash? Maybe it was simply restaurant etiquette. Next it was my turn. I'd just read a book about people doing coke, people just like these, only wealthier, so I knew the procedure. I rolled the gold cylinder between my fingers—like a Monopoly piece—then bent down and sniffed. The crystals stung; my nose turned numb. We scooped up the leftover powder with our fingers and rubbed it over our gums.

It wasn't so bad—I hadn't turned into a fiend yet. But it was still early.

"Angela tells me you're not at Yale anymore," Oleg said, leaning back in his chair. News travels fast. Someone was passing out beers from a six-pack. Nice and cold. Rolling Rock and coke. I wasn't at Yale anymore now, that was for sure.

I popped the top and nodded.

"Yale isn't the end of the world. You know what I mean? It isn't the goddamned cat's meow." Oleg folded the envelope, slipped it into a pocket somewhere.

"Sure. I know."

"But it takes real arrogance to walk out on it, son. That's what I'd say. That's a real future you're giving up. You have everything you want, here."

I shrugged, in a hip way, trying to act cool about not having a future, or having one, either way. Gray and Angela had just skated into the room, but were off somewhere, being solicitous to party guests. Marlou and Dax were involved with themselves as well. So here I was, dealing with Oleg on my own.

"Look. Want to know something, son? Know what got me my place? The restaurant?" He paused, like maybe it wasn't a rhetorical question. "Hard work and determination. No Ivy League in Mother Russia. When I started, I had only my boat. Not even a passport. Me, I'm an American success story." He pointed his finger at me, so sincere he was trembling. I wondered if he was drunk, high from the coke, or just off his rocker. No matter—he had my attention, what he wanted.

"Jews and gold diggers, that's who run your country. I say screw 'em. I have more than two hundred thousand genuine U.S. dollars locked in some bank in Peru; all these conglomerates, they want to buy my jambalaya. They say, 'Oleg, we love your jambalaya, we love your crawfish étoufée, they are so succulent, they are so traditional.' You know something? I got the recipes out of a magazine. *Home and Garden*, I think. It was wonderful. I never saw such magazines before." He paused and held my gaze, eyes aglow. "No, I think it is time for me to expand myself. Time for Big Moe's in Moscow. Big Moe's in Copenhagen. Big Moe's in Yokohama. I'm the one who will bring the genuine Cajun style to the world. Why not? Did Cajuns invent creole? Is it really French, is it really American—these are not very interesting questions. How much money, this is what I like to know. In Russia, we have a saying—I don't remember what it is, but you could always ask the government if you forgot, there was always someone there to look it up. Not anymore. Now everywhere people are on their own.

"But you, son, Angela tells me you have brains. That's important. You've got to be smart in this world; it's all a goddamn quiz show, only no one really cares about the answers, just as long as you look good when you hit that buzzer. Know what I mean? This is a land of individuals, son, a country of opportunity; on our own we're shit, might as well go back to communism or Darwinism or whatever shit philosophy we came from. It's all up to each one of us. Don't let anyone tell you different—each one of us, here we either make or break it, we either skyrocket into orbit or go pffft, down the crapper. It's up to you. The world's at your fingertips, son. *You* control it. Like this desk light. Just hit a button, and boom-o, off it goes."

He pushed a button on the desk lamp, sending the room into semidarkness. I sat there, blinded. Boom-o. I wondered if this was all some ruse: Maybe he was going to murder us in the darkness, use our corpses for some *Sweeney Todd*–type recipe. Maybe human flesh was the secret to his jambalaya. No one acted as if they'd noticed that the light had gone out. Oleg's arm moved in the darkness, and the light flickered on.

"I hit another button, and boom-o, it's on again. Just like that." He paused, giving time for the subtleties of his demonstration to sink in, my eyes to adjust. "See what I mean?" And he pointed his electric finger at me.

I nodded.

" 'I think I am in hell, and I am in hell,' " he said, this time to the light. But he didn't turn it off again. "That's Rambo, by the way."

"Uh . . . Rimbaud?"

"Speaking of hell, want to read one of my poems?" Marlou said. Apparently that's what she and Dax had been talking about, and now she was passing them around. I shrugged, and she handed me a stack of papers. Typed on onionskin, the letters floating out of place—they were anger poems. *dick like a razor . . . her insect lips . . . he bisects my cunt*—the words jumped out and attacked you; it was a full-scale assault. "How interesting," I mumbled, "yes, interesting. . . ." Her father turned up in reference to sharp objects so much that it seemed obvious that she'd had a pathological adolescence. And the word *lesbian*—she used it until I lost count, until it became an idiosyncrasy. But oddly, it didn't seem derogatory in context—she'd taken control of it, reversed it—an epithet that, rather than evade, she'd embraced. You needed to commandeer the terms yourself, I supposed, before someone else came along and did it for you. I suppose that was the lesson I was learning in general.

"That poem," she said to me, tapping the page I was reading, "I wrote that like, like I was seeing something in front of me, and I just copied it down."

"Right," I said. "I know what you mean."

"You know, when I told my parents I was in love with the girl next door"—she was referring to the content of one of the poems here—"Dad threw the goldfish bowl out the window. I knew that would be his reaction. I can't believe what I gave up for that bitch. Those fish were genuine fancy-tailed guppies. Oh, well—shit happens. Besides, Dad's always been a jerk." Everyone nodded, as if they'd heard it all before.

Her story seemed familiar, indubitable, like my earliest memory, or *The Cat in the Hat,* but there it was, nonetheless.

"Excuse me," Oleg said, rubbing his glass against the carpet. "I'm going for more . . . more dip." He left us reading the poems— or rather, we'd left him, engrossed in our meditations. I was relieved, finally, to be rid of him. The others were gone now, too. But then I got nervous, now that it looked like I would get my opportunity alone with Marlou after all, brought together by our common interest in poetry.

"Here," she said, grabbing the papers from my hands. "Read this one."

Each poem had its own story: She wrote this one after her breakup with Margie, that one after meeting Janet, this one after the night she first made crawfish pie. We sat for almost an hour, and soon I knew everything I possibly could about her—I felt like her psychiatrist.

We kept discussing her poems, but after a while, I stopped listening. I was preparing my confession. I had no idea what would happen. I was drunk and feeling debauched and cynical, or I wouldn't have had the courage to do it. I suppose I must have phased out, because she stared questioningly at me for a brief moment, then forgot it and went on telling me about her dangerous-sounding family. The thing was, I could always conceivably go back to medical school, but if I said these words—to a live human being—it'd be the only moment in my life that could never be reversed.

"Marlou," I said, lowering my voice. "I don't know if you've suspected this, but we've got something in common."

"You mean you've got some poems? You'd like me to read them?" She brushed back her hair and started collecting the pages.

"No, I mean, more than that."

I let the comment sit, hoping it might sink in. Marlou knocked the sheaf of papers against the coffee table, straightening them.

I don't know why, but I put my hand on her knee. Hell, I was being so courageous, it seemed like the thing to do, establish physical contact. "Marlou, I want to tell you something. . . . I . . . I'm . . ."

"You're trying to make a pass at me, aren't you?" She stuffed the poems back into the shoe box in the corner. "Jesus, after all the crap I've just been telling you? But that's just how it is with men: Say something, and it goes zip right through the ears. They just don't think with their brains, do they?"

"No, Marlou, I'm not making a pass. I'd never make a pass at you. I'm gay." The words formed, molecular vibrations in the air, just on their own. I'd practiced saying something like that so many times that they had no reality for me. I heard them the way Marlou did, as a bystander.

She paused, half-bent over her shoe box. "Oh," she said, but that was it. I don't know what I'd expected: party horns and streamers, Marlou rushing into my arms like some long-lost sister, reunited as I stepped from the planks of a cruise ship. She crossed her legs on the floor and stared at me.

"Paul Levinson. Gay." She smiled, and dimples came to her cheeks—endearing indentations. She'd been wearing her white cook's uniform, and smiling, she looked like some Louisiana debutante in costume: essentially wholesome and much less to be feared than the bad-girl-librarian image I had of her. "Paul Levinson the Yalie is a fag. Well, why didn't you say so?"

"It's not like I've ever done anything about it. You're the first person I've told."

She just looked at me, smiling, but as my words sank in, the smile disappeared, as she realized I'd implicated her, that I'd thrown the responsibility for my life into her lap.

And it was true—I'd been assuming she'd want to in a way adopt me, show me the ropes, become my gay-world den mother. And I hadn't considered that maybe she had no desire to do any such thing.

"Yes, well, don't think you . . . don't think I'm . . . I've got plenty of ideas. I'm just not sure what to do next."

She put her hand on my leg. "It's okay, Paul," she said, more seriously this time. "We'll talk about it. But now's not a good time. Wait till tomorrow. Why don't you come over? It'll be Sunday, we'll brew a pot of coffee. We'll have a conversation. We'll talk."

"Talk. Okay," I said. "Okay . . . that sounds good." I hadn't realized it, but my leg had been trembling, and by putting her hand there, firmly, she'd steadied it.

"Just ignore Oleg," Angela said as she drove me back to my car. "I don't know what he told you, but he's not even a legal citizen. I don't know what he's doing with a restaurant."

It took me a second to register what she was saying. I was relieved just to get out of the building. My mind was reeling with the alcohol, the coke, Oleg's incomprehensible ramblings, the beginnings of my revelations. It was all bubbling and seething, held back and coming out—and I didn't know if I could keep myself under control.

When we got back to the Mexican restaurant, I couldn't find my car—only an empty space in the street where I'd left it, what seemed like years ago. Had it been stolen, or what? "What the hell happened to it? I left it here myself."

Gray ran down the block to read a street sign. "No parking!" he shouted. "Two A.M. till six."

No parking. No parking. A plot against me, for sure. I looked at my watch. Three in the morning. Shit. Goddamn it. I kicked the nearest signpost and threw a general tantrum. I had to calm down; it was only a car.

"The same thing happened to me last week," Angela said. "Come on, I'll take you."

We climbed into her Mazda and sped off. All throughout the ride, I rambled incoherently. "Who uses the street between two and six A.M.? What crook's going to hide behind a car? Can't the cops just patrol the sidewalk? What sort of neighborhood am I working in, anyway?" I went on and on, but underneath, I was feeling lighter, relieved—cleansed, as if years of accumulated film were lifting from me, layers and layers of grime and particulate matter washing away . . . as if there was nothing underneath those layers, nothing to me that could ever truly be sullied.

When we got to the tow yard, it was like walking on the set of a film, the final rushes of my camera-eye experience—cars all around, stripped or rusted or new, parked at angles. Halogen lamps atop the office sent orange cones of light off the chrome and blacktop—at the perimeters of the yard, the lights ended with scissorlike precision; beyond was only blackness, void, as though we'd stepped onto some hellish geometrical plane floating helter-skelter in the ether. A fat man in overalls sat inside the office, lit from behind, playing solitaire.

We opened the door and asked the fat man about my car, but he just shook his triple chins as if he didn't want any part of it. He told us about another tow company we should try—his competitor, from the gravelly tone of his voice—across town. He gave the following directions: a left, then a right, veer right at the bridge, then two more lefts. He didn't explain further. He wasn't going to be Samaritan about it. We piled back into Angela's car and drove out of the lot.

"Let's drop off Gray on the way. He needs his beauty sleep."

Gray grunted—his eyes were already shut. A minute later he let out a snore like a bulldozer.

We dropped him off somewhere in North Branford, although I couldn't see where we were exactly or how we'd gotten there. Then Angela retraced our path back to route 1B679 (or whatever it was) through some combination of guesswork and memory, zipping across railroad tracks and around sewage treatment plants, under bridges and past tumbledown seafood shacks (at one point I thought we were driving over an oil rig out on the Sound), finding our destination out of some fortuitous conjuction of ineptitude and good fortune.

We pulled in at fifty miles an hour and hurtled to a halt.

There were hundreds of cars here—Chevys, Datsuns, Olds-mobiles, Subarus—and we looked at them all. None were mine. We went to the front office. The guy in charge, some kid with pimples across his forehead like the map of a disease, listed for us all the other tow companies in town.

So we started at the top of the list, and drove to all of them.

"Don't worry," Angela told me. "We'll find it."

We were alone together, late at night, both of us coming down from various buzzes and frantic with searching. If I'd been Gray, I'd have been worried about leaving us like that. He probably would have been worried, if he'd been awake. I felt a bit guilty now about this whole car thing: Angela was being so nice to me, and she had her own life to tend to, working all night and taking care of babies. Whereas I was just passing through her life, as if on holiday. I had no boyfriends or girlfriends, children, mortgages, debt, lost husbands—no heavy Big Moe–managing responsibilities. None of this drama was real to me. My mind was elsewhere. All I wanted was a chance to get myself together.

At the last place, Angela said simply, "Well, we've looked everywhere."

"So now what?"

We sat in the car, in the craggy lot of the bottom-of-the-list tow yard in New Haven. My car gone. Vanished. Maybe we weren't even in New Haven anymore. Angela leaned over the steering wheel, playing with the stick shift, rubbing harder and harder. She was concentrating, preparing, although I didn't know for what. She stopped rubbing and turned to me.

"Paul..."

"It's okay if you want to give up."

"No—we'll keep looking, we'll start over."

"I really appreciate this."

"No problem."

"I really do. I'm grateful. I don't know how I can tell you how grateful I am."

"Don't worry, Paul. It's fine."

"Okay. Thanks. I appreciate it."

We sat there a minute, in the car.

"So what were you going to say?"

She let out a sigh, as though she had something significant on her mind, then smiled, as if to reassure me that I wasn't going to witness anything heavy. "Okay, here it is: What do you think—is Gray too much of a child for someone like me? I mean, a skateboard, really...."

"Is he really that much younger?"

"It's all in the attitude. He proposed tonight, you know? He finally got the hint. So what should I do?" And then, as if reading my objections: "You're the bartender. I hired you to have opinions."

"Angela, I can't tell you what to do." How could she ask me something like that? I didn't know the first thing about relation-

ships, about having an opinion about anything. Besides, anything
that I might say would be so inextricably mixed with my own
unwieldy desires, my own prejudices, I didn't think it possible to
give her an answer anywhere close to impartial.

"It's too bad, Paul, but I just didn't think Oleg was going to
pan out. You talked to him; you know what I mean. Maybe it's
for the best. At least Gray is someone I could really like. Don't
you think?"

"I don't know. Sure. Why not?" She seemed to be going about
it rather cold-bloodedly. But what did I know? The concept of
love was as abstract to me as a series of geometric rhomboids.

Silence.

"Hmmm," she said, rubbing the stick shift again. "Lotta help
you are."

I smiled at her, Mr. Innocence. If she only knew my own
revelations, my transformations—we'd be having a *real* discussion,
all right.

"I'll tell you, Paul, I don't want to handle food service all my
life. I always thought I'd be good at something else. That was the
thing about Oleg. He's going places. He's been places. Think what
a girl could learn. But maybe I don't need to know all that. Gray—
he'll provide a stable life for Sarah, if he doesn't crack his head
open. He'll be interesting on vacation. It's the best thing in town."

"And, uh . . . you think Gray is okay with your family?"

"You mean because he's white? They don't care. I know, it can
be a bitch always having to fall for these freaky white guys. You
know, like Oleg. But it's not that big a thing, really, not if you
don't let it be. Gray's a real sweetie. I don't think he even realizes
I'm black. Although one day he will. But you can't go panicking
about the future now."

I nodded. The car was quieter now; we could hear every
noise—the motor running, the radio soft in the background, the
commercials for home electrical appliances like a tiny man trapped
in the dashboard. All these little voices talking to me. I felt the
need to put my hands to my temples.

"Jesus, Angela. We must both be drunk. You'll never guess
what I told Marlou tonight."

"What?"

"That I was gay."

She laughed. "Why would you tell her that?"

"Well...because I am."

It just seemed remarkably straightforward now. Not worth the effort to conceal it. Unlike it had ever been in the past.

Angela thought for a moment. She nodded her head. "Well, honey, I guess there's really only one thing to do."

"What's that?"

"Go back."

It took me a few blocks after she started driving again to realize she meant: for my car.

Which we found at the very first tow yard, waiting for us just inside the gate (although the fat man was gone). I paid the new attendant fifty dollars' cash—all that was left of this week's tips after booze and coke—and gave Angela a good-bye hug, which she took a little more strongly and perhaps a little more drunkenly than felt comfortable, especially after all that we'd just exchanged.

"So, what about Gray?"

She shrugged. "Things will work themselves out."

I nodded—I understood.

"Look—I wouldn't worry, Paul, about being gay at Big Moe's. It's not like you're the only one working there."

"No—it's a hotbed. Maybe it's something in the red beans and rice."

She gave me another quick hug. Then we got in our separate cars and drove our separate ways home, me listening to the morning deejay to keep me awake, absently tapping out the beat on the steering wheel—this *thing* in front of me called a "steering wheel"—the conversations with Marlou, Angela, replaying in my head, smoothing themselves, my words idealizing into carefully scripted retorts, all the things I wished I'd said, all the perfect scenarios of moral rectitude—while feeling insanely light, weightless, as if I could drive off the planet.

When I got back to the house, the block was dead; it was five-thirty in the morning; I'd journeyed like Céline to the end of the night. In the east, the horizon was turning pink, a flock of birds flapping by overhead, heading south, west; who knew what plans birds had. I pulled off my tie as I got out of the car. A whole night it'd been since I'd woken up yesterday—a whole different empyrean. It was as if time were an envelope: I could just crumple it up and toss it in the incinerator, walk into a totally new time and place, the Year 0. Year of the Snake. Year of the many new voices.

The floorboards creaked as I slipped past George's room, trying not to wake him. The morning light streamed loudly through the living-room windows, too much activity for this time of day. I stripped off my clothes and, in my undershorts, stared into the bathroom mirror: half-hairy bipedal protoplasm, a mass of follicles, skin, and nails, leaning over the sink. Gay follicles. Gay skin. Gay nails. I brushed my teeth, burped, and felt the onset of aftermath.

I took off my underpants and sat naked on the john. Then my stomach twisted; I thought I'd been speared. It was the revenge of the chemicals—I was made out of chemicals, after all; maybe I'd titrated myself to the point of dissolution. I stared at the wall-paper: purple pinstripes, and a crooked patch near the floor, show-ing the void underneath. My last moments could very well be in this bathroom, and I wanted to be fully aware of every detail, aware of the human being who'd laid the wallpaper and left this tiny error, this sign of his or her humanity. I focused on the pinstripes as my sight blurred, my senses reeled, I crashed from the coke, the beer, the bourbon . . . then I was off the toilet and vomiting, clutching the porcelain with both hands and ejecting a steady stream of liquids.

Shit. What would the doctors at YMS have said? *Acute emesis secondary to ETOH and alkaloid poisoning,* they would have said. But I was tired of being intellectual about my symptoms. I just wanted to be sick. I just wanted to be. I felt the porcelain under my hands, my knees on the tile, the smell of Sanifresh and vomit, the sound of my body's recoil and percolation.

When it was over, I looked in the mirror again and washed myself. I was naked, all right, but proud of it. Feet, legs, chest, arms—every part. Stomach empty, I felt better. I went to bed and pulled up the covers. For the first time since I could remember, I slept all day long, like a baby.

When I woke up that afternoon, it was cloudy, threatening rain, but the prospect of rain was nice—the air smelled electric, water from an earlier cloudburst trickling across the sidewalk into pools in the street. I watched from my window, thinking about what I'd done last night. I still felt great, refreshed, relieved. Maybe I hadn't yet fully grasped the consequences. I slipped on a pair of shorts and a T-shirt, and walked over to Marlou's. I listened to the birds, kicked pebbles, watched New Haven conducting its placid Sunday afternoon. It was the beginning of an adventure.

Marlou's apartment was much more homey in the daytime. Stained-glass baubles hung in the kitchen window, through which I could see a pile of cups and saucers in the sink. I rang the bell, and after a few minutes, she showed up at the door—fuzzy blue bathrobe, bunny slippers, rubbing her eyes. I was wide awake. I handed her the paper. She shoved it under her arm, and we went inside.

The party hadn't been cleaned up yet; there were glasses and beer cans strewn about the floor, the bookshelves. Who knew what else I might find if I looked hard enough. Thank God, no sleeping waitrons. I sat at the kitchen table while Marlou turned on the coffee machine. She had spices everywhere, pots and pans hanging from a beam above the stove, but otherwise, it was pretty much a disaster area, considering this kitchen belonged to a cook.

"Do you take it black, with sugar, milk?"

"Anything. I never drink coffee."

She put in everything, lots of it, while I told her about Yale Med, my family, my family's debates.

"I like it at the Moe," I said, "but I'm not going to stay here forever. I'm going back to school. I'm going to learn how to make videos." I was just deciding this business about school as I said it. It seemed the time to be decisive.

She squeezed a dab of honey in her coffee, and stirred. "Oleg's sending me to France next year, to culinary school. If he doesn't weasel out with the money."

"Great."

We discussed all our plans, histories, desires. Well, almost desires. Desires are always the trickiest things to explain to other people—especially in fifteen minutes, when you've got to get to know someone as fast as possible. They always sound so remote, so much as if they couldn't possibly be as overwhelming as they are.

"So last night—what made you decide to tell *me*?" She got up and poured herself another cup, but I refused any more coffee; I was wired as it was. My foot kept tapping against the leg of the table.

"I don't know. That's just the way I planned it. Hell, Marlou, how should I know what makes me do the things I do? I've never said what was on my mind before. I've never been open with anyone. I don't know the first thing about it." I didn't even know how to talk about it. There was so much junk to cut through, so much that I'd kept inside, my mind was a jumble—

How long have you suspected yourself of being gay?
How gay are you?
Have you ever had sex with a woman?
Maybe you're only bisexual.
How committed are you to the gay movement?
What can you tell me about gay clothes/records/books/drugs?
Don't you want to have children?
Don't you want to prevent AIDS?
They don't have gays in Saudi Arabia.
They don't have gays in Duluth, Minnesota.
Maybe it's just a phase.
Maybe it's a fashion.
I think it's a political statement more than anything....

A whole inflated discourse was crashing down on top of me at once—I'd never thought of it as something that might apply to me; it was overwhelming, nonsensical, disorienting. And all those questions of regret: Why had I wasted so many years pretending to be something else? Why should I let other people decide what the divisions are, what the bad words are, what the world is like? But once you started renovating your own little piece of it, you realized that the whole enchilada was fucked up. Priests, parents, newscasters, governments. They had everything wrong. They didn't know what the hell they were talking about. So how should I? Instead of blaming myself, I should have all this time been blaming everyone else. But that idea was just a glimmer—I didn't yet know where exactly I should start. The world was a big place. I simply told Marlou my life—chronologically, indiscriminately, emphasizing everything.

Marlou nodded along as I talked; it was all familiar to her;

she'd lived it herself. The telling was for my benefit. But the talk was liberating, intoxicating—we were floating, headed for maximum entropy, dissipation. "Hell, Marlou, I don't know. Why you? Why last night? I was drunk. I was rash. But now that I've finally told someone, more than anything, I just want to get laid."

She took another sip of coffee and smiled at me, sweetly, with those bad-girl dimples. "Paul, maybe you should meet some of my friends. Or talk to Dax. He's looking for a boyfriend."

"Hold on a minute." I held up a hand. "I didn't say anything about a boyfriend."

I hadn't said anything about Dax, either. I didn't think, if I brought Dax into the picture, that the details of my personal life would remain within my jurisdiction for long. Marlou rubbed her chin. "Hmmm, well, maybe Dax isn't such a good idea, anyway." Thank God. "He's in an intensity mode right now. What you really need is a cheap thrill."

Silence.

"Well... perhaps that's an unfortunate phrase. What I mean is, first... you do... you pract... know about safe sex, right? Like they say in the ads: no fisting, no rimming, use a condom, safety pin, the rest of it. I'm sure you've at least heard about it, haven't you?"

This was all going too fast—I wasn't ready for liberal political description; I just wanted to confess my thoughts. "Let's skip the details for now," I said. I'd ignored everything having to do with sex between grown-ups; it was an embarrassment to me. I needed time to assimilate, bit by bit. Jesus, how would I know anything about making love? How would I know anything at all? I'd only studied bodies; they'd never taught me how to use one.

"Just for the sake of argument, tell me, what's your type?"

"My type?"

"You know, the men. What do you look for in the male physique? What type of boy?"

I didn't feel too comfortable discussing my fantasies with another person. Maybe I wasn't completely ready for this, after all. But I thought about it dutifully. What came into my mind first was Pete, of course. But now I wasn't so sure—personality was maybe a factor after all, when you had to be serious about it, and that might alter the equation. After all, there'd be a person there you'd have to make conversation with when it was over. I thought of Gray, George, Jeff from the bookstore, Oleg—hell, even Fergie might do, if I was feeling especially sleazy (I could see how that sort of thing had its appeal)... so I guess I wasn't that picky after all.

"Actually, now that I think about it, Gray's kind of cute, in an understated way." I was trying to pick a reference she'd be familiar with, surprised at my own conclusion. It was the answer to Angela's question, plain and simple. Still, I thought it was so... queer... to associate the word *cute* with a guy. It wasn't something that another guy was supposed to do.

Marlou nodded. "Did you hear about the wedding?"

"Angela? You mean..." Jesus, things happened fast around here.

"Yep, there's going to be a reception at Big Moe's—we're all invited. Lots of popcorn shrimp."

Thank God, the decision had worked out okay. So why had she even asked?

"But the subject at hand is getting you laid. That really shouldn't be too difficult."

I shrugged. I was twenty-three and starting my adolescence. Making plans to get laid. How juvenile. How goddamned exciting.

"Have you ever been to Vick's? The bar?"

Again I shook my head.

"How about ALAG, the Alliance of Lesbians and Gays?"

"Well, I'm not a student at the moment." I had doubts about a group whose name resembled that of a sedimentary rock. It really didn't need to be this complicated. The bar sounded intriguing, but I knew I wouldn't go by myself; I needed Marlou's complicity. She stood up to pace the room.

"I know, I've got it. Bob. I'll introduce you to Bob."

"Who's Bob?"

"That's it. How about..." She looked at the calendar on the wall, holding up a page. "A week from this Thursday, for dinner? I'll make catfish. Do you have Thursday off?"

"More creole?"

"Hey—give me a break, it's my specialty. I've got the tomatoes."

"Who's Bob?"

"Bob?" She looked back at me, said simply, "Bob. Oh, you'll

love him. You two are perfect for each other. You'll get along perfectly." She took her coffee cup and mine, and dumped them both in the sink. "Trust me."

A week from Thursday seemed an eternity away. In the meantime, Julie and George invited me to go to the beach, to keep me occupied. They said it'd been so long since they'd seen me, they were beginning to wonder if I was still alive. I suppose it was true: I'd been so focused on Big Moe's, I'd completely forgotten about my other friends.

"But it's been a great summer, hasn't it, George?"

"Well, Paul—I wouldn't know."

Pete, Fergie, their lab partners—a whole crowd was coming. It'd be the last beach event of the season. Fergie had recently bought a VW van, so when the rolling study-break pulled up to our house, George, Julie, and I tossed a bunch of blankets in the back, handed up our Styrofoam cooler, and piled in.

"So, Paul, what's new?" Pete asked from the front seat, in his tank top, the same old hirsute gorilla I remembered.

"Nothing." I shrugged. "Too much to explain in half an hour. You?"

He told me about pathology, pharmacology, microbiology, all the women he'd been meeting, all the faculty research—*this* microbe and *that* enzymatic reaction—and I couldn't believe how boring it sounded. I couldn't believe I'd spent a whole year in that environment. But I smiled at him, and tried not to let on that I was falling half asleep. Everyone else told jokes about beta blockers and anticholinesterases. I didn't get them, but I laughed, nevertheless, whenever I sensed they'd gotten to a punchline.

Once we got to the beach, everyone took off their clothes and spread out their towels on the sand. Pete and Fergie ran down the shore tossing a Frisbee. George unpacked an umbrella, chairs, a cooler, pink picnic glasses with pink picnic straws, sunscreen, hats, sunglasses, a toy dog (which Julie's roommate had just adopted). He set up everything with efficient methodicalness. On cue, the dog started barking, pulling weakly on its leash, kicking up spurts of sand. Julie picked up a glass of lemonade, flipped down her sunglasses, and sucked on her straw, while George squeezed a dab of sunscreen into his palm and lotioned her back.

"Watch your hands, George."

"Ah, yes." He turned to me. "Tishman Complaint Number Seven—George is too touchy-feely in public."

Julie gave him a raspberry, then went back to her lemonade.

I placed my towel next to theirs. It was strange for me to see all these medical students half naked. To see their bodies. It unsettled me. George's body looked so thin: the papery texture of the skin, the palms, the way you could see the bones in his chest stick out slightly as he breathed. It didn't look as though that scrawny body could hold the mind, the person, that was the George I knew. "George" was a certain way of answering a question, an inclination for Dirty Rotten Imbeciles and black turtlenecks—not a chest with two pale nipples or skin of a definite hue. I was so used to interacting with his mind, those wry off-the-cuff comments, that his physical presence seemed secondary. And his hands on Julie's bare back struck me as unnatural, out of place, as though he were a stroke victim relearning the most basic of movements.

Julie's body emerged slightly differently—it was more natural to her, already tanning enough to leave lines. But she ought to have been wearing reading glasses, not sunglasses, and her skin seemed particularly delicate, like the leaves of a book someone's neglected to open for centuries. It was the same for everyone: Pete, Fergie, their friends. Without their clothes, they were all pale, small, insubstantial human forms. They couldn't compete with the natural beauty around them—they were simply flesh tones. Pete snapped the Frisbee to Fergie, who snapped it back. Just another pair of prancing animals, pleasant to look at. They moved along the beach, the only people about, but you couldn't say they "took over." It was more as though the beach took over them, subsuming them, until they became inconsequential to the beat of the waves and the blowing gusts of sand.

After some sun, some Frisbee, George asked if I wanted to go for a walk, so we headed off along the shore. We talked idly, George kicking his bare feet in the water. It seemed that he just needed some time away from the crowd, some time to think. Out of nowhere, he said to me, "So tell me, Paul, are you really so happy tending bar?"

"Happy?"

"Yeah. Happy. You know. Are you glad you left school?"

I wasn't sure what he was asking, really. He'd never asked me a question like this before—as if he actually wanted an answer. As if it really mattered. "Well, I'm not going to tend bar all my life. I've got...other things on my mind. But...sure, I'm happy. Life's pretty interesting right now."

"Oh. Well, that's good."

"Why? Is something wrong?"

"No. No...it's just that..."

"What?"

"There's nothing so wrong with medicine, you know."

"No, there isn't," I admitted. "I never said there was." Of course—there wasn't any reason to think George might not be as human as anyone else.

"It certainly pays well. That's a plus. What with the economy getting squeezed, I may not be able to earn what my parents make. I read that in *Newsweek*. I've never been attracted by poverty, Paul. I want a house with a listening room. I want the best stereo equipment available. Not because I want things, but so I don't ever have to give up the music. Do you think it's wrong to actually want those things? I wouldn't know what I'd do, if it weren't for medicine."

"You play keyboards. You could be in a band."

"I know. But I mean, for a living."

"Well, George..." I thought about it for a moment. "No one's forcing you to stay. Or to leave. Or to do anything." I mean, really—I hadn't even figured out how I was going to straighten out my own life. "How're things with Julie?" I thought this might be the real source of trouble.

"With Julie? Oh—fine. They're fine."

But he seemed overly reticent. Or was I reading too much into it? These days, it was increasingly difficult to tell what was true and what was just me. Soon we were walking through an abandoned structure at the far end of the beach, near the water. I thought it might have once been a party room from the heyday of the Connecticut coast: alcoves embedded in the rock that could have once been showers, or some sort of kitchen. It must have been empty for years—cinder blocks crunched under our feet, the walls hid water stains, the ceiling hung awning-like over the far corner, ready to tumble at any moment. We made our way inside, stepping carefully over the barnacles with our bare feet, investigating like archaeologists. When I turned a corner, there was George, standing on an outcropping of rocks near the water, framed in my sight by two walls of cinder blocks. His back was to me. He was contemplating the Sound once again, in that way he had, hands behind his back and staring peacefully, as if waiting for a revelation—George got his instructions from so many obscure sources. And it struck me, as I looked at him, that I was thinking about George not only as a friend, but as something more. It was only for a moment—thinking of him as a man, a being with desires, a locus for others. Did he remember what I'd said to him, that day we were tripping on shrooms? And what had I really meant? I examined my feelings for George with a detail that I never would have allowed before. I felt it incumbent upon me to begin reintegrating all those stray and embarrassing moments of my life, not just those moments in the bookstores or with the pornography, but every intimate feeling or thought I'd ever suppressed. But even now, I wasn't sure what I'd meant; my feelings were tied up with his familiarity, his friendship, my ideas about who he was, about what I thought he wanted, and I wondered if it could simply be that there were different kinds of love, and different reasons for them. But I couldn't be sure, seeing as I didn't even know yet what love even was.

I was eager to get back to the others. Why had we wandered out here alone? The spot was so romantic, I thought he might have led me out here intentionally. Perhaps George was in love with *me*. Perhaps he had his own confession that he was going to make. I don't know why I thought this. If I could have these attractions, why couldn't everyone else? But George wasn't a romantic: hardly ever with Julie, so why now with me? Maybe this was all just in my mind. Did I have any real evidence? I wanted to get back to the group more than ever.

"George!" I called out to him. "It's getting late. You'll catch cold."

He walked back without a word, like a dog answering its master. "It's refreshing, isn't it? The water."

"Uh-huh, George. It sure is."

When we finally joined up with Fergie and Pete, they were in the midst of a debate.

"Look, there's DNA-directed DNA polymerase," Fergie was saying, "and DNA-directed RNA polymerase, so why couldn't there be RNA-directed DNA polymerase? It just seems logical."

Pete sat next to him, mimicking his position, wearing identical sunglasses and staring identically upward. There was something sexual in this medical language, these logic games, I could see it now. That was what the whole medico-scientific system was for. "It's called reverse transcriptase. Don't ask why, that's just what they call it. There's no such thing as RNA-directed et cetera. Look it up. You've got the wrong name."

"Are you sure? RNA-dir-DNA-ase just makes more sense, don't you think."

"You guys, let's not discuss this stuff at the beach, okay?" Julie packed up George's belongings, stuffing in towels and shirts without folding them. "You're going to give each other a mental hernia."

Thursday, and the date with Bob, came without warning. My room was a mess—old televisions, rented videotapes, cut-up photographs, newspaper articles. I searched through my closets for something interesting to wear. I didn't know how to dress, what to bring. Was this really a date? Could you have a date with another guy? Or was it more like male bonding, or a business engagement? I'd seen plenty of examples of guy-girl dates in books, on TV shows, in movies, but for this, I had nothing. I decided to wear a checkered shirt and a tie, and to stop on the way for a bottle of wine—white, for seafood. Why not make it like a commercial? That seemed the safest model.

I got to Marlou's before Bob did—I was fifteen minutes early, but still, the waiting was agony.

"Set out the plates, would you? Wait—first stir the sauce."

I took the lid off the pot. It smelled better than anything at Big Moe's: tomatoes, peppers, garlic, paprika. She'd also made hush puppies, black beans, a pie. Was Bob a vegetarian? I had all sorts of images of him: an International Male, a kid in a mohawk, a Vietnam veteran. We set out three place settings, cloth napkins, and candles. I'd never been so afraid of meeting someone before.

"Tell me more about Bob. What's he like? What's he do?" *Bob bob...bob d'bob...* the word sounded suggestive; maybe he *was* cute; maybe he was a swimmer. I was getting erect. I had to hold myself down, but here at last my senses had come to life, the everyday and the prurient inexorably mixed, the pornographic thrill of an innocent dinner party. Maybe this was how sex was supposed to be—out in the open, in the form of social congregation, rather than stolen in the dark.

"He's a dancer," she said into the plate, rearranging it slightly. "One of Janet's friends." There was a knock at the door. "Oh," Marlou said. She looked up at me and smiled. "There he is."

For a moment we just let him stand behind the door, thinking about his presence, his potential. Then he knocked again and Marlou went to answer.

I heard voices in the hall, then they walked in together. Here he was, Bob: lanky, well-dressed, pink and embryonic, like an unhatched chick, with a pair of horn-rimmed glasses sitting on a tiny, dignified beak. We shook hands; his was warm and squishy, and I too quickly let go.

Marlou made the introductions. Bob smiled, although he seemed nervous, overreacting, his expression a bit exaggerated. He took off his jacket. Marlou left the room to hang it up. Bob and I just kept smiling at each other, not saying anything. This was harder than I'd expected. Bob wasn't anything near as photogenic as I'd imagined. This was a date? It was like meeting your drill instructor, your aerobics partner. Marlou relieved the tension by coming back in the room.

"Smells good, Marlou," Bob said. I wasn't sure how well I liked his voice—a bit artificial, preassembled.

"Boys, tonight you're having Marlou's finest creole."

"It's her specialty," I said. "She has the tomatoes." Marlou and I chuckled; Bob didn't, missing the joke. So I'd won the first round: I'd teamed up with Marlou before Bob could.

At dinner, Bob became animated, more confident, talking about dance steps—after dessert he got up and showed us some. Marlou put on some popular dance beat; Bob started jerking a hand, let the movement spread up his arm, then his whole body. It was like a parody of a Fifties musical, only Bob's physique was wrong for the part. But he didn't care: Soon he was folding his arms, doing the Moonwalk, kicking his legs, and at one point I thought he'd knock over Marlou's bird cage. He wasn't embarrassed by how absurd he looked; he drew attention to his physicality and let other people be embarrassed for him.

I didn't know what it implied, exactly, that Marlou thought we'd be perfect for each other.

After all that activity, he was sweating. We sat on the couch, and Marlou brought iced tea—we were all ready to cool off. Marlou laughed too much, I thought, while Bob told us stories about famous dancers, dance steps, Alvin Ailey, Dancing for AIDS. Then, as if a switch had been flipped, they both aimed their attention at me.

"Paul, where're you from?"

"Indiana."

Bob nodded sagely, Marlou too. I could have said "Neptune" and they'd have nodded the same way. Bob kept making these inside references—Judy Garland, Bronsky Beat, Miss Thing—the gist of which I understood, but whose significance largely escaped me. It wasn't as though he was being intentionally campy—just trotting out the lingo, for my edification, I guess. In between he asked me questions. "Marlou told me you work with her at Big Moe's?"

"Yep," I answered.

Bob kept probing until Marlou excused herself to use the bathroom. Then he leaned forward with what he really wanted to ask. "You know, if you'd like to see any books or things, I've got a bunch back at my apartment." He pushed up his glasses—the one thing Bob wasn't comfortable with was his face; it couldn't settle on any particular expression. I felt a bit sorry for him. If this was his attempt at seducing me, he needed a lot more practice. Jesus—already I knew that, and I'd only been gay for two weeks.

At least, though, I felt safe around him.

"Books?"

"About homosexuality. Coming out. Anything. Newspaper articles. I've got all these cutouts from *Time*, every article they've ever run, ten, I think. Of course, that doesn't count the stuff on AIDS."

"Sure, that'd be interesting."

"You could come over now, if you wanted." He was leaning toward me, barely concealing his expectations, but he *did* have a legitimate reason for inviting me, and besides, I wanted to get to know him; he was gay, like me. I wanted to investigate this new commonwealth, whatever its nature might be—to make up for lost time. Still, between my limpid reaction and his blunt proposal, it would take some deft diplomacy to get me out of the sexual obligation I'd somehow engendered. What had I done, I won-

dered—had I led him on, encouraged him? I'd worn a nice shirt,
a stylish tie, attempting to express my new awareness of myself as
an object of definite mass, potential interest, but I hadn't thought
it overly risqué. Sexual games between people were something
new to me. How could you encourage someone in the space of
an hour? He was the one doing all the moving, the talking, the
looking; I was simply sitting there. I couldn't figure out what I
was missing, what I should have been doing instead. My knowledge
of desire had reached its limits, the limits of intellectualization,
rationalization—which, I was about to learn, in the case of desire,
were approached rapidly.

Marlou came back into the room carrying a plate. Bob leaned
back and smiled. Marlou smiled. I smiled at the two of them.
Everyone was so fucking happy, what were they hiding? "I'd love
to see them, Bob," I said. Which was true—I was dying to see
those articles; it didn't matter to me so much whether I saw Bob
again or not. "But not tonight. Some other time?"

"So what have you boys been talking about?" Marlou asked,
in the most matter-of-fact tone of voice, munching on leftover
seafood. "Making plans to be naughty?"

Bob called me the next day. "Marlou gave me your number,
Paul," he said instead of hello. "Hope you don't mind." He told
me that I should come over and see the articles. I said I couldn't—
I was about to leave for work.

"How about tomorrow?"

I worked tomorrow, too.

"Your next day off?" The voice came puppy-doggish through
the phone, all eager to please and difficult to refuse.

Sunday, I said.

"Great!" He hung up. So Sunday it was.

So I had no backbone. So what else was new?

I clicked the receiver and dialed Marlou. "Tell me, about
Bob . . . does he have a boyfriend or anything?"

"No . . ."

"Has he . . . talked to you about me at all?"

"Paul, excuse me. . . ." Her voice changed suddenly. "There's
someone at the door. Can I call you back later?"

She hung up. So there it was: I was in the clutches of a conspiracy.

□   □   □

Sunday I went over to Bob's. I knew that when I got there, his plans to seduce me would succeed. It wasn't that I outright intended to let him have his way—it was simply that I was so horny, I knew that once things got started, I'd go to bed with just about any member of the male sex. Marlou and Bob must have known that, too. Just the idea of having sex with a guy, no matter who he was, was enough to give me chills. I'd fallen in love with the abstraction "men," and half the human race qualified, including Bob. So I wore a tight-fitting T-shirt and jeans, the ones I liked to wear when I masturbated. If I was going to play out this fantasy, I figured I'd make the most of it.

After I hit the buzzer, he opened the front door of his apartment building, also wearing jeans and a tank top. So we were already half-undressed. "I'm glad you're here."

"Of course."

This second time seeing him, here in front of me, I decided that he wasn't unattractive, just unspectacular. He qualified as a "man," but not overly. I could tell from the unassuming way that he let me lead him back to his apartment that he was destined to be forever unknown, an admirer, a part of the audience. His place was small, meticulously decorated, not unlike my place, and the similarity was disheartening. Maybe I was him, had the potential to be like him, or was becoming him—and he was the thing I'd always been most scared of becoming.

Or maybe not. My feelings about him began to modify. Maybe I shouldn't have been so quick to dismiss his gentler qualities. Maybe "male" could be redefined. He had a softness, a fragility to his limbs, despite their obvious durability. He hung up my coat, offered me a glass of water, brought out the shoe box. He was certainly gracious, well-mannered, polite. He sat on the floor and bent his legs like a Gumby doll, while I flipped through his collected books and magazines. I felt slightly embarrassed for him, having to read over my shoulder, waiting for me to be impressed, or exonerated, by whatever it was he had to show me. He was as much of an amateur at this as I.

Why was I here, was it just for sex, was that what we were waiting for? That certainly seemed cheap, reductive: There had to be more to our motivations than that. But what? I didn't know Bob that well, did I? He might have been someone I'd met on one of my nightly excursions, a lonely boy walking across campus. Meeting him through Marlou didn't change his foreignness—he simply came with a reference.

Bob told me that he thought spinal posture was the key to relaxation; he wanted to give me a back rub to demonstrate, but I declined. So he talked about growing up in New Haven, how he'd never had a best friend; going to SCSU, how they didn't have many good opportunities to dance, and so on, each experience adding to a litany of alienation. Yet he seemed stronger and more sure of himself than he had the week before. We were on his turf now. "You have good gluteal muscles, Paul; you should wear tighter pants. Not those baggy jeans straight guys wear. And I can give you the name of my stylist." He wanted to mold me. I didn't know—maybe I'd let him.

Bob reminded me of a whole childhood world, one I'd thought I'd long left behind—familiar the way all the clothes and toys and stuffed animals from your childhood are familiar, even years later. He was the scared, incompetent child I'd started shunning so long ago, the artistic, unself-conscious, unneurotic self, the faggot in myself that back in third grade I'd already started to shun—and from kindergarten through medical school, nothing about that had ever changed. As the evening wore on, I felt more and more comfortable with him.

"So what should we do now?"

I shrugged. "Whatever."

"Want to watch a video?" he suggested.

"What kind of video?"

He nodded as if I'd said yes, got up and turned on the TV in the bedroom. I followed him in. His television was a mini black-and-white portable, but he had a standard-size VCR underneath, both of them sitting on the dresser. He took a video out of its sleeve and slipped it in. On the tube, the words *Young Stallions* appeared over a Montana sunrise.

I'd seen this one before. The whole supposed story line played out in my mind in an instant. The production values were going to be lousy. They couldn't even get the flesh tones right. We hadn't gotten through the credits, and already I was bored: I was wondering how much money there was to be made in this profession, through how many hands these tapes circulated, those things you think when the fantasy isn't working.

We sat on the bed, watching the seduction scenarios playing out on the screen. Usually, when I watched the videos alone, I stripped off my clothes, played with myself till I came. Bob must have had the same habit—unable to do anything in front of me, he shifted slightly in his seat. Taking his cue, I shifted in mine, but I was too embarrassed to move any further. We watched the whole movie sitting unmoving on the bed, until we were strained, taut, panting. We tried to keep up a pretense of civility. I supposed I wasn't bored *completely*. I suppose you couldn't be. The scenes from the television flickered in a tiny rectangular reflection in Bob's glasses.

After Act III, he stood up and stretched. He started coming toward me. I knew what he was doing; I was nervous... I didn't want to stop it, make any motion that would disturb his momentum. This could be my big moment, the highlight of my life. He put his hand on my leg, started rubbing slowly, working his way up.

I shifted slightly—jerked away, then made the effort to sit still. He took it as a sign of disinterest rather than apprehensiveness.

"If you don't want..."

"Sorry, I..."

I'd made up my mind during the movie to be interested. Rather, as Marlou might have said, my dick had made up my mind for me. I moved my leg closer to him. Bob didn't know how to interpret the movement. We were going to have to talk to each other if we wanted to get anywhere.

He took off his glasses and rubbed his eyes. "You've never done this before?"

I shook my head, quickly. "Should I... take something off?"

He stood there, looking at me with his naked eyeballs, thinking. "Can I kiss you?"

I considered it, then nodded. He bent over—his face came up against mine, his warm breath enveloping my nostrils, his lips mine. A bit livery—I started thinking about corpses, corned beef. This just wasn't the scene as I'd always anticipated it.

His whiskers brushed against me, both stimulating and off-putting—yet it only took a moment, and that ambivalence was overcome, blown away, and I was taken over by years of pent-up fantasy, imploding, solidifying into a realness in my hands, in all my six senses at once. A man in my arms—for real.

"I know," I said, standing up. I pulled off my T-shirt. "Let's jack off." I was in control now, undressing, and he followed my lead. This was how it'd have to be with Bob. I wanted our sex to be hygienic—if I took the lead, we'd stay away from everything unsafe. I'd have my fun; so would he.

Bob undressed. He was hairless all the way down to his belly button; but the dancing could be seen in his arms and thighs, the cords in his shoulders. So I satisfied myself with these.

We sat back down on the bed, naked, our two red erections pointing at each other. Our clothes lay in two neat piles on the floor. So this was it—what I'd been waiting for, what I'd been dreaming about: a naked man in my bed. Or me in his. He wasn't as perfect as my fantasies; one of the basic disappointments of life, to be sure, but I was twenty-three and I'd never experienced this particular disillusionment before. He didn't see well without his glasses...the presence of this nude boy was partly clinical, partly exciting, but the whole experience was much more adulterated than I would have expected. I stared at his penis—the only one, other than mine, that I'd ever seen erect in person—and stroked the skin on his stomach. I had no urge to fling myself at him, but the sensation, the warmth, of another human being—that was all I really needed, as if there were some vital energy transferred by the contact. He smiled while I touched him. The intensity increased, I began to hear voices inscribing themselves on his body....

you know, you've got beautiful eyes...

        ...orbicularis oris, orbicularis oculi

do you want me to take something off?...

        ...the ductus deferens and the rectal vericocities

spinal posture is the key to relaxation...

...reflect the pectoralis major and remove the clavipectoral fascia

haven't we met somewhere before?...

...Jakob-Creutzfeldt disease, a rare subacute spongiform encephalopathy that results in dementia, myoclonic jerks, and often ataxia

lick my nipples; ooh baby, do it to me...

...I'm not going to do it, you do it. Uh-uh, it's your turn to do it.

I explored his body thoroughly, forgetting any misgivings I might have had, any qualms whatsoever. It was a perception multiplied—as if we'd plugged in, doubled, a circuit of energy generating mass, matter generating mind. There was no separation anywhere. But so far it was only motion, me rocking back and forth, and a little sloppy mouth action; I hadn't gotten anywhere specific. I pulled back to look at him, to jerk him off. I sighed, and the heat went down. We faced each other, crossed arms, and went to work—like a bride and groom linking arms for the champagne.

I came right away, and then Bob. But we were still hard. We continued exploring each other for another three or four hours, producing sensations that I'd never even been able to imagine.

When we finally finished, Bob cleaned up with a sock while I put on my clothes. I felt an unintentional affection for him, after what we'd done. We said that we'd be "friends," whatever that meant. But I had no desire to sleep with him again.

I downed my glass of water and told him I had to be going.

"It's three in the morning. Why don't you stay?"

"I really couldn't."

We argued about it for a minute, but he wasn't one to strongly force his opinion. "Well, thanks for coming, Paul," he said eventually, with a straight face. "Call me tomorrow. I mean, later today. Or whenever you feel like it. I'll be here."

"I know."

He gave me all the books and clippings I'd come over for originally. We walked solemnly to the door—his apartment backwards: kitchen, den, foyer—like emerging from the womb.

At the door he put his hand on my arm. "I had fun tonight," he emphasized, while rubbing my arm, as if to keep me encouraged. "For a beginner, you sure know what to do." He gave me a little peck on the cheek, a good-bye kiss. Now he was being my aunt, my dotty aunt Bob.

It was that kiss more than anything that made me feel tainted, feminine, nauseated; I wanted to take the whole evening back. But then, I'd gotten what I'd wanted, hadn't I? I had no excuses anymore. I carried home his shoe box full of newspaper clippings, along with a dozen pamphlets and three or four books. I stayed up the rest of the night reading them, as if cramming for an exam. I couldn't put them down. I spent the whole night learning what it meant, being gay.

8

Metabolism

It took a couple days before I'd registered the full implications. Sex with another guy. Now that I'd actually done it, I'd need to research the part more thoroughly. Homosexuality had been up-welling for over twenty years in this country, still garnered the occasional exposé in the newspaper, and I knew nothing about it, intentionally; I'd been a medical student, I'd lived in an entirely different world. I found George's book titled *The Sexual Behavior of the Adolescent* and flipped through it when he wasn't home: *Roughly 67.2% of the general population has a homosexual encounter by age eighteen.* So I didn't feel too bad. I'd had less gay sex than the average heterosexual.

"Angela," I said at the restaurant, finally getting a chance to corner her. "By the way—congratulations on the wedding. . . ."

"Oh, Paul—don't think like I didn't really appreciate your advice. I just decided that there was no decision to make. I knew, as soon as I got home that night, everything would be all right."

"Yep—I know just what you mean."

After work, I reread everything Bob had given me, this time thinking: Wow, this is me. He had a hundred pieces of information, clippings from *Time* and *Newsweek*, *Firsthand* and *Outloud*, pamphlets, condoms, newspapers, bibliographies. Inside: faggots since the Middle Ages, burning at stakes, mental institutions; families falling from grace, suicide; lesbian torture-cures, witch hunts. But not everything was bleak: In A.D. 300 gay marriage was legal; in the Bible Jonathan loved David; in 1969 gay was good—there'd been druids, priests; a movement in Germany that was the forerunner of gay liberation. A ton of information was available—you just had to hit the sweet spot.

I checked out twenty books from the library and scanned them all in an evening. Just like Stryer and Clemente, they were textbooks of a sort, positing their own elaborate structures, organelles, microprocesses. Only this time, I had a vital interest in understanding them. Apparently, my fortunes rested upon a precarious balance: The great evils—theocracy and latent Victorianism—still lurked, manifesting themselves sporadically throughout the Popular Culture. It was me against the topology of a whole millennium. The books and scraps were talismans, records, sealing each bit of evidence irrevocably into the paper, paste, and ink of history, all the more persuasive for having the status of *the past,* the time before this moment—my Gay A.D. 0. I put the stuff under my bed and slept on it, fingering the chapters as I would a rosary, three times a day.

Even just turning on the TV, I was assaulted: community-service propaganda specials, videos, documentaries, everything I might have ignored before. All those good-looking, querulous demonstrators, locking arms to be toted away by the police—even if they were from the preposterous bowels of Manhattan. I wouldn't have kicked a single one of them out of my bed. I obviously had a lot of catching up to do. I obviously had to stop changing the channels.

So the next morning, I got up early, dressed, and waited for George to come out of the shower. I was going to add my own small motion to the movement. In forty-eight hours, I'd been politicized. It was a mental revolution—a revelation. The answers and accusations were so simple, so self-evident. You had to speak up, be an advocate for yourself—that's what the books all said. It amazed me that I'd never seen that before.

After he went into his room, I knocked and followed him right in.

He sat sideways on his chair, pulling up socks.

"George, have a minute? I've got something to talk to you about."

"I'm in a rush. I'm late for class." He jumped up and combed his hair, not even looking in the mirror. His clock said 9:01. It was a twenty-minute walk to the medical school. So we both grabbed a Pop-Tart, and I followed him out the door.

So how was I going to bring it up? George seemed distant today, not as attentive as he was usually. Maybe it wouldn't faze him. Maybe it wouldn't be any big media event. Maybe, though—and this is what I was hoping most—my honesty would entice him to be, in turn, more open with me.

As we walked, he discussed his rodent research, how it was his job to inject the rats' brains with dye and finally to slice them like pâté on the micrometer; his professor was searching for the neural pathway that would somehow unlock the secret to the "pseudo-psychotic behavior" the rats acquired when they were "reared in isolation with periodic electric shocks applied randomly" as opposed to the "merely neurotic" behavior observed when shocks came "at regular two-hour intervals." George told me he liked the rats, that he wanted to save one and make it a pet. But his professor was, of course, against this. Soon we were at YMS, walking up the larger-than-life marble steps before the rotunda. *Lux-et-Veritas* over our heads—no matter how much the path of my life diverged, the sign was always there over the entrance to the medical school, proclaiming "the eternal verities." How impermanent and subjective they seemed to me now.

The building was empty—just a guard at the desk. "I suppose everyone's already in their lectures, being indoctrinated." That was me, being political. I hadn't even realized that classes had started again. My internal clock had de-synchronized from school time. There were five different halls leading off from this rotunda: Physiology, Neuroscience, Anatomy, Library, Auditorium. The place seemed more of a maze than when I'd first encountered it. On the bulletin board over the north wall, people had posted papers for Thanksgiving parties, ski trips to Vermont, a ride to Boston by September 15th, now past. The rituals of medical education marched on—despite my no longer being a part of them.

"Look, George—I don't know if you've ever thought about this, but I bet you that at least thirty of the people in this building right now are gay."

"Hmm. I guess so."

"Well... I'm one of them." There—it was out.

He considered it for a moment. He wrinkled his brow. "You know, I have a friend from high school who's gay."

"There you go."

"Yep."

Silence.

"Okay. No sweat. So, did you send in the check for the phone bill this week?"

"Uh . . . I think so."

"You'd better check on it. Look—I've got to run. I'm really late." And he disappeared into Neuroscience.

So there it was. No Cardinal O'Connor, William F. Buckley, heterosexist response. No torrid sexual confession. Nothing. I wasn't sure what to do. I stood for about five minutes, staring down the hall where he had gone. Then I walked home, wondering what the apartment might look like when I got there, alone, with no option but to turn on the TV.

I had the rest of the day off, and I spent it fending off feelings, more than political, that I couldn't quite describe: Every love song on the radio caught my ear, every two-cent televangelist roused my ire. Even Oprah was annoying. It wasn't so much George, but my overreading in general. I interpreted everything as a personal threat. I went for a walk. I caught myself not just watching the boys on campus, but actively searching them out—hanging out on open lawns and library steps, where groups of them were likely to accumulate. I sat and stared, eating an ice cream cone, melted cream running in sticky rivulets between my phalanges, daydreaming of forcible assault. Theirs or mine—it wasn't quite clear.

I spotted a particularly attractive specimen and followed him across Old Campus. He was wheeling a bicycle. His physical form—face and body—was so incredible, so absorbing, I couldn't even retain a sense of him as a real being. It was impossible to get an impression of what he looked like: not too muscular, not too tall, not too handsome. Just right. I could only think of him in the negative—what remained was the absolute, the not-known, the perfect. Although I'd have to say that he probably had definite qualities—a dark complexion, at least, and hair on his chest.

He wheeled his bike into a convenience store. I waited outside. I'd never so blatantly lusted after someone before. I was making progress. Or was I? Hell, I told myself, what should I care how queer I acted? In Greece, it'd been butch to be queer; boy-love was recommended for everyone—they'd invented the Olympics, for God's sake. So get with the program.

When he came out of the store, I followed him a few blocks more. Then I forced myself away. It was the same obsessed fascination as when I'd followed Jeff, when I'd wandered the midnight streets. Only now, I wasn't afraid to be acting it out fully, and in broad daylight. I'd learned to enjoy myself. I'd learned to make it ordinary. Although, to be sure, part of the thrill had always been in being surreptitious, in playing the game—but now, the rules were changing seemingly faster than I could keep pace with.

"So," George said to me that night. "Are you cooking dinner, or is it Julie and I?"

"Me. It's me. Afghan lamb curry and brown rice. Just like you wrote on the refrigerator last week."

We didn't talk about—you know—the subject. While I scraped carrots, Julie spread out three different books over her lap and George relaxed on the sofa with some manuscripts. I made a mess, cleaned it, and then it was like every other meal we'd ever shared—dishing out food, munching, talking about art, talking about school. Maybe more about school than about art. The three of us washed dishes together afterward.

"Paul—George told me what you told him," Julie said while George was back in the living room. "Are you in a relationship?"

"If you could order a relationship through the mail, and they delivered it Federal Express, I'd be in one now."

"Well..." She dried one of the plates and stacked it in the cabinet. "Maybe we can think of someone."

"Maybe." I turned to her. "Oh, Julie...you guys are my favorite people in the world. You know that?" And I gave her a hug.

"What's that for?"

"For, you know—being you."

She looked surprised. "Well—that's who we are."

"So who do you have in mind?"

"No one...no one especially."

"Tease...."

Later that night, while George and Julie slept noiselessly on their side of the wall, I turned my stereo down low and wrote notes in my diary, creating a record of all the men I'd followed that day. I catalogued their physiques and then entered them into the data base on my computer. I pulled out some album jackets to read the lyric sheets, looking for secret messages addressed to me. I found a couple. I went into the living room and watched late-night TV, crying at reruns of "I Love Lucy" and "Three's Company"; they seemed so poignant. I felt inexpressibly happy, sad, satisfied, anxious. I watched three episodes of "The Honeymooners" and pined for unreasonable things: winter, old age, Puccini, childhood, a house on Fire Island. If I hadn't known better, I'd have said that I'd just entered puberty.

I decided it was time to make a new video, one of Marlou and her girlfriend. Something more outspoken and direct than anything I'd done before. A full-fledged project had already started to develop in the back of my mind. I just needed some raw footage, something on tape. What I wanted most now was something provocative. So the next afternoon, we took my camera to Broadway and set it up on a tripod in the middle of the sidewalk.

Everything, now, happened to me in a matter of days, even an aesthetic revamping.

"Okay," Marlou said. "How should I stand? Should I throw back my head?" She tilted her head back and let her spikes whistle dauntingly in the breeze, as if that red tuft were a long skein of hair. "How about Janet? Maybe the wounded-vixen look? Go for it, honey."

She cued Janet with an outstretched arm: Janet tried pouting, but the expression of "trying" outweighed the one for "vixen"— it was obvious she didn't have the innate acting talent.

"I don't know about this drama thing, Marlou. Why don't you just smooch naturally. Like I'm not even here."

"You mean like there aren't a thousand curious pedestrians walking by staring at what the three of us are doing?"

I looked at her through my viewfinder. The tape was rolling, red light blinking in the corner. "Yeah. Like that." God, she looked so tough and tall in that leather jacket and those ear cuffs—and she was right about the pedestrians, who were staring at her and Janet, and then quizzically (or else meaningfully) at me, as they entered stage left, passed along the sidewalk, then disappeared one by one off the frame. I think this—the onlookers' intrigued expressions—was actually the shot I wanted most.

"Okay!" I announced. "Action." She took Janet dramatically in her arms, bent over, and they pressed their lips together for a good thirty seconds. Tape rolling. Afterward, Janet wiped her mouth and laughed; she had on a purple T-shirt from Provincetown and her own homemade jewelry. They weren't professionals, but they were having fun.

There was going to be a whole series of these: I taped Marlou and Janet kissing on buses, in parks, in restaurants. I taped the spectators. I taped myself, talking about what I thought of all this taping. I didn't know, exactly, what it was leading up to, but I had an inkling—and I knew that I'd use it for my application to film school; I was going to submit something completely subversive, something that could shake up the world. Or at least the members of the review committee.

I went to a local barber and had them cut my hair. "Give me a flattop," I told her. "Something blue-collar and punk. Whatever you like." It was time for my personal style to start matching my professional content.

She clacked an attachment to the razor and sent it across my scalp, whacking off hair in great swaths.

Afterward, I looked at my reflection in my car mirror. I ran my hand through the bristles. It was vicious, extraneous, sensual. I looked cooler than George. We'd belong in those punk bars now.

I bought a pair of pretorn jeans and wore a bandana Gumby-style on my head. I bought a pair of imitation Ray Ban sunglasses. They were President-Elect, Amateur-Gay-Shock-Video-Directors'-Guild glasses. I designed myself completely in my mirrors—modeling, sculpting, putting every hair and nuance in its place. I was working on a completely different image. I was a chameleon, a reptile, shedding my skin, taking on new colors, new form.

"All right, Paul," George said when he saw me. "I like it. I really do."

But I could tell he was skeptical.

Two weeks later, I got a call from Bob. I hadn't talked to him since that crucial night. I'd been so self-occupied, I'd nearly forgotten about him.

"Paul. It's been a while. How are you?"

"Fine." I pulled on the cord, chewed it to release nervous energy, which had nothing to do with Bob. I had constant vital energy now, tension at a premium, and I'd taken to releasing it any way I could: pacing, chewing, clicking, winding. Nuclear bombs could have been going off, and I wouldn't have noticed.

"I haven't heard from you."

"I know." My words came out mumbled, from the chewing.

"You haven't lost my number, have you?"

"Nope. It's sitting right here on my desk." I opened the flap of paper, which I hadn't touched since the night Bob had given it to me. There was his phone number, already fading.

"I don't want to bother you."

"That's okay."

He paused—was he going to ask me something or not? I was in a hurry; it was my night off, and I was about to start dinner.

"Well, I called to see what you were doing. I thought maybe you'd like to go to a movie."

"A movie?"

"Yeah."

"What kind of movie?"

"Anything you like. Anything you'd want to see would be fine with me."

"Sure," I said. "Okay. Why not?" I sat down, thinking about it seriously only after I'd committed myself. I *did* like going to movies. But with Bob? Was that wise? I didn't see the harm in it; I had nothing else planned that night. But I knew I was getting into a situation that I'd regret.

After Bob opened his door, he stared at my haircut for about thirty seconds, then finally invited me in. He didn't say anything, and I didn't ask. Better not to know. So instead, we talked about the movies. He suggested several esoteric foreign films, but I insisted on a different one, a Hollywood blockbuster called *Aliens Take Miami* that I'd been dying to see for weeks. He hadn't seen it, and I got the sense he had no desire to, but he didn't try to haggle. He told me he didn't enjoy movies involving sex (hetero), Florida (violence), or aliens (the symbolic kind). I assured him the title was a red herring, but he'd turn out to be right, of course— although I'd probably known that beforehand.

At the theater, Bob shuffled nervously for a few moments, then made a confession. "I know you aren't that interested in me. No—no, don't protest." We were standing at the front of the popcorn line, or what vaguely resembled a line. "I'm not totally dense. You haven't called me once since that night. But sometimes these things take time. I just want you to consider everything. Don't make any decisions too hastily."

What decisions? The concessionaire handed us our drinks, smiling. Who knew what the smile hid; maybe he'd overheard Bob's peroration. I didn't care—this was my life. "Okay, Bob. No hasty decisions. But I . . . I think we're going to be late for the previews."

Had I been on Bob's mind all this time? How appalling—maybe he'd been waiting all these weeks for me to call. Maybe he'd rearranged his plans for me, and I'd let him down, without even knowing. I felt like a rat. I wanted to kick myself. I'd never realized that I could unintentionally so affect someone else. God, what a responsibility, if everything you did got caught in the web of other people.

I couldn't concentrate on the movie; I could only think about what he'd told me. Poor Bob. Had he no one better to occupy himself with? When the lights came up, I decided I'd better be as straightforward as possible, before the misunderstanding got out of hand. "Bob, look, you don't think that we've been dating or anything, do you?"

The lady in front of us turned around, looked at who'd spoken—a blank look, like a wall—then turned around again, to shuffle out with the crowd. My attitude was the same as with the concessionaire; I didn't care anymore what people thought.

"Well, no, not exactly. I wouldn't say it was official. But what was the night we spent at my place?" This was something like a line from the film we'd just seen.

A mistake, I wanted to say, but wisely didn't. "Bob, I want to be your friend. I think it's safe to say that much. There's a lot you can tell me about . . . you know, dating." It still seemed reductive to always apply the word *gay*—even though I well knew I was supposed to. "But I don't know about feelings. I think we should leave feelings out of this for a while."

"Easy for you to say . . ."

"I just don't know anything about *having* feelings yet. I don't know what you'd call what I feel about you, or even if I feel anything."

"You need time, Paul. That's all. Friendship is often the best way to build a relationship."

"Maybe." But I wasn't sure. Platitudes like that always sounded too handbookish to me. I doubted that all the time in the world would make me fall in love with Bob. Whatever "falling in love" meant. Somehow, I still didn't think I'd quite expressed what I'd intended to say.

We were just about the last ones left in the theater. The ushers were coming down the aisles, gathering up empty boxes and cellophane. Bob put both hands on the seat in front of him and stood up.

"There *is* something you can help me with, though," I said.

"What's that?" He sat immediately back down.

"I'm working on a tape . . . a 'True Gay Love' sort of thing. It's for my school applications. And I was wondering if there might be any demonstrations or marches coming up or anything. Something to get a picture of. Something to make an impact."

"Gay Pride isn't till next June. That's all I know about."

"Hmmm." I rubbed my chin. "Nothing before that? That's quite a while."

"When did you come out, Paul? Two weeks ago?"

"All right, don't get funny. It's just that, once I decide to do something, I don't hold anything back."

He thought about this for a second. Now we were the only patrons there, and they were cleaning up our row, picking up our litter. Finally Bob gave me his assessment: "Paul, I think you should ease into this a bit more gently. You don't want to be going off the deep end. Take it from me. Really."

"Don't worry, I'm not going off any deep ends." Was that what I was doing? But I thought Bob was talking about something completely different. I thought he was talking about Dax. "Come on. Let's go for some ice cream."

"Ice cream? Sure."

We walked, not talking, to one of those famous nearby stores, where we sat to spoon up our scoops. I still couldn't get all this stuff off my mind, all these esoteric and urgent social remedies. Bob, I thought, had to be the best person to discuss it with. After all, if you couldn't talk politics to the guy who'd given you your first hand job, who could you talk to?

"There's just so much to do, Bob. So much reeducation. You should know what I mean. The public. I was watching the Christian Broadcasting Network last night. I thought I was going to have a coronary. Do people really take that stuff seriously?" As if I were the expert. But I really did believe that my experience, however brief, counted for something.

"Huh-mmmm," he said, the ice cream in his mouth. He swallowed. "You like self-torture?"

"No ... no ... it's just ... arrrghh ..." I threw up my hands and grasped my head. It felt ready to burst. I couldn't contain it anymore. "Whose country do they think this is, anyway?"

"Theirs?"

"It's just too weird. I must be going through some sort of neurotransmitter adjustment. I've never taken anything like this so personally before." I really did think Pat Robertson wanted to assassinate me personally, if he ever got the chance. I'd never worried about any of those fringe-group salesmen before. I didn't know—maybe I was hyperventilating. "Okay, okay. Maybe I just need to meet some progressive people."

"Progressive, Paul? In New Haven? Nah ..."

Even as I sat there, talking calmly, I was winding myself up, being driven by this vision-force that pressed unremittingly against my inner eye, a cylinder of perception that had been developing ever since I'd told Marlou I was gay. My vision was a light, a truth, illuminating every corner of the world. The light drew me, comforted me, but the cylinder was also a filter, polarizing each atom into a binary opposition: spin up or spin down. Every action had become simple to interpret, as good or bad, progressive or un-, because there was only the one standard now by which I thought it worth measuring anything. And just sitting there doing nothing more than talking about it was most definitely un-.

"Oh, Bob. Let's just go. I've got to get some sleep. I think I've had three hours in the last three days." My watch said it was only nine forty-five. I just didn't know what schedule I was on anymore.

"Sleep? Sleep—sure. Sounds good. Mind if I take my ice cream along?" He carried the cup out the front door, eating as we walked, mumbling every response. We were heading straight back to my apartment, out Broadway to Orange Street and then north, through campus, to the burbs.

"It's not like I'm tired or anything. I've just got to go to bed."

"Uh-hmmm ..." He swallowed another spoonful. How much of that ice cream did he have left? He was certainly taking his time. "So will I get to see you again?"

"Sure. Again. As friends."

"As friends. Right. Like we agreed."

But I was hardly listening. I was occupied with my vision—

how it penetrated the world of mere appearances, saw into the most remote of intentions, the ulterior nature of everything, even things I randomly encountered on the street as we walked: hand-bills, movies, diners, ice cream flavors. These subjects, if framed and juxtaposed properly, could surely reveal their inherent good-ness or badness, could be *de-mystified,* based on a scale starting with my own desires as the absolute good (since this was the re-referencing that I'd realized I could—that I should—make). Organizing or reorganizing the world would be a matter of math-ematics . . . that is, morality. Look, see, and circumscribe the prob-lem.

"Good night, Bob," I said, but I didn't even notice when he actually left my side. I was thinking about my camera. That was it, the answer—what I was meant for. It would be the instru-ment for performing this subtraction, leaving the truth for the world. It would be the witness, the testimony, the technology—the *oeuvre* of my body and mind, free to transcend the triviality of individual circumstances. The disparate subjects were begin-ning to coalesce for me—not just the homosexual public affec-tion, but everything. I'd put together a great Enunciator, a magnificent and thorough Talmud. Something with which people could visualize their lives.

But first, I'd need to buy a video editor/enhancer and stereo dubber, with a bypass switch and auto-fader. I had a few tools already, but people's tastes today were pretty sophisticated. You weren't going to impress anyone if you couldn't even do a prop-er mix.

I couldn't even contemplate all the equipment I'd need even-tually. My savings account (the money clip under the socks in my dresser) had only thirty-six dollars. I'd already spent a fortune on tapes, a TV, another used VHS machine. So I'd have to make do with imperfect jump cuts until I could afford the editor. And even that wouldn't get me, ultimately, to where I wanted to be. I'd reached another limit: What I needed were funds, or connections, or something. This medium wasn't cheap.

In the meantime, I'd have to content myself with collecting raw footage. I'd collect as much as I possibly could. I'd log it and put it in storage. The Talmud itself would come later.

I began by posting mysterious messages on the kiosks around campus.

Do not despair. Stop Dancing in the Dark. Listen to your inner voice. You can be stronger. Call the gay info-line: 555–8927.

I'd station myself nearby, and film people as they stopped to read them. My words, once on paper, became an anonymous voice, an inanimate aspect of the landscape, like rocks or concrete, detached from the mind that had thought them. They became simple objects, scratches meant to produce other scratches, and I was the witness to these reactions. I zoomed in on the faces of the passers-by to catch the change in their expressions, while supplying a voice-over: *"Another member of the Eating Clubs stares at his own repression. . . . Will he go on to suppress the rest of us?"*

Was all this recording of strangers illegal? I didn't care—legal/illegal had little meaning to me at this point. I was on a higher mission. I had authority.

I'd go out at night, out wandering the streets of New Haven with my camera. I'd film buses, televisions, street signs, people reading them. I tried double exposures, split screens. I was conjugating a dialectic, a statement. On one side, two men kissing; on the other, Leona's dignified lingerie. I would show all contrasts, all the revelations. People would have to acknowledge my point of view. I'd make them.

I'd come home with pairs of cassettes, screen them till five or six in the morning, eat crackers in bed, transcribe notes to myself on the sides of cereal boxes.

"God, Bob," I said over the phone, twisting the cord. "I think I'm on to something. I think I've got a real statement here. It's coming together."

"What's coming together?"

"I don't know. I can't explain it. All I know—all I know is, I need to get more sleep."

It was at the height of this radical-arts period, what I would later dub my Vertov phase, that my parents called to announce a surprise visit. "We're going to Uncle Jake's on Long Island for Thanksgiving," Mom explained. "So we thought we'd stop in New Haven first. If that's okay with you."

"Sure, Mom," I said. How could any son say otherwise? Even one as revolutionary as I. "Is Dad coming, too?"

"We'll all three of us be there."

"Well, I'll be ready."

Since that day of reckoning in June, I hadn't dealt with my parents except for over the phone, a little more pleasantly each time, as the subject of medical school receded into the past. I should have been prepared for something like this, an ultimate reconciliation. I could imagine Mom convincing Dad of the idea over one of her pot roast and potato specials, spiced with oregano, chicken fat, paprika—the kind of meal she'd simmer for hours until the whole house smelled of it—then afterward taking off Dad's shoes, putting him in front of the television with a beer, making the suggestion while threatening to veto a visit to his extended family unless he first made peace with his immediate one. That's why she'd been the one to place the call. She had a mission of her own.

Already I envisioned the parade of horrors: Mom making Dad hug me. Dad being recalcitrant. Jenny being bored. The three of them talking about new kitchen cabinets and other home furnishings. Me being incomprehensible to the rest of them. Me finally not saying anything and letting them have their way.

It just wasn't that crucial to me anymore—my family, that I impress them. I had my own life to live. My own myths to construct. While my mom was on the phone, I suggested the idea: Why not bring a tape machine to the party? This was my job. My identity. It made sense to give them an opportunity to see me doing it.

"Video, Paul? Video what?"

"You guys. It'll be fun. I'll even edit it and send you a copy. Think of it as a memoir."

"I hate to say it, but it just might be a good idea. Your father might enjoy it."

"I hope so."

"I think so, Paul. I think it'll be a real gesture for him. That you're thinking about the family."

After I hung up, I called Big Moe's and made arrangements for dinner. That's where all the essential taping would take place. Marlou would cook, Angela wait on us, Gray bus, and so on. The tables, so to speak, would be turned. Of course, in a way, I did hope to impress them—with the service, the food, my gustatory friends, with whom I felt something of a protégé. But I wasn't being completely up-front about the video camera—the offer to send them their own version was secondary. What I really wanted was to put them in my collection, my world of the moving image, as yet another element of my haphazard documentary of the world. Their subject title: Family. To be filed between Drugs and Frats.

So call me cynical. But if they were willing to do it, my family was sure to generate some great raw footage. And how could it hurt? Besides, I really did intend to put together their own version of the tape, something they could live with themselves.

The day they arrived, I greeted them out in front of the apartment.

"Paul," Dad said, "it's good to see you"—and he gave me a hug. So I knew, right away, it wasn't as though he'd been mad at me all this time or anything. Just worried. My mother hugged me too, while Dad looked up at our apartment and frowned. He walked inside without saying a word. The rest of us followed.

"Okay," he said, looking around the living room. "It's livable." The thing was, this place was twenty times better than that rat's hole of a dorm, which he'd thought was so neat, but because it didn't promise a secure future, it wasn't romantic to him, it was just a bartender's flop, and all he saw was the cramped kitchen, the leaky sink, the paint peeling off the door frames.

George stood in a doorway, arms folded, watching us.

"George Yan Su?"

"That's me."

They all shook hands.

"So—Paul pays the rent?" Dad in his shirt sleeves and fishing hat—the ultimate tourist, and me the attraction. But I hadn't seen my family in months. And who knew, maybe they'd changed as much as I had.

"Sure, Mr. Levinson. Right on time. I'm the indigent one." (I think all my discussion about my parents' impending visit must have coached George on what to say.) "We haven't seen him around much lately, though," he added, on his own, but I couldn't argue with the truth of it.

Meanwhile, Mom inspected the "quaint design" of our miniature kitchen cupboards (wondering aloud if Sears could do a similar "treatment") while Jen checked out my record collection. "What time's dinner?" she called from my bedroom.

"Five o'clock," I yelled back.

"You cut your hair, didn't you, Paul?"

"Looks good, huh?"

They stared at me like a bunch of cows. This was my apartment. My haircut. I don't think they understood at all.

"So where's your video camera?" Jenny asked as she came out of the bedroom. "Aren't you supposed to be making a movie of us?"

"Don't worry. It's waiting at the restaurant."

Later, I met my parents at their hotel. Dad and I had put on suits and ties, Mom and Jen their best temple dresses—our standard going-out outfits. It wasn't the right kind of Yuppie/casual to after-theater vogue appropriate for the Moe, but my parents wore the same blue suit and dinner dresses to every occasion, regardless, and I wasn't about to try to inculcate them with a new sense of fashion. I drove them up to the restaurant, my ancient Honda spitting gaskets on the way, with Dad's knees in his lap and Jenny's dress getting caught in the door. But we got there in one piece and finally fell out of the car.

As for the camera, I didn't know what they would say when they actually saw it sitting there, on its tripod. I knew its physical presence was bound to be more provocative than just all my talk about it. It penetrated the atmosphere, an interloper, insectlike and science-fictiony. But when they spied it, they didn't react, they seemed to accept it as a natural part of the landscape. Angela took us to the table, carrying menus. It was only four-thirty, and the place was nearly deserted—more homey and less spectacular in the daylight. The camera equipment was already rolling (thanks to Gray), mechanisms locked in place.

"Hey, kiddo, you going to introduce me to your family?"

I introduced them.

"So this is the show?" Dad asked right into the aperture, taking notice for the first time. "Is this thing on?"

"Is this thing on?" we would see, and Dad's nose heading toward us.

Then Angela stood in front of the camcorder as she passed out the menus, and I tried to motion her away. She was too close— all we'd see would be a blurry uniform, a uniform blur. She never got the idea, but after a while, she moved around the table.

"Paul, honey, are you going to leave the camera running the whole evening?"

"Well, if I'm going to tape dinner, I don't see any other way to do it."

"Cool," Jenny said. She ate a muffin. "It's like the time you taped the TV, right?"

We all looked at Dad. Had he understood the implications?

"What?" he said, and acted surprised. "This is for posterity. The Levinson Family Eats Cajun. Maybe it'll get its own series."

"That's the spirit, Dad." It'd been too long, I thought, since we'd been on the same wavelength.

Dax came over to take our order. "Mr. and Mrs. Levinson, tonight's menu is exquisite—don't you agree, Paul?" and he winked at me. "But let me just tell you the specials...."

He prattled on, while Mom and Dad stared at the menus. Jenny was the only one whom I could see ever really enjoying a place like this, or people like this: the way the picture frames matched the color of the carpet, the way Dax flourished his pen after completing the order, bringing it in toward his body the way a baton twirler would embrace a toss. It was the first time I'd ever thought of Dax as someone possessing talents. Every touch, every detail, took practice and planning, demanded appreciation. I could see Jen maybe one day bringing a date here. She even knew what to order, while Mom and Dad contented themselves with T-bones.

"I thank you, Mr. and Mrs. Levinson, for your thoughtful selections this evening, and your choice of Big Moe's fine authentic Cajun cuisine." Dax bounced away, and we stared after him—an irrepressible ham.

"Honey," my mother said. "Is this really going to work, if everyone knows the camera is here?"

"What do you mean?"

"Maybe it would have been better to hide it, and not tell anyone. Then they wouldn't have acted any differently."

"Mom. You wouldn't have wanted me to do that, would you?"

"No. I'd have murdered you."

Dad munched thoughtfully on a cracker. "No one else is going to see this tape, are they?"

"Who else would I show it to?" But he didn't look convinced. I must have sounded a bit disingenuous. Dad could probably sense my ulterior motives. I'd forgotten how well he knew me. Sometimes that could be a problem. But I didn't think I could reasonably explain myself—the aesthetic prerogative. I thought that my family's cooperation was something, simply, that they owed me. After a lifetime of having it the other way, for a change *their* surfaces would belong to *me,* and circulate as currency in my world.

Dax passed out our salads.

"Dad—if you want me to turn it off, I will."

He looked at me, thinking. "No. No—keep it on."

So I did. The salads went calmly along, like any other night out with the Levinsons. Only we were alone. And at the same time, we were being watched by a hundred anonymous eyes, making us all super-self-conscious.

"I think it's a novel idea, Paul," my mother whispered, more for my father's benefit than anyone's. "Just like something you would think of." She put her hand to her mouth. "Oh—you don't mind that I said that, do you?"

If we were going to spend the whole evening talking about the camera, it would defeat the point.

"No, Mom. It's okay."

"Why don't you stop the tape and rewind. . . ."

"He can't do that. Right? That's not the idea."

"Right, Dad." He had always understood my intentions better than anyone. Too well, it seemed.

"No. Please, rewind it, Paul. I don't think that what I just said should be on there."

"Mom, don't worry." Already, I regretted this whole idea. I could foresee everything my family was going to say all night—it's a nice place and how's your job and what's the waitress's name again, darling? And do you like living with George? And wait, let me rephrase that. It was as if I'd already seen this show, or I was sitting at home watching the tape at the same time as I was living through it.

I concentrated on the food. The étoufée was tender and tangy, as always. But my mind wasn't too much on my palate. I didn't know what my parents thought of the steaks. They'd said they were "very good." That was what they always said about everything.

Marlou came out after we were almost finished.

"Mr. and Mrs. Levinson, I'm Marlou Toussaint, your cook tonight."

They stood up to shake her hand. Actually, my father started to stand up, then stopped, realizing he wasn't going to reach her full height.

"Your son is quite a gregarious young man."

"Indeed." They perked up at that. Anything a woman had to say by way of an innuendo was news to them. I myself wasn't sure just where she was heading.

"He's making a lot of new friends these days."

"Oh?" Mom said dramatically.

"Don't act so surprised," I told them, and glared at Marlou.

Jenny giggled and took a drink of water.

"You'd better watch out, Marla," Dad said. "Have you asked Paul how he plans to support a family?" This was apparently his idea of a backhanded joke, with a pretty firm backhand.

"I don't think I have to worry about that," Marlou said, and winked at me. Fortunately, my parents were slow enough, they wouldn't draw any conclusions.

"Well—he's basically a good kid." He sat back down and looked at me. "Paul, I have to admit—it took a lot of courage for you to leave school. I have to admit. You were right: You have to learn about the world for yourself. But I think *you* should admit, honey, now that you've been out for a while, that perhaps it was something you just needed to get out of your system?"

"Dad, let's not bring this up right now."

"Poppa," Mom whispered. "Don't spoil Paul's nice dinner."

"I'm not spoiling. I'm just asking a question."

"I like where I am, Dad. I have no plans to go back. I'm going to school for video. You know all that."

"There's video medicine. . . ."

"Can't we . . . can't we for once have a conversation about something else? Why don't we talk about René Magritte or Karl Jaspers?"

"Here we go," Jenny said. "Why don't we talk about Jenny Levinson? Has anyone thought of that?"

"Paul, Dad . . ."

"Well," Marlou said over the din, and smiled pleasantly. "I'll just head back to the kitchen now."

We stopped talking, all four of us. We knew the routine, where each line of argument was going. It was pointless to pursue it. So we went back to eating our meal in silence. If there was one thing we could all agree on, it was not making a scene.

*   *   *

"You know, Paul, your father's not lying—he really was proud of the way you stood up to him."

We were standing outside the restaurant, Mom and I, waiting while Dad and Jen used the restrooms. The meal had gone okay—I supposed, once Dad dropped the subject—although we'd never gotten into the conversation I'd wanted.

I didn't know how to respond. Mom was being confidential, which was unusual for her, and she was telling me something that I wasn't sure what to make of.

"He didn't come right out and say it, but I think he'd been pushing you for a reaction. Like tonight. So you were reacting. He just needs to understand the depth of your conviction. He's had some disappointments in his life."

"Of course—of course. I didn't mean to lose my tone of voice. I just don't want to keep having to feel like I owe him something."

"No, Paul, you needn't feel that way. Just because you've had a nice home, a nice education, all the advantages."

"I didn't mean that. . . ."

"Oh, Paul." She hugged me. "I just don't want you to forget that your father only has your best interests in mind. He'd do anything for you. I want you to understand him a little better. I don't think he's that easy to understand. Neither are you, you know."

"*I* don't even understand me, Mom. So how could anyone else?"

"It's been hard on him since Sammy died." She was getting into new territory here. She stroked my chin, lightly, as though there was something interesting about my skin. She always got touchy this way when she was being nostalgic. "Your father always had mixed emotions about my brother. Did you know that right after we all met, they ran off to Mexico?"

Of course I knew that—I'd heard the story maybe a thousand times.

"Just try to imagine your father with long hair and a poncho, drinking a bottle of Dos Equis. That was pretty startling back then, for a good Jewish young man. You know, Fred failed all his courses that semester; he ended up having to retake them over the summer. Sammy didn't have classes to worry about; he'd been back from Korea for a while and was doing door-to-door by then. He'd had most of Fred's same teachers—they were my teachers, too. He told Fred he'd arranged it so we could hand in our final papers a week late. He hadn't arranged anything, of course. That was their first falling-out. It lasted a month. Fred didn't want anything more to do with our family—he almost even broke off our engagement."

She'd never mentioned that part before. . . .

"You see, Paul, this is what I'm trying to tell you. Sammy was a big influence on your father. I think that's why they'd always been so close. They had plans you've never heard about—minerals, junkyards, political campaigns. Sammy making hundreds of dollars a week just from knocking on strangers' doors. Fred was always in awe. He was sure he could have made a fortune, that Sammy could have made them both a fortune, if only Sammy didn't lose his seriousness halfway through every deal. To be fair to Sammy, I think your father overestimated him. We who'd grown up with him had learned to take him with a grain of salt. You know how your uncle Sammy was; he couldn't pass by a racetrack or an airport without having to buy a ticket."

"I know." I couldn't help but smile at the memory.

"Well, maybe you could humor your father a little. Tell him that you're still in touch with the people at Yale. Tell him you're thinking about your future. He's worried about you. He thinks you're going to turn out like Sammy."

"Mom . . . I'm not going to lie." They knew all about my plans for school. *School to make videotapes? Isn't that what the instruction manual is for?* They hadn't been too impressed, but I thought they'd accepted it. I thought they'd appreciated school as school, whatever kind.

"Then don't lie. Just be a little more tolerant of him. Let him think you're being responsible. Even if all it takes is just a little effort on your part, it can mean a lot."

"Okay. I'll make an effort."

"Thank you, honey." She hugged me, the good old Mom hug,

full throttle. We both saw Dad and Jen coming out from the restaurant. "I just wanted you to know these things, Paul. You haven't been home for it, but I think you should be aware."

Dad walked up to us, chewing a toothpick, smiling. He ruffled my hair. His mood had totally changed. Maybe all it took was some thinking about attitudes.

"Kiddo," he said to me, putting his hand on Jenny's shoulder. "You know, I didn't mean to pick on you in there."

"It's okay. I shouldn't have snapped back at you either."

We stared at each other.

"Shake?" Dad held out his hand. When I reached for it, he grabbed me, as if taming a bear. "Aw—Paul. I should just leave you alone. You know the best thing to do with your life."

I squeezed him. "If you say so." It felt so good to be on these terms again—I'd always known he'd eventually come around.

We let go. Mom and Jenny were watching, smiling, as if they knew this was going to happen, as if this was what the whole trip had been about.

"So what are you going to do with the equipment?" he asked me.

"Leave it, for now. I'll come back for it later."

"And the tape?"

"Right here." I took it out of my pocket and showed it to him.

"Well, we'd all like to see it, I'm sure. But some other time? I think we can remember dinner at least for the rest of the evening."

"I'm sure." So my father had finally accepted my decision. And it was amazing, that it really did, after all, make a difference.

After they left town, I watched the tape in my room, logging the sequences I wanted to save. I'd stop the machine and write down the time code. I had a little book bound with a rubber band. Afterward, on my computer, I linked all these things together, I printed out a log. This was my form of calming ritual.

What a show. Here we were, on TV, The Levinson Diaries. How quaint we all seemed. Sit at the table, talk about the camera, eat our food, the whole night replayed. Jenny, Mom, Dad, Paul— each in our familiar weekly roles. Overtop, though, was something else, a ghost: Dad, not who he was. Dad younger, regressing, not belonging at that table at all—his gestures, his comments, his reaching for the garlic bread, all meaning something else, all meaning something in a vector away from *me,* as if his ghostlike subimage would superimpose and obscure the first. Mom's story had stayed with me, and it made me see our family scene in a different light. I'd never imagined it so vividly before, my father's history, even though I'd heard it since birth. Maybe, after all, our family would be more interesting from his point of view than from mine—maybe Dad's story was the real one, and *I* was the supporting player. The stories altered as they circulated, as they were retold. You couldn't reconcile the truth of them all, you couldn't use them with complete impunity and then be free of them: not unless you were Lyle Montgomery Cash, not unless you were a completely different person in every situation—no ties, no obligations, no history—because there was always an outline of who you were yesterday, following you, dogging you, wanting to hold you in. There was always an obligation engendered to someone. And Lyle Montgomery Cash was a criminal, an outlaw, a wanted man.

I sat in front of my television for hours, watching all these scenes, all these carefully logged scraps of audiovisuals. I ejected the tape of dinner, put in others from the whole past year—lamp poles, Marlou and Janet, architecture, torsos—and I saw how they, too, had different meanings than I'd first intended, loosened ghosts, wandering images that depolarized and ebbed in other directions, that scattered wherever, sometimes even contradicting the point I'd been trying to make. There was just no possibility of complete control. And it occurred to me, as I watched these things, that you could no more rightly chart the world with videotape than you could with chemical equations.

And that's how I saw, like a million stars, the infinitudes of possible points of view. The variegation of thought, the spaciousness of time—there was no need to be so didactic in my work, in my life, in my attitude about the world. There was room for us all. Even Pat Robertson. Maybe. The serendipity was more interesting, anyway. And as the pressure that I'd felt so strongly in my head for the last few months for the first time began to subside, I finally fell asleep, television talking.

I woke up to white noise and the sound of George moaning my name. He'd somehow gotten into my room. He seemed to be having some sort of crisis.

"Paul, Paul . . . oh no, oh, I shouldn't have done that. . . ."

"Done what?" I sat up in bed. It was three-something in the morning, one of those numbers on the alarm clock you hardly ever get to see. What was going on? I rarely saw George anymore, let alone found him bursting into my room in the middle of the night.

"It's not going to work. I can't find the mustard. How are you supposed to get this thing on...."

"George, what the hell are you talking about? What's going on?"

"Paul?" When the light came on, I saw that he was in his pajamas, sitting in a chair by the door. He looked so anachronistic in those clothes, like a little boy who hadn't realized he'd grown up. I hardly ever saw George after he put on those pj's; that was usually Julie's privilege alone. But she was sleeping in her own apartment tonight.

"Oh, hell," he said in a different voice, a wide-awake voice, rubbing his eyes as he sat in my chair. "I must have been having some sort of dream."

"You're telling me."

He shook his head. "It was so bizarre. What was I saying? I don't remember anymore. Something about mustard. Did we have pastrami for dinner tonight?"

I really wanted to know what he'd dreamed. He'd been mumbling about stranger things than deli items, and the dream-words still hung about the room, affecting his speech, remnants of dust and cobwebs. I watched his lips, wondering if there couldn't be something more to it that he was hiding. Here was George, wandering into my room in the middle of the night, and this seemed to be the genuine relationship I'd been cultivating all this time—not Bob, not any of the others—but this companion whose friendship might have little to do with physical attraction after all.

"It was a giant pastrami. With fourteen arms and one of those skullcaps, and it was chasing me down the block. Definitely. I remember now. I had lunch today with Julie's parents." But there was something in the offhanded, overconfident way he'd said that, something that reminded me of the white lies I used to tell, that made me think he hadn't dreamt anything like that at all.

"George, can I ask you a question?"

"Sure. Why not?"

I hesitated. Did I really want to say this? Did I really want to make it a big deal? Especially now that none of this world-change seemed so dramatically urgent anymore? I didn't know. "We've known each other for a while, haven't we?"

"Sure."

"And we're pretty good friends, wouldn't you say?"

"Sure. Best friends. Why? What's on your mind?"

"Okay. You know how I told you I was gay, and you didn't say much about it, and things just went on as they were?"

"Uh-huh."

All at once, I knew I was wrong. It was the moment of having to go through with it. But I had built up too much momentum to stop. "Well, George, it's just a sense I've been getting. When we talk, there's something going on below the surface. I don't know what it means. I think, I don't know, that maybe you're attracted to me."

Silence.

"You don't have to say anything about it, if you don't want." It wasn't as if I was in love with *him* or anything.

"Paul. That's pretty interesting." He raised his eyebrows. "At least—yeah, I can see—we usually have a meeting of the minds. But it's nothing like that."

"Uh-huh."

"I mean, I think of you as a friend. It never occurred to me that, uh ... Have I done anything to give you this idea?"

"I ... don't know."

He thought about that. He seemed to be running through a record of our relationship in his mind.

"It's just that—it's not like, from my point of view, that it's impossible."

"Well," he said finally. "I think you shouldn't worry about it."

"Sure," I said, eminently agreeable. "Of course." But I wasn't going to let go so easily. "And ... there's nothing else, then? Nothing else to it? I mean, it seems like *something's* bothering you." It just seemed so remarkable that I could understand him so well. That we could have so many of the same interests. It couldn't be that I'd simply imagined everything.

"I ... don't think I have to share everything with you, do I?"

"No," I said, surprised. "No, you certainly don't."

"Okay, then." And he stood up. "By the way. Guess who I ran into today."

"Who?"

"Your friend Dr. Sparrow."

"Oh . . ." I wasn't ready to think about Sparrow. It wasn't as if I'd left medical school because of him, but I could see how, from a certain point of view, it might look that way. And I didn't want to have to address that misperception. It seemed inevitable that George and Dr. Sparrow would meet up. They might even have been conspiring about me behind my back.

"He says you should give him a call."

"Of course he would. Actually, George, I'd like to. . . . Maybe I could even get a recommendation from him." I hadn't really thought, these days, of getting in touch with him. I hadn't thought much about Yale at all. George took out a piece of paper and laid it on my desk. It was Sparrow's home phone number.

I stared at it. Maybe it was, after all, time to start reviving contact with my past. Maybe this was the sort of thing my mother had had in mind. I pinned the paper to my corkboard.

"George?"

"Yeah?" He stopped, stood in my doorway.

"I've been listening to the new Agnostic Front."

"You've got it?"

"Yeah . . ."

"I didn't know it was out."

I got out of bed and loaded the CD player for him. It clanked a few seconds, and then they came on, manufacturing their industrial noise and jackhammer guitars.

"Fantastic band, man," George said, closing his eyes and sailing with the groove. " 'Victim in Pain.' 'Toxic Shock.' Classics."

"I don't know. I'm learning to like it. I'm learning to cultivate the right mood." I snapped my fingers a few times, even though there wasn't much of a beat to speak of.

"Okay. Pretty good, Paul. Work on it."

The band played, the metal crashed.

"Well, I'd better get some sleep. Class tomorrow, you know."

"Yep. I know. I know just what you mean."

He smiled at me. Then he gently closed my door.

9

Psychology

The first night Bob had ever taken me to a gay bar, we'd gone to Vick's. I was nervous about it, but excited too; at that point, I had reached the stage where nothing could discomfit me. The bar was in an anonymous wreck of a building, in a section of town I'd walked through before, without knowing what was there. A bouncer had carded us, then Bob led me in through the narrow, Art Deco door, the only thing about the tumbledown facade that had been rebuilt. So much subterfuge, it was like going into a speakeasy, a whole underground world. Inside was fully high-tech: loud music, milling crowds, people dancing—boys with boys and girls with girls. My first reaction was that it seemed so much more democratic than heterosexual dancing, which always had boys or girls left over. The pairing was both startling and refreshing, exhilarating, like a dousing in cold water. Neon lit the dance floor and strobes flashed over the faces. The boys were wholesome Yale types; the girls wore cardigans and pants. Friends congregated along the aisles, talking and drinking beer. Dozens of burly bartenders in tuxedos rushed back and forth behind the bars—it looked like the evacuation of a Paris hotel. Glitz and glitter everywhere. I'd never known such a Valhalla existed; it was like waking up in Oz—I finally understood Bob's reference.

While we walked, I had catalogued all of the:

boys in T-shirts
boys in suits and ties
women in suits and ties
boys in drag

boys who looked like Rob Lowe
boys who looked like George Will
women with key chains
boys in cowboy hats
girls go-go-ing on top of speakers
boys go-go-ing on top of speakers
womyn
men with tattoos
women with tattoos
women with designer jeans
librarians
half-naked boys with massive, sweaty chests
and a group of people dressed like the characters from
    The Rocky Horror Picture Show, in a corner, handing out
    condoms and blending into the crowd

They were all dancing and swirling, swirling and dancing. It was Friday night. A never-ending party.

And it was like that first time tonight, at Vick's, my first night out after my parents' visit: the evening strange and full of possibility.

"What do you think?" Bob said. "Pretty good crowd. Looks mixed. In fact, I think I see a straight couple dancing on the floor, over there."

We stared.

"No, wait, he's a girl."

"Excuse me, Bob, I'm going to get a beer. You want anything?" I already knew he didn't drink, but waited for him to shake his head anyway. I looked for the least-crowded bar, started making my way over. Once I was out of Bob's line of vision, I slowed down, took more of a look around. At the boys. It was open season.

At the bar, someone tapped my shoulder. "Pete DuPree, I thought it was you." A woman's voice—I couldn't place it at first, and when I turned to face her, it took a moment to recognize . . .

"Veronique! Veronique Maria Sebastian Contessina Lake."

"You remembered."

"Who could forget? All those names."

"Let's ignore that regrettable period of my life, shall we? Just call me Veronica." She looked practically ordinary, in a regular dress, only she did have two large slivers of quartz hanging from her earlobes, dangling gamely. A change from Angela, all right. She was smoking, too, so at least she was recognizable.

"I'm Paul, by the way, not Pete. Pete's the one who's going to be the orthopedic surgeon."

"Paul, Paul, right. Sorry. How imbecilic." She moved like a Nile River queen, upper body along a horizontal, feet glued to the floor, very hypnotic. "Paul, I want you to meet some friends of mine. This is Jaime and Jeff."

Jeff? I shook hands with two dark-skinned men, both in suits and ties. "Jaime is a law student, from Argentina. Jeff's a senior in economics. Paul's—what are you doing now, Paul?"

"Tending bar."

"Oh, yes. That's right. A bartender."

"At Big Moe's."

"At Big Moe's."

They both smiled at me, Jaime only briefly, Jeff giving a slightly longer nod of recognition, as if indeed we knew each other—which was hard to tell, under these lights. I ought to have been non-plussed by Veronica's presence here, in Vick's. But I was too excited to connect things logically. It just somehow made sense. Besides, you tended to expect anything from someone who'd spin circles in front of a bunch of medical students.

"How is medical school these days, Veronica?"

She told me about classes, classmates, but I didn't pay much attention—I was watching Jeff. Could it really be him? The Jeff of my year-ago wanderings? The possibility was distinct, but I couldn't remember. Had "Jeff" really been his name? Had I heard it right? Had he even looked anything like this? It was impossible to remember, genuinely, to know if it wasn't just my need for completion. He surveyed the room as we stood there, then tapped Jaime on the shoulder and whispered in his ear. I wondered about this seeming ghost from my past, why he was here, what his interests were, what might have happened to his cohorts. Periodically, he would look at me, notice that I was staring at him, and smile—the self-confident grin of one of the ancient Yale rugby players, whose black-and-white photographs adorned the walls of every pub in New Haven.

"So how do you know Veronica?" Jeff asked over the din.

"Oh—we met at a party." I didn't feel like telling Jeff that I'd left medical school. It wasn't just that I didn't want to have to explain my reasons: I didn't want it to be the first thing he knew about me. Maybe I was being a bit disingenuous—I preferred not to impress him with my credentials. I wanted to see if he'd first be impressed with just myself.

"Come on." Veronica tugged Jaime's shirt sleeve. "I've spotted a table."

"Would you all excuse me for a moment?"

I went back over to Bob. "Bob, this place is great. I've met some friends—they've asked us to sit with them."

"Friends?" He seemed shocked. Was it that shocking? Maybe it was: He'd been standing alone, gazing at the patrons, lost. Seeing Bob here, alone, I wondered why I hadn't noticed it before—there were other people out there besides Bob. He was wearing a too-small Izod, meant to be sexy, but all it did was emphasize his dumpiness, the round shoulders. Why did I consider myself so tied to him, just because he was the first? Why couldn't we simply be friends—as I understood that word to mean—as someone you didn't have to change for?

"There's this guy, Jeff. Someone I might know. I have to get a chance to talk to him. You don't mind, do you?"

Bob shrugged. What else could he do? He pushed through the crowd, trying to keep up with me. He was probably thinking, *Oh, what monster have I wrought?* But once you're a monster, it's too late for regrets. I found Veronica's group, made quick introductions, and we sat. Jaime talked about Argentina in clipped English, while Jeff nodded along, adding comments about economics. All these men, all gay—I was in heaven. Veronica kept watch on the dance floor, where the more androgynous of the crowd swirled to strains of Olivia Newton-John, lost in their own little time warp. I didn't know if she was gay, straight, or progressive. I didn't know the situation between Jaime and Jeff. But these mysteries made the moment all that much more savory, enchanted, a destiny that could play itself out in many ways. Bob watched the dance floor, too, absently tracing lines on the table, sending out bored-waves like a radio tower.

"Jeff, where are you from?"

"Tulsa." He said the word slowly, with precision, looking into my eyes—as though he'd named the town just for me.

I'd planned it so I was sitting across from him. We talked about his youth, about Tulsa; with the loud music, the other people at the table disappeared, and I saw only him—his face, the smile, the lips, his modest but heartrending accent. Now, as I said, I wasn't sure if this was the same Jeff of my previous encounter, my earlier fantasies, or even, indeed, if "Jeff" was the name I'd heard all that time—perhaps I'd not heard the name right, or perhaps I was projecting back into my memory and somehow revising it to the name Jeff, or the semblance of such a name. Could there really be this essential atomic element, this individual fact named "Jeff," that I'd randomly encountered, and perhaps had randomly encountered again, at some mathematically calculable and presumably verifiable present time point? Or, in fact, was "Jeff" a quality of mind, an indeterminable state of grace that had insinuated itself into my life, in some breathtaking and beautiful way, and which might soon find itself more fully flushed out, the way a painter flushes out the color of a sunset? The latter seemed less precise, but for me, more true to life. And even if this were Jeff D and not Jeff A, B, or C, could I in fact know an original Jeff with any more certainty? Maybe it was precisely "his"—or "my"—mistracking that intrigued me.

I talked to him, being forward, loquacious, but it just came so naturally, I didn't even think about it. My most intimate feelings came pouring out—"I'm working on a video; I wish I'd lived through the Sixties; I don't want my life to go by without having any fun." I'd have corrected the omission about medical school, but now it seemed awkward, so I let it be. Some of the things I said surprised even me; yet it never occurred to me that the picture he might form could be any different from myself as I conceived of me, at that moment.

Jeff replied, apparently, with equal candor. He told me he was twenty-one, that his father had plans for his career as a brilliant economist—Tulsa was in bad financial straits, and his father's business needed a good, Yale-educated economist—and it all struck me with just the right amount of familiarity.

"I've got eleven goddamn credit cards. Do you believe that? Thanks to my daddy. Want to see them?" He fanned them out on the table. "Visa, Visa, Gold Card, Visa, American Express, Visa, Sears, MasterCard, Diners Club, Dillard's, Visa, and oh yeah, J. C. Penney." He finished with a laugh and tossed out the plain brown card on top of the pile. "So that makes twelve."

We looked at his credit cards.

"Have you ever had a dream where you're your daddy? You know you're him because you're wearing a suit, or black leather shoes, these clothes you can't afford. And as your daddy, you kill little boys by slicing their throats with a knife? White boys, black boys, all of them you kill because they're innocent and sad." He was just throwing this out, apparently rhetorically. "I wrap my arm around the boy's forehead, start to see the blood, then wake up. I think it must be something sexual, don't you?"

"You've got a beautiful smile," I told him. "I like it when you smile." It was the most logical reply to make.

"Thank you," he said, and smiled fabulously for me. He took a sip of beer, then collected his credit cards. "I don't mean to sound crazy. I just have bizarre dreams sometimes."

I understood what he meant. He still sounded crazy to me. But it was the cutest thing I'd ever seen, the way he blushed just because I'd given him a compliment, and that was all I cared about.

I went straight home from the bar—George was out, and so were the lights, but I couldn't sleep. I was wound. It was destiny. I searched through my old college textbooks, for *Poetry*, the book. I flipped the pages. Blake, Spenser, Shakespeare. I copied down the most mawkish poems, changing all the pronouns to *he*. I addressed an envelope (his address was listed like an answered prayer right in the phone book), then decided it'd be more chivalrous to hand them over in person. It was an irresponsibly sentimental thing to do, but I loved it. Finally I had a Romantic self-image suitable for worship. I went to sleep clutching the sonnets in one hand, the phone book in the other.

I slept for four hours. I woke up at sunrise and couldn't fall back to sleep. I brewed a pot of coffee. George woke up ready to head off to the library.

"Hi," I said as he came padding out of the kitchen.

"Bye," he said back, opening a granola bar as he left. With school, and Big Moe's, that was just about how much I ever saw of him every day.

I let enough of the morning pass to be polite—watching TV, eating breakfast, pacing the room. When I dialed Jeff's number at ten thirty-four, he was in; he sounded wide awake.

"Jeff?"

"Uh-huh. Sure."

"This is Paul. Paul Levinson. I don't know if you remember. We met last night."

"Sure, I know who this is."

Bingo. Now what?

"Would you like to get together? Do something? See a movie? Anything?"

"A movie, huh? Hold on, let me see what Jaime's up to."

Before I could say anything more, the line went blank. Jaime? I'd forgotten about Jaime. Maybe they were . . . but Jeff had given me no indication, had he? They lived together, this was de facto evidence of something. Or was it? How could I let myself fall in love before getting all the information? O desperate, fatal error!

Jeff came back before I'd finished agonizing. "Sure, I'll go. Jaime's going to Washington for the evening. He didn't tell me till just now, of course. So it looks like I'm free."

Praise be. Jeff's accent was so soft and feline, it was like a whisper saying *Hold me, caress me, love me.* "Great," I told him, waiting for further instructions.

"What movie did you want to see? I've got something in mind, myself."

"Anything. What?"

"*Aliens Take Miami.* Heard of it?"

So the tables were turned; it was poetic justice, as they say in the preface to *Poetry.* But I wasn't about to repeat Bob's mistakes. At least, that's what I told myself. Jeff was already standing outside the theater when I got there.

"Good to see you, Paul."

"Same here." We shook hands vigorously, but not overly long, implying that there was nothing special to be inferred from it. I had no clue what he thought of our haphazard date, or what, if anything, he thought about me. I still couldn't believe it was happening—the time alone with him, his agreement to come along, to be the person I'd always dreamed of meeting. He let go of my hand, and I followed him inside, trying to imagine what he might be thinking, staring fawningly at the back of his head.

The lobby was still plastered with the same cheap cardboard theater cards: male movie star with Uzis, buxom female with diamonds, both surrounded by palm trees, as if summing up the legal limits of What the Public Wants—misogyny and bullets in a tropical venue. Same 1930s retro decor, same smirking concessionaire. Déjà vu. The situation woke me up a bit—I thought about Bob, the way I'd abused him. But what could be done about it now? I'd call Bob later, when we got home. I'd make it up to him.

"If it isn't too personal," I said to Jeff—taking Bob's role— "are you and Jaime . . . ?" I left the blank intentionally (tactfully, I felt) for him to fill in.

The concessionaire—the same one as before—smiled at me, as though we were sharing our own little secret.

"How do I know about Jaime?" he snapped, unexpectedly. "Jaime hides behind what he hides behind; he has no idea of himself. He conveys one thing and says another. All right, so maybe he has to be that way, somewhat. His father is some sort of head of security for the Argentine government. But I think I deserve a little more respect on a Saturday night, even from a G-man. Or a G-boy. Don't you agree? Running away to Washington just like that. He's just too incomprehensible to have anything that you might call a relationship. I really shouldn't be telling you all this. Don't tell Jaime I've said anything about him, will you?"

He hadn't told me anything; he wasn't even talking to me, but looking at his movie ticket. I noticed the way his hair fell over to one side, as if listing in a storm. It wasn't nearly so dark under the lights of the theater lobby; that seemed to be his Southern heritage, the sunny summers of Oklahoma, leaving highlights.

"It's okay. I won't say anything. Go on."

"Maybe we're nothing more than roommates, okay? And then, maybe not. Why should you have to pin it down, anyway? I mean, if everything's okay for the two people involved, why try to define it, kill it, just so you can supply answers to other people's questions?"

"I didn't mean to ask anything. . . ."

"What Jaime wants is unpredictable; it changes from day to day. Today he wants to go to Washington. You know, there's freedom, but there's such a thing as being there, too. Sometimes, Paul, I think I could be psychotic, if it weren't for the order of day-to-day experiences, Saturday coming before Sunday, that sort of thing."

It was non-sequitur remarks like those that had attracted me to him the night before. There was something romantically self-destructive about him, his haphazard logic, as though at any moment he might implode, leaving only a vapor of atoms. Such willful self-contradiction! I wanted to solve his riddle, sublimate him into a solid. Or was his potential mental instability all a pose, a ploy, to elicit sympathy? He averted his eyes as he talked, but glanced up occasionally when he thought I wasn't looking, to gauge my reactions. Sneaky bastard. Poor SOB. I felt all manner of incompatible things about him at once.

We watched the movie: murder, hetero sex, violence, palm trees, hetero sex, death, palm trees, hetero sex, car chase, brief self-conscious parody of latent homoeroticism, broken palm tree (attempt at symbolism), death. You had to lower your IQ to understand the plot, especially the second time, but at least the stunts gave you some sort of adrenaline rush. That had to be worth something.

Afterward we went to a nearby café, found a table amongst the crowd of assorted beats, hippies, and punks. The waitress took our order. I stared at Jeff while he stared back. God, he was so debonair. Could he really be interested in me? We talked idly about the movie, about the food. He spoke favorably of both, so I did the same. I sipped my mocha and he drank his soda. In my pocket were the love poems; I kept a tight grip on them with my grimy little hand.

"Jeff, I've been searching for the right words, and, well, I guess I just have to come out and say it."

He shrugged. "If you have to."

"Well, I'm not sure what the right procedure is, exactly, but we're having such a good time and all, I'd like to know if you'd want to—"

"Look—let's not talk about this now." He finished his soda, sipping loudly. Then he put down the empty glass. "Besides, talking is for MacNeil/Lehrer. It's bad luck." He checked his watch. "Okay, now I'm late. I was supposed to call Daddy at eleven."

"On a Saturday night?"

"He's got a deal in the works. Oilmen don't take any holidays, you know; they're constantly on the go." He paused. "Unintentional rhyme."

"Why don't you call from here?"

He looked around, then grabbed his jacket, rising. "No, I need my spread sheets; they're at home."

The next thing, we were out the door; I was following him

home—he walked too fast for me to keep up, let alone have a conversation. I kept in mind my gullibility; I didn't know whether to believe him about this appointment. It was a plausible enough excuse. But that was what Jeff was about, it seemed—this change of mind, this evasiveness. Why would someone make up a complete lie about spread sheets?

"Here's my phone number. My address. My place of employment. My social security number." I wrote it all down for him. "Can I call you tomorrow? That's really all I was going to ask."

He took the slip of paper from me. "Sure. I may not be home, though. Jaime's schedule, you know."

We buzzed into the apartment building and stood in the hallway, the wooden 3B tacked haphazardly on the red kindergarten-looking door. No one else around.

"Well, good night," I said, standing there. "I had fun." Then, startling both of us, I leaned forward and gave him a kiss.

It was like:

I lose sense of where his lips end and mine begin. My legs disappear and we become two heads, attached at the face. We float three feet over our torsos. We don't glance up or down, but looking into his eyes, I see clouds, my future, dinosaurs, an apple. We dissolve into atoms; the atoms swirl and slowly float away.

The kiss ended and I caught my breath. He just stood there, key in hand, forgetting to unlock the door.

"Call me," I said. "Won't you?"

"Sure. Sure—of course."

Eventually he unlocked and went in, just dumbfounded, not once looking as if it'd dawned on him what had happened. His insouciance disappointed me more than anything else he might have done. The kiss had been a test, and he'd evaded it, just as he had everything else. He'd simply gone inside, declining to offer any interpretation at all.

So I left his doorstep and walked outside—the clear sky, the stars. What a night. I was rich. I'd gotten everything, just about, that I could have ever hoped for.

□   □   □

But once in bed, I couldn't get to sleep. I kept replaying the evening. "Let's not talk about this now." What did that mean? Did it mean, *I'm in love with you*? Or, *I'm not in love with you*? What had made him end it so quickly? Was he afraid? Was he shy? I told myself it was fruitless to try to guess, but that didn't stop me. I formulated all sorts of hypotheses. I imagined that he was scheming to find a way to be rid of the ineluctable Jaime. Or that he was simply confounded by the prospect of my interest in him. By eight-thirty, I had Jeff calling me that morning to confess his obsession. By ten o'clock, I had us married and living happily ever after in Kauai.

I'd forgotten to give him the poems. I thought now that maybe I never would. Maybe they were too silly—they'd only backfire. I put them in my desk, hoping they might one day become a mutual source of amusement.

I called him six times. He wasn't home all day, as he'd warned. I knew I should have just waited for him to call me, like he'd promised. But I couldn't get him off my mind. He was a tune, one you don't necessarily like or dislike, but one that grows more significant the more it skims round your brain. And then you all at once realize that you've been whistling it for hours. Jeff—his swagger and talk and crashing wave of hair—had gotten inside me, and I couldn't get him out. I lay in bed and let my fingers walk over me, here and there, imagining it was him.

It was fruitless to stay home waiting for him to call. I went over to Bob's. I needed to keep myself occupied. I needed someone semirational with whom I could talk things over.

"Bob, Bob, I think I'm falling in love. It doesn't look good."

"In love?"

"It's Jeff. That guy we met Friday night."

"You really do things fast, don't you?"

"Love...love...love....I never knew what the word meant before. I'd had no idea. It's amazing."

We were on his bed—me lying on my back, staring at the ceiling, Bob sitting next to me, occupying space. Jeff, Jeff...I'd known him for two days, and I couldn't even see now what he looked like, couldn't recall an image. I was blinded by my emotion for him...for Jeff, the boy, the man, his lips, his hair, our conversations (an hour and forty minutes' worth, all totaled), for each word he'd pronounced—*my daddy's business; neat aliens, huh?*—or

the way he'd repeated *Visa,* over and over, with that slightly Southern twang, so that it was almost *Veysa.*

"You're not in love."

"Yes I am. Maybe before, I wasn't sure what love was, but now,
there's no doubt. Once it hits you it's like getting religion, you just
know."

Bob shrugged. He got up and walked around the room, grabbing two of the Pet Rocks from off his desk. "It sounds like you've
got a crush, that's all."

"No, Bob—he likes me, I know it. You were there on Friday.
You saw the way he looked at me."

"I didn't see anything special, myself. Maybe it was you, the
way you looked at him. Maybe that's all you saw, what you were
hoping to see." He kept his back to me, rolling his pets in his
hand.

"Not so, Bob. I know it's not so." Then I crossed my arms.
"Hmmph, just listen to the way I'm talking." I sat up. I couldn't
believe that I was doing this—a grown man, swooning. Over some
man with what color eyes? I couldn't remember the details—if
indeed they were even worth bothering about. Jeff's face was a
blinding light, on top of it that golden hair. Bob was right, I wasn't
looking clearly at the facts. Who cared? Facts were for sissies.

"This really isn't good," I heard myself say. "I think I'm hope-
less."

Bob fell silent. I lay back on the bed and stared again at the
ceiling. It was a useful distraction—a blob of paint here, a scratch
there—but the more I stared, the more the reticulations came out,
pulsing out and pulsing in.... Maybe the psilocybin was having
an aftereffect on my perception. Maybe that's all my experience
was—just chemicals. Then what responsibility did we have? Or if
not chemicals, then hormones, behavior patterns, gene segments,
some unlikely synchronization of the control centers in my brain.
Would having the map solve the problem? In such a biological-
determinacy mood, it was easier to quiet the nagging worries, like
maybe that talking about all of this in front of Bob was yet another
example of my taking him for granted.

Was I attracted to Jeff and not Bob because Jeff had money,
status, his father's watchful eye, a sense of angst—all those things
I'd willfully refuted? I liked to think not, but there it was, staring

me in the face. Maybe I hadn't really escaped the things I thought I had.

"Listen, Paul, let me tell you something. Maybe this will shed some light." Bob stood at the other end of the room, talking, but I was so caught up in my own dilemma, staring at the ceiling, I barely perceived him. "This goes quite a ways back, to my childhood. I wasn't as snappy a dresser then as I am now. It's true. I was clumsy. I wasn't in touch with my inner color sensibility. Why do you think they call it color coordination? It's all interconnected. I couldn't catch a baseball, or pick a shirt that matched my shoes, or any of those other survival skills that even the most unathletic children do so well. I was always put on the sidelines. But the side became my center, that's how I kept my balance. The first thing a dancer needs to develop is a sense of relationship. On the side, I could feel what others had neglected; they were my specialty, things like beauty, poetry, motion, grace. But I didn't know what those words meant; it was before I had names for my feelings. I was ten and caught up in the world—I had no idea about the cause of things."

Was there going to be a point to this? "You know, Bob, the thing about love," I said, ignoring him, starting to talk over him, in fact, each of us lost in our own separate talk, "is that you just can't conceptualize it. You can't analyze it. All you can do is experience it. I'm lying here on your bed, thinking about myself lying here on your bed, a person in love. I always do this—look at myself from above, study the machine of myself, through a mental microscope. But as soon as I say the word *love*, all that tortured self-awareness implodes, and I fall back to being totally in myself, totally one. That's never happened to me before...."

"...dancing just evolved from that. But it wasn't enough just to dance. I wanted to be good. I wanted something for *me*. In gym class, all those schoolboys in the gray 'Property of Roosevelt High School' sweatshirts, they couldn't square dance. They laughed and made fun of it, but they couldn't do it. The gymnasium filled with the squeaks of stumbling tennis shoes. But I could do it—not only square dance, but two-step, disco, jitterbug. All of it. I just didn't think about it, about what I was doing, and then I wasn't afraid anymore....

"...So how does love work? It's all controlled by the chemicals, it must be. Endorphins, maybe. Endorphins that seek out their endorphin-receptors in the brain. Certain physical attributes: When you see these things, smell things, hear things, it causes an aminergic release....

"...But most, you've got to forget yourself when you dance. Just move your body. Move your leg, your foot, instep, big toe, and on, toe by toe. Arms, torso, hands, neck, jaw, fingers, shoulders, back. I was so caught up in it, for a while all I cared about was dancing myself, dancing my Self. Get it? I used to think I was the only person in the world. But things change, of course. I met another dancer, this guy....

"...the amines cross the synapses and find their appropriate love receptors. Then the chemical energy gets translated into electricity. But what are the factors? What combination of elements turn it on? Turn it off? If only there were a way to elucidate it....

"...he was in college and I was sixteen. This was in the community dance ensemble, Bridgeport. They classified me with the adults by then. A bit premature, but I didn't argue. Greg was so sweet. He taught me so many things, dancing too, of course—that's all he cared about, teaching. He understood life enough to know he didn't understand a thing...."

"...Someone could decipher the code. The proper sequence of molecules. The age-old love potion. I think the amygdala has to do with it somehow. That's the primitive part of the brain—our animal ancestry. It curves around the hippocampus. Maybe love is no more than that, plugging into our animal brain, our primal codes...."

"...But that's what I'm trying to tell you, Paul. I'd forgotten that dancing is a *pas de deux*. When we danced together, he held his arm along mine, we looked into the mirrors. We mirrored each other. Dancing and sex were two sides of a coin: In the hall we moved like lovers; at home we choreographed our fellatio...."

"...But I don't know. All that isn't the same as *being* in love. That's just *talking* about love. Taking love apart. Being in love is completely different."

Bob turned to face me. "God, you really bring back memories. I haven't thought about Greg in ages. I made a dance about him, though." He stood for a minute, staring at the floor, concentrating—he was going to dance for me, maybe lift himself off the ground by sheer willpower, take off into flight. Then he shook his head. "Sorry, Paul." He looked up and tried to smile, his feet crossed. "It must be a bad night. I can't even remember the first step."

I called Jeff all day Monday, too, and still no answer. Where could he be? What had I done wrong? Oh, Jeff—if only you could know my anticipation.

On Tuesday, the phone rang while I was cleaning dishes, just at the moment I'd forgotten about it. I knocked over a lamp, a juice glass, a stack of George's sheet music in my leap for it.

"Paul. Hello. How are you?"

"Great. Jeff—you called. How are you?"

Nothing. Then . . .

"Could I maybe see you?" He sounded out of breath, as if he'd just gotten home at that moment. "I mean, can I come over? Tomorrow? That is, if you want me to."

"Come over? Sure, of course." Mr. Cool. "Tomorrow's fine. Tonight's fine, too. Why not right now?"

"Well, tomorrow would be better. I'll be there after dinner. Around seven." And he hung up, just like that. I held the receiver, thinking about the luck, like being hit by lightning.

So I'd been right, and Bob had been wrong. Hallelujah! For the first time since I'd met Jeff, I felt calm, assured, on top of things. And vindicated. I called up Bob immediately, to gloat. My prey was coming to the den, without my having done a thing.

"Sure," Bob said. "For now. But don't say I didn't warn you."

The next morning was glorious—I didn't have to go to work, so I simply did all the relaxing things I could think of: watch MTV, go for a jog, log scenes in my notebook. Life was a perfect moment. I generated more ideas for videos than I normally produced in a month.

Jeff showed up before I was ready; I'd just finished dinner and a shower. I slipped on the first ratty T-shirt in my path and answered the door while trying to smooth back my hair with my hands. He walked in as if coming right over the phone line from the day before—still agitated, or nervous, or whatever it was that had provoked him to call. He paced the room, not looking at me. It reminded me of the odd way he'd invited himself over: distractedly. But then, that seemed to be the way with everything Jeff did.

I showed him around the apartment, nervous, not knowing, really, what I should say.

"What's all this?" He'd spotted my video equipment. By now I had a sizable collection: three old VCRs, an editor, CDs for music, tapes of every format, whatever I could beg or borrow. Once people knew you were interested, it snowballed. My bedroom was like a warehouse; you could hardly see the bed, the desk. It was as if, all this time, I'd been preparing all this equipment for Jeff, his arrival, to somehow impress him.

"Here, I'll show you."

I aimed the camera at him. I had it set permanently on its tripod, the monitor continually feeding copy to the TV, like in a department store. "Don't look into the camera. I've got you in profile."

While I taped him, he played with the levers on my editor. It was a cheap piece of junk; I'd bought it from a mail-order catalog. It couldn't sync with any smoothness. That didn't seem to concern Jeff, however. I watched him in my viewfinder, checked it with the picture on TV, making sure it was all recording.

"This is pretty neat stuff. You never told me you did this."

"Yes I did." I talked not to him, but to the television, where he reappeared, facing in an off angle—where I'd redirected his profile, framed his body. "It's all I talked about the night we met."

"Well, it's pretty cool." He stood up and walked offscreen, or toward me. He still hadn't mentioned the reason he'd come over. Maybe he didn't have one. I looked up from the viewfinder.

"It's like that movie, right?" he said. "You bring people here and film them, and then they want to have sex with you."

"No—never before."

The words came out as a proposition, an open question, although I hadn't intended them that way. But once said, I didn't back down; I waited for Jeff's response.

"Why don't I tape you?"

"Me?"

"Sure. You're not against it, are you? All you camera people, get you in front of one, and you fall to pieces, don't you?"

"No. . . . Sure, go ahead. I don't think I'll be very interesting on camera, though."

Jeff took the tripod from my hands, undaunted. He was exercising what seemed his natural tendency, to take control of the perspective. Normally, I would never have relinquished it, but with Jeff, the situation was different; resistance didn't seem to be an option. I was too curious about him—I'd do anything he wanted, simply to find out what might be on his mind.

"Well?"

"Lie back. I think you're too tense. That won't tape well, will it? It'll look artificial."

I tried to relax, which only made me more uptight. I wasn't sure where he was going with this; perhaps it was his plan to seduce me outright—what he wanted all along, why he was out of breath when he'd called me. Or perhaps I assumed too much, projected too much of my own scenario on to his intentions. I knew there had to be something else that was motivating him, even if I didn't know what. He talked while he filmed me, and while he talked, he held the camera by one leg of the tripod, leaving the other two spokes to point aimlessly in the air, as if deliberately mocking any natural grip.

"It's about Jaime. Why I'm here. Whatever was going on, let's just say that it's over now. Let's say it's definitely over. And . . . well . . . I wouldn't ordinarily ask this of someone I'd just met, but I already feel like we've known each other for a long time. I feel like we're already close friends, Paul. So, basically, I want to know if you'd move in with me. Jaime's moving out next week, and I need the rent, and it seems somewhat providential, that we met and all. . . ."

It was like a dream come true, that he should propose something so romantic, so immediate. And the way he was taping me, as if to secure my steadfast agreement. As if to make it all seem preordained. I could see myself on the television, mouth open, ready to reply.

But I held back from answering. A voice inside was skeptical, urged me to examine the angles, told me something didn't add up. Could I really trust him? Could I be sure this wasn't all some sort of ruse? Why all of this good fortune, so quickly? We hardly knew each other. I decided to give this voice credence, to play it somewhat safe, which surprised me, after all I'd made of this wild infatuation, my great spontaneity. Maybe it was something in his tone—a line that I thought I'd heard before.

"If you have enough for the deposit, you could even give it to me today, seeing as it's the end of the month."

"I'll have to think about it, Jeff. I've got a roommate, you know. We've already got a lease. I can't just walk out on it." Really. What would George have said?

He put down the camera. He came over and gave me a kiss, one more passionate than anything I'd ever considered giving him. We scraped teeth, bit each other's lips, played with each other's tongues. It was a kiss without end, without being, for in that moment, I would have done anything he wanted, gone anywhere, transformed myself in any manner whatsoever. I became his desire—his desire became our desire, a perfect union. But then he stopped. He backed away and wiped his mouth—the way a clown might, in pantomime, leaving me breathless.

"Well." He shrugged. "I offered. Think it over." And just like that, he left.

I worked the following three days straight—barely able to concentrate—but the next weekend, I went over to his place. He lived not three blocks from George and me. He was dressed strangely when I got there—not the suit and tie I'd first met him in, but something ragged and ritualistic, a suede vest, with tassels, and jade jewelry. He smiled gapingly as I beheld whatever it was about himself he was trying to show me. Hell if I knew—he was a different person every time we met.

"You like the getup, huh?"

"Sure."

"I thought you would." He handed me a shot of schnapps, and kept a second for himself, as if inviting me to join a Native American peace treaty.

We downed them simultaneously.

"Come at me," he said, putting his glass on a table. "Come at me." There was a glow in his eyes. He'd maybe already had a few shots beforehand. He went to sit on the couch, facing away from me.

"Put your hands around my neck. Come up from behind and put your hands around my neck."

I did as he asked.

"Say 'You're a worthless little shit.' "

"I'm not going to say anything like that. That's sick."

"Just say it. Please." He sounded upset, as though he might cry.

I felt foolish, embarrassed, an actor performing without any idea of the script. I put my hands on the back of his neck. "You're a worthless little shit," I said, shivering at the words, which to me sounded like some sort of evil incantation. And I thought just how much he seemed like a boy, running on guile and improvisation, despite the largeness of his frame.

As I held him, he closed his eyes and sank further into the upholstery. I didn't squeeze him, apparently, as hard as he wanted, for he flopped his arms and acted disappointed.

"Paul..." He breathed. "You're not going to try being nice to me, are you? I hate it when people try being nice. It's so vulgar." Then he grabbed my arm. He pulled my hand in front of him, looking at it closely, as if examining for defects, for the secret of its working. He meshed his fingers in mine and squeezed, then turned and smiled at me. He was so pleased with this simple action, which seemed to have taken years for both of us to come to, in our own individual ways. Then he placed my hand back on his shoulder.

"Okay, Daddy, we're not going to be rude to our guest."

His body felt so light, pliable in my hands, like a bird's. And the warmth of him, the solidity, filled me with a sense of longing, the urge to protect him. I sensed the need he had to have me standing over him, to have me witness his self-defamation. It impassioned me all the more.

"All right, pal—time's awastin'. Enough games. Let's see what you're made of."

He stood up from the couch and came around—wrapped his arms around me, kissed me, slipped me his tongue. It all happened before I had a chance to think about it, react, and by the time I was in his embrace, I was completely swallowed into his field. My senses fogged over. He stripped off my T-shirt, had me naked before he'd even taken off his pinky ring.

"Let's go to the bedroom."

Those magic words—the ones I'd been waiting for all my life. Once there, he had me stand, undressed, while he simply looked or touched. He had complete control of the situation, and that was as sexual as the rest—this question of power, of using it, of constructing the fantasy. He wanted to arm wrestle. From there he got even more athletic. But once we were in bed, he gave up all pretense to this game of "fraternity foolhardying" and started licking up the inside of my thigh. He panted like a dog, then smiled at me, as if to say, *Get it?* I wondered where he'd learned his maneuvers, his caprice, especially seeing as he was nearly three years my junior. As for myself, I could barely take in my surroundings; all there was for me was (1) his chest, or (2) his legs, or (3) whatever erogenous nibblet appeared next, one by one, each part of his body a gift presented anew. Events went so fast, I lost their order. We tangled our legs and disheveled the sheets, yet even so, I felt only half there—already I anticipated being finished with it, searching for a Kleenex or a sock. My mind participated on two levels—the one enthralled by pure lust, the other repelled by Jeff's emotional guard, the way he placed my hands in certain positions—for I was beginning to understand, on some deep level, that the Jeff I was in love with was only a mask, a screen upon which I'd projected my own yearnings. And a pretty good licker, once he let himself go. But behind that—I still had no idea. He wouldn't let anyone know, perhaps ever. And I understood the fact with even more certainty by making love with him.

Afterward, we lay in his bed, completely still, limbs entwined. A breeze blew across my leg, ruffled the hairs near Jeff's ankle. It seemed so completely intimate, that a single breeze could touch us both. Maybe it was still possible for us to find some sort of spiritual communion, what perhaps I wanted most from him. Jeff was apparently asleep, but I wasn't sleepy at all—I lay and watched him breathe. Maybe I didn't, yet, feel the type of love that came with years of shared experience, familiarity, trust, but I *did* feel something for him. I was intrigued by his humanity, his existence as a living creature in this world, and who knew—that might be a form of love as well.

But what was most valuable to me was having the chance to examine, at my leisure, a living, breathing body. His rib cage rose and fell rhythmically. Life flowed over his skin in luminescent currents. The few hairs on his chest gathered into a fine, wispy line that ran down to the grove in his stomach. He was a real animal presence, a cat or cougar: At any moment he might open his plaintive eyes and look at me. He might become animated, a force to be reckoned with.

Or he might wake up and ask for a teddy bear.

I looked around his bedroom, his possessions, and thought about what it'd be like to live among them. They were so different from my own. He had a telescope, a basketball, a pennant from Yale, a half-read mystery novel. Just like any all-American boy. How comforting such things must have been to him.

Jeff opened his eyes, just as I'd foreseen. Had he been awake all that time? Had he been aware of me watching him? His face was once again blank, and he simply stared at me, composed, expressionless. The way he'd so casually gotten rid of Jaime, if indeed that was what he'd done with him, weighed on me, as if I could just as easily be next. Los Desaparecidos. Perhaps some of Jaime's political instability and intrigue had infected Jeff, had made him the mystery he was. Did I want to get involved with someone who might have contracted danger like the flu? But then, the story of Jaime could very well have been Jeff's invention, or exaggeration, designed to give his life some extra flair and drama.

"Jeff, about moving in . . ."

"I've already arranged for someone."

I didn't say anything. I simply looked surprised.

"You hesitated. You didn't give me a firm commitment. How should I know? This other guy, he was ready to move at the drop of a hat."

"What other guy?"

"Oh, jealous? Don't worry, he's only some dupe in my accounting class. Not someone of our breed. He won't be getting a piece of your action. We just might have to meet over at your place for a few weeks, that's all."

The thing was, I had been ready to decline moving in. I had too many reservations about throwing in my lot with someone like Jeff so quickly. But now that I'd been preempted, I wasn't going to show my hand. I wasn't going to give him any more information than he absolutely needed.

I didn't even realize that he'd practically implied we were going steady. I hardly realized it even after we were.

□   □   □

We saw each other regularly over the next few days. Several times I considered calling the whole thing off—I already could sense that it had no chance of ultimate success—but I couldn't bring myself to get rid of him; I looked forward to seeing him too much, found the whole thing too stimulating to renounce. I kept hoping that I would find out something about him that would change him for me, make him more gentle and predictable, more like the Jeff I'd expected, the one from the bookstore, my dreams. But time showed this to be less and less likely. When I began talking about my videos, Jeff would visibly tune it out. His eyes would glaze over and he'd bury his head in the *Wall Street Journal* or, of all things, a *Playboy*. We went out to dinner, out dancing, made love, but talked to each other less and less. His new room-mate had moved in, apparently, immediately, and because Jeff didn't want to tell him he was gay, now we met strictly at my place.

I'd briefed George on everything that was going on, and he was eager to meet my first romance. He was making himself a pineapple-fudge milk shake, grinding up a real live pineapple in a blender, along with the Hershey's hot fudge, speckling pulp and chocolate all over the walls as it splattered out the top.

"You'll like him, George. He's . . . interesting."

"Paul," he said, off the subject, "you don't think I'm becoming boring, do you?" The blender caught something solid and buckled; he grabbed the lid and put it through a battery of speeds, until it digested the chunk and smoothed to a steady hum. "You know, I'm constantly afraid that one day I'm going to wake up and go to walk the dog and bring in the paper, and that'll be it—I'll get in my BMW, turn on Barry Manilow, and dissolve into a pile of tax-deductible charity donations and reinvested capital gains."

"You'll never listen to Barry Manilow, George." But it was true that I hadn't heard any annoying industrial noises coming from his room lately. And I all at once understood his fear—of getting stale, of becoming yet another statistical success.

"I'm sure you're going to be a fascinating doctor. You'll be a doctor to the stars. You'll probably wear a black leather smock. You'll play the Dead Kennedys in the waiting room. I want you to be *mine*."

It was clear, though, that compared with Jeff, my feelings for George had never been romantic. I'd simply appreciated him. Maybe he just appreciated me, too. And the thought of that only made me appreciate him even more. Funny, how that was easier than love.

"Here," he said, pouring his concoction into a paper cup and handing it to me. "Taste this for me."

But in the question of getting one side to meet the other, it was Jeff who was the squeamish one; he would only come over when I assured him George wasn't home. He didn't like anyone else knowing our maneuvers. He didn't like talking about Jaime. He didn't like talking about his family, or his past. This didn't seem like the way you could make a life with someone for long.

Whenever I discussed these things—my family, my past, myself, my plans—it bored him, but nothing bored him more than when I discussed "politics," which for Jeff included everything from the plots of my favorite films to my video application. Despite having finished my Vertov phase, I was claiming that my work would "combat stultifying ideologies" and contribute to "the general raising of consciousness." Perhaps he could discern the hyperbole. Whenever he sensed the subject about to come up, he'd yawn visibly and head for the refrigerator. I had to admit, though, that there was something tremendously satisfying about having a man, yawning, padding around my kitchen in his underwear, who at any moment might get it in his head to pull down my jeans and suck my cock. Whenever this happened, I asked him if we shouldn't use a condom—after all, if there was any disease that I'd become an overnight expert on, it was AIDS—but he just laughed, as if I'd suggested hari-kari or becoming macrobiotic. Instead, he put to work a technique he'd learned would instantly silence my objections.

"Paul," he'd say afterward. "Lighten up and enjoy life for a while. Sometimes you can be a real stick-in-the-mud."

I knew he was right, in a way, even though it was a strange message to be coming from Jeff. I wondered if I wasn't being a curmudgeon intentionally. If he wasn't somehow provoking me.

But I was quickly losing patience. If he wasn't going to adapt to my life, I wasn't going to wait for him. I'd put everything on hold since the day we'd met. But after two weeks of Jeff, I was ready to go back to my cameras and tapes, back to working on all the plans I'd had before we'd met. Other than his cuteness, his wit, his schizophrenia, and the incredibly fun and neurotic sex, he just didn't, after all, have that much to offer.

So I stopped waiting for his calls. I stopped going out of my way to alter plans. It was time to put the burners on, give him a taste of his own medicine. I'd been getting my fill of excitement lately, my fill of romance. For a change, all I wanted was a little stability.

I told Julie and George I wanted to take them out to dinner. This was the best way to get Jeff off my mind for a while: to find myself again in my friends.

It was a seafood place—we shared fried clams from a basket, drank beer, generally had a good old commiseration. The clams were huge—New England sized, fresh out of the water—and they'd given us enough to last a week, for about the price of a six-pack.

"It's good to see you, Paul," Julie said. "You've seemed preoccupied lately."

"Ever since I left Yale," I told them, my mouth filled with fried food, "my head's been swinging through so many drastic permutations, I'm dizzy. Love, hate, this, that. It's hard to know what's true anymore. You know, first you live by one set of rules, and then one day you wake up and have to learn another just the opposite. And then you realize that they're all just as arbitrary. I only have myself to rely on. I just need to gather myself together. I need to calm down." I was only just beginning to realize how turbulent my life had become since leaving Yale. How many changes I'd been forcing myself through. And how difficult it was to come up with a system of life totally on your own—with hardly any help from anybody.

"You think you've got problems," George said. "At least you have time to figure things out. This medical-school routine leaves a lot to be desired."

"Really?"

So he was finally opening up. I looked at Julie, but she simply shrugged—she wasn't going to speak for him.

"I knew there was something, George. I knew I wasn't wrong. You and me, we think too much alike."

"No, Paul, it's not that. You left medicine to do something hard that you love. I genuinely love medicine. I love lots of things. Most of the rest of it, the music and fashion, it's my free time, time for myself, time to be someone else every now and then. But medicine is different. You can't mess around. I don't know if I can stick with it. It's not that the material's so difficult. It's no harder than college. Easier, in fact. There's just so much more of it. More every year. I miss having those other lives."

"It's an entirely different kind of crisis," Julie added.

"You won't quit," I said. I didn't think, though, that his crisis was necessarily all that different.

"No. Of course not. I never said anything about quitting. What would I do if I quit? How can you just quit doing what you love?"

"Listen, George. Everything we love is hard. That's *why* it's hard."

"That's why we love it"—Julie.

"Here here."

And we toasted. George raised his glass too, if reluctantly.

We went back to munching our clams.

"So what's it like to be free of it?"

"Of what?"

"Medicine. The whole preplanned path."

"George . . ."

"I'm just asking, darling. I just want to know. Maybe if I know what I'm missing, I won't miss it that much."

I told him . . . well, I don't know *what* I told him, exactly. It was like being someone new, the person I always used to feel guilty about being—because it was a waste of time, a dalliance, unproductive, not good for the complexion—but the person I'd always wanted to be. But I didn't put it in those terms exactly, the terms of a magical transformation, of alchemy . . . perhaps because I wasn't that new person yet, completely—because I possessed the remnant of the urge to explain things according to a rational hypothesis. I told him something about psychology, about defense mechanisms. Whatever it was, I think he could tell it was eighty percent bullshit.

"Maybe you'd like to get back into it some? Earn some extra money?"

"What do you mean?"

"He's not interested, George."

"Wait a minute. What does he mean, earn some money?"

"You remember Veronique? She's working on a project in the lab next to mine. She needs some healthy male volunteers."

"Sure—Veronica." I reached for a handful of seafood.

"He's been asking this of everyone, Paul. Don't let him pressure you."

"I'm not pressuring him, darling. No pressure. Not me. Wouldn't think of it. I'm just going to lay out the facts."

It didn't matter. I knew right then—whatever it was, I was going to do it. Especially for money.

It turned out that she was doing some sort of pharmacological research—it wasn't going to be any actual treatment that I received, just a bolus to test my kinetics: heart rate, blood pressure, urinary retention. Preliminary data. All they needed were some raw numbers. All they needed was a solid biological machine to test the stuff on. A no-brainer—any spinal preparation could do it.

And the money.

"You just lie there for six hours, and then they pay you?"

"Basically."

"George . . ." she warned. "Paul—I don't think it's quite that easy."

"How hard could it be? As long as it isn't going to turn me into a vegetable."

"If it does, Julie and I will be the first to file your lawsuit."

George had a consent form for me to sign the very next morning: *I hereby release Yale New Haven Hospital from responsibility for any physical or mental disconnection I may suffer. . . .*

"So what are *you* getting out of this, George?"

"Subscription bonus." He handed me a pen. "Free issue of *Neocortex Monthly.*"

As soon as I finished signing, I got nervous about it—all those plugs and wires, and me, totally at the mercy of the inanimate needles and machines, some abstract nurse measuring my fluids, Veronica—of all people—with a voltameter. It struck me as something dark, erotic, and sinister. But that was what had intrigued me in the first place. So I wasn't going to back out now.

It took elaborate preparation: I had to round up six hours of cassette tapes, leave messages for Bob and Jeff, switch schedules at work. Then, inexplicably, I found myself once again walking the venerable trek up the medical-school stairs.

It'd been so long since I'd been here, in this environment, it all seemed strange, alien: the white walls, the elaborate machines, the scurrying nurses and residents, the IV stands like signposts every few yards. It was all part of a definite and completed time of my life, one I'd forgotten more and more with every passing day.

"Hello, Paul," Veronica said throatily. She was leaning against one of the doorways, smoking. It was like a scene from a Mae West movie. She tapped the ashes into her open palm. "So how's it feel to be back?"

"You're allowed to smoke in here?"

"No."

"But I'm not really back, am I? It's like coming back as a cadaver—I'm just here for your edification." I gave a nod at her cigarette. "I hope you'll put it out before you hook me up to the oxygen."

She dropped it on the floor and crushed it with her heel—just the way Sammy used to do it. Maybe there was something transcendent in that gesture. Maybe that's why I'd always liked her. "Ready? No last-minute cold feet?"

I shook my head.

"Okay—follow me."

She led me into another room—smaller, almost a closet, perhaps the place where they kept the extra heart monitors—and handed me a smock. "You haven't eaten anything in the last hour, have you?"

I shook my head and pulled off my shirt. She sounded like a doctor already. "So just what are you researching? What sort of drug am I getting?"

"It could maybe possibly be for asthma," she said, coughing. She smiled. "You think that's funny? I shouldn't even tell you that, Paul. It could ruin the blind."

"Any psychedelic side effects?"

"Don't count on them."

"So, Veronica—you're doing this for your research? What ever happened to kwashiorkor? AIDS?" I hated to press her. I was just curious—about Δ, change from baseline, how people changed over time.

"Oh . . ." She flipped her hand, as if it wasn't even worth mentioning—her way of being embarrassed. "That was the trendy period of my life. I've gotten more down to earth these days.

Pulmonary work—there's a good living in it. I like the sound of the word. The lungs have a comforting consistency to them. And the professor—she was nice."

"Well, can't argue with consistency." I slipped my arms into the smock.

"But you know who's doing AIDS work? You'll never believe it."

"Who?"

"Ferguson."

"You're right—I don't believe it." I tied the ribbon behind my back. Imagine that. Fergie cloning HIV. So my predictions had been wrong—but that was life: marvelous, unpredictable, divergent. "Voilà. Next?"

"This way...."

She led me into the room next door, where she had me lie down on the bed while she put on the sphygmometer cuff and the squishy ECG probes under my gown. A male intern wheeled in a tray of needles.

"Oh, you mad scientists...."

"Don't worry. Ned will be doing all the injecting. This sort of thing gives me the willies."

"How reassuring." Ned swabbed my arm. "Veronica, have you ever seen that film, *Hisss* or *Slither* or something, where they turn the high-school quarterback into a snake? A takeoff on *The Island of Dr. Moreau.*"

"Nope."

"I used to fantasize about that movie."

Ned stuck in the needle and then hooked up the IV. How familiar it was, yet the pain—that was something different, the view from below. The purpose to everything they were doing was a mystery to me, something I didn't—didn't want to—understand. I just exhaled and put my trust in them. It was the best thing to do. I had no power now, no hope for control, no inside knowledge. I was just the patient.

"Uhhh..." Veronica said, with a face, when some blood got in the line, and Ned had to play with it. She looked away. "Sorry, Paul. Faint heart. Maybe by third year I'll get the hang."

She sat facing away from me, flipping through a magazine, while Ned turned on the machines.

"Lie back. Relax. We'll start slowly. Now, don't be tense. That's better.

Are you comfortable? Do you want some water? Don't move; you'll disturb the readings. Some people panic; I don't think that'll happen. You might feel a bit of discomfort—that's to be expected. Okay. Feel it? Slightly giddy, jittery, as if something's going on inside? Good. That's us in there. You're doing fine; you'll be done in no time. Remember, we're monitoring every-thing. There's nothing to worry about."

"I hear you're seeing a lot of Jeff these days."

Whatever they were giving me, it wasn't placebo—I could feel my heart starting to race, my head fog. "Did you hear that from Jeff?"

"Around."

"Hmmm." I closed my eyes for a moment—I saw the bar, Veronica smoking, Jeff and Jaime. A whole different time and place, a whole different circumstance. I was starting to be there. "Where'd you meet them, anyway?"

"Oh—you know, the usual places."

I nodded at that. I understood. The need for understatement. Veronica was too interesting to be located specifically. I decided to listen to the Walkman to keep me occupied, hooked up my ears as my mind wandered. I mouthed along with the Talking Heads, the bongos and guitars, as my own electrolytes were amplified.... The voices and the needles filled me. I was totally embalmed, invaded, liberated....

"Hope you brought a lot of tapes, Paul. This will take a while."

I nodded placidly. Random thoughts floated through my head, moment to moment, in my study-chemical haze. How easy it was to be simply a mine, a farm, a field. Here I was, earning money as a *human organism,* not through any effort of will. What was will? Maybe it was merely a vestigial instinct, an autonomic reflex. That's why we always had to struggle—against a world set to read you in only one way, the way of the machine. Even people, that's how they preferred to operate. My parents knew nothing of this, the mechanics underneath the world. That's why we saw things so differently: I had a philosophy when on drugs, I could see inside things.

I thought I caught a glimpse of the readings coming out of the machines—

Thrombocytes: 2.3 × 10^5/cu mm.

Follicle-Stimulating Hormone: 7.0 mIU/mL.

**Test Substance Excretion: 3%. Outside predefined limits.
**Flag **Flag **Flag

A whole minefield, I was. Zillions of bits of data. Let them record each one. Let them reconstruct the original. Or at least an approximation: my mother's face. My father's voice. The lyrics of David Byrne. These were the sorts of particles getting into the observation of things, things like here comes Ned to change the IV. Hello, Ned. I'm trapped supine on the bed. I'm being read. I look like I'm dead. It's all in my head.

He patted my arm and smiled down at me. "You're doing just fine."

Afterward, Veronique handed me my shirt, watched as I tucked it in—in the meantime she'd gone home, she'd eaten dinner, she'd read a few pages of pharmacology. I was light-headed, tasting zinc in my mouth, hungry as hell.

"What'd you have for dinner, Veronica?"

"Mashed potatoes and meat loaf. I ate at the school cafeteria."

"Sounds great. I'm starved."

She spun in a circle, lab coat billowing, then flared out her arms and stopped—as if summing herself up for me, her eccentricities, one more time. "So, Paul. I'm curious. You remember that picture you took of me?"

"The one with the ophthalmoscope? The one they showed on TV?"

"Yep. Well, now I've got my own picture of you, in a way. Now you've done something for me. It's a bit like getting even."

"A bit. Isn't it?"

"Yeah. Well, no—not really. But it sounds good, doesn't it?"

I shrugged.

"I think they must have some of that meat loaf left. If you really want some. But I'd have thought you'd rather eat at that haute restaurant of yours. Wouldn't you?"

I shrugged again. "Everything gets old, Veronica, after a while. Everything."

*   *   *

Being in the hospital reminded me that it was high time to call on Sparrow. I couldn't put it off any longer. He agreed to meet me at a bookstore/café on Chapel Street. This was it, our reacquaintance. It'd be meeting him all over again, a chance to do it right. I was sipping mocha when I spotted him walking through the door—it was Sparrow all right, but in a sweater, with a satchel over his shoulder, distinguished gray hair: He didn't look like a doctor at all. More like an itinerant poet. My kind of old man.

We shook hands, and he ordered a cheeseburger.

"Paul. I'm so relieved to see you. I've been worried that I've done something wrong."

"Wrong?"

"The way you suddenly dropped out of sight. I was afraid you might have thought I'd been leading you on a wild-goose chase. I was just trying to help. It's too bad, but I can't promise everything, you know. I think we must have crossed wires somehow."

He seemed genuinely upset. It was an apology. I'd have never expected one from him, I'd have never thought I'd deserved it. . . . "It's all right, Dr. Sparrow. Perhaps I took it too personally. I expected too much. It's my fault for losing touch."

My reassurances cheered him, so we chatted idly for a while. Sparrow told me he'd started teaching camera presence and presentation to a group of freshmen medical students—the future TV docs of the world, something like overeducated weatherpeople. Meanwhile, the waitress brought Sparrow's plate.

"Cheeseburger isn't exactly the special here, you know."

"I don't really go for this bean sprout trend." He took a healthy bite from his burger, juice dripping down the corner of his mouth and collecting on his lettuce. He wiped his chin with a napkin, his hand trembling, perhaps a little more so than I remembered. "Sorry. I haven't eaten anything yet today."

Twenty-four and seventy-something. It was an odd friendship, one I should have pursued more vigorously. Sparrow was the only one for whom I'd ever done anything of note, my only professional contact, and if I was going into video full-time, his input would be worthwhile. Hell—his friendship was worthwhile, no matter what it meant professionally.

"You know, Dr. Sparrow, I've been planning to go back to school," and I told him all about my plans, my future, my videos— especially the one for the application. I described the "plot," as it were, as it had modified, mellowed, since my first preliminary radical sketches.

"And you want me to review it for you?"

"Actually . . ."

"Yes?"

"Actually, I was hoping I might be able to use some of your equipment. I'd like to do some postproduction work."

He nodded sagely. "Ah . . . by the way, Paul, you know, I myself have given up my clinical practice. It's just too hard mixing television with medicine."

I could have told him that last year.

"I knew you'd find that droll. I wasn't seeing any patients, anyway. I've done medicine for years now, and you know what? It's easier to mix TV with the *appearance* of medicine. The appearance works so much better. Appearance is what TV is all about. But you don't need patients for appearance. I'm going to do appearance full-time: I've been asked to be the spokesman for a series of antacid commercials."

"Sounds lucrative."

"Money? Who needs it? I do it for fun."

That, at least, I understood.

"It's talking to the public, making things easy to understand. It's what I do best. And I have all these medical students to take care of. Paul—I sincerely hope you haven't been mad at me."

"No," I said, surprised. "I've never been mad." It was untrue, of course. But it was the best way to answer him. "The antacid thing sounds good. I think anything that you like doing is a good idea."

"That's good. So we have the same philosophy. I don't want to think that I did something to make you radically change your life."

"No, Dr. Sparrow, it's not like that at all." If anything, I was envious of him. But I had that feeling about a lot of people.

"Okay. About the studio." He told me that the time wasn't going to be free—they routinely rented it out. So I told Sparrow how much money I'd saved up, and we struck a bargain: I would give him all I had, and he'd convince his producer to let me have the place, and one of the assistant editors, for a Saturday afternoon.

"Paul, I've got to go now." Laconic, as always. "But we'll stay in touch? It was good seeing you again." He crumpled up his soiled napkin and set it by his plate. His hands were still messy, and he gestured at my unused one. "Can I?"

I nodded, and he took it. "Yes—stay in touch. I'll have to call you for the keys."

So Sparrow gave me the use of his studio, and I gave him my napkin. Considering the difference in the extent of our experience, I thought it a fairly even trade. And in the end, who knows—Sparrow's brief tutelage could have been the one thing that really made a difference.

I went home and prepared three tapes of rough cuts. I brought them with me to the studio on Prospect Street, along with some three-quarter-inch tape, some posters, some photographs, Sammy's lithographs of Paris, some rhythm-and-blues CDs. All the things I'd collected. Sparrow wasn't there, but the assistant editor, Ralph, met me at the door and gave me a quick tour of the place. The tape room was kept at a nippy fifty-six degrees, for the equipment. Sparrow had warned me about that; I'd worn a sweater.

In the studio was all sorts of medical equipment, stuff set up for Sparrow's final episode of "Health Beat"—ECG machines, NMRs. And over here, this was where Sparrow sat . . . the mahogany desk . . . the steps. I walked up them, to see what they felt like. It was all tinfoil and painted cardboard. The room was small, cramped, much unlike the sense you got on TV. And the sets weren't real, just cardboard boxes, flats and cycloramas. All appearance, like he'd said. But now it was my turn to create the image. It was *my* game we would play, *my* version of the hoax that we would all believe; I'd reverse Veronica's polarities, send the information back *into* the body, into the brain, to be focused on the head of my tape machine.

Ralph patched my cassettes through a time-base corrector and then sent them to the monitor. On Screen 1 came pictures of my parents eating, pictures of myself stripping off my clothes, Janet and Marlou's romance (soft focus), interspersed with Sammy's lithographs. Scene A, Scene B, Scene C, just as it said in my log book. I'd even snuck some tape of Jeff asleep, his rhythmic rib cage rising and falling in the dark. My inspiration: I was going to structure this like one of the psych films. There were even a few scenes that I'd staged, using George in his lab coat, pretending to be a psychiatrist. Or maybe he was a surgeon. His specialty was meant to be unclear.

"Under conditions of isolation and afamiliarity, the subject rapidly presses the lever until a pellet is dropped," George said, waving a pointer. It had little to do with the keys and inserts I'd planned to have surround him. But in a peculiar way, it worked.

"What now?" Ralph would ask, sitting at the console with his eyes on the oscilloscope. I stood next to him, feeling the power of the place, the worlds you could circulate—whatever you could imagine—like having access to an entire culture's Command and Control. Ralph didn't seem fazed by any of the semi-nudity or otherwise controversial pictures I had up there playing in front of us. He was a professional, concerned with the transitions, not the content. Although, watching my tapes in this sterile milieu, in front of this staid technician—where all he'd seen for years must have been beer commercials and colorization—I had to admit that some of them seemed more transgressive than I'd first imagined. I wasn't unhappy about that, though.

"Do a dissolve just as his finger reaches the X ray," I'd say, or something like it, and Ralph would obediently key in the next frame.

I'd come a long way from those few simple photographs of a year before. It was amazing what you could do, the authenticity you could generate, the more equipment you had access to. The more people you knew. And I had something definite to say now. Even though I wasn't sure, exactly, what it was. But it was something I could feel, and I could sense when I'd gotten it just right, when something on the tape made me bristle with satisfaction.

For the coup de grace, I used the "Health Beat" swirling caduceus to open my show, which happened to be queued up on Reel 2. Ralph showed me a way to change the animation so that it looked like the snakes came alive, came off their posts, did something like a little snake dance. So I used it over the final credits. You could have called it symbolic—of this, or that, or perhaps something else. But I thought it just looked cool.

When I was done, I put the cassette in my backpack and walked home. All this work, the bits and scraps of a whole year, now reduced to a fifteen-minute spool of tape. It was like having trapped the world, preserved it from mistake and dissolution—

or, at least, salvaged a little corner of it. At home, I screened the tape once, to make sure I'd gotten all the cuts I'd wanted, to make sure it all looked perfect. Which it did, as far as I could see. It had the sort of semi-medical texture I'd been hoping for, as if the bodies on the film had all been built from a stockpile of used neurons, leftover muscles, neglected enzymatic reactions. It was the medical frame that most gave it that sense, but the colors, the body tone—it all lent itself to this empirical appearance, at least in my mind. I had no idea what anybody else might make of it... and realizing that, I decided that I couldn't bring myself to watch it again. I just wanted to launch it into the world with its own independent existence, and get it over with. I just wanted the judges to judge it. I was ready to start thinking about making something new.

"Well, Dr. Sparrow," I said over the phone. "It's all finished."

"Finished, huh? I'll have to take a look at it."

"Okay. I'd appreciate that. But there's no need to say anything. Anything critical, that is. Just let the experience wash over you."

"Uh-huh. I can see it already. It sounds just like you. I'll keep my criticisms to myself."

A pause.

"So—weren't there some recommendations that you wanted me to fill out?"

"Yep, yep... and thanks, Dr. Sparrow. Thanks so much."

"Don't mention it, Paul. Not at all. It's my pleasure. I'd do it for anyone."

I sent the recs to him in the mail. Then I made six copies of my tape, and posted it to all the schools I was considering, with a personal essay for each one. I wasn't taking any chances. Come September, I was going somewhere.

That same day, Jeff called.

"Paul, where have you been?"

"What do you mean?"

"I don't know—I don't know. You just don't seem to be around anymore, Paul. You're never there when I call."

"Well, Jeff." It had taken him that long to realize? "I left you a message. I've had some things to do. I have my own life, you know."

Our discussion grew, stage by stage, into a full-blown argument. Apparently, I hadn't been home when he'd wanted to see me (although his emergency had no particular reason). I'd been at the studio, producing my tape. For the first time, he was genuinely yelling at me: *I've been trying to reach you for days. Why weren't you at the whatever? I called to tell you to be at the whatever at whenever o'clock, and you weren't there, you weren't even home.* I wanted to tell him off. I wanted to tell him not to be an asshole. But I felt sorry for him. I didn't know what pressures he was really under, what preconceptions. Worse—I was starting to not care.

After an hour of it, he calmed down; he was simply telling me, "Look, maybe we shouldn't try to spend every moment together anymore"—as if it were his idea. "There are some things about you, Paul. Things that just strike me as a bit weird."

I just shrugged and said nothing.

"By the way, I'm watching the game this afternoon. You want to come over?" Completely forgetting all we had just said.

"The football game?"

"Yeah—the football game."

"Okay. Sure. I'll be over." Even if I'd given up hope for the future, I still wanted for us to talk, to work out some sort of mutual understanding—at least get back on cordial terms. Even though I knew that whatever was final between us, given both our personalities, couldn't allow for half-measures.

It was only as I was about to hang up that he told me he was having some other friends over, as well—"but that's okay, you can stop by anyway." He emphasized that he wasn't "out" to these friends, that I shouldn't do anything suggestive while I was there, I shouldn't get into any discussions of an intimate nature.

"No intimacy?"

"No fag stuff. Get it?"

I went over anyway.

He sat in front of the television with these economist friends of his and his roommate's, watching football: They cheered every ten minutes or so and threw beer cans across the room. Not very economical, if you'd have asked me. A pile of aluminum had accumulated around the trash bin. Newspapers were strewn across the floor and feet were propped on coffee tables.

"All right! Wow!" they yelled at the tube, in chorus, a whole crew of five or six.

"Want some pretzels?" Jeff's roommate asked, oblivious to who I was. I shook my head.

Jeff himself, though, wouldn't even acknowledge that I was there, not even during the commercials. We all watched the television, but I was seeing a different program from the rest of them: They saw the TDs, the offsides, the interceptions. I watched the inserts, the keys, the spectacular ADO digital effects. It was a whole different experience. They wouldn't have seen what I saw, not even if I'd explained it to them. It was probably the same the other way around.

All afternoon, Jeff and I didn't exchange a single word. He didn't even look at me. I could understand his need for secrecy, but he could have devised some signal, or the slap and dash of affection that even straight boys manage to show for each other, even Pete and Fergie. But he'd never shown me any of that anyway, not even when we were alone.

"Jeff!" I called during the postgame, after hours had gone by, still unable to get his attention. "Jeff! Hey—aren't you even going to say hello?"

"What? What?" Finally, he came over to me. He was visibly upset. He was squeezing his thumb inside his palm. He put his hand on my shoulder and forced me out the front door.

"Look, Paul, let's don't make a scene, okay? We'll talk later. Not now."

"Maybe I shouldn't have even bothered to come over."

"Well, maybe you're right."

We stared at each other. His eyes were stones. We were conducting this whole breakup in looks and secret code.

"So are you going to come in and watch TV or not?"

"What's the point? You won't even talk to me. You won't even go for a walk."

"Paul . . ." he warned.

"What? What? Isn't this more important than your football buddies?" *This*, I said, meaning *me*. But my only hope was to play his game.

He shrugged, as if to say, *Yep*.

"So, fine. Go have fun." I pushed my beer into his chest. He grabbed it from me, to keep from spilling it. Then I turned around and went home, not once looking back.

I knew he wouldn't call me again.

Jeff. He was a creature of two minds. One pulled left and the other right. He didn't know where he was. He had no center, nothing to locate. I could never interpret his intentions. I read him as a collection of random impulses, even though I was sure that, to his mind, he had a logic, within which everything he did had a strategy. But hell if I knew what it was. Peel away the layers, the games and pretenses, the dodges and assumptions, and what was left? Only my stupidity. Only my own wishful thinking. But this time, at least, his message had been unmistakable.

As soon as I got home, I called Bob; I wanted to take him out to dinner and apologize for the sometimes lousy way I'd treated him. And I wanted solace. Bob was always there, always to be counted on. That had to be worth something. I figured it was worth at least a steak dinner. And me telling him so. Why, only now, did I realize how easy it was to talk to Bob? Even if we didn't always know what the other was talking about, or pay close attention, we didn't mind simply listening to each other's voice.

Bob cut his steak into tiny cubes and ate hungrily—I could barely bring myself to touch mine.

"From what you've been saying, sounds like he's had a pretty harsh childhood. You deserve better than that, Paul. I don't think you need to see him again." Bob—always so sure about what was good for me.

"Don't worry, Bob. I'm ready to give it up. Like I said before: It might take me a while, but once I decide something, it's decided."

Throughout dinner, I drank three beers, maybe four, maybe five. It was such a classic maneuver—I couldn't resist. "Bob. Bob d'bob...you're a real pal, you know that?" Thank God, Bob—he had the guts not to say, "I told you so." I slapped him on the shoulder a couple of times. "Who needs a boyfriend? Who needs Jeff? Not me. You know there's a wedding reception at Big Moe's next week? My roommate and his girlfriend are going. And Marlou of course. Maybe you'd like to come, too?"

"A wedding? You mean with a boy and girl? With hors d'oeuvres?"

"Sure. And popcorn shrimp. Come on, come on; it'll be stupendous. They're friends of ours."

"Well..."

"We can't live inside our little boxes forever...."

By the end of the night, I could barely get out of the chair; Bob had to drive us home.

I thought I'd managed to fall out of love with Jeff. I thought I'd gotten free of his influence. But I'd been wrong. After Bob dropped me off, I closed my bedroom door and had a good sob. I figured it didn't hurt, for once, to let myself wallow in my misery. The sadness was, in its own way, as romantic as falling in love had been—it was all part of the same story, all an education, all an experience. I'd never enjoyed just letting myself go like that. Perhaps I had been milking the whole affair, all this time, for more than it was worth, and I just wanted to finish it the same way. Or it could have been, simply, that for one incalculable evening in my life, I was pretty goddamned drunk.

So we all went to that reception—George and Julie, Bob, Marlou, the whole crew. It was one of those elaborate restauranteur traditions. After the dinner rush, after the small private wedding, they closed the restaurant and held an all-night bash—rows of food set up along all the tables: egg rolls, meatballs, ribs, tenderloins, fish, breads, cheeses. A different pan for every table. They opened up the bar and served drinks, beer, everything. It was help yourself. It was eat all you can. It was time to make a memory.

Angela had asked me to take pictures. So I had my video camera rolling. The natural highlight was to be when she and Gray cut the cake. They did it perfectly—slightly self-mocking, feeding each other, dropping crumbs, fully immersed in the moment, in both their invention and their parody of it. Angela came over afterward and gave me a great big hug. I hardly knew them anymore, they were such a perfect twosome, a modern example of romance.

Afterward, I interviewed each guest and shot some scenes of candid affection, my specialty—all that kissing and hugging, Marlou and Janet, George and Julie. It would all come together eventually, it would all get ordered into videotape sequence. That was just the way I saw things.

"Angela, Gray, I'd like you to meet George, my roommate. And Julie, his girlfriend."

They all shook hands.

"Congratulations, folks," George told them. "It must feel nice."

"Yeah," Gray said, pulling back his hair. "It does."

"Here here," I said. All my friends together, for the very first time. They all looked great.

"It certainly took him long enough to come around. Over a month."

"So I guess now I have to work on George here." Julie tugged his arm.

The four of them talked as if they actually had something in common, as if they did this all the time, when in fact they'd probably never meet one another—on equal terms—again. After a while, they broke up for refills—cocktails, shrimps, mingling with the others. Meanwhile, I started shooting again; I circled the room, I elicited a reaction from everyone I could.

"Hell, Marlou," I said hours later, changing cassettes. "These shindigs are exhausting. Maybe I should be charging them. How much more?" My watch said four-fifteen. There'd been a time when the middle of the night would have been peak creative time for me.

She and Bob were sharing a slice of wedding cake. Janet was there, too. They were all sitting placidly in chairs by now. They acted a lot more run-down than they had the last time I'd cruised by.

"Till dawn, at least."

"I think it's starting to die. I think I see people starting to go home." Julie and George, for instance, had left hours ago. It was amazing that so many people could be so happy for such a young, extraordinary couple.

"It's just your imagination."

"At any rate, I'm done taping."

She nodded. "That reminds me. How're your applications coming?"

"It's all in the mail. I'll be hearing in a few months." I pulled up a chair and sat down. I'd had enough with the camera. Sure, it was my job now—taping people, filling drinks, being in service. And I really was happy being able to do it. But four-fifteen A.M. was enough for anyone. "You know, I've been seeing a lot of medical-school people lately. I've been thinking about when I first got here, about this guy who got arrested the first week. Have I ever told you guys this story?"

They shook their heads. So I entertained them for a while with tales of Daniel, his exploits, his stratagems, his attitudes. I didn't really miss him anymore—it just struck me as an interesting adventure. A good anecdote. Something to share with your friends. "You know, I wonder whatever happened to him."

"There's no way to know, is there?"

"No—and that's the one thing, the annoying thing, the thing I've just realized."

"I hope you'll let us know what happens to you, Paul, when you go off to school...."

"Don't worry. I'll keep in touch."

"Paul, you fool—you haven't left yet." Marlou—she was still eating, Janet on her knee, massaging her girlfriend's neck with one hand while spooning cake in her mouth with the other. Such a delicate balancing act for such a tough and skinny woman. "Are you still seeing Jeff?"

I looked at Bob. He smiled at me. We understood the significance of the subject. "No—no, I don't see him so much anymore."

"Too bad."

"No. Not really."

"It's true," Bob said. "Can't you see it on his face?"

The party didn't last till dawn—everyone left by four-thirty, and I drove home, full, floating, pleased. Satiated. An evening to remember, another scene for my diary, maybe even the beginning of my next project, whatever it might be. When I got to my room, there was a note taped to the door, from George.

Great party, Paul. Thanks for inviting us.

And that's how I slept, wrapped in the comfort of my friends.

But at six A.M., I awoke with a start. I sat upright in bed. Something had happened. Outside, the sun was just rising, birds chirping; it was as if the birds had woken me (which was absurd; I'd never been woken up by daybreak before). Dawn after all. And I realized what it was—right at that moment, I knew that what I'd told them was true: that I didn't mind about Jeff. That of course there'd be others. And so I let go of my resentment. What, really, could I hold against him? He'd done me a favor, he'd been a willing participant in my life, and even if he didn't love me, he'd shown me that *I* could care about me, and that was all you could ever ask of someone. And now, awake, at sunrise, I was having a vision: A snake, following the rays of the sun, was coming through the window, and the snake said to me, *I am your animal. You can*

shed your skin, but you will always be complete. Do not be disheartened.
There is nothing and no one you cannot be.

And the snake made me see a thousand things at once: myself
in third grade, Pinewood Elementary, walking down that endless
corridor. Angela not wanting to do the Moe all her life. Leona's
contests. My father's escapades in Mexico. Veronica reading her
charts. Sammy in Korea. Jeff and his friends. George studying for
his Boards, passing this test, that test, going on to the next phase,
the next stage. Me, going from one adventure to the next, pro-
gressing from goal to goal, never necessarily concluding anything
but always moving on, transforming, getting older, setting tasks
and achieving them. All of us—our desires never really having a
reality as expansive as our ambition, a vista onto which they can
unfold, until we look back and see just how far we've come. And
that was it, the secret: I'd come to this point. I'd found out who
I was. And it was with something like an electric shock that I united
mind and body, animal and machine, and woke up whole.

I landed back in bed, still naked, with a mental thump. Here
was my body. I opened and closed my fist. My hands didn't look
like mine anymore. They looked like my father's—an adult's. I
flexed my legs. Chest, cock, skin, fingers. I was so filled with eroticism and potency, I felt tremendous. I grabbed the mattress, the
sheets, the blankets, and squeezed. I'd never been so conscious.

"Happy birthday, Paul," I said to myself. And I really did feel
ready, and eager, to begin my life once more.